The formation of the Tuigan charge was clear now, though the sun at the enemy's back and the high, waving grain sometimes hid the horsewarriors from Azoun's sight. As the king had guessed, the khahan had organized his warriors into three rough lines, each about three men deep.

At a few hundred yards, the bulk of the enemy reined in their horses and stopped. A group about half the size of the Army of the Alliance, perhaps fifteen thousand men, raced

THE EMPIRES TRILOGY

HORSELORDS
David Cook

DRAGONWALL
Troy Denning

CRUSADE
James Lowder

FANTASY ADVENTURE

The Empires Trilogy: Book Three

James Lowder

Cover Art
LARRY ELMORE

To Beth Anderson, Dawn Colwell, Robert Cole, and all the teachers at WHRHS for getting me started; to my families in New England and New Berlin for helping me along the way; and, most of all, to Debbie, for understanding, support, and proofreading beyond the call of duty.

—JDL

CRUSADE

©Copyright 1991 TSR, Inc.
All Rights Reserved.

Distributed to the book trade in the United States by Random House, Inc., and in Canada by Random House of Canada, Ltd.

Distributed in the United Kingdom by TSR Ltd.

Distributed to the toy and hobby trade by regional distributors.

FORGOTTEN REALMS and the TSR logo are trademarks owned by TSR, Inc.

First Printing: January, 1991
Printed in the United States of America.
Library of Congress Catalog Card Number: 89-51890

9 8 7 6 5 4 3 2 1

ISBN: 0-88038-908-7
All characters in this book are fictitious. Any resemblance to actual persons, living or dead, is purely coincidental.

TSR, Inc.
P.O. Box 756
Lake Geneva,
WI 53147 U.S.A.

TSR Ltd.
120 Church End, Cherry Hinton
Cambridge CB1 3LB
United Kingdom

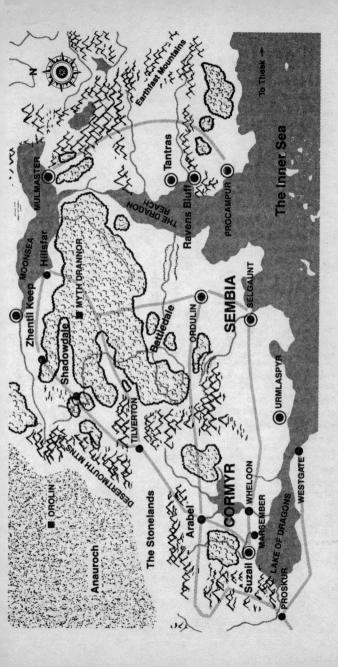

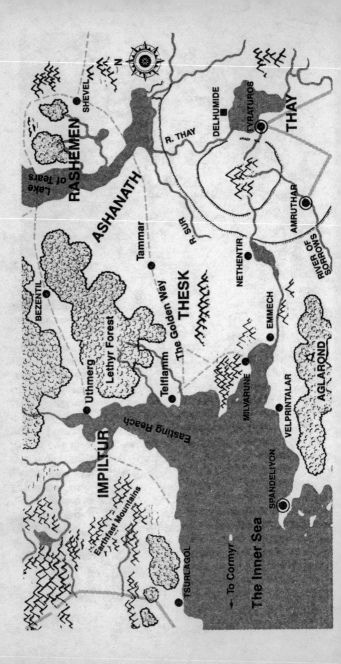

- 1 -

The King's Men

King Azoun IV of Cormyr paced back and forth before a window in his castle's highest tower. After two or three steps in the circular room, the king paused and threw open the wooden shutters. Restlessly clasping his hands behind his back, he looked out on Suzail, the capital of his rich and expansive kingdom. What the monarch saw of the city from that vantage troubled him greatly.

Suzail sprawled contentedly in the bright, early spring sunshine. As on most mornings in good weather, crowds filled the narrow streets, heading toward or returning from the capital's bustling marketplace, doing what people in most of western Faerun's larger cities did each day. Servants ran from their masters' homes to shops, then returned with goods purchased. Watchmen, dressed in the livery of their office, settled disputes and kept the peace. Wealthy merchants argued among themselves about the price of ivory or cloth or wheat. Freebooters and sailors wandered through the various inns and taverns, searching for a new adventure or just a good barroom brawl. In all, Suzail looked that morning much like it had for all of King Azoun's twenty-five-year reign—peaceful and prosperous.

Unclasping his hands, Azoun ran his fingers through his silver-shot brown beard. "Why hasn't it affected them, Vangy?" the king asked without turning around.

"Eh?" a voice sighed. "What did you say?"

Azoun turned slowly to face Vangerdahast, royal magician of Cormyr, chairman emperius of the College of War Wizards. The paunchy mage was hunched over a chessboard, staring intently at the finely carved ivory pieces. In the bright cold light from the window, Vangerdahast looked to be the veteran of fifty winters or so. Azoun knew better. Despite the color in his wrinkled cheeks, his steady gaze and steady hands, the royal magician was well over eighty. His magic had helped him stave off old age for many years now.

"Why hasn't the Tuigan invasion affected my subjects?" the king repeated. "Do they think the war won't touch them at all? They're going about their lives as if nothing is wrong."

Straightening his back with a short groan, Vangerdahast cast a quick glance at his opponent in the chess match—a short, stout man with gray hair and sparkling blue eyes—then turned to Azoun. The mage recognized the puzzled tone in his king's voice, which told him that Azoun was genuinely bothered by the subject he'd broached. Vangerdahast had heard that inflection many times since he had been hired by King Rhigaerd II, Azoun's father, to tutor the young prince in heraldry and ethics. However, the tone had never been so prevalent in Azoun's voice as it had been since the Tuigan horsemen interrupted trade between Faerun and the eastern lands of Kara-Tur a little over a year ago.

"Actually, Your Highness," Vangerdahast began, "you've already answered your own question, though calling the Tuigan incursion a 'war' might be a bit premature." When Azoun didn't object, the wizard continued. "The barbarians have done little so far that really touches the lives of the average Cormyrian. Since they charged through Rashemen into Ashanath last fall, they've not moved west. Must I remind you that the nearest Tuigan is well over one thousand miles to our east, on the other end of the Inner Sea? Having barbarians camped there is hardly a direct threat to Cormyr."

Vangerdahast's opponent in the chess game moved his queen and smiled. "What about lost revenue? Haven't the attacks on Thesk and the countries around it slowed trade?" the stout man asked. "Surely the guilds care about the money."

"The guilds, especially the trappers, are the biggest opponents of any military action against the Tuigan," Azoun noted. He shook his head. "They feel we should wait until the barbarians threaten Cormyr directly before spending money to fight them."

"For once, the guilds are correct," Vangerdahast said a bit peevishly. "The Tuigan are not an immediate problem." The wizard looked at the chessboard, noticed that his opponent wore a grin, and cursed softly. "You're supposed to announce your move, Dimswart. Now, what did you—ah, the queen."

"And I believe that's checkmate," Dimswart stated flatly. "Your chess game really hasn't improved in all the time I've known you, Vangy." The gray-haired man, also called the Sage of Suzail, knitted his fingers behind his head and leaned back against the room's whitewashed wall.

Snorting in irritation, Vangerdahast stood up. "We've more important things to do in the castle than play games all day. Now that you're retired and all your daughters are married, I suppose you do little else but pore through obscure texts and hover over chessboards. Why, even the supposed 'Sage' of Shadowdale, Elminster, does more important work than you."

Dimswart's smile faded, and he opened his mouth to reply to the royal wizard's insult. It was common knowledge that Vangerdahast held a longstanding grudge against the legendary sage and wizard, Elminster—though the origin of the feud was long forgotten. So to have Vangerdahast compare one unfavorably to him was quite a barb. The stout sage never had a chance to reply, though, as Azoun cleared his throat noisily, signaling an end to any further digressions.

"My esteemed royal wizard is correct," the king said as he placed a hand on Vangerdahast's shoulder. A slight smile crossed Azoun's lips, but its warmth didn't quite reach his dark eyes. "There are important matters to consider at the moment, the most pressing of which is the crusade."

Vangerdahast frowned at the use of the word "crusade." Azoun noted the expression on his friend's face, then turned back to the window. "I know you object to my plan. However, I've considered the matter carefully, and I believe that it will be better for Cormyr and the rest of Faerun if I follow my own best judgment . . . despite opposition from the trappers. After the discussions I've had with the leaders of the Dales and Sembia, our own lords, and a few others, I believe I can recruit a large number of allies. If they agree to support this venture, I will lead it."

Slowly Azoun rested one hand on the edge of the window and bowed his head. "The Tuigan are hurting the entire continent of Faerun," he said, anger in his voice. "Including Cormyr. And if these barbarians, these 'horsewarriors,' are harming my people, I must challenge them. A crusade is the only way."

Vangerdahast's frown deepened. He stalked to Azoun's side, his heavy brown robe hissing along the ground as he walked. "Look there," the wizard said, pointing out the open window. "The nearest Tuigan raider is in Ashanath, half a continent from here. You can't possibly think they'll invade us soon. And can you really tell me that the horsewarriors have put a serious crimp in our economy?"

Raising his head, the king looked out at the city once again. In the direction Vangerdahast pointed lay Suzail's docks. The port was busy, as was usual for that time of year. Ships bearing the colors of countries and free cities from all over the Inner Sea dotted the piers, and Cormyrian traders bound for those places and more filled the rest of the harbor. Hundreds of sailors and longshoremen swarmed over the docks, loading and unloading cargo. Cloth and livestock, gold and ivory, art treasures and other, more precious things poured into the city by the hour.

Azoun slowly traced a path with his eyes from the dock to the foot of his tower. Closer to the piers, the king saw dozens of inns and businesses, all bustling with trade from the harbor. Moving his eyes over the slate or wooden roofs of these establishments, the king saw the wide, dusty thoroughfare called "the Promenade." This street, like the docks, was filled with traders from throughout Faerun and other parts of Cormyr. As Azoun watched, wagon after wagon of goods rolled past, not to mention the mob of merchants and citizens who trod the Promenade as they went about their business. The noise of the people in the streets mixed with the shrill cries of the seabirds that lofted over the harbor, creating the backdrop of sound Azoun had grown accustomed to in his years in Suzail.

The king's eyes crossed the Promenade and lit upon the sprawling, interconnected buildings that made up the royal court, the seat of Cormyr's bureaucracy. Just the day before, he'd received a report that the royal tax collectors expected a rise in income this year from tariffs levied on merchants.

"No, Vangy," the monarch said firmly. "I can't tell you the invasion has ruined our economy. In fact, the Tuigan have had little *direct* effect upon our trade."

The paunchy wizard nodded, as if prompting a student to develop a single correct answer into a more complex conclusion—as if Azoun were still a young prince in his tutelage. When the king only continued to gaze out at the city, Vangerdahast sighed.

"Come now, Vangy," Dimswart said as he leaned forward. "You know as well as I that trade with Ashanath, Thesk, and Shou Lung is only a small part of Cormyr's shipping industry."

Vangerdahast moved away from Azoun, toward one of the two large tapestries that hung on the circular room's cold, white walls. The finely crafted hanging depicted a joust, complete with heavily armored knights wielding ornamented lances. One cloth warrior, his silver thread armor looking faded with age, leaned forward on his mount and pressed his lance against the splintering shield of his adversary. The other, a gold-clad warrior, seemed to be slipping off his horse, frozen eternally on the brink of defeat.

"We don't have strong ties with the Shou people," the wizard noted absently as he stood between the knights and his king. "Not yet, anyway. That was the reason Azoun and I attended that trade conference in Semphar last year, the one that was supposed to solve the problems the Tuigan were creating for commerce."

"It could have been a very productive conference, too," the king added. "Representatives from Shou Lung and many of the western nations interested in trading with them showed up. The whole thing was pointless though; a barbarian general—I believe his name was Chanar—took the city hostage, surrounding it with armed troops."

Azoun laughed bitterly. "General Chanar wanted to deliver an ultimatum from the Tuigan leader, their *khahan*. We were supposed to recognize this barbarian, Yamun Khahan, as emperor of all the world."

"What an unwashed brute that general was," Vangerdahast said with a chuckle, tracing the figure of the golden knight in the tapestry with his finger. "You could almost see the fleas hopping around on him."

Smiling at his friend's sarcasm, Azoun walked to the wizard's side. "I'm sure General Chanar had just ridden for days, Vangy. He was a warrior, not—" The king paused, then waved his hands in front of himself, motioning toward his silk tunic, fine, purple surcoat, and expensive, perfectly crafted dragonskin boots. "He wasn't a politician."

"Speaking of politicians, Your Highness, do you think one of your enemies is stirring up the guild masters?" Dimswart asked. The sage leaned over the chessboard and started to rearrange the pieces, setting up for a new game.

The paunchy wizard dropped his hands to his sides and slapped his thighs. "Perhaps the Zhentarim *are* baiting the guild masters. That doesn't mean their objections to the crusade are unfounded. The trappers will gain little revenue from the venture. In fact, they'll end up paying for the crusade in higher taxes on the furs they bring to the city for sale." He scowled and shook his head. "Your Highness, I can only imagine the damage that you'll do to yourself politically by running off to the other side of the Inner Sea to look for a war."

Vangerdahast's shoulders sagged then, as if his anger had fled suddenly. "I've heard your arguments, Azoun, and I can see that they have *some* merit. However, I still don't understand why you need to rush off."

"Have you forgotten my duty?" Azoun asked, a touch of

pride in his voice.

Vangerdahast shook his head. "Your duty is to Cormyr, not Thesk or Rashemen. I've told you a thousand times before, you—"

Laughing, Dimswart cut in, "Vangy, you miss the point completely."

The king's eyes grew dark again. "We've had this argument before. Cormyr is more than the lands that lay between lines on a map. We are only one country, one power amongst a dozen in Faerun. If one of our neighbors falls, then we fall, too. My duty to Cormyr demands that I help avert a crisis that could threaten any part of the continent."

The wizard turned away from Azoun. "As I've I told you every other time you've wanted to help the Dales or Tantras or Ravens Bluff, you shouldn't go looking for trouble."

After reaching into his pockets, Vangerdahast dug out the components to a spell and muttered an incantation. "Look," the wizard cried as a glowing map of Faerun appeared, superimposed on the tapestry he had been studying only moments before. Rivers and mountains, deserts and glaciers, cities and countries all appeared faintly in the air, the armored warriors from the hanging showing vaguely through them all.

The kingdom of Cormyr lay on the northwest end of the Inner Sea, also known as the Sea of Fallen Stars. To Cormyr's north were mountains, then the arid, inhospitable Stonelands and the vast expanse of the great desert, Anauroch. The merchant kingdom of Sembia, equal in size to Azoun's domain, was located directly to Cormyr's east. The Dales, to the northeast, were a loose confederation of small farming communities. Unlike Cormyr, with its hereditary monarchy, and Sembia, with its merchant oligarchy, the Dales were strongly democratic. Together, Cormyr, Sembia, and the Dales made up much of the "Heartlands" of Faerun.

With their varied political outlooks, it wasn't surprising that the three core countries in the Heartlands often suffered long disputes. The multitude of independent city-states—places like Tantras and Hillsfar—that were located close to the larger nations often found themselves caught between bickering giants. Still, Cormyr, Sembia, and the Dales were lands where peace flourished; their disputes were never serious enough to create permanent rifts.

And they always agreed when it came to matters involving Zhentil Keep. Though only a walled city just to the north of the Dales, Zhentil Keep was the focus for much of the evil in the Heartlands. Only out of necessity did Azoun and the other lawful rulers deal with the dark priests who controlled the Keep.

But it was not to Cormyr or the Dales or even Zhentil Keep that Vangerdahast pointed when the magical map came into focus. The wizard's finger drifted east of the Heartlands, across the land of Impiltur, to the eastern end of the Inner Sea.

"For the horsewarriors to get from where they are now," the wizard began, directing their attention to a spot hundreds of miles beyond even the end of the Inner Sea, "to our forests, they'd have to go through Thesk, Damara, Impiltur . . ."

With each new nation or free city he mentioned, Vangerdahast unfurled another of his pudgy, large-knuckled fingers. Azoun and Dimswart merely waited for the royal wizard to finish his tirade.

"And depending upon the route they take," Vangerdahast concluded, turning sharply to face his king, "it's conceivable that Yamun Khahan, 'emperor of all the world,' could lead his barbarians through Zhentil Keep before he came south to the Dales." The map disappeared, and the wizard stood in front of a plain tapestry once again.

"That's a fine hope," Dimswart noted after a few moments. "It would be nice to see the Tuigan try to storm the black walls of that wretched, evil place. However, it's more likely the Zhents would join the Tuigan—or at least guide them toward the Dales and us. For all we know, the Keep might have struck a deal with this khahan already, like the Red Wizards of Thay did last fall."

Azoun considered that possibility for a moment, then shuddered and dismissed it. He could only hope that the leaders in Zhentil Keep had more sense than to believe the

Tuigan would leave them alone if they appeared to offer no resistance. The messages he'd received lately from Lord Chess, the nominal ruler of the Keep, all indicated that the Zhentish would support any sane plan against the raiders. Azoun knew that Chess could be lying just to keep the Dales and Cormyr off balance, but he had to hope otherwise. Even a rumor that Zhentil Keep planned to cooperate with the Tuigan, like Thay had done a few months earlier, would give the guild masters who opposed the crusade a stronger argument.

"We'll never have the opportunity to see what Zhentil Keep would do in that situation for we cannot—no, *will not*—wait for the Tuigan to arrive on our doorstep," King Azoun stated firmly. "If I have the support of the rest of Faerûn's leaders, I'm going to stop Yamun Khahan long before he reaches us."

"And the guilds?" Dimswart asked.

Without pause, Vangerdahast replied, "We could toss the leaders of the Trappers' Guild into the tower until the crusade is over."

Azoun shook his head. "And make martyrs of them? Hardly." He glanced out of the open window again and added, "The guilds will simply have to follow my commands in this. There really is nothing they can do to stop me."

Dimswart and Vangerdahast knew from Azoun's voice that the discussion was over as far as the king was concerned. The tower room fell silent. Abruptly a sharp breeze from the open window carried the noise from the street to the tower and made the tapestries flutter on the wall. The air in the room, a little thick with the smell of the musty old books piled neatly near the window and the oiled wooden chess set over which Dimswart still fussed, lightened for an instant with a breath of sea air. If only for that moment, the tension in the room seemed to dissipate—until a loud rapping sounded at the lone entrance to the tower, a heavy, iron-braced trapdoor.

"Ah, that will be Winefiddle," Dimswart noted as he stood and moved quickly to unlock the entrance. The sage slid the bolt back noisily, then said, "Speak the password and enter," his foot planted firmly on the door.

"Don't be ridiculous," came the muffled response, followed by another loud thump on the oaken door. After a barely suppressed chuckle, the unseen man added, "I have a message for the king, Dimswart, so stop this nonsense and let me up. You'd think you were Vangerdahast, asking for a password."

The wizard cocked an eyebrow as Dimswart pulled open the door. Winefiddle, a rotund man with thinning brown hair and puffy red cheeks, shuffled up the stairs into the room. "You'd think *I* was—," he huffed as he climbed into the room. Then the fat man saw the royal wizard standing before him, his arms crossed, tapping his foot.

"Both you and Dimswart have succeeded in annoying Vangy this morning, Curate Winefiddle," Azoun noted as the priest faced the fuming mage. The quiet, happy cleric usually had a soothing effect upon the king, and that day was no exception. He forgot about the Tuigan and the crusade for a moment and smiled. "This is just like old times."

Vangerdahast snorted. "Yes, Your Highness, this rather is like the times you 'went adventuring' with these oafs. It's a wonder you all weren't killed any number of times."

"That we survived some of those adventures is due partly to you, Vangerdahast," Winefiddle said sincerely. He shifted the sack he carried to his left hand and wiped the sweat from his brow. "If you hadn't been so conscientious about following Azoun around, the King's Men would have perished any number of times." Noting the astounded look on the wizard's face, the cleric straightened his light blue tunic and headed for a comfortable chair on the other side of the room.

"You see, Vangy, someone appreciates you," Dimswart said, sitting back at the chessboard. "Even I admit that you saved our lives once or twice when we were tearing up the countryside as the King's Men."

The room was silent again for a moment as all four of them dusted off memories of the King's Men. Dimswart, then a mage of little renown, and Winefiddle, a novice in the temple of Tymora, the Goddess of Good Fortune, had formed the group, eager as they were to seek fame and fortune in the wilder parts of Cormyr. They were soon joined by other Cormyrian adventurers, including a highly skilled swordsman who called himself Balin. In reality, this noble cavalier was young Prince Azoun.

The prince had no trouble keeping Balin's true identity a secret from the world at large. Few people knew what Azoun looked like, and even fewer expected him to be roaming the countryside with a troupe of minor adventurers. After two or three months, though, the young cavalier revealed his identity to the group. Dimswart had uncovered the prince's secret after their first adventure together, proving himself to be a noteworthy sleuth even then. Winefiddle and the others were astounded at the revelation. This information changed little, however, as the King's Men were more interested in saving damsels from ogres than getting mixed up in Cormyrian politics.

And that went double for Azoun himself. Riding with Dimswart, Winefiddle, and the three other members of the group gave the prince a chance to escape the pressures of life in the castle. Vangerdahast covered for Azoun whenever possible, telling King Rhigaerd that his son was on an expedition to a distant shrine or library. Frequently the royal tutor would furnish an excuse to the king, then go hunting for the boy himself. He often found the would-be heroes in dire straits.

"Remember the time we stumbled upon that goblin camp in the mountains near High Horn," Azoun said with a chuckle. "They were sure we were spies—"

"And then they decided that Winefiddle was a cleric of some terrible, evil elemental god," Dimswart added, smirking at the rotund curate. "Just because a rock tumbled off a cliff and hit one of them as it tried to grab him."

Winefiddle frowned weakly. "You're both lucky they thought that, too. The beasts made short work of both of you before they tried to grab me. Those horrible little things were ready to kill us all." He rubbed his stomach. "I still have a scar where one of them prodded me with a spear."

The cleric paused, toying with the plain silver disk that hung around his neck. Talking about danger or even discomfort made Winefiddle nervous. He, for one, did not miss his life as an adventurer. "And if Vangerdahast hadn't come along when he did," the curate added, "they might have killed us anyway. I was getting tired of acting like an elemental lord."

The royal wizard nodded slowly as a reply, then sat down at the chessboard, across from the gray-haired sage. "The curate's right, you know. You're all very lucky not to have been eaten by any one of those monsters you pestered."

The comment stung Azoun like the flick of a whip. "We did far more then 'pester' creatures, Vangy," he said hotly. "The King's Men did some good in the short time they were around."

The king paused, as if daring someone to disagree. He knew that none of his friends would think of it, however. "What about that caravan we saved from the hill giants in the mountains west of here? Or the children we rescued from the zombies that raided that farm outside of Tyrluk?"

"They were fine adventures, Azoun, weren't they?" the royal magician stated more than asked.

King Azoun recognized the wizard's bait and responded to Vangerdahast's real question. "They were, Vangy . . . but I don't think the crusade will be an adventure at all, and that's certainly not why I'm organizing it."

"Are you so sure of that?" the wizard asked softly.

Azoun did not answer, and resumed pacing instead. Vangerdahast sat, drumming his fingers on the chessboard, while Dimswart and Winefiddle exchanged concerned glances.

Then the curate's eyes grew wide, and he leaped out of his seat. "The message!" he cried. "I almost forgot about it!"

Winefiddle noisily dug through his sack. "One of the pages gave it to me when he saw that I was coming to see you up in the tower." Wine bottles clinked together, papers and scrolls rustled, and loose coins clattered against everything else in the rough brown bag. "Here it is!" he exclaimed at last.

The parchment Winefiddle held aloft was crumpled

slightly, but Azoun could see that it was an important message even from across the room. Bold black and red ribbons, secured by a thick wax seal, dangled from the paper. Vangerdahast abruptly snatched the letter from the curate's hands and gave it to Azoun.

The king looked at the wax. A phoenix clutching a hammer in its claws was imbedded there. That imprint told him that the message was from Torg mac Cei, a dwarven king from the Earthfast Mountains. After closing his eyes and whispering a short prayer to Torm, the God of Duty, Azoun snapped the seal and read the missive.

As his eyes raced down the page, Azoun sighed. A slight smile bloomed on his face, then disappeared. The king handed the parchment to Vangerdahast and headed toward the trapdoor. "Excuse me, my friends, I have some important people to contact right away."

As he started down the stairs, the king turned and added, "We'll talk again soon, Dimswart, Winefiddle." He smiled again briefly and looked at his stunned royal wizard. "We should confer, Vangy. I need your advice on obtaining the use of a large number of ships."

The wizard, sage, and cleric stood dumbfounded as Azoun rushed down the tower stairs. After the footfalls on the stone steps grew distant, Vangerdahast pulled open the letter. "It's from King Torg of Earthfast," he told the others as they moved to his side.

"A message about the crusade, I assume," Dimswart noted. "I can probably guess what it says."

"Well, I can't," Winefiddle said, turning his holy symbol over and over in his hands. "Please read it aloud, Vangerdahast."

"No," the wizard muttered, handing the letter to the priest. "It's short. You might as well read it yourself."

Winefiddle glanced at the dwarven runes at the top of the page, then read over the lengthy listing of Torg's titles and genealogy. Vangerdahast was correct about the body of the missive: it was brief. The text was also written in perfect rows of neat letters.

I have consulted our war council about the barbarian

horsewarriors, the letter began. *You are absolutely correct in your assessment of the situation. Therefore, I pledge, as ironlord of Earthfast, to lead two thousand dwarven troops under your banner against the Tuigan. I also have a brilliant human general in my city at this time who will join the conflict. We await your arrival to begin this crusade.*

Winefiddle stopped reading, then a shudder wracked his heavy frame as he saw the final lines of the message: *My troops and I will gladly lay down our lives to the last warrior to stop the invasion. I know that you and your troops will certainly pledge the same.*

The cleric held the parchment out to Dimswart, who had returned to his seat at the chessboard. The sage waved the letter away. "Torg has offered troops to support the crusade. You could see it in Azoun's face as he read the note." Dimswart picked up the white king from the chessboard and looked at it intently. "Those of us who think the crusade is a good idea can only hope now that the other kings and lords will follow Torg's lead."

Vangerdahast sighed. "Azoun is a very, very persuasive man. The leaders of Faerun will do as he suggests."

As one, Dimswart and Winefiddle looked to the royal magician. Vangerdahast stood at the window Azoun had occupied earlier, looking out over Suzail. "The question is no longer 'will Azoun lead the crusade against the Tuigan?'" The mage turned to face the king's two friends, who both saw the sadness in his eyes.

"Suzail will pay dearly for this. Azoun simply doesn't know what a real war takes out of a people." The mage breathed another ragged sigh and turned back to the window. "And he's underestimating the opposition of the trappers.

"No," he stated after a moment, "the crusade will go on. The question to be asked now is, can Azoun pay the price for fighting this war?"

- 2 -

The Council of Suzail

Initially at least, King Azoun had far more trouble recruiting support for the crusade than Vangerdahast had predicted in the tower on that day. It wasn't that the monarch's persuasive powers were less than the royal wizard claimed. In fact, Azoun and his wife, Queen Filfaeril, had spent much of the winter speaking to their nobles and their neighbors; most of the rulers considered a preemptive attack on the Tuigan vital to preserving their countries, their cultures, and, most importantly, their treasuries.

In politics, however, rhetorical support and actual support sometimes have little in common. As the time for action grew near, few of the statesmen who seemed eager to lend troops to Azoun followed through on their promises. The source of this change of heart could be traced to a simple fear of popular unrest.

As in Cormyr, certain guilds throughout the Heartlands opposed any proposed crusade. Guilds were an important part of commerce and even everyday life in Faerun. Each trade, whether it be thieving, forestry, or smithing, had its own guild, and to become a lawful, certified member in any profession meant joining the appropriate organization. In this way, guilds insured that standards be met in the production of crafts and prices remained reasonable. The guilds also represented their members before governments, provided retirement funds, and even took care of members' widows and orphans.

Not all guilds stood against the proposed crusade. The armorers, fletchers, bowyers, and swordsmiths all stood to gain from the war. Even the teamsters and shipwrights knew that they would see an immediate profit from the expedition against the Tuigan. The merchants who stood to garner little from the conflict—the trappers who worked the Heartlands' wildernesses; the tanners who made leather from animal hides; even the butchers, who would lose business since the army would kill and dress its own meat knew only that higher taxes would come their way.

To counter the fear of guild opposition to the crusade, Azoun held conferences with those lords he could visit personally and dealt through messengers and magical communications with those located farther away. He encouraged the leaders to put the Tuigan matter before their people, allowing them to comment on the proposed crusade outside the restrictions of guild politics. Surprisingly, it was only a vocal minority that opposed the venture; most of the people supported a peremptory strike against the barbarians.

By weakening the nobles' fear of popular unrest, Azoun won back most of the troops committed to him during the winter. With the promise of strong dwarven support, the king won a few more tentative troop commitments. His charisma won still others. Finally, after a seemingly endless parade of small conferences, King Azoun called together all the leaders who he felt might support his cause.

"If I can persuade the Dales and Sembia to give me troops," the king said as he straightened his ornate ceremonial tunic, "I will stop the khahan before he breaks out of Thesk." He paused. "I do wish the queen could attend the meeting today. But . . . other matters of state demand at least one of us be present in the royal court."

Vangerdahast, sitting at a table covered with various parchment notes, nodded absently. "Don't forget to remind them of the dwarven support Ironlord Torg promised." The wizard rubbed his eyes slowly and put down the letter he was reading. "The Lords of Waterdeep send their regards."

Azoun froze. "They're not dispatching a representative to

the meeting?" His sharp tone was muffled by the carpets and tapestries that covered the cold stone walls of the study.

"Far too busy running the 'City of Splendors.' " Vangerdahast shook his head. "No. That's not quite fair. They note here—" He picked up the parchment again. " 'Though we recognize the importance of quelling the Tuigan incursion, we do not feel that it would be prudent for us to commit any of our forces at this time.' "

"I don't really blame them," the king sighed. "They lost a sizable part of their city guard during the Godswar."

The wizard nodded. "If Cormyr had been attacked by a troop of creatures from the Realm of the Dead, horsemen eating up territory on the other side of the continent wouldn't be our priority right now, either."

" 'The gods save men from some disasters only to thrust them into the middle of others.' " The king opened a dark wooden chest and took out a ceremonial sword. "Isn't that how the old saying goes?"

The heavy, earthy smell of pine wafted from the open trunk. Azoun inhaled deeply, soaking in the familiar, comforting scent. He closed his eyes for an instant and let the tension flow from his neck, then his arms, then his back. When he opened his eyes again, Vangerdahast was looking at him curiously.

"Nervous, Your Highness?"

"This is a very important meeting, Vangy. I can save hundreds, perhaps even thousands of lives if I—sorry, *we*—can persuade the people to our plans."

"This crusade is your plan, Azoun, not mine."

The king smiled warmly. "I know that you don't think a strike against the khahan is important, Vangy, but you've been invaluable to me in the last tenday. A few of the dalelords are here only from your prompting. I appreciate your aid."

"You're wrong about one thing, Azoun. I do believe that the campaign to stop the Tuigan *is* necessary. The khahan is a bloodthirsty savage intent on destroying as much as he can in as short a time as possible. The frightening old woman here to represent Rashemen at the meeting convinced me of that."

As Azoun turned to face the wizard, he couldn't hide his surprise. "If you agree that the crusade is necessary, why don't you agree with my plans?"

"Because I don't think you're the right person to lead the armies." The wizard raised his hand before Azoun could respond. "Not that I think you incapable of commanding the troops or making sound decisions . . . I just don't know if you realize what you're getting into."

A puzzled look replaced the shock on the king's face. "Why help me further my plans at all, Vangy?"

"I am, above all, your servant." The wizard bowed his head formally.

"Not friend?"

Vangerdahast was gathering the scattered stack of letters. He paused and studied the king. "Yes. Friend, too." The wizard fumbled with the stiff papers, then added, "But in the matter of the crusade, I will be of more aid to you as a servant of the crown."

The king strapped on the brightly gilded scabbard. "And why is that?"

"As your obedient subject, I will organize the crusade." The wizard stuffed the papers into a worn leather satchel, considering how to word the rest of his reply. After a moment, he concluded, "As your friend, I'd try to stop you from making what I see as a grave mistake."

Azoun shook his head. "I don't understand how can you separate your allegiances. I can only do what I think is right. And what's right is always right. The situation shouldn't have any bearing on it."

Anger clouded the wizard's features. He dropped the satchel onto the table, then quickly moved to the king's side and pulled the ceremonial sword from its scabbard. "You've been in battles before, Azoun, but never in a war. Charging into combat by yourself to face an ogre just isn't the same as leading thousands of men onto a battlefield."

The wizard slashed at the air angrily with the ornate weapon. "And you've grown more accustomed to ceremonial blades than real ones, Your Highness."

Azoun was more surprised by the anger in the wizard's voice than his actions. He gently took the saber from his friend's hands and replaced it at his side. "I know far more about warfare than you, Vangy. I've stood against enemies who should have beaten me, creatures that might have killed me with a single, bloody swipe. Perhaps—"

"That was more than twenty years ago," Vangerdahast interrupted. "Look in the mirror. You're not a young man anymore."

The silver-backed, full length mirror that stood in one corner of the room was an expensive rarity in Cormyr, but the king really wasn't concerned with the mirror's pure glass or the intricately wrought wooden frame. What caught Azoun's attention was the middle-aged man he saw reflected in the looking glass. His earth-brown eyes still gazed alertly back at him, but the king saw that the rest of his face and frame was showing the wear of his fifty-three years.

The most noticeable signs of aging visible to the king were the streaks of silver in his brown hair and beard. Azoun had been graying for much of the last twenty years, though, so that wasn't a surprise. Today, however, the creases around his eyes looked deeper, the bags under them a little darker, his cheeks more hollow and sunken. Although he exercised every day with sword and shield, the king's shoulders were bent, no doubt from the hours he spent poring over books or decrees in his study or the tower room. The king dismissed those things and decided that he was tired after the long nights of planning he'd gone through recently.

"Perhaps I am a bit worn down," he said brightly, "and I know that I'm no longer a young man . . . but I'm more experienced now than I ever was when traveling with the King's Men. Besides, I'm willing to gather strong, intelligent advisors about me."

The wizard didn't respond to the obvious compliment. "The dalelords will probably be waiting downstairs by now, and the others will be arriving shortly."

"Then you should make sure that the 'frightening old woman' from Rashemen is ready to address them," Azoun told Vangerdahast. He glanced into the mirror once more and straightened the ceremonial purple sash across his chest.

"You can joke about that woman because you haven't had to spend much time with her, listening to her tales about the Tuigan invading her land," the wizard said, picking up his satchel and opening the door. "I'll see you in the meeting hall in a few moments," he added as he left the room.

The king stared at the closed wooden door for a moment, not really seeing anything. He considered what Vangerda-hast had said about his inexperience, then frowned. The wizard was right: He had seen battles, but never a war. Cormyr had been at peace, apart from a few border skirmishes, for his entire life.

Spinning abruptly on the toe of one highly polished boot, Azoun turned toward the high, dark-wood bookshelf that covered an entire wall of the study. He walked briskly to the shelves, his heels thudding on the carpeted floor.

As he got close to the rows of ancient tomes he kept in the study, Azoun could smell the familiar, musty odor of old, well-read books. He ran his index finger along the spines of the mostly leather-bound volumes, searching for a particular book, a fifty-year-old family history.

Though most of the older books did not have their titles embossed on their spines, Azoun had little trouble finding the one that he wanted. It had a worn red cover and was the thickest volume in the study. The king quickly located the tome between his own treatise on the history of polearms in warfare and a collection of notes on falconry. He pulled the book from the shelf and headed for his desk.

A small, thin black tube rested on the dark oaken desk. As Azoun sat down he lifted it, and the rod of steel that the tube had covered cast a bright yellow-white light over the desk. The glowing rod, a simple piece of shaped metal with a spell cast upon it, was a product of Vangerdahast's magic; the radiance cast by the steel augmented the weak natural light in the study.

Gingerly Azoun unsnapped the chipped metal band from around the book and allowed it to fall open. A tight, neat script covered the yellowed pages, broken only by a hand-

ful of beautifully detailed illuminations, some done in ink
laced with gold or silver dust. The king flipped cracked
pages until he reached the section detailing the end of his
grandfather's reign. Azoun III had died when his son was
only six years old. The king's brother, Salember, had taken
control of the kingdom as regent until young Prince Rhigaerd grew old enough to seize the throne.

Azoun knew the family history's version of what happened next almost by heart. The wear on the pages certainly attested to this particular chapter's use over the
years.

Civil war, the section began, *was almost inevitable from
the day Salember, "the Rebel Prince," became regent. Salember was a shiftless, lecherous traitor to Cormyr's crown,
and within a year after taking hold of the government, he
began plotting the demise of Prince Rhigaerd. The details of
the Rebel Prince's crimes against our fair land will not
darken these pages. It is enough to note that the bloody revolt that eventually claimed Salember's life was of the regent's own making.*

The king licked his dry lips and continued to read.
The text on the next page, under a stylized rendition of
Rhigaerd II, Azoun's father, leading troops against his uncle,
contained the information for which Azoun searched.

*Cormyr has been cursed—or blessed—with few wars.
The War of the Regency, however, should remain a bloody
reminder of what grief war can bring. In 1260 and 1261, the
span of the conflict, the land was wracked with strife and
famine. In the Battle of Hilp alone, three thousand men died.
Corpses rested in the fields instead of crops in the fall of
that year, and plague ravaged the countryside.*

*Few were prepared for the sacrifices the conflict de-
manded. However, as King Rhigaerd, ruler of Cormyr at the
time this history is written, so rightly points out—*

" 'War is an endeavor never entered into lightly, though
there are many reasons to fight,' " the king quoted as he
closed the tome. He heard his father's voice behind those
words, heard his strength and his commitment to the land.

"I've found one of those reasons, Father," Azoun said softly as he covered the light. "Now I must convince the others that I don't enter into this conflict lightly."

*   *   *   *   *

The crowd gathered in the castle's large meeting hall that day included representatives from Sembia, the Dales, the various free city-states around the Inner Sea, and many of the most important Cormyrian nobles. Each dignitary was allowed, by Azoun's consent, one advisor or guard at the meeting. Some representatives, ever fearful of assassination attempts, brought powerful wizards or well-trained warriors with them. Others required only the company of a scribe.

All were there to hear Azoun give one final request for aid. Most did not know that the king had asked a representative of Rashemen, a country far to the east of Cormyr, a country already overrun by the Tuigan horselords, to speak to the assembly. Azoun hoped that the old woman would be able to sway the politicians who were still reluctant to commit any sizable number of troops or large sums of money to the crusade.

The king was wondering just how effective the woman would be, when a page knocked on the study door. "The lords and ladies are all gathered, Your Highness," the young boy said, bowing deeply. His mind racing ahead, full of speculations about the meeting's outcome, Azoun absently dismissed the youth and left the study.

The hallways the king paced through on his way to the meeting were a sharp contrast to his study. No soft carpets lined the hard stone floors, and no richly woven tapestries covered the whitewashed stone walls to prevent drafts. Where they butted against the castle's outer walls, the corridors were bordered with small windows. These cast only weak light in most places. The real light sources for the hallways, in fact much of the castle, were small metal globes that had been magically prepared to cast light continuously. Shadows hung thick in many places despite the regularly spaced magical globes.

Pages bowed and soldiers saluted as Azoun made his way to the court's central meeting hall. The king snapped automatic greetings to some of the servants and courtiers whom he passed. To others he simply nodded. By the time he reached the meeting hall, its doors guarded by a dozen well-armed soldiers, Azoun had gone over the outline of his speech three times.

Whatever comments he had prepared about Tuigan troop strength and the khahan's tactical abilities flew from Azoun's mind when he entered the hall. The burst of loud laughter that greeted him as he opened the door drove such organized thoughts away and replaced them with unsettling confusion.

The herald standing inside the hall started as the monarch entered, and the grin on his boyish face weakened to a faint smile. He quickly bowed to Azoun. "His Highness, King Azoun of Cormyr," the herald announced loudly, and the laughter died away.

The stylishly dressed men and women who sat at the three long trestle tables turned from something at the front of the large room and faced the door. Those few who were sitting immediately stood. All bowed to Azoun in the silence that had suddenly overtaken the room.

"Please, my friends," the king said, "there's no need for that. We are here as allies, to solve a common problem." He slowly scanned the crowd, meeting the gaze of as many people as he could. "Let us relax and speak as friends."

The lords and ladies, magicians and generals, visibly relaxed, and a murmur of renewed conversation washed over the room. Many of the thirty or so people sat down again. When they did, the king saw a handsome, dark-haired man sitting alone in front of the room. The blood-red shirt the royal bard wore was neat and proper, and it mirrored the embarrassed flush on his face quite well. Azoun smiled and walked to the young man's side.

"No doubt you were the cause of that outburst when I entered the room," the king said. "Just what story were you telling them, Thom?"

"I was trying to lighten the mood a bit, Your Highness," the man said, bowing his head and hugging his harp tight to his chest. His fingers slid nervously over the whales carved into the instrument's neck. "Vangerdahast told me to play for the gathering until you arrived. They were all rather somber . . . so I told them the tale of Sune and the hayward."

Azoun flinched slightly. That particular story of Sune Firehair, the Goddess of Beauty, was one of Thom Reaverson's better. Still, though not vulgar, the tale was a bit bawdy for mixed company. "Was that a wise choice, Thom?" the king asked, turning to look at the gathered nobles. Various polite excuses ran through his mind as he studied the assembled rulers of the most powerful cities and countries in Faerun.

"They requested it, milord."

"What?"

Thom smiled and pointed to an attractive young woman. As the king watched, the Cormyrian lady tossed her head back slightly, laughing at another noble's jest, letting her hair dance luxuriously around her bared shoulders. "She asked if I knew that particular story," the bard quietly told the king. "When I said yes, she requested I tell it. I tried to suggest another, more appropriate tale, but the other lords and ladies followed her lead."

King Azoun sighed, then smiled. "Thank you, Thom. You did the right thing. They probably wanted a little light fare to cut the tension before the meeting started." He pointed toward the doorway. "I'd like you to remain in the meeting hall, but at the back of the room. Observe what you can. We'll talk again later."

The bard nodded, then quietly moved from the front of the room. A few of the nobles applauded Thom, and he smiled and bowed in response. As the bard reached the door, Vangerdahast and a very, very old woman entered.

"Time for us to begin," Azoun announced, and the assembled men and women took their places at the long, polished wooden tables. Chairs lined one side of each table instead of the benches often used with them, and the three tables themselves formed a large **U**. The opening in the tables' arrangement faced the front of the room, where Thom

Reaverson had played and Azoun now stood.

The room in which the dignitaries gathered was large and had a high ceiling, with brightly colored pennants hanging from the rafters. The king had purposefully chosen the meeting hall, located deep inside the castle, because it had no windows, a single door, and thick walls of stone. If someone thought to assault the assembled leaders, he would have found the task difficult, if not impossible.

Still, though the hall was secure, it was rather drab, apart from the pennants hanging near the ceiling. Barren stone walls, whitewashed like all the walls in the castle, surrounded most of the room. Brightly glowing globes hung at regular intervals around the hall and sat upon each table, but shadows crept into corners and made many a face look far more ominous than it did in daylight. The only unusual ornamentation, a large, colorful cloth-and-thread map of Faerun, covered much of the wall behind the king.

Azoun stood framed by the tapestry, waiting for the assemblage to settle down. After a moment, he inclined his head slightly. Everyone recognized the subtle request for silence. Vangerdahast and the old woman continued toward the front of the room as Azoun said, "May Torm, God of Duty, help us discover our responsibilities to Faerun, and may the gods of all gathered here aid them in their search for the best path to the truth."

By now the royal magician had reached the front of the room. A servant quickly brought a chair for the old woman, but she waved it away silently. Her tight-skinned, age-spotted face remained impassive and unreadable, even when Azoun smiled at her in greeting. Looking at the woman, the king realized why she so unsettled Vangerdahast. A prominent, knife-thin nose jutted out from between her close-set violet eyes, and it, like the rest of the woman's thin face, was covered with ash-gray skin pulled taut. In all, it seemed to Azoun that he was gazing at an ancient, but well-preserved corpse.

"Go ahead, Vangy," the king said softly as he pulled his eyes from the old woman's steady gaze.

Vangerdahast patted his beard, and his eyes seemed to

lose focus under the bushy covering of his eyebrows. He inhaled deeply once, then again. Closing his eyes, the mage started to mutter a low, rumbling incantation. The few wizards in the room, members of various delegations, leaned to their companions and whispered that the royal magician was casting a spell to detect scrying. If anyone was attempting to magically eavesdrop on the conference, Vangerdahast would be able to ferret out their spell.

At the front of the room, Vangerdahast's chant grew louder, more frantic. His hands wove a complex pattern in the air. Without warning, he raised his fingertips to his temples, opened his eyes, and uttered the spell's final word. A brilliant blue-white flash burned through the room.

"By Mystra's wound!" Vangerdahast cried. The wizard covered his eyes and fell backward onto the floor.

The skittering sound of swords leaving their sheaths and daggers sliding from boot tops hissed in the room. A few well-trained soldiers, guards for various dignitaries, crouched next to their lords, ready for battle. A mage cast a spell, and a glowing sphere of protection appeared around one of the dalelords.

The few Cormyrian guards in the room rushed to Azoun's side, but the king paid them no attention. "What's going on, Vangy?" he asked as he helped his mentor from the gray stone floor.

The wizard rubbed his eyes with both hands and muttered curses under his breath. "Someone close by had a very powerful spell locked on this room. That flash was caused by my incantation uncovering the other mage's scrying spell. Their contact with the room has been severed."

Many of the dignitaries relaxed, but few of the bodyguards put their weapons away. A large, middle-aged man slammed the hilt of his broadsword against the tabletop, breaking the room's uneasy silence. "If we could trace that spell," he growled, "we'd find a Zhentish agent to be the spellcaster."

"How do you know that, Lord Mourngrym?" asked a quivering merchant from Sembia.

All eyes turned to the nobleman who had spoken first:

Mourngrym, lord of Shadowdale. The dalelord frowned as he slipped his broadsword into its jeweled sheath, but when he saw that he commanded the room's attention, he straightened his thick-muscled frame to its full height and smoothed his immaculate, stylish surcoat. Almost casually he cast an appraising eye over the crowd and drew his mouth into a hard line in the midst of his neatly trimmed beard and mustache. The politicians in the room who were allied with the dalelord would later call the look on his face as he spoke benign, even paternalistic. Those who thought less of the nobleman labeled the expression condescending.

"Who else but Zhentil Keep would want to spy on this gathering?" Mourngrym touched the symbol of Shadowdale—a twisted tower in front of an upturned crescent moon—which lay over his heart on his impeccably tailored surcoat. "We from the Dales know of the Keep's evil better than anyone."

Vangerdahast shook his head and stepped forward. "The mages at the Keep would have used a far more subtle spell than the one I discovered."

"What about the Trappers' Guild, then?" the dalelord returned. "I hear you're having trouble with them about the crusade."

"A few grouchy hunters hardly constitute 'trouble,' " Azoun offered. He bowed slightly to the delegates from the important merchant kingdom of Sembia. "Though we certainly have the highest respect for our trade guilds."

The leader of the Sembian delegation, Overmaster Elduth Yarmmaster, stood. A rather flabby man with a relaxed, almost discourteous air about him, the overmaster was resplendent in rich purple robes that morning. "We have heard of the trade unrest in your land, Your Highness, and it does trouble us. However, isn't it more likely the Tuigan themselves are spying upon us?" He waved a fat-fingered, gold-ringed hand in lazy circles. "They, above all, would dearly love to learn our plans."

"You obviously know little of the Tuigan."

The voice was low and gravelly, but strong. All heads turned to the front of the room, where the old woman stood. She regarded the assembly coldly, through hooded eyes. After running her fingers along the fold of her plain white wrap, the woman added, "The Tuigan do not value magic as we do, and they care little for what you do here in Cormyr."

Gasps and mutters answered the woman's slight. Vangerdahast and Azoun both stepped to her side and held up their hands in an attempt to calm the crowd.

"Do not quiet them on my account, Azoun of Cormyr," the old woman said flatly, turning her sharp gray features toward the king. "Once they hear the wisdom of my words they will be respectful enough."

The muttering grew angrier, and Azoun silently wished that they had not been blessed with the woman's presence. She may have won Vangerdahast to his side, but she was about to alienate most of his allies. "Please, noble lords and ladies, Fonjara Galth is a representative from Rashemen. Hear what she has to say."

When Azoun identified the woman, the assembly quieted almost instantly. Though many in Faerun traded with Rashemen, which lay on the easternmost fringes of the "civilized Realms," few westerners were very comfortable in the presence of that country's people. Ballads often referred to Rashemen as the "Land of Berserkers," for many of its inhabitants were savage, relentless fighters. More mysterious still were the country's rulers. A *huhrong* nominally guided the land from his steel-walled palace in the city of Immilmar. In reality, a powerful, secretive group of witches held the reins of Rashemen's government.

Though the witches rarely traveled outside their country without adopting foolproof disguises, the lords and ladies who stood and sat in shocked silence wondered if Fonjara might indeed be one of Rashemen's real rulers.

The short old woman held her body still, her thin, bony arms folded across her chest. She surveyed the room for a moment, paying particular attention to the wizards who waited, slack-jawed, for her to speak. "I will not pretend or play games with you. I am here on behalf of Huhrong Huzzilthar, lord of Immilmar and commander of our standing army—and the sisterhood who also rule the land."

Gasps and murmurs washed over the room anew at Fonjara's overt reference to the witches. A faint, fleeting half-smile crossed the woman's gray face as she listened to the astonished hum from the nobles. A few of the Cormyrian lords looked to Azoun and Vangerdahast for some kind of confirmation. The king and his advisor remained stone-faced as best they could, though Azoun was finding it difficult to contain his excitement.

"My people have battled the dire Red Wizards of Thay, our villainous neighbors to the north, for many years," the woman rasped after a moment. "We have kept those vile sorcerers in check with little help from the rest of Faerun. Now, we face another threat, the Tuigan—and our magic and the bloodied steel of our bravest warriors are not enough to stop this barbaric horde."

For the first time since reaching the front of the room, the old woman moved her body. She unfurled her spindly arms and traced a complex symbol in front of her. Fonjara's voice remained low and threatening, and her incantation sounded more like a curse than a chant. Not even Vangerdahast could identify the spell she was attempting to cast, the power she was trying to summon. In less than a minute, the witch pulled a tiny pouch from her bone-white robe and emptied its contents into the air.

The faintly transparent image of a squat, unwashed man, wearing heavy leather leggings and soiled scale mail, appeared next to Fonjara. His long reddish hair was bound into braids, which fell below the simple silver helmet he wore. The ghostly image turned, unseeing, to the crowd, and Azoun noticed the pale, jagged scar that ran across the bridge of his nose and down his cheek. A second scar, grayer and therefore probably older, pulled the man's upper lip into a slight sneer.

"This is Yamun Khahan," the old woman noted, "self-proclaimed emperor of all the world—at least an image of him as he currently is. Presently, he is in camp with one hundred thousand warriors in Ashanath, near the Lake of Tears, immediately to the west of my country."

After a moment's pause, Fonjara Galth wrapped her arms tightly around herself again. Turning only her head toward King Azoun, she hissed, "This is the man who will gladly destroy all of Faerun if given the opportunity. He will attempt to kill anyone who stands in his way—even a king."

Her statement was no revelation to Azoun or the nobles gathered in the court, but coming from the witch's lips, it sounded ominous, like a promise of events that must inevitably come to pass. Cormyr's ruler shuddered slightly, but shook off the feeling of dread immediately. He walked close to the Yamun Khahan's slightly flickering form.

The witch looked at the king, then at the nobles. Slowly, methodically, she began a description of the typical military encounter with the horsewarriors. Fonjara detailed the terrible slaughter and suffering that had been inflicted both on Rashemen's army and its civilians. Looks of shock and disgust hung on most of the faces in the room. Only then did the witch smile very slightly and note, "And they will continue across all of Faerun like this unless they are stopped. Ashanath is a thousand miles to your east, but the barbarians will not stay there for long."

Fonjara's steady, icy gaze fell upon Azoun. "In addition to the five score thousand Tuigan with the khahan, there are, perhaps, twenty thousand or more still in my land. We have eliminated at least five thousand Tuigan soldiers since early last winter, when they first entered our borders."

Overmaster Elduth Yarmmaster, leader of the Sembians, ruffled his thick purple sleeve, then tugged at one of his flabby chins and stood up. "Excuse me, er, Lady Fonjara, but it seems to me that twenty thousand soldiers should not be a problem to Rashemen's legendary army."

"If we had only to face the Tuigan, there would be no problem at all," the old woman rumbled. "However, Zulkir Szass Tam, the undead ruler of the Red Wizards of Thay, made a pact with Yamun Khahan: if the Tuigan would pass through Rashemen instead of Thay, he and his wizards would part the Lake of Tears, allowing them easy access to the open lands beyond." She regarded the room coldly. "The countries of Ashanath, Thesk, and eventually your own lands."

Vangerdahast cleared his throat noisily and added, "The Red Wizards of Thay have used this attack as a convenient diversion. Their armies of gnolls, goblins, and even undead creatures have been expanding their borders. Aglarond, Thesk, Ashanath, and, of course, Rashemen are currently fighting two wars—one with the Tuigan, the other with the agents of Thay."

"So who are we supposed to battle on this crusade: Thay or the barbarians?" a gruff, unshaven commander from Tantras called out.

Fonjara uncurled, then clenched her gnarled fingers impatiently. Azoun looked away from the conjured khahan and said, "The Tuigan. The local armies can handle the incursions from Thay. For now, at least, the Red Wizards seem to be testing the waters and aren't launching any large-scale invasions."

Mourngrym, lord of Shadowdale, sighed and shook his head. "What you're saying is that we'll be fighting this khahan and his horde without any help from the people we're saving."

King Azoun frowned. "You're helping yourself, too, Lord Mourngrym. The Tuigan could cross Faerun and be sitting on our doorsteps in a little over one year."

The dalelord waved his hand in front of him, dismissing the idea completely. "That's all as may be, Your Highness."

Vangerdahast, his face flushed with anger, started to speak, but Fonjara held up a bony finger to stop him. The wizard swallowed his retort as the witch moved cautiously across the room. The conjured image of Yamun Khahan blinked, then disappeared as Fonjara reached the spot where Mourngrym sat.

"You would like to dismiss the Tuigan as easily as I have banished the noncorporeal khahan who stood before us," she began, leaning slowly toward the dalelord.

Shifting uncomfortably in his seat, Mourngrym said, "You must realize that we have problems of our own." The unassuming, bespectacled scribe at the dalelord's side nodded, but remained as silent as he had throughout the meeting.

Fonjara narrowed her eyes and whispered, "How old is

your child, dalelord?"

Mourngrym Amcathra snapped to his feet, his handsome features contorted in anger. "What's my child have to do with this?"

"The twisted tower that you call your home will not save you from Yamun Khahan if he reaches the Dales." The witch spread her fingers like talons and raked the air in front of Mourngrym. "Not even the great Elminster himself, who I understand resides in Shadowdale at present, could stop a thousand Tuigan arrows from striking you, or your wife, or your young child."

The dalelord sputtered, then began, "Elminster could—"

"—do nothing," Fonjara finished for him flatly. Her violet eyes paled, almost to the color of her ash-gray skin. "Magic is always a force to be reckoned with, but the horse-warriors vastly outnumber the wizards you could muster to fight them."

"By the way," Vangerdahast chimed in, the sarcasm evident in his voice, "where is Elminster?"

Mourngrym's scribe stood. The short, inoffensive man had a slightly vague look about him, which was heightened by the casual way he cleared his throat before he spoke. "He was too busy to come, Master Vangerdahast."

Fonjara cackled low in her throat and turned away from the dalesmen. Azoun arched one eyebrow and asked, "Too busy, Lhaeo?"

The dark-skinned scribe glanced around the room, then resettled his spectacles on his nose. "His exact words were, 'Let the kings and nobles go off and—' " Lhaeo paused and swallowed hard " '—play at war. My time is far too valuable.' "

"Unsurprisingly," Fonjara noted as she returned to Azoun's side, "your wizards will be far more interested in poring over the contents of their libraries than in saving the ground those same buildings stand upon."

As Mourngrym and Lhaeo sat down, the beautiful, dark-haired woman who had requested the Sune tale from Thom rose to her feet. She'd had enough of the dalelord's stalling and wanted to get the real agenda for the meeting underway. "For those here who know me not," she began, "I am

Myrmeen Lhal, lord of the Cormyrian city of Arabel. The people of my city are ready to pledge three hundred soldiers and thirty mages to the cause."

The Cormyrian lords and generals gave a short but enthusiastic cheer. King Azoun bowed his head in acknowledgment. "My thanks, Myrmeen. And what of the rest of my nobles?" He smiled secretly; one could always count on the beautiful lord of Arabel to cut to the heart of such matters.

A gaunt man stood up, ringing his hands nervously. Tiny beads of sweat worked their way down his pale face and into his overly starched white collar. "Ildool, the king's lord in Marsember, pledges, uh, the same as Myrmeen Lhal."

"What?" Vangerdahast snapped. "Marsember is at least twice, if not three times the size of Arabel." The royal magician looked to the wizard who sat at Ildool's side and asked, "Are you sure you've counted correctly?"

The young wizard frowned in response to Vangerdahast's steady glare, then fluttered through some papers. "Lord Ildool is mistaken," he said after a moment. "These calculations tell me that King Azoun can expect eight hundred men-at-arms, seventy wizards, and—" the mage paused and looked up at Ildool, who rubbed his hands with a bit more speed and nodded, "—and as many ships as we can spare to transport you to the east."

Azoun smiled and moved quickly to Ildool's side. "My thanks. The valor of your subjects reflects well upon you." The gaunt man stopped twisting his hands and bowed to the king.

"It's the least I could do," he concluded and sat down with a flourish.

Vangerdahast rolled his eyes and muttered, "No doubt," under his breath.

The other Cormyrian lords followed the lead set by Myrmeen Lhal and Ildool of Marsember. Before the representatives from Sembia, the Dales, or any of the free cities around the Inner Sea spoke, Azoun had gathered ten thousand warriors and almost three hundred wizards for his crusade. But this was as the king had expected. Azoun knew that his nobles—even Ildool—were generally loyal and that they would raise as many troops as possible. In fact, the nobles owed him a certain number of troops in lieu of their own military service under Cormyrian law. The real question remained the free cities, the Dales, and Sembia.

Sembia declared its intentions first. After the Cormyrians had all pledged their troops and ships to further their king's mission, Overmaster Elduth Yarmmaster heaved his bulk to a standing position and addressed the assembly.

"I will not promise Sembian troops to the crusade."

Chaos erupted in the room. Azoun stood, shocked into silence, at the head of the assembly; this was not what he had expected at all. Sembia was a large country, a very important part of the Heartlands and vital to the effort against the Tuigan. Azoun badly needed the merchant nation's support.

A few Cormyrian nobles, including Myrmeen Lhal, voiced not-so-veiled threats to the Sembian dignitaries sitting near them. The merchants, for their part, either sat silently, ignoring the jibes, or noisily gathered their papers in preparation to leave. Mourngrym and the other dalelords huddled in smug satisfaction, certain that they were not alone in their belief that fighting other peoples' battles was a mistake.

The overmaster rapped his flabby fist on the table. "Sembia will, however, give any ships the crusaders need, as well as money for mercenaries and supplies."

That promise only quieted the room slightly, but it was all that the Sembian leader was willing to offer. His country did not have a large standing army, and if Sembian commoners were going to be recruited, Azoun's personality would not be enough to lure them into battle with the Tuigan.

Azoun understood the Sembians' military position. Though he did not relish the idea of fighting alongside mercenaries, the king knew that he had little choice but accept them if he wished to stop Yamun Khahan.

"Your offer is generous," Azoun said as loudly as he could, short of yelling. "We appreciate it greatly."

The Cormyrian nobles took this as an order for silence and immediately quieted down. The overmaster's offer, while doing little to sway the dalesmen, was generous enough that the representatives from the free cities of Tantras, Hillsfar, and Ravens Bluff all agreed to raise contingents for the crusade. Azoun was glad for this, not only because the troops raised from Hillsfar and Tantras promised to be well-trained warriors, but because the free cities could provide more wizards for his ranks.

Finally, after the representative from Ravens Bluff returned to her seat, Lord Mourngrym ordered his scribe to pack up their papers. "You've done nothing—other than let an old woman threaten me—that might persuade me to join the fight."

Vangerdahast, who was resting in a straight-backed chair, pointed at the dalelord. "You've chosen to find no reason to join us," the wizard said bitterly.

"If that's your opinion," snapped a red-haired general from Battledale, "then we all might as well leave right now!"

Azoun shot an angry glance at his friend. It was clear that Vangerdahast's approach would only alienate the dalesmen further. "Please, friends," the king began, "how can I convince you of our task's importance?"

"It's not the importance of the crusade that eludes us," Mourngrym told Azoun. "However, Your Highness, you seem unable to see that any troops we send to Thesk will be men who can't stand with us against the Zhentish if they decide to attack."

"And if the Tuigan didn't try to magically spy on us at the start of the meeting," someone noted from the crowd, "then it was certainly the Zhentish."

Mourngrym nodded his approval of the comment. After glancing around for effect, he added, "I don't even see a representative from Zhentil Keep here."

"Of course not," Azoun said calmly. "I did not invite their ambassador. We will hold separate meetings after I know your dispositions."

The soldier from Battledale snorted a laugh. "We can hardly give you our 'disposition' until we know what the Keep intends to do." The steady light from the magical globe on the table cast ominous shadows on the man's face. His flaming red hair only made him look all the more demonic.

A few of the others gathered in the room bristled at the dalesman's impertinence. Mourngrym was known to be a good ruler, protective of his people, so they could excuse the edge in his voice. But this man, a member of the Battledale militia, was intolerable.

Lord Mourngrym recognized this, too, and quickly moved to head off a nasty confrontation. "Thank you for your input, General Elventree." He turned to Azoun, and the hard line of his mouth softened slightly. "If Your Highness can secure the cooperation of the Zhentish, we will consider raising troops for the crusade."

Cormyrian nobles smiled at the concession, but the other dalesmen's objections to the offer were apparent on their faces. "However," Mourngrym added, more to his fellow dalelords than to Azoun, "any troops levied from the Dales will be put under commanders from the Dales."

After a short silence, Azoun nodded slowly. "There is nothing more for me to say, then. Unless someone else has something to add, this meeting is at an end." The king waited for a moment, then bowed his head again in prayer to the God of Duty.

As soon as the prayer was over, Mourngrym again signaled to his scribe, who quickly gathered up his papers. "We appreciate being included in this conference, Your Highness," the dalelord told Azoun, a genuine warmth in his voice, "but waiting here any longer might be counterproductive. We wish you luck with the Zhentish. We will await Your Highness's word on their reply."

With that, Mourngrym snatched up his fur-trimmed cloak and headed for the door, his scribe in tow. The other dalesmen—including General Elventree from Battledale—quickly followed the lord, leaving a subdued, milling assembly in their wake. The Cormyrian nobles and other representatives soon paid their respects to Azoun and left, too. When Fonjara Galth made her way from the room, Thom Reaverson was at her side. The royal bard, prompted only slightly by the king, was intent on learning more of Rashemen. Within half an hour, Azoun was once again alone with Vangerdahast.

The king sat on a table's edge, studying the tapestry that hung at the end of the hall. He had stood in front of the hanging for the entire meeting, but only now considered the backdrop from the assembly's perspective.

Woven from threads of gold, silver, and other precious metals, the tapestry depicted the continent of Faerun, with Cormyr purposefully prominent at its center. Around the hanging's edge, the artist had placed renderings of Cormyr's kings from the last thousand years. Azoun saw his forefathers, from Pryntaler to his own father, Rhigaerd II, staring emotionlessly at him from the wall.

"My father had them leave Salember, 'the Rebel Prince,' off the tapestry, even though he ruled the country for almost eleven years," Azoun said absently.

Vangerdahast took a seat behind the king. "If Salember had been the victor of the civil war, your father wouldn't be on the tapestry and I daresay you probably wouldn't be alive."

Azoun frowned, thinking about all he knew of Salember's reign. "He wasn't a bad ruler, Vangy—Salember, I mean— and some say he had a right to the throne."

"Why bring this up now?"

Shifting to face his advisor, Azoun mulled over a thought for a moment, then said, "I wonder how my ancestors will portray me, Vangy. I've been a good king, but I could do something so wrong that all my good deeds would be forgotten. Salember forces me to remember that."

" 'You will make history,' " the wizard quoted from his old lessons to, then, Prince Azoun, " 'but history can unmake you.' "

Azoun laughed and nodded. "What will history say about the council today?"

Raggedly Vangerdahast sighed and drummed his fingers on his not inconsiderable paunch. "You controlled it as best you could, I suppose."

"If that's the best you can say, we're in sorry shape."

The wizard rubbed his eyes and started to add something, then stopped. In actuality, Vangerdahast wasn't quite sure what to think of the meeting. He settled for a noncommittal reply. "At least your nobles followed your lead."

Azoun was quick to pick up the hesitancy in his advisor's responses. "As we expected," he noted as he studied Vangerdahast's face for some clue as to his true opinion. "But what about Sembia, or, more to the point, the Dales?"

The wizard shrugged. "We got what we could from Yarmmaster and Sembia. Their army is so small it has trouble keeping the peace at home, so we shouldn't expect anything other than financial support."

"I'm still not all that comfortable with hiring mercenaries, Vangy."

"You have no choice," the wizard replied. "At least Sembia will pay for some of them."

"And the Dales?"

"Not even a witch from Rashemen could predict what they will do," Vangerdahast said flatly. "It mostly depends on your meeting with the Zhentish delegate two days from now." The wizard paused and stood up. "Even if you do get Zhentish support, you're going to have trouble placing the dalesmen in the army."

"Ah, Mourngrym's ridiculous demand for dalesmen leading themselves."

"Ridiculous?" Vangerdahast repeated, his eyes wide with surprise.

Azoun nodded, wondering why his friend was taken aback by his comment. "I'll not have anyone undermining my command of these forces, Vangy. For us to succeed, there must be one clear leader on the expedition."

"You're being inflexible."

"Not inflexible, Vangy. I'm right. Military history shows that—"

Vangerdahast threw his arms into the air and looked up at the ceiling. "One minute you're damning fickle historians and the next you're basing your army's organization upon their advice."

Azoun scowled and crossed his arms over his chest. "I find good advice where I can."

"No, Azoun," Vangerdahast began, then shook his head. "It's just like Alusair used to—"

All the color drained from the king's face at the mention of his youngest daughter. Vangerdahast saw the pained expression that took hold of his friend and instantly regretted the slip. The princess's opinion of her father's stubbornness was, however, a very valid point to bring up.

It was Azoun's inflexibility that caused his conflict with Alusair. No one really believed that it was entirely the king's fault his daughter had run away four years past, for Alusair was as headstrong and willful as her father was sure that she had a duty to the state. Still, if Azoun hadn't pressed her to abandon her desire to see the rest of the world before settling down to a life of royal responsibility, she wouldn't have fled. And though Azoun had offered a generous reward for her return, Alusair remained hidden from even Vangerdahast's considerable magical talent.

All these facts, and more personal things, raced through Azoun's mind. Vangerdahast bowed his head and mumbled, "I'm sorry, Azoun."

The king closed his eyes for a moment and banished the memories as best he could. "As I was saying," he began dully, trying to avoid the topic altogether, "it is important that one person be recognized as the crusade's leader. For this venture to be successful, we need to dissuade our soldiers of their national loyalties. We should fight as one, and this means Mourngrym's demand for dalesmen leading dalesmen is utterly impossible."

"Have you even considered letting another man lead the crusade?" Vangerdahast asked quietly.

"Cormyr is committing the most troops," replied Azoun sharply. "Are you willing to give them over to another leader?"

"That depends upon who stepped forward," Vangerdahast said, though there was little conviction in his voice. His spirit still muffled by his painful error, the wizard meekly returned to his seat.

"Who, Vangy? Mourngrym, perhaps? How about the Sembians' mercenaries? Would they have my training in strategy? How about that hotheaded general from Battledale—Elventree?" The king hammered the table with a fist, anger roiling inside of him. "I am the only one to lead this crusade. I am the best trained. I—"

Azoun ran a hand through his beard and straightened the scabbard at his side. When he spoke again, Vangerdahast heard the cold resolve in his voice. "I know that I'm fighting for what's right. I fight for Cormyr and for Faerun, not for myself."

A deeper sadness took hold of the royal magician as he realized that Azoun was correct. There was no other ruler in Faerun better suited for the crusade, no one who could muster as many troops or lead them against the Tuigan with as much zeal. The wizard pushed himself up from the table and headed toward the door.

Azoun moved to Vangerdahast's side, putting a hand on his shoulder. "I want you to see that I'm right," the king said softly.

"Your Highness knows this matter best. As your servant, I will support you in any way I can."

Vangerdahast heard Azoun's sigh. "And as my friend?"

The wizard gazed deep into the king's oak-brown eyes. "As your friend I am sorry that you are the best man to lead the army against the horsewarriors."

"Then that will have to do," Azoun said. He took his hand off Vangerdahast's shoulder. The wizard turned and exited the room, leaving the king alone to study the faces on the tapestry once more.

– 3 –

Razor John

"Sure flights! Razor points!"

The fletcher's cry rang out over the marketplace. Other wandering sellers called, "Nice red apples!" or "Boots mended! Leather repaired!" The fletcher's call, borne by his deep, resonant voice, carried over these and other noises.

"Sure flights! Razor points! Buy your arrows from John the Fletcher! Only the best from Razor John!" Pausing a moment to settle the heavy cart in his hands, John the Fletcher took in the sights and sounds of Suzail's market.

It was a beautiful morning. Winter was finally loosing its grip on Cormyr, and the sun shone brightly in the cloudless azure sky. The nights were still chilly, of course, but the days were getting more and more pleasant all the time. The nice weather brought people out to the market, so merchants and shoppers now crowded the open area reserved for tradesmen like John. A few permanent tents and stalls dotted the dusty expanse, but the place was mostly packed with small-time sellers and farmers. Shoppers bustled from one stall to the next. Cooks frowned at unripe imported fruits and vegetables, and merchants smiled endearingly, trying to lure people toward their goods. Ham and beef and other, more exotic meats roasted over small fires, sending tempting smells and black, greasy smoke twisting into the air. Pack animals brayed, gulls screamed overhead, and people jabbered and bartered, creating a steady, roaring hum that would hang over the square until the sun set.

"Morning, milady," John said to a passing flower peddler. He lifted his black felt hat with one gloved hand and grinned at the pretty young woman. John had seen her around the market before, and by the purple sash she wore around her waist, he could tell that she was a maiden looking for a mate.

She passed the fletcher by without so much as a second glance. John shrugged, hefted his cart again, and set off toward the docks.

"Sure flights! Only the best from Razor John!"

The fletcher had walked but twenty yards or so, calling out his wares, when a stout man signaled him to stop. The man's sunburned face was almost hidden by the fur cloak he wore over his earth-brown tunic. The fletcher immediately assumed him to be an itinerant mercenary from the grimy, unkempt state of his dress.

"What'll it be today, good sir?" John asked as he unrolled the cloth on the top of his cart. A dozen different types of arrows and crossbow bolts lay on display.

The man glanced at the weapons, then looked to the fletcher. "I heard you call 'Razor John.' Is there anyone else in the market who uses that name?"

John rubbed the dark stubble on his chin. "Not that I know of, though I'd wager there are other fletchers in Suzail who go by the name of John."

The fur-clad man nodded. "No, my good man. If you are *the* Razor John, then you're the only fletcher I seek." He picked up a silver-tipped longbow arrow and turned it over in his hands. Sunlight glinted off the finely honed arrowhead.

"You've got a good eye," John noted casually, studying the customer. "That type of arrow is one of my specialties."

"You make the arrowheads, too?"

"Aye. I've been trained as an arrowsmith as well as a fletcher."

The man looked at John suspiciously. "Do you pay dues in the Fletchers' Guild *and* the Arrowsmiths' Guild?"

John shrugged his left arm toward the customer. "Of course," he said, slapping his hand over two patches tied around his arm. The small leather circles had the symbols of the Fletchers' and Arrowsmiths' Guilds stamped into them. "Licenses are up to date, as well."

An odd smile crossed the man's face. "A guildsman. Good. I'll take two hundred of your silver-tipped arrows, then."

John raised one eyebrow in surprise. He was accustomed to selling such quantities of arrows, but only to ships' stewards, the royal guard, or the city watch. "My apologies, good sir, but I don't have that many on hand." John rolled the cloth display aside and opened his cart. He removed four batches of ten arrows each.

"I don't need them right now," the customer said. "I'll be in the market to pick up the rest in—" John held up one finger. "A tenday, it is."

They discussed how and where John was to deliver the arrows. The terms were simple enough, and the fur-clad man paid the fletcher thirty pieces of silver as a down payment. John was pleased with the sale, for it seemed to indicate that his reputation as a craftsman was spreading. Still, he wondered why the man wanted so many arrows.

"Outfitting a mercenary company?" John asked as he pocketed the silver coins. "The king is going to be hiring well-outfitted sell-swords for the crusade against the barbarian invaders in Thesk."

The man's sunburned face paled noticeably. "You'd sell arrows to someone supporting Azoun's foolish plan?" he asked, his lips curling into an almost feral snarl. "I'm tempted to cancel my order, even if you are a guildsman!" Not taking his eyes off John, he slipped his hand into his purse and removed a small leather badge similar to the ones the fletcher wore—this one, though, bore an open, jagged-toothed bear trap stamped into it.

John stared at the badge. The man wasn't a mercenary; he was a trapper. The opposition the Trappers' Guild was fomenting against the king was rumor throughout Suzail, but the trappers had yet to brave any truly public statement of their opinion about the proposed crusade. Suddenly, the fletcher realized that the grimy trapper might be needing the arrows for just such a statement.

"I may be a guildsman, but I'm also a good subject of the king," John said gruffly. He dug the silver coins out of his pocket and dropped them into the dirt. "I'll not be selling weapons to malcontents for them to use in a revolt."

"Better a malcontent than a fool," the trapper snapped. He quickly snatched up the coins and turned to go. "You'll remember this when the king's tax collector takes your shop away." Without another word, the fur-clad man disappeared into the crowded marketplace.

John simply shook his head in dismay and packed up his cart. He'd heard a great deal about Azoun's crusade—and the trappers' opposition to it—in the last few tendays. It was common knowledge that the king was meeting with important nobles and even the leaders of Sembia and the Dales, trying to get their cooperation. The fletcher wondered for a moment if he should report the trapper to the city guard, then decided he would that evening.

Not that he thought the trappers posed any real threat to the king. Azoun's army, known as Purple Dragons, could certainly thwart any minor uprising. More importantly, Azoun was going to make a public speech that very afternoon—a speech, rumor had it, in which the king would formally announce the crusade. After the official declaration of war, the government would swiftly equip the crusading army and move it to the east. If the trappers hadn't yet done anything to unify the scattered groups that were against the venture, it might soon be too late.

Shielding his eyes, John looked into the sky and estimated from the sun's position that he had enough time to make one delivery before the king's speech. He quickly lifted the wooden cart and set off for the Black Rat, a tavern near the docks, east of the marketplace. On his way through the crowded streets, the fletcher thought not of battles in faraway lands, but of the apprentice in his shop. He'd have to visit him before his delivery at the tavern.

A few blocks from the Black Rat, John left his cart at home. The fletcher lived above his forge and workshop. He sometimes sold his wares from the shop, but it was located far from the market. John found that by traveling part of the day, showing examples of his work, he could drum up much more business than came looking for him.

His apprentice was a young lad with sandy brown hair and nimble, long fingers. As the fletcher entered the bright, open-fronted shop, the boy was stripping feathers, preparing them to become fletching. "Take time out at highsun to hear the king," John told the boy, examining his work over his shoulder.

"Thank you, Master John," the apprentice chimed.

The fletcher laughed. "It's your duty to King Azoun to listen to his proclamations, Loreth, not a gift I can give you." John tossed some poorly prepared fletching onto the dirty wooden floor and patted the boy on the back. "Take more care with these. Tell Mikael and Rolf at the guildhall that I'll have work for them for the next few days. You'll be busy, too," he added as an afterthought. Then John gathered up the arrows he needed to deliver at the tavern and left.

The Black Rat was crowded when he arrived. Smoke hung in the low-ceilinged taproom, making the dark interior only darker. Two dozen men and a few women squatted on wobbly chairs around uneven tables, smoking pipes, eating breakfast, and telling wild tales.

"No," John heard someone yell, "storm giants are at least twice that size!" He turned to see an elf wearing leather armor. The exotic-looking man, his fine-boned cheeks flushed with wine or the argument in which he was engaged, leaned back in his chair and gestured wildly.

A squinting, tomato-nosed dwarf sitting across from the elf folded his arms across his long, white beard and barrel-like chest. "Bah!" he rumbled. "I've killed more giants in my time than you ever saw!"

The elf leaned forward, made some comment about orcs, and continued the argument more quietly. John couldn't hear what was said next, but he caught snatches of dozens of other conversations, some more interesting, some less than the one going on between the elf and dwarf. Mixed in with these, men and women called for the barmaid. The woman usually responded with a shrill, "In a minute."

Over this cacophony, the fletcher heard someone yell,

"Hey, Razor John! Over here!"

He scanned the room for his customer, a sailor named Geoff from a Sembian merchant ship. Eventually the fletcher spotted the man sitting at a table near the back of the room. Pulling the bundle of arrows close to his chest to avoid jostling anyone in the taproom, John made his way to the sailor.

"Well met!" the Sembian said, clapping John on the shoulder as he reached the table. "I see my arrows are ready."

John smiled amicably and opened one of the bundles. The arrows it contained had the standard shaft and fletching of those used by many hunters. Their heads, though, were quite different from those on typical, pointed hunting arrows. Shaped like crescent moons, these arrowheads were meant primarily to cut through rigging on ships.

Geoff glanced at them and nodded. "The pirates off the Turmish coast will be surprised to see these slash through their lines." He slapped down a few gold pieces in payment, then signaled to the barmaid and motioned for John to join him at the table.

"I suppose you're waiting to hear King Azoun's speech this afternoon," the sailor said once the barmaid had delivered an ale for John and another for him.

The fletcher sipped the warm, bitter brew and nodded. "I've heard he's going to announce another heir is on the way. I don't much believe that, though."

"Nah," Geoff snorted. "He's much too old." When he saw John's scowl, he added, "Not that I meant that as disrespectful or nothing."

A brawny, ham-fisted man, sitting at the next table, spun and grabbed the sailor by the collar. "You just wish you had a king like Azoun," he snarled. "All you've got is your pitiful merchants' council."

The Sembian pulled away from the bigger man, but knocked over his own mug of ale in the process. The heavy metal tankard bounced off the table, spewing ale everywhere, and clattered to the floor.

Whole tables quieted quickly at the first sounds of conflict. A member of the king's guard who sat near the door stood and started to move across the room. However, Geoff was neither drunk enough nor foolish enough to start a fight in a Cormyrian tavern, especially by insulting the king who was perhaps the most popular leader in Faerun.

The Sembian reached over and snatched John's mug. "To King Azoun," he called, "the bravest ruler on the continent." No one in the room considered the sailor's toast genuine, but it was a suitable apology. After raising their own mugs, the tavern's patrons turned back to their business and the Purple Dragon returned to his seat.

Geoff bought the ham-fisted man a drink and replaced John's. Silently, he said a thanks to King Azoun for forbidding anyone from bearing arms not bound by peacestrings in the city. Then, after a few moments of small talk, he awkwardly excused himself and left the Black Rat, intent on returning to his ship and fellow countrymen.

As the Sembian took his leave, the big man from the next table leaned toward John and grumbled, "He didn't belong in here in the first place."

The fletcher agreed. He didn't much like Sembians. They were far too interested in money and leisure rather than honest hard work. And they had little in common with Cormyrians, as far as John was concerned. Sembians had only a weak loyalty to their country, and their rulers were salesmen, like many of their subjects. They didn't even have a strong standing army.

"If His Highness does call this crusade," John said to his countryman by way of a reply, "you won't find many Sembians on the battlefield—not unless they're mercenaries."

"You mean you haven't heard?" the man exclaimed, pushing a lock of his curly blond hair from his eyes with a meaty hand. "We *are* going to Thesk to fight the barbarians. Tuigan, they call them. Azoun had a meeting with a bunch of nobles a few days ago."

John nodded. "That's what the king will announce today, I suppose."

"Aye," the brawny man said, his voice betraying his excitement. "He'll be calling for volunteers. A friend of mine from Arabel told me just yesterday that Lord Lhal has already started rounding up soldiers and wizards."

"Azoun should be able to raise quite a few in Suzail," John noted, finishing off his ale.

With exaggerated motions, the big man slapped himself on his broad chest. "And I'll be one of the first to sign on!"

"And me," said a woman from a nearby table. "I'll be going, too, Mal. I wouldn't let you gather all the glory for yourself."

"I'd expect as much, Kiri," Mal replied, breaking into a loud, jolly fit of laughter.

John turned to look at the woman called Kiri. She was thin, but had a slightly round face. Her feature were attractive but unremarkable—except for her eyes. Kiri's eyes, sparkling brown and full of laughter, drew the fletcher's gaze instantly. He felt himself grin rather fatuously when he saw her. The grin widened when Kiri smiled back at him affably.

A few others adventurers sitting near John broke the spell as they loudly informed anyone who'd listen that they intended to go to Thesk and fight the barbarians. Drinks were bought, bravery and the king saluted. John wondered how many of the would-be Tuigan-slayers would actually ship out when the time came.

"And what about you, fletcher?" Mal asked. "Are you going to stay here with the children and old folks?"

"I don't know," John replied pensively. "I haven't really thought about it."

That was the truth, too. John put little stock in gossip, and that was all he'd heard concerning the crusade. Still, if the king himself asked for soldiers, the fletcher would probably volunteer. He was a brave man and a good archer. Above all, John the Fletcher was loyal to his king and country.

Azoun IV had ruled Cormyr for John's entire lifetime. In his twenty-one years, all of which had been spent in Suzail, he'd known no other monarch. Every year since he could remember, John had devotedly pledged his allegiance to King Azoun at the High Festival of Winter.

Like most other commoners in Cormyr, John knew that his king belonged to House Obarskyr and that his land's calendar was based upon the date Azoun's family had established themselves as rulers in Suzail. This information, along with a smattering of math and the rudiments of Common, the trade tongue of the Inner Sea, was all John had gained from his brief formal education.

Still, this was enough to instill a great sense of loyalty toward Azoun in John. To the craftsman, the king *was* Cormyr, not just a representative or a figurehead, but a real embodiment of everything that was good about the land. And since Cormyr, and especially Suzail, had flourished during Azoun's reign, John could only assume that the gods of Good approved of the monarch.

"If King Azoun is going to lead the armies," Razor John decided aloud after a moment's pause, "then I suppose I'll go."

Mal immediately bought John another ale, but the fletcher drank only a little of the murky, pungent liquid before he announced that he was off to the castle to hear the king's speech.

"Why?" the burly, blond man asked, scooping up the fletcher's unfinished drink. "The wizards'll make sure Azoun's voice carries over the city. We're just going to go outside."

The woman Mal had called Kiri stood up and attempted to pull the big man from his seat. "Let's go with John," she said between tugs. "I don't think I've ever seen His Highness in person before."

Mal sighed, shrugged out of Kiri's grasp irritably, and downed the rest of the ale in one, long gulp. "All right, all right. We'd best get moving."

So Razor John, Mal, and Kiri made their way out of the Black Rat and started off in the direction of the palace.

* * * * *

"Pawn to king's four."

Queen Filfaeril smiled warmly and scanned the chessboard with her ice-blue eyes. "Your game has become rather predictable, husband," she said, moving her hand to the board. She lifted a knight of purest ivory. "Knight takes pawn."

Consternation crossed King Azoun's face. "You know that I'll take that knight with my queen," he said. "Losing it for a pawn seems rather pointless." The king slid an onyx queen across the board and picked up the white knight in one smooth motion. "Queen takes knight."

Filfaeril studied the board for a moment, then moved her bishop. "Bishop takes queen." Azoun cursed softly. "In three moves I'll have you in checkmate," his wife added.

Azoun lifted a rook, then moved it closer to his king.

The queen's smile faded. "Are you sure you want to play this out?"

"Of course. I never quit before the game's over."

Positioning her queen to place Azoun in check, Filfaeril prepared to finish the game. As she had guessed, it lasted only three more moves.

The king and queen set the pieces up for a future game. When the board was reorganized, Azoun asked, "Am I really that predictable?"

The queen considered her answer for a moment, then nodded. "There are certain things I can count on you to do, and others I can count on you never to do."

"Such as?"

Filfaeril picked up a pawn. "You don't trade pieces well, my husband. That's why you didn't see my logic in sacrificing the knight."

Azoun took the pawn from his wife's hand and replaced it on the board. "There should be some way to win that doesn't involve losing one piece for another."

"As I said," the queen repeated as she smiled and took her husband's hand, "there are certain things I can count on you never to do."

The king laughed, patted Filfaeril's white, slender fingers, and stood up. "I guess I'm still mulling over what Vangerdahast said the other day after the meeting. I don't really think of myself as inflexible, predictable." Azoun paused and looked into his wife's eyes. "Still, what he said about Alusair . . ."

Filfaeril saw the pain in her husband's face when he mentioned their daughter's name. What had happened with

Alusair pained her, too, though she knew that Azoun considered himself directly responsible for driving the girl from home. "Alusair was willful, my husband," she said after a moment. "Much like her father."

The queen rose and moved to Azoun's side. She embraced him tightly. "If you're looking for proof that you're a good father, Tanalasta should stand as example enough."

Azoun nodded, though the furrow in his brow did not lessen. He certainly loved Tanalasta, his eldest daughter, and she had given him plenty of reasons to be immensely proud of her. Still, she lacked the spirit, the fire her younger sister possessed. No, Tanalasta's devotion could never cover the rift between the king and Alusair.

Filfaeril knew this, but had hoped her words would pull Azoun from the dark mood into which he had fallen. She caressed her husband's cheek and turned his eyes toward hers. "And you have me. You are not so unbearably rigid that I cannot love you."

That last comment brought out Azoun's smile again. Looking at his queen, he noted that she was as lovely now as the day they'd married. Many around the court said that Filfaeril was classically beautiful, and Azoun agreed. The queen's delicate features seemed to have been smoothed out of the purest alabaster. And fifty years of life—thirty in the court—had done little to dull this loveliness. Even the wrinkles that pulled at the corners of Filfaeril's startlingly blue eyes seemed intentionally carved there by some artist.

But it wasn't simply for her beauty that Azoun had first fallen in love with his queen. Filfaeril was far more than a nobleman's statuesque daughter; she was a bright and insightful woman, as well. In fact, she had won Prince Azoun's love more by her refusal to surround herself with flattering courtiers than by her slender figure and flowing blond hair. Filfaeril's ice-blue eyes were lovely to behold, but the young Azoun had quickly learned that they saw through illusion and idealism, down to harsh reality.

Finally Azoun mocked a sigh and said, "Yes, at least I have you." Filfaeril wrinkled her brow in feigned anger, and Azoun kissed her, long and tenderly.

After a moment, the king heard Vangerdahast clear his throat noisily. He glanced at the study's door to see his advisor standing there, red-faced and fidgeting, staring at the ceiling. "Come in, Vangy," Azoun sighed. "I suppose it's time for the ceremony and my speech."

Filfaeril leaned close to the king and whispered, "We'll continue our discussion later, Your Highness." The queen gently pushed herself from Azoun's arms and moved toward the door. "I'll be waiting for you both in the throne room," she announced as she left the room.

Vangerdahast waited until the queen closed the door behind her before he spoke. "Yes, it's almost highsun. I've already cast the necessary wards on the platform. Are you ready to begin the procession?"

The king looked down at his ceremonial uniform. The purple surcoat was embroidered with thread spun from platinum and gold, and the hose were woven from the finest imported silk from Shou Lung. Azoun didn't like the outfit much; he considered it gaudy. It was, however, necessary for him to wear it in the formal crowning ceremony that was to precede his public address.

Straightening an epaulet, Azoun said, "I suppose I'm ready to begin. I just wish we didn't have to make such a production out of this."

"If you wish to—"

Azoun quickly held up a hand. "I know, Vangy. An emphasis on pageant today will help to convey the crusade's importance." He moved to the window and looked out on the inner bailey. Servants and messengers rushed from the castle to the gate, their hurried pace an indication of the day's importance.

"We should go, Your Highness."

Azoun watched a page, who wore the royal purple, rush from the keep and hurry past the gatehouses. The sight reminded him of an errand he had assigned to the royal wizard earlier that morning. "Any news from Zhentil Keep?" the king asked as he turned to his advisor.

The wizard spun about abruptly and headed through the door in an effort to move Azoun toward the throne room.

"Actually, I did receive a message from the Zhentish hierarchy just before I came to get you," the wizard noted quietly. He bowed in response to a guard's salute as he and the king entered the drafty stone corridor, then added, "They're sending someone to talk to you about the Tuigan tomorrow."

Azoun stopped short. The wizard took a step or two past the king, then wheeled about. "So soon?" Azoun exclaimed. "That doesn't give us much time to prepare."

Vangerdahast hooked an arm around the king's elbow and started walking again. "I believe that's the whole idea, Your Highness."

Queen Filfaeril was waiting in the throne room when Azoun and Vangerdahast got there. Crowds of musicians and nobles filled the long, sumptuously appointed hall, waiting for the king to arrive. Handmaidens straightened the queen's long dress of lavender silk as the royal steward ran to the king and announced that his crown, scepter, and medallion—the trappings of his heritage—were ready. Vangerdahast left the king's side without any leave-taking and went to find the other royal wizards who were to participate in the ceremony.

Azoun soon joined his wife near the large, ornately carved wooden thrones that dominated the front of the hall. The queen already wore the symbol of her office—a small but beautiful silver crown. The white metal seemed to glow around Filfaeril's golden hair and catch the blue in her eyes. After nodding a silent greeting to his wife, the king took his chain of state from the spot on his throne where it traditionally rested. The thick gold chain felt reassuring in Azoun's hands as he lifted it over his head. The gold medallion had a skillfully wrought dragon, *guardant* and *statant*, covering its entire face.

Next, the steward solemnly presented the king's crown, couched on a pillow of pure purple silk. Everyone in the room bowed as Azoun reached for the bejeweled crown and lifted it.

Gold, silver, and gems twinkled in the sunlight streaming in from the stained glass windows lining the throne room as Azoun studied the crown. The sinewy, lithe form of a dragon curled around its rim, and the monster's head reared, openmouthed, at the headpiece's front. A priceless wine-red ruby stood captured in the dragon's open jaws, throwing off tiny, enthralling beams of light. This crown— the most ancient of three possessed by the king—was only used for very special occasions. Azoun wondered how many Cormyrians had ever seen this particular artifact as he placed it on his head.

Finally the steward, still bowed, presented the king's scepter. Like a vine, a slender, scaled dragon curled around the two-foot-long staff from tip to crown. A glittering, golden head, like that of a mace, topped the scepter. The king grasped the staff firmly and held it outstretched toward the hall. The crowning was complete.

"Arise, subjects," Azoun said formally, repeating the ancient rite. "Look upon your king."

That said, he glanced around the throne room and found that the procession was ready, filed neatly into rows that would fall in line behind him and Filfaeril as they left the hall. All that remained now was for the king to lead the nobles to the Royal Gardens, where the speech was to occur. Taking a deep breath, Azoun turned to his wife and smiled, then started through the room.

Drums rattled softly, marking a slow cadence for the parade. Azoun and Filfaeril reached the center of the room, and Vangerdahast, accompanied by a few other mages, moved into place behind the king and queen. Next came the nobles, then a contingent of the king's guard, then a few musicians. In all, forty people walked through the castle's halls. A few servants and guards stood in the corridors, bowing as their king passed by, but most of the keep's staff was assembled outside, in the castle's inner bailey.

The king moved quickly through the bailey, the large open courtyard inside the castle's high stone wall. Occasionally Azoun nodded to a familiar servant or knight as he made his way out of the southern gate. The trumpets called almost continually once the procession reached the open air outside the walls. The music of expertly played instruments mixed with the loud roar of the drums in the blue sky.

Animated by nervous excitement, the crowd milled restlessly outside the keep, waiting for their king and queen to walk slowly past. The procession, almost mindless of the masses, kept the castle's sun-bleached walls on their right and made their way through the cheering throng to the gardens at the rear of the keep. The trumpets blared more loudly as Azoun and his entourage approached the castle's western corner.

Even that pompous heralding couldn't completely drown out a louder, more insistent noise.

"Can you hear that?" Filfaeril whispered in Azoun's ear. Turning his head slightly, he listened. High, gray stone walls still stood between the king and the Royal Gardens, the location of his speech. Despite this barrier, the blaring trumpets, and rumbling drums, he could hear the Cormyrians gathered there. By the time the procession reached the westernmost tip of the wall, the murmuring crowd collected outside the walls drowned out even the musicians.

As the king rounded the corner into the gardens, Vangerdahast gave a signal. On the battlements, the line of trumpeters snapped to attention. The brightly colored pennants hanging from their instruments flapped in the breeze. The crowd grew louder, more anxious.

With almost military precision, the royal wizard glanced toward the handful of mages who stood with him. At his nod, a fat, balding wizard started to weave a spell. He was joined by a stooped old woman and a pock-faced young boy. The three sorcerers mumbled incantations and traced obscure patterns in the air. Suddenly, simultaneously, they stopped and nodded at Vangerdahast.

The paunchy wizard winked at Azoun, then signaled the trumpeters along the wall again. They, in turn, lifted their polished brass to their lips and blew. A single high, clear note rang out over the gardens. Thanks to the spells cast by the wizards, the trumpeters' call didn't stop there. All over Suzail, no matter where he was, each Cormyrian citizen heard the note as if he were standing at the foot of the wall, before Azoun's keep.

"Good luck, Your Highness," Queen Filfaeril said softly. She reached down and squeezed Azoun's hand for an instant.

The king smiled at his wife warmly, then strode through the garden. The procession followed behind Azoun as he climbed briskly onto the large wooden platform that had been built at the garden's edge especially for the speech. When he reached the top of the stairs and stepped onto the broad, polished deck, King Azoun looked out over hundreds and hundreds of people.

He glanced back quickly at Vangerdahast, who was only then clearing the last step onto the platform. The gray-bearded old man bent over, winded after chasing the king up the stairs. Finally he took a deep breath and stood. The other wizards had joined him by now, and together they softly repeated their incantation, this time directing the spell at their monarch.

Azoun thought he saw a small, intense spark of blue-white light form in the air in front of the wizards, but before he could focus on the spark, the spell was complete and the ember disappeared. He felt a sharp, burning prickle in his throat as he turned back to the milling throng.

"My people," the king said, and his words called through the entire city.

A thousand eyes looked up at Azoun from the Royal Gardens. Nobles with spyglasses lined the roofs of their homes to the north of the keep and watched the king. He, in turn, looked out on the sea of faces and smiled. He saw respect and awe and, perhaps, a little fear there. Those looks, the wide-eyed faces, momentarily eclipsed the speech Azoun had prepared in his mind. A warmth, a feeling of paternal duty and love, now filled the king's thoughts.

"My friends and countrymen," King Azoun said, correcting himself. "Faerun is in great danger, and I need your help." He paused then, and let his subjects realize that he was asking them for assistance, that he needed them.

That fact alone would have shocked most of the throng into silence, but the intensity and emotion in Azoun's voice fell upon the crowd and riveted them in place. Throughout the city, smiths put down their hammers and shipwrights lay down their awls, clerics put aside their holy books and tutors let their students set down their grammars and writing tablets.

From where he stood, near the garden's edge, John the Fletcher couldn't see Azoun's face, but he imagined it was dark with passion. He'd never been closer to the king than he was that day, not even when Azoun had opened the previous year's spring fair, only a few hundred feet from his shop. John's proximity to the monarch made him happy, and the craftsman listened intently as Azoun described the Tuigan menace and the plight of Thesk and Rashemen.

"I'm not in this to help witches or foreigners," Mal grumbled. A jowl-heavy baker held up a flour-covered finger and shushed the warrior. Mal scowled, but held his tongue. Silently John said a prayer of thanks that the warrior hadn't started a fight with the fat man.

On the platform, Azoun was warming to the topic, falling into the same impassioned argument he'd used on some of his nobles to gain their support. "But the horsewarriors threaten more than our neighbors to the east," the king said, waving an open hand toward the horizon. "No. The Tuigan will not be content with that end of the Inner Sea, nor will they be happy if they conquer the Dales or Sembia."

Azoun ran his gaze slowly over the crowd, letting their expectation of his next words build for a moment. He could sense in their expressions that he'd won many of his subjects over already. "Do you know what else they want?" the king asked softly.

A ripple of hesitant answers rolled over the crowd. Azoun heard a few of these replies, and they revealed the names of his people's fears. He singled out some and used them as rallying cries.

"Will we let the horsewarriors take our land?" the king asked.

The crowd shouted a ragged reply of "No!" and "Never!"

Azoun balled his hands into tight, quivering fists and held them in front of him. "Will we let the horsewarriors take our homes?"

"No!" the people screamed. Men and women mirrored the king's stance, holding their own fists clenched before them.

Out of the corner of his eye, Azoun saw that a few of the guards that lined the platform to either side of him were shouting with the crowd.

At the garden's edge, Razor John felt the hair stand up on the back of his neck as he screamed his reply to Azoun's challenge. He glanced at Mal and Kiri, and saw that they, too, were caught up in the king's speech. In fact, almost everyone around the fletcher seemed to be shouting his or her defiance to the Tuigan threat.

Everyone, John realized, except a lone man, who stood next to the fat baker. He was tight-lipped and rigid, as if immobilized. Thin, almost emaciated, the man stood silently, his hard gaze locked on the stage.

The fletcher stared at the man for a moment, mesmerized by the contradiction he presented in the wildly screaming crowd. The rigid, green-clad man didn't notice John's gaze, though, as he stiffly pulled his tattered forest-green cloak a little tighter around his shoulders. He narrowed his eyes and glared at the king on the stage.

"Will we let the horsewarriors take our lives?" Razor John heard Azoun cry. A unified reply went up, and people raised their fists into the air. The fletcher glanced back at the platform and saw that the crowd again mirrored the king's stance. When John returned his gaze to who seemed to be the one silent person in the gardens, he saw that the ragged man had pulled a rolled, yellowing piece of parchment from under his tattered cloak.

He held the scroll up quickly, and his lips began to move. Because of the shouting, John couldn't tell if he was actually speaking. No one else seemed to be paying attention to the tight-lipped man, so John was the only one who saw the parchment he held in his bony fingers begin to glow with a pale red luminescence.

For a moment, the light puzzled the fletcher. Then the realization dawned on him: The man was casting a spell.

"I challenge every able-bodied citizen of Suzail," Azoun continued from the stage. "Citizens from any part of Cormyr. Be prepared to help me to defend our country."

The crowd roared, and John looked quickly from the

glowing paper to the platform. "No!" he cried.

Shoving Mal out of his way, the fletcher lunged toward the assassin. He was too late. A second before Razor John touched the man's torn and threadbare surcoat, the parchment disappeared in a gout of red-orange flame.

Three things happened at once.

Azoun had just told the crowd that they should report to the city watch to sign up for the crusade. The king was about to inform them that several churches devoted to gods of Good were ready to enlist volunteers, too. He never got the chance.

A pinpoint of red light arched from the crowd and sped toward the stage. As it got closer to the king, it grew larger and larger, until, at last, it resembled nothing less than a miniature sun, blazing toward the platform. The ball of fire singed the hair of those it passed over and blinded those foolish enough to look directly at it. It left a trail of smoke and the smell of burned skin in its wake.

Razor John saw none of this as he slammed into the assassin, knocking him to the ground. The fletcher rolled on top of the man and grabbed him by the shoulders. Only after the assassin's elbow smashed into John's ribs did he realize that the ragged man was far stronger than he looked. That blow was the only one struck, as the fletcher's work-hardened muscles were enough to pin the man until help arrived.

"The city'll thank me," the man rasped over and over.

After the incident earlier that morning, the fletcher was only slightly surprised when the man's tattered green cloak flew back and revealed the bear trap badge of the Trappers' Guild bound to his thin arm.

On the platform, Azoun had only a second to react to the fireball rushing at him. Turning toward his wife, the king made what he knew was a futile effort to shield her from the blast. A few guards stepped toward the king and queen, but no one was fast enough to block the doom that hurtled toward the stage.

For his part, Vangerdahast seemed riveted with fear. In truth, he was reciting a brief but sincere prayer to the Goddess of Magic that the wards he'd placed on the stage held.

The fireball struck the front of the platform. All the king, the queen, or the others on the stage could see was a splash of brilliant red, though they could faintly feel the heat from the blast. Still, the flames never touched them. The magical attack struck the invisible wall Vangerdahast's wards created in front of the stage and exploded.

Guards and nobles hustled Azoun and Filfaeril off the stage, back through the gates and into the keep. Once he was sure that the king was safe, Vangerdahast returned to the platform to assess the damage. Though his vision was slightly blurred from observing the fireball too closely, the royal magician could hear the screams and smell the burned flesh quite clearly.

The wards had kept the king safe, but hadn't protected the people standing close to the stage.

- 4 -

Allies and Enemies

Vangerdahast paced around the barren, chilly cell for a moment, then spun about sharply and slammed his fist on the dark wooden table. "Are you mad?"

Laying a restraining hand on the wizard's shoulder, Dimswart the Sage tried to repeat the question more neutrally. "Please, Bors, try to explain to me again why you thought you needed to kill King Azoun."

The thin man pulled his tattered cloak tight around his shoulders and glared up at the sage. A spiteful look pulled his features into a squint on his narrow face. "I'll tell ye no more than this: I did it for the good of the city. The crusade'll ruin us all."

"This is getting us nowhere," Vangerdahast grumbled. He turned to Bors and shook a pudgy finger at him. "If you know what's good for you, you'll tell us where you got the scroll and who put you up to this."

The trapper closed his eyes and ran his hand over the leather guild patch tied around his arm. It was an action he'd repeated many times during the long night's interrogation. For a moment, the close, stone-walled cell grew quiet.

Dimswart rubbed his red, puffy eyes and looked down at the notes he'd compiled. Bors—that was the only name the man had as far as they could learn—claimed to have acted out of public spirit in his attempt on Azoun's life. A down-and-out trapper, barely making enough to pay his guild dues, the would-be assassin was sure that the expedition against the Tuigan would ruin the meager life he still had. Killing Azoun was the only way he knew to stop that disaster.

"What about guild members buying weapons, arrows and the like?" Dimswart asked, turning his gaze to the only other item in his notes. The fletcher who had captured Bors in the Royal Gardens had also told the king's guard about another trapper, one who had tried to purchase a large number of arrows the morning of the attack.

"I don't know nothing about that," Bors grumbled. "This ain't guild business. I meant only to harm Azoun."

Vangerdahast cursed bitterly. "Well, you certainly did more damage than that, didn't you? Fifteen dead. Twenty more horribly burned." The wizard leaned close to the man and added, "The gods will not look kindly on this, and I'm sure you'll be visiting the Realm of the Dead very soon."

For the first time during the long hours of questioning Bors's face betrayed something other than rigid anger. The flickering light from the single tallow candle that burned in the cell revealed the fear on the thin man's hateful face. That expression lasted only an instant.

"I've told ye that I'm sorry for harming those poor folk unfortunate enough to be standing near the stage," Bors said, his voice low and even. "But I can't show ye my soul, so don't second guess the gods as to my punishment . . . if they see fit to punish me at all for trying to save innocent Cormyrian lives from a needless fight."

Dimswart rolled up his parchment, put away his ink and stylus, and abruptly rose to his feet. "Come on, Vangy. Let him rest. We've learned all he's going to tell."

The royal wizard glanced once at Bors, then called for the guard. A helmeted man appeared, wearing the purple dragon, symbol of King Azoun, emblazoned on his tunic. The long sword he wore at his side hung down past his woolen breeches and almost to the heels of his high, soft leather boots. The guard quickly opened the iron-braced door and let Dimswart and Vangerdahast out. "Make sure the prisoner doesn't kill himself," the wizard noted as he left.

Vangerdahast walked stiffly down the tower's broad stone steps. Through the arrow loops cut into the thick walls every ten feet or so on the stairs, he could see the first feeble rays of the morning sun. The light cast flowing ghostly images before Vangerdahast's eyes. The wizard staggered for a moment, but leaned against the cold gray wall before he could fall.

Dimswart patted the paunchy old man lightly on the back. "Not used to staying up all night anymore, eh, Vangy?"

The wizard shook his head and frowned. "These are strange days, Dimswart," he said, continuing down the steps, this time at a slower pace. "At the moment, I wonder if I shall ever sleep again."

The sage moved to Vangerdahast's side. "I believe him, you know—about not serving the guild."

"Eh?"

"Bors," Dimswart began again. "I think he's telling the truth. You can see it in his eyes." He paused for a moment, then added with a slight smile, "Besides, my sources tell me that the guilds would plan something far more elaborate than one man reading a spell from a scroll."

Again Vangerdahast steadied himself with a hand against the wall. After four or five stairs, he stopped and turned to the gray-haired sage. "I find it hard to believe that he actually had enough money to purchase a scroll of that power."

Shaking his head, Dimswart folded his arms across his chest. "I don't think the fool who sold the scroll to him realized what he had. Or perhaps it was stolen and some wandering thief wanted to be rid of it. There's a thriving black market for magic in any city the size of Suzail."

"And the money?" the wizard asked impatiently.

The sage smiled, this time a broad, self-assured grin. "He had to have a little money from winter trapping. He probably spent all of it on the scroll. Did Bors look like he'd eaten recently to you?"

"So this was his last hope," Vangerdahast concluded, stroking his beard. After a moment of thoughtful silence, he conceded, "It makes some sense, I suppose."

The wizard and the sage walked the rest of the way down

the tower without saying another word, lost in their own theories about the assassination attempt. They crossed the frost-covered courtyard to the main keep the same way, and only spoke when they'd entered the palace and reached the antechamber to the king's quarters.

Azoun was sitting in a corner of the small room, tugging at the corners of his mustache, when Vangerdahast opened the door. The king still wore the clothes he'd changed into immediately after the attack: a plain tunic and breeches, with high, black boots. A thick purple cloak hung carelessly from his shoulders, probably put there by Queen Filfaeril sometime during the night.

Vangerdahast couldn't help but feel the monarch looked as if he were stranded on some desolate stretch of beach, shipwrecked and alone. The room's few candles and the thin sunlight from the window cast deep, aging shadows on Azoun's face. After the sage and wizard had entered the room, Vangerdahast cleared his throat noisily. When Azoun looked up, his dark-circled eyes and pale complexion only heightened his appearance as a lonesome castaway.

"We're done interviewing the trapper," Dimswart noted softly.

"Is Zhentil Keep involved? Or the guilds?" The king asked the questions casually, offhandedly. This wasn't the first time someone had attempted to take his life; conspiracies and failed assassinations had become a part of Azoun's everyday existence.

Rubbing the knotted muscles in his neck, Vangerdahast eased himself into a padded chair. "Your friend, the 'Sage of Suzail,' believes Bors was working alone. He has a few interesting points, but I'm not convinced. We've heard the trappers are gathering weapons, too. This could mean trouble."

Dimswart shrugged. "That was an awfully sloppy assassination attempt for one sponsored by a powerful guild."

"I thought the people, the merchants would understand. I thought they'd be the first to see how necessary this is." The king turned toward the window, which overlooked the gardens, and noticed for the first time that the sun was coming up. "We've been up all night," he noted absently.

"You should rest, Azoun," the royal wizard said, concern coloring his voice. "The special envoy from Zhentil Keep will be here late this morning to discuss the crusade."

Inhaling deeply, then sighing, Azoun stood. The cloak slid from his shoulders and dropped into liquid folds of fine cloth at his feet. "It's all getting out of control," he said, half to himself. "I can't let that happen."

As Azoun paused, standing lost in his own wandering thoughts, Dimswart noticed that the king's age dragged heavily upon him. Azoun's shoulders stooped slightly, and his arms and legs seemed slack. "Vangy's right. You need to rest."

The king snapped out of his reverie and looked at the sage. "Did I hear you correctly, Dimswart?" he asked, a trace of a sad smile on his lips. "Did you actually agree with Vangerdahast?" The gray-haired man nodded, though he found he couldn't return even his friend's half-smile.

"I suppose you're both right," the king concluded at last. He walked to the nearest candle and snuffed it out. "I tried to sleep earlier. It didn't do me much good."

"Perhaps a spell, Your Highness?" Vangerdahast offered helpfully.

"Or a mixture of herbs?" added Dimswart.

The king shook his head. "No, no. I'll go and lie down beside Filfaeril. Try to sleep on my own. Spells or potions might leave me unfit to meet our guest later this morning." He shuffled to another candle and extinguished its flame, then turned to the gilt door that led to his inner chambers.

Silently the king left the room. The gilt door slid noiselessly shut, and the wizard and sage were left in the antechamber. Vangerdahast squeezed the flame out on the room's sole remaining lit candle.

"Good night—or should I say good morning? Thank you for your help, Dimswart."

The sage frowned and gestured toward the gilt door. "Will he be all right?"

Nodding, Vangerdahast mumbled something about the trials of kingship and all men needing rest. The wizard then hustled Dimswart from the room and told the guards standing watch outside to knock in three hours and keep alert. Before Vangerdahast closed the door to the antechamber, Dimswart asked, "He's paying for the crusade already, isn't he?"

The royal wizard didn't answer as he shut the heavy door. As quietly as he could, Vangerdahast picked up the king's cloak, hung it over his own shoulder, and dragged the padded chair closer to the window. He lowered himself slowly into the chair, his old joints creaking, his brown robe folding around him. Finally, pulling the cloak up to his chin, he glanced out at the blue morning sky. It was chilly, but he guessed that the sun would burn the frost from the air by highsun.

Azoun will have to pay far more than one sleepless night to stop the Tuigan, was the wizard's last thought before he lapsed into a shallow, fitful sleep.

The guards knocked on the antechamber door three hours later, as instructed. Vangerdahast started awake. His none-too-rested mind immediately called a defensive spell to the fore, but the groggy old wizard recognized the soldiers before he had a chance to make a mistake.

The sun was high over the gardens when Vangerdahast glanced out the window. He reckoned that he and Azoun had at least an hour before the special emissary from Zhentil Keep made his appearance. The wizard shivered slightly and rubbed his arms through his woolen robe. Winter still hadn't been completely banished from Cormyr, and it was certainly making its presence known that morning.

Wondering if the king had managed to sleep at all, Vangerdahast crossed to the king's bedchamber and knocked. When he got no reply, he slowly, quietly open the gilt door. It slid noiselessly open on oiled golden hinges.

To the royal wizard's chagrin, King Azoun was awake. He stood across the large room, near a multipaned stained glass window that depicted a twisting purple dragon. The king traced the dragon in the glass, running his fingers over the purple, burgundy, and gold fragments. The light from the sun shot through the window and cast the king in a bath of deep, beautiful color.

"Your Highness," Vangerdahast began, "I—"

Azoun turned sharply and held a finger to his lips. He motioned toward the large, white-draped canopy bed that dominated the room. Seeing that the monarch pointed to his still-sleeping wife, Vangerdahast nodded. Azoun cast one longing look back at Filfaeril, then followed the wizard into the antechamber.

"My apologies for intruding, Azoun," Vangerdahast said softly as he closed the gilt door. "How was your rest?"

"I feel fine, Vangy." He moved restlessly to the window and added wryly, "Until I saw your expression just now, I almost suspected you of casting a spell to restore me."

"Not against your wishes," the wizard said, coming to the king's side.

"No, I really didn't think so."

Noting an irritability in the king's voice, Vangerdahast decided to tread carefully with his questions. It was obvious Azoun had slept little. "Are you ready to meet with the Zhentish envoy?"

The king chuckled a humorless laugh and pushed himself away from the window. "I must be," he said firmly. "I can't let madmen or intractable dalesmen or anything else get in the way of this crusade. I must be ready."

Without waiting for a reply, the king spun on his heels and headed out into the hall. The wizard trailed behind him, making mental notes of the orders the king snapped off. Finally, Azoun reached his study. Before he opened the door, he noted that a sizable reward should be sent to the man who'd captured Bors in the crowd and that the would-be assassin's trial should be convened immediately.

"He'll almost certainly be put to death," Vangerdahast replied, watching the king's eyes for a reaction.

Azoun's expression, a mixture of cold resolve and vague distraction, didn't change. "If he hadn't killed those people it might have been different. I have to uphold the law. I want the masters of the Trappers' Guild called to court, too. They have much to answer for."

Vangerdahast hesitated before he replied. Anger, not just irritability, had a hold upon the Cormyrian king, the wizard realized. It was very much unlike Azoun to act that way, but, then, the last few days had been unusual themselves.

"Perhaps I should reschedule the meeting with the Zhentish envoy," Vangerdahast ventured, hoping that his friend might recognize the cause for the suggestion.

Azoun's forehead furrowed deeply as he narrowed his eyes and glared at the wizard. That expression was only temporary. The dark look on the king's face passed as quickly as a lone storm cloud on a bright summer's afternoon. Vangerdahast silently breathed a sigh of relief.

"That won't be necessary," Azoun noted, clasping his hands together in front of him. "Besides, if I don't convince the dalesmen that we can leave in the next tenday or so, the Tuigan will conquer most of Thesk. At that point, we might as well do as Lord Mourngrym suggests and wait for the barbarians to show up on our doorstep."

Vangerdahast sighed and hoped that the king could shake off his concerns long enough to parley with the envoy that afternoon. "Should I bring our Zhentish visitor here when he arrives?" the wizard asked as he turned to leave.

"No," Azoun replied. He opened the study's door. "I want to skim a book or two and clear my mind. Bring the envoy to the throne room."

Vangerdahast raised an eyebrow. "You don't usually meet mere envoys there, Your Highness."

The king smiled—a little wickedly, Vangerdahast noted with mild surprise—and said, "No doubt the ambassador will know that and expect a more casual greeting. I think it wise to keep him off balance, don't you?"

The royal wizard returned the king's smile, though his was undoubtedly tinged with a mischievous malice. "Of course, Your Highness," he said. Vangerdahast bowed, then hurried down the hall, his concern for Azoun lessening as he pondered the king's strategy.

Azoun quietly entered the study and sat at his desk. First, he scribbled a note to Torg, the dwarven king of Earthfast, informing him of the crusade's status. That done, the king opened the large, leather-bound book that lay on the desk. For a short time, he read and reread the passages describing the "black days" under Salember, the Rebel Prince. The citizens of Cormyr, and especially Suzail, were reportedly very supportive of the crusade. Despite this, Azoun wondered—as he had for much of the night—whether or not his people really did believe his plans to be in their best interest.

The king knew that history might report him to be the next traitor to Cormyr if Bors was an accurate manifestation of his subjects' true feelings about the crusade—*his* crusade. What his descendants thought of him mattered to Azoun more than it probably should have, so before he headed to the throne room to meet the Zhentish envoy, he devised a plan by which he might discover the people's real opinion of the crusade and uncover any plots the trappers might have hatched for open revolt.

Putting that plan into action would have to wait for the following night, when he'd have a chance to make a suitable disguise.

*   *   *   *   *

The royal chamberlain, decked out in his finest costume, entered the throne room. He strode pompously to the center of the large hall and bowed to the figure on a throne at the room's opposite end. After a few moments of silence, which seemed to the Zhentish envoy like an hour, he sharply rapped the tip of his gold-shod staff on the polished marble beneath his feet.

"Your Highness, may I present Lythrana Dargor, special envoy from Lord Chess at Zhentil Keep."

The introduction rang through the room, echoing off the stone floor and beautiful stained glass windows, eventually getting lost in the rich tapestries that covered most of the walls. Special Envoy Dargor stood patiently still, despite the fact that she had been told in Zhentil Keep not to expect any formality when dealing with Azoun IV.

On the throne, the king tapped his foot, silently counting off the time before he would allow the Zhentish politician to advance. He fidgeted slightly and toyed with his long purple cloak. At Azoun's side, Vangerdahast stood, resplendent in his most colorful robe. A closer look at the wizard would reveal red, bloodshot eyes and a slight pallor about his cheeks, but he hid his exhaustion almost as well as Azoun masked his.

After a short time, when Azoun felt certain the wait must be seeming like an eternity to the visiting dignitary, the king sat up straight and said, "Let her advance, Lord Chamberlain."

The chamberlain bowed again and turned to Lythrana. She straightened her gray blouse, petulantly brushed a stray strand of raven-black hair, then started toward the king. Her high-heeled boots sent sharp, cracking footsteps throughout the hall, and her black, high-collared dress hissed where it dragged along on the floor behind her.

"It is a pleasure to finally meet Your Highness," Lythrana said in a low sibilant voice after she bowed.

"We are pleased that Zhentil Keep sent such an accomplished politician to discuss Faerun's needs," the king responded. Though Vangerdahast chuckled inwardly at Azoun's use of the royal "we," an affection he rarely adopted, he knew the king was serious in his praise of the Zhentish envoy. Lythrana Dargor's reputation as a shrewd negotiator was well known throughout the lands around the Inner Sea.

Noting the king's praise with a slight smile, Lythrana said, "On my way from the Keep, I learned of the recent attempt on your life. Lord Chess would certainly wish me to send his hopes that you escaped unscathed."

"This was the first you'd heard of the attempt?" Vangerdahast asked, a bitter taint of sarcasm edging his voice.

Spreading her long-fingered, white hands open before her in a sign of peace, the sultry envoy said, "It is natural for the king's worthy advisors—" she bowed slightly to Vangerdahast "—to suspect Zhentil Keep in this matter. We make no secret of the methods by which we solve our problems, or the gods we worship." The envoy brushed her long bangs out of her eyes. On her forehead lay a circle of black, surrounding a white, grinning skull—the symbol of Lord Cyric, the God of Death, Lies, and Assassination.

"We appreciate your honesty," the king said coolly.

Again Lythrana nodded and let her hair fall back over the symbol of her god. "While we are being honest, Your Highness, might I be so bold to ask why the Keep was not invited to the general meeting you held with your nobles, the Sembians, and the dalesmen?"

Vangerdahast shifted his weight, suddenly uncomfortable at the bluntness of the discussion. The wizard glanced at the king and was a bit surprised to see that Azoun was taking it all in stride. "The others were not in the right spirit to discuss plans for a foreign war in front of a Zhentish representative," he stated without hesitation. "Had you been at the meeting, I might not have found the other politicians very cooperative. Still, the lack of an invitation did not prevent you from spying on the conference."

Lythrana studied the king for a moment, puzzled by his honesty. She close to ignore the accusation, tacitly confessing the Keep's guilt. Instead she noted, "I infer from your comments that your crusade is gathering the support it needs."

"I told Lord Chess as much when I requested a special envoy."

After a moment of tense silence, Lythrana turned her green eyes back to Azoun. She forced her face to show a calm she did not feel. "It is a crisp, clear day, Your Highness, and I understand you have marvelous hunting a short ride to the north of Suzail. Could we not discuss your crusade under less formal circumstances?"

Azoun paused, perhaps a little too long, and tried to think of a way to politely decline Lythrana's request. He felt far too tired to ride and really didn't care much for hunting. Lythrana had probably guessed that, Azoun decided. But as soon as he had realized that the envoy was expecting him to decline, he smiled as brightly as he could and said, "Of course. Vangerdahast," Azoun added to his slightly shocked friend, "please have the groom prepare my horse and ask the royal huntsman to gather a suitable hunting party."

To Lythrana, who was staring in undisguised surprise at

him, the king said, "Hawk or hound, Lady Dargor?"

"Hound," she replied, then motioned to her dress. "Perhaps I suggested this too hastily. I'm not quite attired—"

The king smiled graciously. "That shouldn't be a problem. We'll find you something to wear." That said, he sent the royal wizard away to prepare for a hunt.

"While we wait for Vangerdahast to get things ready," the king commented smoothly after his friend had departed, "let us discuss the Tuigan threat to Zhentil Keep."

Realizing that she was being overwhelmed by a far better politician than she, Lythrana Dargor smiled and let the king of Cormyr expound upon the menace of the horsewarriors. They had a leisurely stroll around the castle, Azoun alternately relating the history of each ancient family artifact they passed in their walk then describing the preparations for the crusade.

Within an hour, they moved the discussion outside, onto Suzail's main road. As the royal procession moved through the city, Azoun realized that it was a very good thing for the citizens to see him alive and healthy after the assassination attempt. Crowds quickly gathered at the side of the Promenade, cheering the monarch as he made his way to the northern gates of the city.

As soon as the hunting party was clear of the tent city that clustered around Suzail's walls, they let their horses speed over the open road. The chilly air whipped cloaks and made eyes water, but Azoun found it revived him. Though he didn't enjoy hunting, he did love the feeling of freedom riding a powerful horse gave him. So, grimacing against the chill breeze, Azoun pulled his purple cloak tight over his fur-lined surcoat and let his horse race on.

Eventually, the party slowed down again. As they brought their horses to a canter, the master of the hounds gathered his barking charges closer to his lead. The busy, thriving farms that surrounded Suzail had given way to wilder country, and the king and his party found themselves surrounded by thicket-covered fields and sparse forest. Azoun trotted his horse to Lythrana's side.

"Will this do?" he asked politely. "I suspect these fields and stands of trees might hide a suitable wild boar or two."

Lythrana nodded. Her green eyes were red from the wind, but that didn't dull their intensity. "This is as good as anywhere."

Signaling to the master of the hunt, the king took a barbed spear from a young squire. He handed the weapon to Lythrana, then took another for himself. The king's huntsmen hurried off into the woods with the hounds in search of game. Only when they'd flushed a large boar or stag from the trees would the hunt begin for the nobles. In the meantime, a handful of guards spread out around the tall grass in the clearing to protect the king.

While he waited, Azoun resumed the discussion of the crusade he'd begun earlier with Lythrana. As the king had expected, Lythrana knew a great deal about the Tuigan presence in Rashemen and Thesk. However, he was surprised to learn that the leaders of Zhentil Keep thought a peremptory strike against the barbarians a very wise idea— as long as it was accomplished by the other nations of Faerun.

"If you understand the importance of the crusade," Azoun said to the envoy, "you must also see the importance of a temporary truce with the Dales. I need Mourngrym and the others to commit troops. They won't if they think you'll attack the minute they're gone."

Lythrana squirmed in her saddle slightly. The tight riding breeches and warm woolen jacket she had obtained at the palace itched uncomfortably; she was far more accustomed to silk than coarser, more functional fabrics. "Do you think the dalesmen will believe any pact we sign?" she asked.

Azoun sat up straight in his saddle. "Of course," he exclaimed, "but only if you also agree to send crusaders to Thesk as a sign of good faith."

Poking the ground idly with her spear, Lythrana considered Azoun's suggestion for a moment. "It's unlikely," she finally concluded. "Unless we get something in return—other than the satisfaction of doing good." She almost spat the final word.

From her tone, Azoun knew Lythrana already had a price

in mind. "What do you want?"

"Darkhold," she said matter-of-factly. "The Keep wants you to stop harassing the patrols from Darkhold."

"Out of the question," Azoun snapped. "The citadel of Darkhold houses criminals and brigands. They prey upon our western border. I could never—"

Azoun saw Lythrana's cool smile and stopped speaking. "You didn't expect me to request something silly, like food or trade agreements, did you?" she asked. "Zhentil Keep has an . . . interest in Darkhold, and your patrols are jeopardizing that. If you want the Keep to sign a pact with the Dales, you'll have to sign a pact with us."

A high, shrill note echoed over the field. Azoun turned toward a copse of trees a hundred yards to the east and pulled his spear into battle-ready position. The latter action was really a reflex, borne of both battles fought when younger and training in the law of arms. The trumpet was always a call to attention and action.

Lythrana's horse pranced nervously, and she pulled her spear up from the ground, too. "I leave again for home late tonight, Your Highness. I'll need your answer right away."

Anger swelled inside Azoun, a black, choking gall that almost made him tremble. All he wanted was to fight the Tuigan, to help Faerun—all of Faerun, including Zhentil Keep. Yet, it seemed that no one truly saw the importance, the urgency, of his task.

Azoun frowned. He simply couldn't accept that kind of deal with the murderers and highwaymen who inhabited the citadel of Darkhold.

Before the king could give Lythrana his answer, though, the master of the hunt broke from the trees and rode toward him. The huntsman's large black horse swept through the tall grass like a ship on choppy seas. As soon as he was near, the hunter dismounted and bowed his head. "The dogs have found nothing," he reported. "Would Your Highness like to move to another spot?"

Azoun was relieved by the news, but he was not going to let Lythrana know that. He knit his eyebrows in feigned consternation and frowned. "This land should be better stocked. Our foresters are not keeping the poachers away, it seems." Turning to the Zhentish envoy, the king added, "We have royal lands only a few miles from here that are sure to provide you some sport."

Lythrana shook her head, tossing her black hair as she did so. "If Your Highness doesn't mind, might we go back to the city?" she asked. "I believe I underestimated how tired my long journey has made me."

It took only a signal from Azoun to throw the assembled nobles, huntsmen, and guards into motion. Within minutes, the dogs were gathered and the king's party was riding at a leisurely pace toward Suzail.

"I've never hunted boar before," Lythrana noted idly as she rode beside the king. "Though I've heard the beasts are much like the Tuigan."

"What do you mean?" the king asked.

Lythrana rested her cold green eyes on Azoun. "We've had scouts—spies, if you will—come back from Rashemen and Thay with reports about the Tuigan." She kicked her horse into motion when it stopped to graze. "They're beasts: ruthless, cunning, and amoral. Like boars, the horselords won't tire and won't stop trying to kill you until either you or they are dead."

"Then why won't you help me against them?" Azoun snapped.

Lythrana saw that his brown eyes were flashing with anger. The nobles and huntsmen moved away in respectful silence. "We will," she said quietly. "After we have your word about Darkhold."

Azoun pulled his reins and stopped his horse. The party halted around him. "We will discuss this further over dinner," he growled. With a quick strike of his heels, the king pushed his brightly caparisoned horse into a trot, then a gallop. As he rode, Azoun let the cool air wash the fury from his heart. He allowed the birdsong he heard and the bright sunshine dappling the road ahead of him to soothe and relax him.

All the way back to the city, he turned the problem over and over again in his mind. At first, he saw no other alternative but to refuse the Keep's proposal—and lose the support of the dalesmen and any troops he might gain from Zhentil Keep itself. Many of Azoun's own subjects had been victimized by the roving bands of thieves and slavers who used Darkhold as a base. Time and again, Cormyrian merchants had complained to the king about the powerful citadel. Azoun had done his best to curb the raiding parties coming from the stronghold, but Darkhold itself was located outside of Cormyr's borders and protected by powerful magic. Destroying the citadel utterly was out of the question. Still, Azoun knew that it his duty to combat the evil based there.

As the miles wore on and his initial anger and revulsion at the idea wore off, the king began to wonder if a flat refusal was all that wise.

I am serving my gods by fighting the men of Darkhold, he decided without much thought. But do I further my cause more when I combat lesser evil like that or when I battle a massive evil like the Tuigan?

An answer did not come to Azoun easily, and when he had tentatively decided on a course of action, he wasn't sure that it was the right one. In fact, he changed his mind on the way to Suzail, then once more as he prepared for dinner.

* * * * *

That evening, Lythrana and Azoun were joined by Filfaeril and Vangerdahast in the castle's vast formal dining room. A long, highly polished table of pale wood stood in the room's center. Curtains of deep red velvet covered the windows and reflected dully in the polished oak floor. Together, the floor and the wall hangings first echoed, then damped the high, sweet notes from Thom Reaverson's harp as he played a light tune.

The meal passed swiftly. Vangerdahast spent some time in idle, pleasant chatting with Queen Filfaeril. Azoun and Lythrana kept to themselves, but for very different reasons: the Cormyrian king pondered the growing price of the crusade; the Zhentish envoy silently wondered at the meeting's outcome.

"That will be all, Thom," Azoun said as soon as the meal was over. He pushed his untouched plate of imported strawberries away and signaled for a servant to clear the table.

Turning to the king, Vangerdahast rose to his feet. "I think I will retire, Your Highness. The matters left for you to discuss do not require my presence." With a stiff bow, the wizard shuffled from the dining room.

Within minutes the table was clear and only Azoun, Filfaeril, and Lythrana were left in the cavernous hall.

"I find it hard to believe Vangerdahast has lived over eighty winters," Lythrana began casually. She stretched luxuriously, once again comfortable in her tight black dress. "He seems no older than fifty. In fact, someone at the Keep mentioned he looked about that age ten years ago, too."

Azoun cast a disinterested glance at the envoy. "He's a wizard, Lady Lythrana. It should be no surprise to you that he ages little; such practices should be common among the mages at the Keep, too." He looked to his wife, who was oddly subdued in the presence of the exotic envoy. "But my advisor's age isn't what we're here to discuss."

"The demands haven't changed, Your Highness. Let Darkhold go about its business unmolested for one year."

"And?" the king prompted.

Lythrana paused. "We sign a pact with the Dales. You get the dalesmen to provide you with archers for the crusade."

"That's not enough," Azoun said sharply. His voice echoed from the floor. "There are at least one hundred thousand Tuigan in Thesk right now. I want Zhentish troops to stand with the rest of Faerun."

Lythrana leaned back from the table. She started to speak, then swallowed her words and sighed.

"You're afraid of them too, Lythrana," Azoun rumbled. "I can see it in your eyes when I talk about them." He stood up and turned his back to the table.

The emissary bowed her head. "Of course I am. I was one of the people the Keep sent to spy on the Tuigan." She pulled down the high collar of her black dress. A long red scar marred her otherwise perfectly white shoulder. "I was the only one of my party to escape alive."

The king whirled around. "Then help me. Give me troops."

Lythrana met Azoun's gaze again. "I want to," she hissed after a moment, "but the Keep won't. Not without something in return."

The king paused. He knew that this was all the envoy had to offer, that Lythrana would not, could not concede him anything else. The king's course was set; Azoun had decided after the hunt that reasons of state demanded only one decision from him. "We'll leave Darkhold alone for two seasons," he said at last.

"No. A year."

Azoun sighed, then nodded. "A year."

The words burned like acid in Azoun's soul. He knew that he was allowing the network of evil that connected Zhentil Keep and Darkhold—the Zhentarim—free reign to attack travelers and raid caravans, but he saw no other solution. If the Tuigan came to Cormyr, they'd cause a thousand times more suffering than the troops in Darkhold could ever create. He needed the archers from the Dales to stop that from happening.

Azoun pointed a slightly quivering finger at Lythrana. "Darkhold will be left unhindered for a year," he said, "but I want troops. And if I don't get them, or if Zhentil Keep stands in the way of this crusade again, I promise you that Darkhold will be crushed to rubble."

Lythrana was shocked into silence for an instant. "Of course," she agreed after a time. "Zhentil Keep wants the Tuigan stopped as much as you."

The Zhentish envoy looked over at the queen, who sat quietly at the end of the table. "Are you taking notes?" she asked, her words mixed with puzzlement and sarcasm.

Locking her ice-blue eyes on Lythrana's cold stare, Filfaeril smiled pleasantly. "No," she said. "The crusade is Azoun's matter."

Lythrana arched a thin black eyebrow under her raven-dark bangs. Noting the look on the envoy's face, the queen added, "However, if Zhentil Keep breaks its word and attacks the Dales or Cormyr while the king is in Thesk, I will be here to mount an army against you."

Narrowing her eyes to green slits, Lythrana studied the queen more closely. Filfaeril looked delicate, with her pale skin and long golden hair. Even the filmy rose-pink dress the queen wore made her seem fragile. But as the envoy looked into Filfaeril's eyes, she caught a glimpse of something—a hardness, perhaps—that worried her. "Zhentil Keep does not take threats lightly," Lythrana said at last.

The king leaned on the table with both hands. "Be assured, Lady Dargor, neither Queen Filfaeril nor I ever make idle threats. We do not like to deal with the worshippers of evil gods, but you are the lesser of two bad options."

Lythrana stood slowly. "Zhentil Keep never assumed you would regard us as anything but a 'necessary evil.' " A false, cold smile crossed her face, then she bowed. "We should end this meeting before either of us says something . . . regrettable. The papers detailing the treaty will be ready in an hour?"

When King Azoun nodded, Lythrana bowed again and moved toward the door. "I will send word as to how many troops you can expect and where they will meet you."

As the echoes of the envoy's retreating footsteps died in the large room, the king put his hands on Filfaeril's shoulders. The queen pursed her lips. "I don't trust her for a moment," she noted. "Still, I suspect the Keep isn't foolish enough to break a truce."

Azoun smiled weakly. "They certainly must see that if I can raise an army of thirty thousand to fight a foreign war, the force that would rise against them if they foolishly attacked the Dales would be ten times that size."

The door slid open, and Vangerdahast briskly crossed the room. He looked expectantly at Azoun, who only nodded.

"The Keep will send troops?" the wizard asked expectantly as he got nearer.

"They haven't said how many yet," replied Azoun, "but I'm sure I can get at least fifteen hundred men-at-arms from them." He squeezed Filfaeril's shoulder and added, "We should be ready to send the first troops to the east within twenty days."

– 5 –

The Black Rat

Arrow loops were the only source of natural light in the tower's lower floors. As a result, rooms located there were usually dark, dreary places, even during the daytime. King Azoun didn't mind the deep shadows. In fact, he welcomed the darkness as he stood quietly on the bottom floor of his fortress's northeastern watchtower, for the shadows hid the monarch's growing anger at the soldier who stood before him, his tunic rumpled, his boots unpolished. The guard also had his sword drawn, and a broad smirk lined his thick-boned face.

"So tell me again, old man," the guard grunted at the king. "Just what are you doing down here? Don't you belong back in the main hall with the rest of the relics?"

Azoun narrowed his eyes and cursed silently. The piggish man who stood before him, dappled in the late afternoon sunlight from a nearby arrow loop, was being far too obnoxious to be tolerated. "I told you, my good man," the king said softly, "I'm looking for the captain of the guard. I have a message from His Majesty. Now, are you going to let me deliver it or not?"

The soldier rubbed his poorly shaven chin. "I don't know. I mean, I can't be too careful about who I let roam around the keep." He paused for a second and scratched a particularly hairy spot at the corner of his jaw.

It was obvious to Azoun that the guard was simply being difficult to someone he saw as a harmless old civil servant. "Kind sir," he pleaded, "I must be on my way. The king will be very cross if I don't deliver this message soon."

"All right, but just you remember that Sergeant Connor was nice enough to let you pass," the guard warned, finally stepping out of Azoun's way.

Smiling, the king stared at the soldier's round face. "Oh, yes," he said. "I'll remember." To have you demoted and fined for harassing one of my servants, Azoun added to himself. The ruler of Cormyr bowed fatuously and limped out of the tower into a corridor inside the castle's outer wall.

The king wore the guise of a royal messenger that afternoon: a fine black tunic with a purple dragon sewn across the chest, rough woolen pants, a dark cloak, and low-cut leather shoes. He carried a heavy cloth satchel and a rolled, sealed piece of parchment, official-looking enough to fool almost anyone he met.

Azoun had done a little to change his features, too. With the help of some dye, the king's graying brown hair and beard were now completely white, and some cleverly applied greasepaint had enhanced his wrinkles and paled his skin so that the monarch looked like a veteran of seventy winters instead of fifty. A little well-placed grime covered his normally spotless hands and hid the marks left by the rings he wore as ruler of Cormyr.

It wasn't surprising that the guard didn't recognize King Azoun. Few of his servants and even fewer of his subjects ever got close enough to the monarch to get a good look at his face. Nor was his visage on any of Cormyr's coins. Even without the simple makeup he now wore, Azoun could stroll into most taverns in Suzail without being recognized.

Still, the king didn't take any chances. Whenever he wished to move about the city unencumbered by his personal guard, he donned a disguise and slipped out of the palace by way of the secret door near the tower he'd just left. His great-great-grandfather, Palaghard II, had ordered the secret door be built so he could rendezvous with his various mistresses. Azoun had never used the exit for that specific purpose, but he had thanked Palaghard's lust more than once when the door allowed him to escape unnoticed into the Royal Gardens, then into the city itself.

The king continued to affect a limp as he moved down the dark, seemingly airless corridor, counting paces for a hundred yards or so. Suddenly he stopped, looked up and down the hallway, and listened for the sound of guards nearby. When he heard nothing, he felt the cool stone walls for a hand-sized indentation. Once Azoun found what he was searching for, he checked the hallway one last time for guards, then pressed a hidden lever.

With a low, muffled rumble, the secret door opened. Sunlight flooded the corridor as a four-by-four stone sank into the ground, revealing a tall, thick, cleanly trimmed hedgerow. Azoun squinted at the sudden burst of light and quickly moved into the concealing shrubbery. He fumbled for the hidden release on the outside of the castle for only a moment, then the door slid shut to the sound of stone faintly rubbing against stone.

"Wait a minute, Cuthbert," someone muttered in a deep voice from a few yards away. "I just heard something moving in them bushes next to the wall."

Azoun crouched down and held his breath. Though the secret door was mechanical, magic kept it relatively silent. Still, the king couldn't hide the sounds of his movement in the hedgerow. A sword poked through the evergreens just above his head.

"There's nothing in there," another voice, probably belonging to Cuthbert, said. "And if it was something, it'd more likely turn out to be a rat than a man. Castles attract scavengers like that. Why, I once saw a rat the size of—"

"You've told me that story fifty times if you've told it to me once. Anyway, I'm just doing my job," the deep-voiced man told his companion. He thrust his sword into the bushes again. "I've got a duty to the king, and I intend on doing my best to fulfill it."

Azoun smiled at the sincerity he heard in the guard's voice. It was a welcome change from Sergeant Connor's thinly veiled threats. I'll have to find out who that soldier is and have him commended, Azoun noted to himself. Perhaps I'll even promote him into Connor's job inside the tower.

After a few moments of silence and a few halfhearted sword thrusts into the hedges, the guards moved off. Azoun listened to their footsteps on the gravel path as they walked away. The king also heard one of the guards ask, "I suppose you're going to sign on for that crusade the king's mounting?" The other guard either nodded a reply or had moved too far away, for Azoun never heard his response.

As quietly as he could, the king took off his cape and tunic and unloaded the satchel. Inside the pack was a thin, unlined cloak and a worn, colorless tunic. The livery of a court messenger was fine for getting Azoun out of the keep with few problems, but the king knew that he'd never get honest answers from the townsfolk if he was seen as a member of court.

And honest answers were what Azoun wanted more than anything in the days after the assassination attempt. Of course, Vangerdahast hadn't found it surprising that one of the king's own subjects would try to kill him because of the crusade he proposed. To Azoun, however, the whole affair was mind-boggling.

The Cormyrian king had never doubted that it was his duty to gather the western forces under his banner and stop Yamun Khahan and his barbarians before they had a chance to destroy any western cities. The monarch knew that he had a responsibility to protect Faerun and his own kingdom. He was prepared to sacrifice a great deal—even his life, if necessary—to be certain that the horde never reached the heavily populated areas around the Inner Sea. Perhaps foolishly, Azoun assumed that his people would understand the war's necessity, even share his vision of the West united against the invaders. And he'd dismissed the rumblings from the guilds, for the merchants always complained about any venture that would increase taxes.

The assassination attempt had shown the monarch how wrong he had been to do so. Now Azoun wanted to know if the Trappers' Guild itself had sponsored the attack. And if the guild did foster the attempt on his life, the king wanted to see firsthand how many of his subjects were in unrest. He realized that any strong popular revolt while he was away on crusade might be difficult to quell. Filfaeril was certainly capable of leading the loyalist forces, but the king didn't want to make such a dangerous possibility more likely by ignoring it.

"Reports can't reveal half of what I'll discover myself," Azoun whispered as he stuffed the royal livery into the satchel and hid the bag in the bushes. Then, as quietly as possible, the king pushed his way through the hedgerow.

"Hey, you!" someone yelled. "Get out of those bushes. You'll not be using the Royal Gardens for a chamber pot!"

Azoun blushed and turned to see the royal gardener, a thin, choleric man, shaking a rake at him. So much for stealth, the king thought. Holding his hands before him, Azoun said, "Sincere apologies, my good man. I dropped a coin, and it rolled into the hedge."

People were beginning to stop and stare at the irate gardener and the red-faced old man at whom he was yelling. The Royal Gardens were open to the public during the day, but usually few commoners strolled around the northeast corner of the keep; the rest of the gardens were far more attractive. Still, there were enough people gathering to make Azoun nervous. If the guards should come back, he might be taken in for questioning. The king shuddered in embarrassment at the thought of explaining to the captain of the guard why he was skulking in the bushes, dressed as a down-and-out merchant.

"My apologies, sirrah," Azoun called as he pulled his cloak around his shoulders and walked briskly toward the path that lead out of the gardens.

"And don't come back!" the gardener yelled, tossing his rake to the ground. A few of the half-dozen people gathered nearby laughed, but most just shook their heads and went about their business.

Azoun was soon outside the Royal Gardens, standing on the dirt road that wound through the houses of Suzail's noble families. Unlike the other streets in the city, this one was devoid of garbage. The nobles paid commoners to keep it that way, just as they paid the men to fill the deep, muddy ruts that formed in the dirt street during rainy weather. In all, it was probably the nicest stretch of road in all of Cormyr, and the ancient, landed families—like the Wyvernspurs—didn't allow just anyone to wander down it.

That made the presence of a crowd of average citizens, following what appeared to Azoun at first glance to be a traveling priest, that much more of a mystery. Twenty people, most dressed in dirty, threadbare clothing, walked at the cleric's heels. The men and women at the rear of the crowd all leaned forward as they moved, straining to hear the priest's words. The gathering soon stopped, however, and the cleric raised his hands high above his head.

"Friends, I come to you with a message from Lady Tymora, the Goddess of Luck, the patron of adventurers and warriors," the cleric said as Azoun moved toward the crowd. When the king got close to the rest of the audience, he reached down and put his hand around the small cloth sack that hung at his belt. Cutpurses and pickpockets often worked crowds like this one, and Azoun knew better than to leave his silver unprotected.

The cleric smiled warmly and continued. "I've gathered you here so that you can see what good fortune may bring." He pointed to the beautiful, three-story facade of Wyvernspur House. "These people have been graced."

A murmur of approval ran through the crowd.

The cleric spun around and pointed at his audience. "Are they better people than you?" he asked, raising his voice slightly. "Are they more worthy people than you?"

"No!" someone yelled.

"Of course not," a man close to Azoun hollered in a deep, rumbling voice.

"They don't even work for what they have," a woman cried. Another murmur ran through the crowd, this one tinged with anger.

"But there you are wrong!" the priest said, pointing at the woman who had spoken last. Again his voice grew a little louder. "The people who live along this street, even the royals who live in the grand palace—" The cleric threw his hands into the air, gesturing toward the castle that stood at the other side of the gardens as if he'd just seen it. "They've all paid for what they own. Do you know how?"

A few people muttered, "No."

The cleric raised his voice and clasped his hands together in front of his chest. "Do any of you know how?"

"No!" a few more commoners cried. "Tell us!"

Another warm smile crossed the cleric's face, and the man dabbed sweat and pushed a few strands of dark, matted hair from his brow. "Yes," he said softly, "I'll tell you."

Azoun felt a dull anger welling up inside of him as he watched the cleric play the crowd. He'd seen bullfights in the south, and the toreadors had toyed with the bulls in just such a way, forcing the beasts to dance like trained bears. The king couldn't be too angry, though; he'd used some of the same rhetorical tactics himself when giving his speech to the crowd in the gardens. As the smiling priest paused, waiting for anticipation to build in his audience, the king studied him closely.

The cleric's hair was dark brown, almost black, and combed back from his broad forehead. Deep blue eyes lay under the man's thick eyebrows. His most startling feature was his mouth, which was somehow amazingly expressive. With just the twitch of a lip, the cleric could convey more than most people could with their entire body. Azoun silently noted that the tongue inside that mouth was most likely gold-plated, probably forked, too.

Whatever else there was of the cleric was hidden in a thick brown robe, which was itself very clean, even newly laundered. That fact alone made the cleric stand out in the crowd of grubby peasants that surrounded him. A small silver disk hung at his throat, a symbol of his devotion to the Goddess of Luck. Since the cleric was facing west, whenever he moved, the late afternoon sun glinted off the disk and flashed into someone's eyes.

The priest finished mopping his brow. "These people have won the favor of the Goddess of Luck because they've helped themselves, taken their destinies into their own hands." He signaled to a young boy in the crowd, who moved forward, carrying a small wooden box.

"But what can we do?" asked a pathetic-looking old

woman. She held her bony arms outstretched toward the cleric, and her shapeless gray frock shifted on her thin frame.

Without a word, the dark-haired cleric took the box from the boy's hands, held it out to the woman, and opened it. A large golden coin lay in the velvet-lined case. The coin was a gold lion, if Azoun guessed correctly, and like the cleric's holy symbol, it caught the rays of the afternoon sun and flashed them at the old woman. This time it was a gasp that escaped from the crowd.

Servants from Wyvernspur House now lined the street in front of the manor, and a few noblemen and ladies peered at the gathering from open windows. Azoun knew that it was only a matter of time before a contingent of guards arrived to break up the cleric's meeting.

"Lady Tymora visits the Realms from time to time, and when last she was upon this continent, the Goddess of Luck blessed this coin for our temple." The cleric picked up the gold lion and flicked it high into the air with his thumb. The coin arced into the sky, then stopped and spun in the air. Everyone on the street—the crowd, the servants, the nobles, even King Azoun—found himself staring at the gold piece hovering and twirling above them.

"Accept her into your lives, and Tymora will bless you, too," the cleric said to the sea of upturned faces before him. "But only if you prove your worth, only if you tread the way of the faithful."

A few people grunted curses and looked away from the floating coin. "Here comes the plea for copper pieces," a young blond man near Azoun grumbled. A few commoners simply walked away.

That didn't phase the cleric at all. "Yes," he said to the young man near the king. "One way for you to prove that your heart is ready for the goddess is for you to donate money to her church." A few people nodded, their suspicions confirmed. They started to leave.

"What Tymora really wants from you is a commitment to adventure, a promise to trust in luck and forge your own destiny." The priest paused for a moment and looked into the eyes of the dozen or so people left in front of him. As he locked gazes with the king, the cleric added, "Tymora wants you to go on the crusade."

The statement hit Azoun like the flat of a sword wielded by a fire giant; his head swam and his eyes blurred for a moment. When the king looked again, the cleric's gaze had moved on, latching on to other people in the crowd. The dark-haired man was still talking, saying things about the crusade and how Tymora would reward anyone who trusted in her enough to face the barbarians. The king wasn't really listening.

Instead, Azoun was trying to reconcile his initial reaction to the cleric with the message he was preaching. Somehow, coming from an overpolished orator, a common manipulator of words like that worshiper of Tymora, the call to arms sounded crude. It was obviously effective, though, for when Azoun focused again on the priest, he saw that a half-dozen men were gathered around him, evidently still interested in following his advice.

Before the king could speak to the cleric, however, a patrol of six guards came marching up the street from the east. Without hesitation, Azoun turned to the west and walked away. The soldiers ignored the old man in the tattered cloak and moved straight toward the cleric and his audience. From the windows overlooking the street, the noblemen shouted a few cheers and cries of support for the soldiers.

When Azoun was fifty yards or so away, he looked back at the scene, only to see the cleric in a casual, friendly conversation with one of the guards. After a moment, in which time the priest introduced all of his new recruits to the soldiers, the worshiper of Tymora held his right hand open, palm up. The spinning golden lion dropped softly into the cleric's grasp. Azoun shook his head and strode toward the waterfront.

Two hours passed as the king wandered through the streets of Suzail, in the general direction of the Black Rat, a tavern near the docks and marketplace. The late afternoon sun was just reaching the horizon, so many of the businesses were closing for the night. Some shopkeepers busied themselves with securing the awnings and heavy wooden shutters on their open-fronted shops. Other merchants—including all the bakers, butchers, and other food peddlers Azoun saw—were still standing in their storefronts, hawking their goods at the tops of their lungs, trying to sell what perishables they could before they closed for the night.

The king walked to a bakery and leaned against the corner of the building. The white-bearded man who ran the shop scowled at the king, but didn't chase the loiterer away. For the next few minutes, Azoun simply stood on the corner, taking in the relaxing smell of warm bread and watching his subjects as they went about their lives.

"Tell your master that this is the finest bread I have," Azoun heard the baker tell a young serving girl who'd come to pick up part of her master's evening meal. The girl smiled as if she'd made a special deal with the merchant, then ran off. In a few minutes, another girl in the low-cut blouse of a serving wench came to the shop. The baker told her the same thing he'd told the last customer.

Across the narrow, rocky street from the bakery, a weapons crafter kept shop. At the same time the second serving girl was passing by him, the king watched as a small, even scrawny man stormed up to the smith across the way and unwrapped a sword.

"This weapon isn't balanced correctly!" the man bellowed. "I was guarding a caravan in the Stonelands. When we got attacked by goblins, I used the sword and nearly cut off my own leg!"

When the weaponsmith didn't reply, the warrior smashed the heavy pommel of the claymore against the store's weather-beaten counter.

The dark-skinned crafter looked up at last, contempt in his eyes. "I warned you when you bought it, Yugar. That sword's just too damn heavy for you to wield correctly."

"Ha!" the overzealous warrior cried, snatching up the monstrous two-handed sword again. "I can use any weapon that'll fit in my hand. I'm Yugar the Brave!" He said the last as if it should mean something to anyone who heard it. No one passing by so much as took a second glance at the young braggart.

The smith dropped the whetstone he was using to sharpen a tiny, jewel-handled dagger and stepped out of the shop. He grabbed Yugar's arm and wrested the claymore from his grasp. "If you're so brave, why aren't you signing on for the crusade?"

Without pausing, Yugar picked up a slightly smaller sword from the smith's display—rather awkwardly, Azoun thought—and said, "I am . . . I think. I've heard there's good money to be had if I sign on as a mercenary."

The king winced. Traveling through the city, he'd heard many people discussing the crusade. Most of the merchants were complaining about the new taxes that were being levied to defray the cost of the expedition. Azoun had heard only two craftsmen talking about the crusade with any enthusiasm. However, one of these men was an armorer, the other a weaponsmith. They had far too much to gain from a war to be considered fair representatives of the people.

The king had also overheard many warriors like Yugar, hungry only for money, and a few who only wanted adventure. Still, the guards and churches had reported early that day that over a thousand people had already signed on for the crusade. Azoun had spent much of the morning dispatching letters to the various nobles who had promised armies, asking them to gather in Suzail as soon as possible. The crusade was, without a doubt, going to become a reality very shortly.

Despite this, the trapper's attack still plagued the king. And before he could leave Filfaeril in command of Cormyr, he needed to know that he went with his subjects' blessing. Few people seemed willing to talk about the guilds in detail, though the assassination attempt was the subject of much idle speculation.

Azoun hoped that the adventurers and guildsmen who frequented the same tavern would prove a greater source of information about the Trappers' Guild and public sentiment about the crusade than the merchants he had encountered so far. At the very least, a visit to the Black Rat would provide an excellent escape from the court, if only for one night. He had, after all, frequented the Black Rat in his days with the King's Men.

As the king was remembering a few of those happy hours, the baker came out of his shop, scowled at the loiterer again, and slammed the awning closed. Azoun took the hint and headed for the docks.

By the time the king got to the tavern, the sun had set and a bright moon hung over the city. The air was very chill, and Azoun could see his breath as he hurried along. Occasionally a lantern or candle flickered in an open window, but most of the shops and houses were completely dark. This wasn't surprising, for few people traveled the streets of any city in Faerun at night, especially one the size of Suzail. It was commonly said that only criminals, fools, heroes, and gods walked a city's streets after dark. That statement was generally quite true.

While the night watch made regular patrols in Suzail, shadowy figures still skulked in and out of alleyways, waiting for unwary travelers or drunken adventurers to stumble into their traps. Creatures that would never roam the streets during the day came out to scavenge through the offal and garbage dumped unceremoniously out of windows into the thoroughfares. And though Azoun had secreted a small dagger in his boot when he'd left the castle, he felt much safer when he finally passed through the door of the Black Rat.

"For the last time, no!" a barmaid screeched. She slammed a mug down on the table nearest the tavern's front door and slapped the one-eyed man sitting there. A burst of loud, raucous laughter rumbled through the room in response. The frumpy, fat-cheeked barmaid took a curt bow—one much too low for a woman with any modesty, considering the cut of her dress—and sauntered back to the kitchen.

Azoun started at the disturbance, then shivered at the wall of warm air that washed over him as he entered the tavern. He hadn't noticed how cold it was outside until then. The king glanced around the room for an open table, saw quite a few, then moved toward one close to the small fireplace that dominated the taproom's northern wall. The dozen or so patrons of the Black Rat watched Azoun cross the room, then went back to their drinks or their games of dice.

"I'd do anything for that girl, and this's what I get!" the one-eyed man yelled. Azoun noticed that he was slurring his words slightly.

"Bring back the head of one of those barbarians the king's so hot on killing," a mournful-looking man called from a table near Azoun. "That'll win her heart."

The barmaid walked out of the kitchen and went straight to Azoun's table, ignoring the rude comments from most of the drunkards in the taproom and the protestations of love from the one-eyed man. The king politely ordered an ale, then leaned back toward the fire.

The woman smiled in gratitude at the respect shown her. "Ale's free tonight," she said. "One of our patrons was recently rewarded by the king, and he left gold to pay for drinks." After another brief smile, she blew a coil of red hair from her eyes and went for the drink.

"Alas," a lean, dark woman sighed as the barmaid left the room. "She's given her love to another, Brak. You'll never have her now. Her smile gives her away."

A few men chuckled, but Brak, the one-eyed warrior, stood up. "What?" he snarled, pointing at Azoun. "That old coot?" The king's shoulders sagged. The last thing he wanted was trouble.

The barmaid returned with Azoun's ale, gave it to him, then got Brak to sit down. "There's no one but you," she teased and pinched the man's ruddy cheek. "But I'll love you more if you prove how brave you are on that crusade. Perhaps I'll love you most of all if you don't come back."

There was more laughter, but one man, clad in shining chain mail, stood up and lifted his mug. "I say we should raise a toast to King Azoun . . . the only king in the West worth following into battle. Long live the king!"

After the trials of the last few days, Azoun felt his heart leap as the patrons of the Black Rat, both men and women, lifted their mugs and called out, "Long live the king!"

That phrase always made King Azoun think of his father. Rhigaerd had loved to hear men shout that toast, and few nobles had missed the opportunity to please him with it during his reign. Azoun usually found the phrase troubling, since many of the courtiers assumed it was a sure way to win favor. The phrase had fallen out of use at court, but it obviously hadn't in the city. The king didn't find this particular toast lacking in sincerity or enthusiasm, however.

He smiled to himself beneath his powdered white beard. "Yes," Azoun agreed softly. "Long live the king."

"And your damned guild brothers will pay for their grumbling," the mail-clad warrior added, swinging his mug toward the table by the door. Brak grumbled something under his breath, but remained silent.

Azoun didn't miss the reference to the trappers and quickly moved to the table of the man who'd made the toast. "May I join you?" When the man nodded, the king took a seat on the rickety bench across from him. "What was that about the trappers, young man?" he asked in a soft voice.

After a long swallow of ale, the warrior leveled his gaze on the king. "A guild should be responsible for its members." He cast a withering glance at Brak, then added, "He's an influential member of the Trappers' Guild, so—"

Abruptly Azoun held up his hand. "The attack on the king," he finished. "So that's the source of your animosity." He studied the man across the table for a moment before he asked his next question.

He's probably a mercenary, the king decided. The warrior was by no means unhandsome, but the look of dogged obstinacy that clung to his square features made him appear contentious. After a moment, Azoun reconsidered his opinion. The man was fastidiously dressed; his mail shone as if recently polished, his leather breeches and silk surcoat were spotless. No, not a mercenary, the king concluded. More likely a paladin of some lawful order.

Azoun leaned close. "The name's Balin," he said. "Well met . . . er . . ."

"Ambrosius." The man reached out and clasped Azoun's forearm in a traditional greeting. "Ambrosius, Knight of

Tyr." A slightly puzzled look crossed his face as he let the king's arm go.

Without letting it register on his face, Azoun cursed to himself. The man *was* a paladin, a holy knight of the God of Justice. Such warriors were difficult to fool, and it seemed for an instant, when Ambrosius had grasped his arm. . . . The king smiled wanly through his powdered beard and started to rise.

"No need to hurry," Ambrosius said flatly, clasping a strong arm around Azoun's wrist. "I am always at a loss for personable men to share conversation with me here." When the king hesitated, the knight whispered, "Do not make a scene, good sir. I simply want to know for whom you spy."

With a sigh, Azoun took his seat. "I am here on the king's business," he replied. "Is my disguise so poor that you can see through it so easily?"

Ambrosius thrust his square chin out and looked at Azoun with that expression of doggedness. "Your arm is far too muscular for a man of the age you pretend to be," he whispered. "I do not approve of spies or subterfuge. I've learned long ago to ferret out such as you."

The knight paused, then asked, "My toast to the king was sincere. What does His Highness wish to know?"

"The feelings of his subjects on the crusade," Azoun replied. "As well as the disposition of the Trappers' Guild toward the king himself."

Ambrosius laughed, a deep, robust sound that came from his heart. "The first is a simple matter to discern. There are hundreds of the king's loyal subjects—myself included— who have signed on already for the crusade." The paladin leaned back in his chair. "The other is more complex."

After rubbing his chin for a moment, the knight of Tyr smiled broadly. "But, again, there is simple way to the truth." Without pause, he turned to Brak. "Ho, trapper! This man wants to know your guild's attitude toward the king," he said truthfully.

The bar quieted slightly, and Brak stared at the paladin and the king like an enraged cyclops. "I don't want to answer to the likes of you, Ambrosius," the trapper slurred.

The reason for that would have been obvious to anyone in the Black Rat who knew Ambrosius to be a paladin. Such holy knights, because of their devotion to their gods, were sometimes gifted with the power to detect evil in other men's hearts.

"You needn't fear answering unless the trappers *were* in league against the king," Ambrosius announced. Now the bar was silent, and everyone looked toward Brak. The one-eyed trapper shifted nervously in his seat. "Best answer right away," the paladin added after scanning the room. "It seems there are many here who wonder what your guild has been up to."

A tense silence followed. Brak took a long sip of ale and wiped his mouth with the back of his callused hand. "The Trappers' Guild didn't have anything to do with the attack on the king," he grumbled. He met Ambrosius's steady gaze with his one good eye. "But we don't make no secret of the fact we oppose the crusade."

Ambrosius said nothing as he returned to his seat. Most of the patrons at the Black Rat turned back to their drinks and their private conversations, though a few still watched the trapper and the paladin. Azoun shook his head. "You could have asked the same question without revealing me as the king's man," he said.

"As I said before, I have no use for spies. You get more by asking questions directly."

"I take it the trapper was telling the truth?"

"Of course," Ambrosius replied. "Brak knows me far too well to consider lying."

After talking with the paladin for a time, sipping on the inn's dark, bitter ale, the king stood and headed toward the door. Brak scowled slightly as Azoun passed, but the drunken trapper was quickly dragged back into an animated conversation about the Tuigan. Azoun heard someone say, "There's no way we can lose with the armies of Faerun brought together like that!" He offered a silent prayer that the man was right, then moved once more into the cold night air.

This chill is the last gasp of winter, Azoun decided as he

hugged his cloak tighter around his shoulders. That means the Tuigan are probably on the move again in Thay. The armies of Faerun can gather none too soon now.

And from all that Azoun had learned that day, he was sure it was safe to proceed. The people of Suzail supported his crusade, despite the seemingly isolated unrest amongst a few of the guilds. Though the merchants grumbled about the taxes, the king knew that they rarely stopped complaining about such things. More importantly, the king felt secure that the would-be assassin was working alone.

Azoun shivered in the frosty air and pulled the worn cloak tighter still. The tattered disguise tore under the strength of his grasp. He looked at the ripped cloak and smiled.

On days when he had been in a good mood, Azoun's father had called his son's interest in the theater and costumes a waste of time. At times when the hawks refused to cooperate or the nobles were particularly fractious, King Rhigaerd II had given Prince Azoun's hobby a few less diplomatic titles. At that moment, as he made his way through Suzail, the king of Cormyr thanked the gods that he'd chosen the Black Rat to visit. He smiled with the knowledge that his penchant for disguises had indeed served him well.

- 6 -

The Goddess's Hand

Azoun sat back in the cushioned chair and allowed himself to relax. It was the first time in two tendays he'd taken such a luxury.

"One day out, many more to go, eh Thom?" the king asked absently.

The bard sat at a steel-legged wooden table, taking notes for the crusade's annals. He finished a sentence or two, then looked up and nodded. "By the time we get to our destination, I should have the section on the crusade's organization completed."

Azoun closed his eyes and rested his head against the cabin wall. "Let's hope the battles don't prove any more difficult than raising the troops has."

Thom Reaverson didn't answer; it was obvious Azoun didn't expect one. Within a few moments, the king had drifted off to sleep, lulled by the gentle rocking of the Cormyrian carrack as it made its way across the Lake of Dragons. The bard listened for a moment to the creaking of the ship and the sounds of the crew going about its business abovedeck. After a while, he turned back to his work.

Thom dipped his quill in a cup of water, then scratched it across a square of dried ink. After reading over the last sentence he'd completed, the bard continued his account of the twenty-one days between the assassination attempt and the departure of the king's ship for the east.

The scutage—or shield tax—levied by King Azoun against the Cormyrian nobles has provided him with almost ten thousand troops and the money to raise two thousand more. Surprisingly, many of the nobles have decided to accompany the king themselves, so Azoun can count on a large, well armored cavalry to lead his attacks. No doubt these nobles see the importance of the cause.

Thom considered crossing out the last sentence. The bard felt that, as official historian for the crusade, it wasn't his place to editorialize. Pondering the point for a moment, he decided to let the entry stand. There could be little other reason for the nobles to join the crusaders, Thom reasoned, so that claim actually isn't simply my opinion.

The bard inked his pen again and continued.

Added to the troops King Azoun has gathered from the Royal Army and the populace of Suzail itself, Cormyr has given a total of twelve thousand brave archers, knights, and men-at-arms to the cause. These troops have been organized into one army under King Azoun IV of Cormyr, together with the soldiers levied from other parts of Faerun.

Thom stretched and moved his ink-stained hand over his mouth to cover a yawn. After closing his eyes for a moment, the bard shuffled through the other papers spread out on the table. Moving carefully to avoid smudging the still-wet ink on the page in front of him, Thom slid a particular sheet of parchment out from under the rest. He glanced at the list scrawled hastily on the page, then carefully added its contents to the annals.

The twelve thousand Cormyrians will be joined by soldiers from many parts of Faerun in this battle. The following is a rough estimate of the troops committed by those in Faerun allied with King Azoun.

Sembia	*money for 4,000 men-at-arms*
The Dales	*4,000 men-at-arms (mostly archers)*
Tantras	*1,600 men-at-arms*
Hillsfar	*600 men-at-arms (mostly cavalry)*
Ravens Bluff	*2,400 men-at-arms*
Other Cities	*3,400 men-at-arms*

The dark-haired bard turned over the sheet that held the original list of troops and added the numbers. He hastily noted that figure in the annals.

These troops will be joined by at least two thousand dwarves under the command of King Torg, from a city in the Earthfast Mountains. Zhentil Keep has also promised one thousand soldiers, who will be meeting the army at the northern end of the Easting Reach. All told, the crusaders should total over thirty thousand when they meet the Tuigan.

The last line of the paragraph barely fit at the bottom of the page, even with Thom's tight, controlled handwriting. He studied the finished sheet. When he found no major blotches of ink or dirty fingerprints on it, Thom gently blew it dry. After a moment or two, he put his initials in small, barely legible letters at the sheet's lower right-hand corner. That done, the bard gently laid a thin blotting paper over the new page and put the two under a large, heavy book.

Thom Reaverson packed up his papers and put his ink and quills in a small wooden box that had Cormyr's emblem carved into its top. The box and fine writing tools it contained had been a gift from King Azoun, one of many rewards given to Thom for accepting the duty to chronicle the crusade. The bard would have gladly faced a dragon for the prestigious title of court historian, and he saw the gold and gifts the king had offered him as a sign of the monarch's generosity. Still, the pen set was special to Thom Reaverson, for it had come to symbolize for him the trust Azoun had in his skills.

With his tools and the pages of the ever-growing chronicle stowed securely in a cabinet, the bard quietly made his way from the king's cabin. He nodded to the guards as he left and told them that Azoun was sleeping and was not to be disturbed. On his way up to the deck of the tri-masted carrack, Thom met Vangerdahast, who was working his way stiffly down the steep wooden steps.

When the wizard spotted Thom, he stopped his descent. "Is the king awake and well?" Vangerdahast asked, his voice weak and a little strained.

Thom's sympathy went out to the old mage immediately. It was clear from the color of Vangerdahast's face that his constitution was not up to the challenge of the gently swaying ship. "He's well," the bard answered, "but not awake."

"I hope he knows that we have a meeting with the generals in an hour or so," the pale wizard said testily.

"I'm sure he left word with a servant, Master Vangerdahast," Thom replied, steadying himself on the stairs as the ship heaved deeply to one side. "The rest will certainly do him good."

Scowling at the motion of the ship, Vangerdahast nodded and said, "He's certainly been tireless these last few tendays." The ship dipped again, and the wizard cursed softly. "I'm going to lie down myself, Thom. If I'm not at the meeting, send someone to fetch me."

The bard backed down two steps to the landing and allowed Vangerdahast to squeeze by him. Though the *Welleran* was one of the most luxurious ships on the Inner Sea, the cabins and walkways were still very cramped. Only after the wizard closed the door to his cabin did Thom climb up to the deck, into the red glow of a beautiful spring sunset.

Some of the crew were eating their supper in various spots on the deck. They gulped watery stew and washed it down with warm, dark ale. Around them, other sailors went about their duty, securing sails or climbing into the fore rigging toward lookout positions in the masts. Thom got out of the way as best he could, positioning himself near the port railing.

Far to the north lay the coast of Cormyr—or perhaps it was Sembia by then, for all Thom knew. Dozens of other ships dashed through the water nearby. Most of them were spectacularly rigged carracks from the Cormyrian navy. With their large aft and forecastles, and three masts decked with canvas sails and multicolored flags identifying vessel and port of origin, the carracks were the sturdiest ships in the crusaders' fleet. Others nearby were less impressive merchant ships or mercenaries' vessels. Of course this was only a small part of the massive caravan to the east. Ships had been leaving from Cormyr for days now, heading toward the free city of Telflamm, the gathering point for the armies.

It's no wonder Azoun is exhausted, Thom decided silently. In just the last few months he's brought everything together. And not even that damned attack in the Royal Gardens has been enough to shake his dedication to this venture.

Thom couldn't know that a secret trip to the Black Rat had countered any doubts that Azoun had had about the crusade—even the ones planted by the assassination attempt. In the tenday that followed the surreptitious visit to the tavern and the meeting with the Zhentish envoy, the king had indeed attacked the Tuigan matter with renewed vigor and enthusiasm. Supply lines had been quickly established, ships and troops gathered together, and final messages dispatched to King Torg and the witches in Rashemen. He'd even appointed an impartial seneschal to oversee the trial of the imprisoned trapper.

That dedication had paid off for Azoun, and Thom could see the success manifested in the high-spirited crew around him and the fast-moving troop and supply ships crossing the Lake of Dragons. After watching a dark-hulled cog, the *Sarnath*, come even with the *Welleran*, then pass it, the bard let his thoughts wander to the battles that loomed in the future. For the next hour, he wondered what his part would be in the conflict.

Thom's reverie was broken by a large, callused hand on his shoulder. "Time for the meeting, Master Bard," a deep, soothing voice said.

Thom turned to see General Farl Bloodaxe, commander of the army's infantry. The bard knew the soldier well, for he was a frequent guest at Azoun's palace. Farl looked particularly dashing that night as he stood, one hand planted on his hip, the other grasping a line overhead. The final light of the setting sun cast deep shadows on his ebony skin and glinted in his green eyes. The wind tugged at the loose-fitting white shirt the general wore. That, coupled with his silver-buckled boots and tan breeches, made him look more a pirate than an infantry commander. It wasn't an image Farl fostered, Thom knew, for the general was a well-known supporter of law and order.

Thom smiled warmly. "Thank you for reminding me, General. It's not hard to lose track of time completely when watching the sea pass by, especially after it gets dark."

"I traveled by ship quite a lot when I was a younger, you know," the general noted, leaning on the railing. He looked up at the stars, just becoming visible in the night sky, and added, "It's the one thing I miss most about my days as a world traveler."

"Too bad Vangerdahast doesn't share your enthusiasm for ships," the bard said. "He looked quite ill when I saw him earlier."

The general took a long last look at the dark water rushing by the ship. "We'd best be going, Thom. The meeting will be underway by now."

Farl Bloodaxe was right. When he and Thom reached the king's cabin in the aft castle, Azoun was unrolling a map, talking about the reorganization of the troops that would take place once they were gathered in Telflamm. Vangerdahast, still slightly pale, sat by an open window, taking in deep breaths of the cool air. Finally, at either side of the table, the crusade's two other generals stood, listening intently to the Cormyrian monarch.

"After seeing the ships to Telflamm, I'll be going north up the coast to deliver supplies to King Torg and rendezvous with the troops from Zhentil Keep," Azoun said. "The dwarves, being creatures of the earth, won't travel by boat, so—" He stopped speaking when Thom and Farl entered the cabin.

"My apologies, Azoun," Farl said sincerely.

"Yes, milord," Thom added. "It's my fault we're late. I was mulling over a song at the railing when the general reminded me about the meeting."

"Leave it to a bard to forget an important meeting because of a song," one of the generals said gruffly. "Never did see much use in having them along on campaign. They can even be a downright nuisance. Why, once—"

"Please, Lord Harcourt," Azoun said quickly, preventing the cavalry general from launching into one of his endless war stories. "I chose Muse Reaverson to come along as court historian, not as an entertainer. I'd rather you didn't insult him."

Looking a bit shocked at the reproach, Lord Harcourt

rubbed his long white mustache and mumbled an apology. He shifted uncomfortably in his hauberk under the king's gaze. Silently Azoun wondered if the cavalry commander ever took the chain mail shirt off, for he was the only armored man in the cabin.

Farl laughed and added, "Or you'll end up looking like a fool in the chronicles. Eternal infamy is a high price to pay for a minor insult."

Though both Thom and Azoun knew the infantry commander meant that last comment as a joke, they both frowned—each for a different reason. The barb brought the family history's disturbing depiction of Salember to Azoun's mind, while Thom simply felt a little insulted that someone could even suggest he would use the position of court historian to settle personal grudges.

The third general cleared his throat noisily. "You were saying, Your Highness, you'll meet with the dwarven lord and the Zhentish . . . troops in the Great Dale." The impatience in the red-haired man's voice was barely hidden, but his hatred for the soldiers from Zhentil Keep was not.

"Yes, General Elventree," Azoun replied coldly. "Thank you for reminding us of our business."

Lord Harcourt and Vangerdahast both scowled at Brunthar Elventree. Neither man liked the general who was to lead the archers on the crusade. The red-haired warrior was a dalesman—a military leader from Battledale, more specifically—and he had been given the position in Azoun's army only as a concession to Lord Mourngrym and the other dalelords. The king had thought the appointment of a dalesman to lead the archers in combat a wise move, despite his earlier reservations. Elventree's election pleased the dalelords, and Azoun had hoped it might give the army a new unity.

The appointment seemed to be accomplishing just the opposite. General Elventree could barely conceal his dislike of the other generals, especially Lord Harcourt, whom he felt was elitist. He had also rubbed Vangerdahast the wrong way almost immediately by claiming that no battle was ever won through magic. Elventree didn't conceal his hatred of the Zhentish either, and he proved time and again that his temper could flare as brightly as his striking red hair.

Azoun did what he could to keep the dalesman in line, but he secretly worried that Brunthar Elventree's myopic bigotry was only a prelude to the problems he would face later in uniting the soldiers as an efficient fighting force.

The king broke the tension that had settled over the room by introducing a topic he'd discussed only that morning with Thom. "Before we begin in earnest, gentlemen," he said calmly, "I propose we adopt a single name for the crusading army."

"Yes," Vangerdahast said from his seat near the window. "A single name will help bring us together."

For the first time since they'd met, all three generals agreed. Farl Bloodaxe and Brunthar Elventree nodded, while Lord Harcourt added a hearty, "Here, here!"

"Any suggestions?" the king asked.

After a moment's silence, Lord Harcourt tugged at his long white mustache and said. "I place the title 'Knights of Faerun' under consideration."

"All right, Lord Harcourt," Thom said as he noted the name on a clay tablet. "What about the name you mentioned to me earlier, Your Highness?"

"The Alliance of the West," Azoun offered. "Or just the Alliance."

"I don't have a suggestion myself," Brunthar said. "But I like 'the Alliance' much better than 'the Knights of Faerun.' After all," he added sarcastically, "we aren't all going to ride horses into battle."

Vangerdahast cut in with another possible name before Lord Harcourt could respond to the dalesman's snide comment. "How about 'the Confederacy of Western Powers'?"

"Too long," Farl said. He glanced at the map, then concluded, "The Alliance is the best, I think."

Thom Reaverson noted his approval, as did Vangerdahast. Only Lord Harcourt paused before throwing his support to the title. The king thought that he saw the old cavalryman pout slightly before he mumbled, "You have my support, Your Highness."

"Fine, then," Azoun said brightly. "Now we can get to more important business." The king pushed a book onto one corner of the map to stop it from rolling and pointed to Lake Ashane, otherwise known as the Lake of Tears. "This is where the Tuigan started their invasion of Ashanath."

"And by now," Vangerdahast offered, "they are certainly through Ashanath and into Thesk." He walked slowly to the map and traced west from the lake. "The Tuigan probably haven't reached the town of Tammar, which is halfway between the Lake of Tears and the place where we'll land. However, the city will likely fall before we enter the conflict."

Farl rubbed his chin. "What about local resistance?"

"Either wiped out by the Tuigan or caught up in skirmishes with the Red Wizards of Thay," Azoun replied. He shook his head. "We can expect only a small addition to the army once we muster outside Telflamm."

Each man was silent for a moment, caught up in considering the hard times that obviously lay ahead of the Alliance. The wind whistled through the open window in high, haunting fits. The breeze had grown so steady, in fact, that Vangerdahast reluctantly closed the heavy leaded glass. The groans and creaks of the wooden ship and the shouts of the men on deck filled the momentary silence in the cabin.

"Then we'll have to arrange the army as best we can," Brunthar Elventree offered at last. "Take advantage of what we have."

As the generals set about organizing, then reorganizing the army into fighting units, Thom Reaverson scratched notes into soft clay tablets. Parchment and ink were too expensive to waste on note-taking, so the bard always took down ideas and important information on a clay tablet. He would later meticulously transfer those same notes to paper and wipe the tablet clean to be used again.

The discussion lasted for hours. As the subject turned from troop organization to supply lines to potential battlefields, the lantern that hung from a beam at the center of the cabin swayed more and more. The wind soon howled outside the ship, though that sound couldn't drown out the deep, tortured creaking of plank on plank. At first the signs of the incipient storm didn't alarm King Azoun or the others in the great cabin. However, when waves started breaking against the heavy windows at the end of the room, Azoun and Vangerdahast decided to go on deck to see what was happening.

Sailors were rushing everywhere, and as the king reached the deck, he was stung by a hard, cold rain. He motioned for Vangerdahast to stay below, for it was clear that aboveboard on the ship was a dangerous place to be. The royal wizard still felt weak from his earlier sickness, so he didn't even consider arguing. As Vangerdahast shuffled back to the great cabin, Azoun pushed himself toward the railing.

The king soon found that it was difficult to see. Storm clouds had blotted out the moon, and the fierce wind made any other light source almost impossible to maintain. The rain slashed across the sky, almost parallel with the sea, and waves reared up over the railing and crashed down with frightening speed and power. The king shielded his face as best he could and struggled toward the wheel, where the *Welleran*'s captain stationed himself during a storm.

Before Azoun could take three steps away from the railing, a sailor ran into him, knocking him to the deck. The youth didn't stop to apologize or even help the king to his feet. Instead, he dashed to the railing and emptied a large coffer he held in both hands into the water. Azoun gasped; he saw glints of gold and silver as the metal in the box spilled into the sea.

"All the treasure in my cabin," Azoun heard a shrill voice cry. "Into the water with it!" The sailor spun around and dashed toward the voice.

A wave crashed onto the deck and slammed the king into the nearest section of gunwale. Azoun stood as quickly as he could and grabbed a line. As he wiped his wet hair from his eyes, a strong, dark hand clasped onto his shoulder.

"I thought you might want some company up here," Farl Bloodaxe yelled, trying to be heard over the wind, "when Vangerdahast came back without you."

Azoun nodded and looked toward the wheel. "Have you seen Captain Merimna, Farl? I heard his voice a moment ago."

As if in reply, the shrill voice relayed another order from the rain-darkened ship, then Captain Merimna himself stumbled toward Azoun. "Into the rigging and clew up the topsails! In the studding sails!" he cried, his right hand cupped next to his mouth.

"Captain Merimna," Azoun called.

The *Welleran's* gaunt commander turned his face toward the forecastle and yelled, "Bring out all the gold. Dump it over the edge and give Umberlee her due!"

Farl grabbed the sea captain and spun the man around. A sudden fork of lightning split the sky and illuminated him. The captain was soaked, like everyone else on deck, and his sodden royal blue uniform clung to him heavily. He didn't seem to notice the rain; his eyes, huge with terror, were focused on some vague, distant threat. "Umberlee's due," he mumbled.

"May all the gods of Good protect us," Farl muttered. "They didn't give the Goddess of Oceans enough tribute before we left!" The soldier gripped the captain with both hands now. "That's it, isn't it?"

Merimna nodded, then pulled away from Farl and rushed toward the bow. Another wave washed over the gunwale, and both Azoun and Farl lost sight of the gaunt captain.

"What is it, Farl?"

"The captain didn't offer a sacrifice to Umberlee before we left port. If we don't appease her, we're all dead men." In the darkness, Azoun could barely see his face, but he could tell from Farl's voice that he was frightened.

"From that look in his eyes, I'd guess Merimna's useless to us now," Azoun said. "I know you've had a little experience with ships like this, so take command and keep us afloat." After a second, he added, "I'll find suitable tribute."

Without waiting for a reply from Farl, the king struggled toward the hatch. The ebony-skinned general was already barking orders. Shouts from panicked sailors and the noise of masts bending in the gale obscured what the man said, but Azoun was certain that Farl Bloodaxe could get them through the storm.

The king burst into the great cabin, cold and shivering. "We've offended Umberlee," he shouted. "No one offered her tribute before we left Suzail."

Vangerdahast cursed loudly. Thom Reaverson said a quick, silent prayer to Lord Oghma, the patron god of bards, asking for his protection from the storm. Barring that, Thom prayed that a suitably glorious tale would be written about them. Brunthar Elventree, on the other hand, whispered something to Mielikki, the Lady of the Forest, asking that he be allowed to see the trees in Battledale again.

Lord Harcourt leaned forward in his chair and steepled his fingers. "We need something of great value right away," he noted stoically. A wave crashed against the stern, shattering a pane of leaded glass. "We lost a flagship this way, back in the Year of the Dragon. Nasty business." He tugged at the corner of his mustache and frowned. "It's our responsibility as flagship to make the proper sacrifice. If she's not happy with the offering, Umberlee will take the flagship instead. Oh, anyone in her way will be sunk, but she'll head straight for us. . . ."

Azoun pulled open a chest and uncovered a few brilliant, multifaceted gems. Brunthar emptied a dozen gold pieces from a leather bag at his belt and dumped them on the table. Vangerdahast and Thom did the same. Lord Harcourt stood and walked to the center of the room.

He glanced at the gathered wealth and shook his head. "Umberlee wants something we value. Something important to us. We must—"

The sound of splintering wood and tearing canvas stopped the cavalry commander from continuing. Farl Bloodaxe's voice carried over the chaos on deck, and the men in the great cabin could hear his commands over the storm. From what Farl was telling the crew to do, Azoun concluded that one of the masts was breaking.

After running a hand through his wet, tangled hair, Azoun reached up and steadied the swaying lantern. He paused in that position to think. Across the table from the king, the royal magician and the dalesman pelted Lord Harcourt with questions. Some of their queries were drowned out by the wind and water whistling in through the broken window.

Like Azoun, Thom Reaverson stood silently in thought. He braced himself against the cabin wall and listened to the thud of waves crashing against the hull and washing over the deck. A hundred stories of misadventures at sea filled the bard's head, and he briefly reviewed each one for something that might help. Then an idea came to him, not part of a particular story, but related to all of them. He walked to the cabinet, opened it, and took out the finely carved wooden box containing his pen set and the completed pages of the crusade's annals.

As the bard left the cabin, Azoun turned to follow; Lord Harcourt, Vangerdahast, and Brunthar Elventree were too caught up in their argument to notice. The king found Thom Reaverson tossing page after finely lettered page into the sea. Rain slashed the sheets and the wind whipped the water-laden parchment, then dashed each page into the waves.

"Thom, wait!" Azoun cried as the bard tossed the last page over the side and lifted the finely carved box above his head. Another flash of lightning zigzagged a wild path across the sky, and the king saw sailors lining the rails to either side of the bard, tossing coins into the water.

In the instant of absolute blackness that followed the lightning strike, Thom hurled the case. The king reached the bard's side in time to see another fork of lightning split the night and strike a nearby cog. The bolt splintered one of the smaller ship's two square-rigged masts and set its canvas ablaze. It was the first time Azoun had realized that the storm had tossed them so close to other ships in the armada. Flames eagerly licked the cog's second mast, and soon it was burning brightly.

The eerie red glow from the burning cog cut through the night and the storm, illuminating the churning sea. The king glanced out at a few of the parchment pages bobbing on the waves.

"Why?" Azoun asked.

Thom didn't answer, but kept his gaze locked on the spot where he'd guessed his gift to Umberlee had hit the water. "Look," he said in a voice that was barely heard over the storm. He pointed to the waves.

When Azoun saw what Thom was pointing at, he gasped and gripped the railing tightly.

Against the backdrop of the burning cog, a forty-foot-high, forked wave had risen out of the ocean. The wave curled in breakers both to the left and right and moved with unnatural slowness toward the *Welleran*. "Lady Umberlee herself! The goddess's hand!" Azoun heard a sailor cry from nearby. "We're doomed!"

"Try and turn her about!" Farl Bloodaxe yelled from somewhere on the deck. "This'll swamp us for sure."

But the wave continued to move toward the king's carrack, slowly blotting out Azoun's view of the burning cog. A burst of wind pushed cold rain into the king's eyes, so he shielded his face for a moment. When he looked up again, the forked wave, its breakers never falling, was only fifty yards from the ship. It reared even higher for a moment, then collapsed, slapping the surface with a terrible roar.

Everyone onboard the *Welleran* who saw the unnatural wave fall braced for the terrible aftershock. The collapse of the forty-foot-high wall of water should have sent huge waves out all around, but it didn't. Instead, the storm died abruptly. The wind lessened, the sea calmed, and soon only a steady rain fell on the king's carrack.

As Azoun, Thom, and the crew looked out at the now-calm waters, they saw hundreds of blue-white points of light sinking below the surface. The light diminished as the glowing coins sank into the sea. Closer to the surface, dozens of sheets of parchment, tangled and torn, shone more brightly. Finally, a small box with Cormyr's symbol prominent on its cover bobbed on the waves, casting a bright light.

Thom Reaverson turned to King Azoun. "I'm sorry, milord. Of the things I have on the ship, I valued them most."

Azoun watched the pages and the box sink beneath the

water, their light dimming as Umberlee drew the offerings to the bottom of the sea. "I'll replace the gift, Thom, but I can't give you back all your work."

The bard shook his head. "Our work, Your Highness. The annals told of everything you've done up until now to organize the crusade." He glanced at the points of light falling beneath the water. "Perhaps that's why Umberlee accepted the pages and all as a suitable sacrifice. They tell why we're here."

Farl Bloodaxe clapped Thom on the back as he reached the bard's side. "You may have saved us all," he said, exhaustion apparent in his voice.

The king cast a glance at the mainmast, then looked at Farl. "Will we need to make for shore? From the orders you were giving, I thought the mast was splintering."

The infantry commander shook his head. "We lost some rigging, and the masts were sorely tested by the storm. I've given command over to the first mate for now. He's inspecting the masts and the sheets to make sure we're still seaworthy, but I think the ship will be able to go on."

The rain continued to fall, so Azoun moved the discussion back to the great cabin. Thom Reaverson stayed on deck for a short time, watching the cog burn itself out, then slowly sink. The *Welleran* picked up some of the survivors, as did the dark-hulled Sembian ship that had passed the king's carrack earlier.

Before he left the railing, the bard took one last look into the sea. The blue-white lights that marked his sacrifice were gone. As he gazed into the inky water, Thom Reaverson wondered if Azoun or anyone else could truly understand what he'd given up. The pages that Umberlee had taken could never be exactly reproduced. They might have been his best work, now lost to the world.

Then again, Thom realized suddenly, perhaps the new annals he would write would be better. He returned to the great cabin to begin his notes anew, hoping that the goddess's hand had granted him an unintended favor.

- 7 -

Blood and Thunder

T he storm caused by Umberlee's wrath was the last bad weather the fleet saw on its way across the Inner Sea. Most of the days were bright and breezy, and the cogs, coasters, and carracks made good time toward the free city of Telflamm. Still, each day presented new problems for the ragtag navy and the soldiers unaccustomed to life at sea.

This particular morning, on a Sembian ship in the crusaders' fleet, Razor John rubbed his shoulder in a futile attempt to work out a knotted muscle. The fletcher's back had begun to ache continuously after his first night aboard the dark-hulled, square-sailed cog, and he'd been unable to shake the pain since. The constant damp and perpetual hard labor he faced each day only aggravated the problem.

Sighing, John pushed his rough, spray-soaked blanket aside and sat up. Like most of the other passengers onboard the *Sarnath*, he slept on the open deck. In fact, the shortage of storage space on the cog meant that many of the sailors and soldiers on her slept, ate, and passed their free time on deck. Still, Razor John was a hearty soul, and he quickly acclimated to the everpresent dampness and the aches it caused.

He couldn't get used to the lack of privacy. Only high in the rigging could anyone escape the bustle of the deck, and that was certainly not the safest place to be. Four sailors had already plummeted to their deaths from the masts, the victims of a single misplaced step. Picking up half the survivors

- 112 -

of the ship struck by lightning during the storm hadn't helped the overcrowding either. The refugees from the burned ship had swelled the ranks aboard the *Sarnath* almost to capacity.

Clasping his hands high over his head and stretching again, John said, "Time to get up, Mal." When the snoring lump next to the bowsprit didn't move, the fletcher kicked it softly with a toe.

"Leave me be, son of a Sembian pig," Mal grunted. He pulled his blanket up over his head, muttering incoherent curses.

Razor John frowned. Mal—or Malmondes of Suzail, as John had discovered his full name to be—had proved himself quite adept at starting brawls with comments like that one. Though Mal was seemingly a good-hearted man, the fletcher found it hard to see beyond his many prejudices. The fact that John, Mal, and their other companion, Kiri, were traveling on a Sembian cog only made the problem worse.

John nudged the ham-fisted soldier again. "Don't give the first mate an excuse to start in on you again, Mal." As the lump beneath the spray-soaked blanket grumbled, the fletcher pulled on boots and placed a shapeless felt hat on his mop of sandy hair.

"Won't get up again, eh?"

Razor John started, then turned to face the person who'd just posed the question. "No, Kiri," he said. "Just like every morning."

The thin, brown-haired woman handed John two hard biscuits and a piece of fruit. The fletcher let his gaze wander over the woman's lithe form to her slightly round face. As usual, her brown eyes were bright and made John glad to see her. In fact, he had recently found himself using images of Kiri and her smile as shields against the boredom and fatigue that assailed everyone aboard ship.

"Don't fret, John. If Mal sleeps for much longer, we'll split his morningfeast." Kiri began to juggle the biscuits as she waited for a reaction from the blanket-covered warrior.

She didn't have to wait long, for Mal soon rolled over and

scowled at her. The blond soldier quickly held one of his large fists in front of his eyes, shielding them from the bright morning sun. "Only you would think of something that low, Kiri *Trollslayer.*"

The soldier spoke the woman's name with as much venom as he could muster so early in the morning. He knew that Kiri hated her family name of Trollslayer. She hadn't revealed it to John or Mal at all; they had learned it from another adventurer onboard the *Sarnath.* Kiri had denied the name at first, but then reluctantly admitted that her father was indeed the famous Cormyrian freebooter, Borlander the Trollslayer.

"At least I have a family name, Mal. I know who my father is," Kiri now retorted, trying to show as little annoyance as possible.

Mal laughed a deep braying laugh. "Ha. Good one, Kiri." The woman knit her brows in confusion. Her reply had been far from original. But then, she realized, Malmondes of Suzail was far from witty.

Both Razor John and Kiri Trollslayer shook their heads as Mal lumbered to his feet and stumbled to the galley. They both found the warrior trying on their patience, but he seemed completely devoted to them. In fact, John and Kiri found it difficult to get away from him for more than a few minutes at a time. And though they enjoyed what little time they had alone, for now, at least, the couple was resigned to Mal's presence. There was simply nowhere on the ship to hide from him.

"By the Goddess of Pain, I hate that name," Kiri cursed softly but passionately as soon as Mal was out of earshot. She kicked the soldier's blanket up against the gunwale and sat down on the bowsprit.

John looked at her sympathetically. "Are you ready to tell me why yet?"

Kiri sighed and glanced around. A Sembian sailor swabbed the deck nearby, while two others just free of watch curled up against a nearby hatch to sleep. "With that kind of name—," she began, then stopped abruptly when one of the dozing Sembian sailors looked up at her.

"Mind your own damned business," Kiri snapped. She leaned toward the sailor as if daring him to reply. He snorted a laugh, then turned and at least pretended not to be listening.

Razor John moved closer to Kiri. "Go on," he urged. More than anyone the fletcher had met—including the flower girl in Suzail's marketplace—she ignited his interest. The more he knew about her, the better.

Kiri locked her sparkling eyes on John's face and smiled. "People expect me to be some kind of professional troll killer. I've never even seen a troll in my life. One might come up and bite me, and I wouldn't be able to tell it apart from a tax collector."

The Sembian sailor rolled over again. "Have you heard the joke about the tax collector?" he asked, ignoring Kiri's angry stare. "No? All right, what's the boldest thing in Faerun?" When no one replied, the sailor said, "A tax collector's shirt. It hangs around the neck of a thief every day."

"That isn't the way I heard it," Mal said, standing above the sailor. A look of confusion crossed his thick-boned, fleshy face. "I thought the joke was about Sembian millers."

For an instant Kiri considered telling Mal that the sailor had just finished a joke about King Azoun, for that would certainly provoke the warrior into hitting the nosy sailor. She relented, deciding that a fight would mean another run-in between Mal and the first mate. No one needed that. "He just got it wrong, Mal. Hear any news in the galley?"

The blond soldier shoved a whole biscuit in his mouth, chewed twice, then swallowed. "Yeah, actually I did. One of the cooks heard that the captain of Azoun's carrack, the, uh—" He scratched his head in confusion.

"*Welleran,*" John said between bites of fruit. He glanced at Mal and realized that the thickness of his facial bones accentuated the bewildered look that often clung to the warrior.

"Yeah," Mal said, "the *Welleran*. Anyway, the captain supposedly took some of the gold that was meant to be sacrificed to Umberlee before the fleet left Suzail. They say that he was the cause of that storm."

"They going to give him a trial?" Kiri asked, leaning back

against the railing.

Mal wiped his mouth on the sleeve of his coarse woolen shirt. "Nah. He's dead. Got washed overboard during the storm."

"The gods take their due," Razor John noted. Kiri nodded, and Mal just scratched his chest through his damp clothing.

A voice from the rigging broke the silence that followed the fletcher's comment. "Ship off the starboard!"

The companions squinted until they saw a small speck near the horizon. In minutes, the *Sarnath*'s bow had been realigned toward the dot. John, Kiri, and Mal sat near the bowsprit for a time, watching the other ship grow larger and larger. The first mate, a cross, foul-mouthed woman, came by soon and sent them to their morning tasks.

Mal muttered defamations against Sembians, dalesmen, and anyone else he could think of as he made his way to the ship's hold. John didn't envy the soldier his duty, which was to feed, clean, and exercise the horses stored in the deepest part of the ship. The animals were kept in slings much of the time to prevent injury. That captivity made them high-strung and skittish, though. Many was the day that Mal came back from his duty with a bloody bite mark or large purple bruise from one of his charges.

Kiri cheerfully went to her station in the rigging. The daughter of Borlander the Trollslayer had keen eyes, so she was often assigned lookout duty. Despite the fact that her job was more dangerous than Mal's, she relished the time it gave her away from the crowded deck. She'd even invited John up into the masts on occasion, but the fletcher found the heights too unsettling to stay there long.

Razor John spent his days working on arrows and fletching. Azoun's generals had made it clear to all the ship's captains that weaponsmiths, including fletchers and bowyers, were to be given the time to work on tools for the crusaders. Without the freedom to stroll, selling his wares, John found the work a little tedious. Still, if he closed his eyes and tried to ignore the slight swaying of the deck, he could picture himself back in the marketplace. The noisy bustle of sailors and soldiers, the salty tang in the air, and the cry of seabirds lofting over the ship certainly made it easy to imagine the *Sarnath* as an extension of Suzail's market.

The fletcher was letting his mind wander over his days in the marketplace when he heard Kiri's voice from high on a mast. "Ship close to the starboard."

"Signal her," came another voice from the deck. John listened for a reply, but if there was one, it was lost in the murmur of the people nearby.

Quickly John stacked the shaft he was working on to the pile he'd finished in the hour since the ship had first been sighted. He stood, stretched, and glanced at the ruined carrack that foundered a few hundred yards from the *Sarnath*.

The derelict ship's rigging hung loose, and its sails were shredded and limp. Gulls stood unmolested on the rail, a clear indication that something was wrong onboard the trimasted carrack. For ten minutes, the *Sarnath* tried to raise a response from the ship, which someone eventually identified by its serpentine masthead as the Turmish vessel, *Ouroboros*. No one on the transport replied to the shouts or signals from the Sembian cog.

"The *Ouroboros* is part of the crusaders' fleet," a sailor told John. The fletcher frowned and wondered if he knew anyone who'd shipped out on the now-abandoned vessel.

A sharp rap on the shoulder brought John out of his contemplation. "Ho, fletcher," the first mate snapped. "Come with me. I've got some real work for you." She spun around and pushed her way across the crowded deck.

Razor John sighed, then followed. The first mate had decided shortly after the start of the trip to make his and Kiri's life miserable; the fight Mal had started with her the first night out from Suzail was certainly the reason. Still, the fletcher knew it was futile to argue.

"Help lower that," the first mate told John. She pointed to a small boat that hung at the rail. Without a word, he went to work with three others, lowering the craft and its two passengers into the water.

One of the men in the boat was a Sembian sailor. The other was a young, gold-haired cleric. His robes and the holy symbol around his neck indicated his worship of

Lathander, the God of Dawn and Renewal. "I'll signal you if I need help," the priest shouted as the sailor took up the oars and started to row toward the *Ouroboros*.

The first mate placed a rough hand on the shoulder of the captain, who now stood nearby, and said, "We should be ready to attack if need be." She pointed to the wallowing carrack and added, "This might be some kind of pirate trap."

The captain, a slothful, careless man with a few days growth of beard darkening his cheeks, simply nodded. He scanned the seemingly abandoned ship with watery gray eyes, then turned his attention to flicking the smaller spots of dirt from his soiled white and gold uniform. This was a scene that Razor John had seen repeated in various forms throughout the voyage. It was clear, to the fletcher at least, that the first mate actually ran the *Sarnath*.

"All right, fletcher. Get your bow and get right back here." The first mate cupped her hands over her small, cruel mouth. "All archers to the starboard rail. Bring your weapons."

The cry was relayed around the cog, and John listened to men and women grumble as they gathered up their weapons from the spots where they slept. The fletcher took his longbow from his bed near the bowsprit and returned to the first mate's side.

Much of the ship's attention was focused on the little boat as the sailor and the cleric made their way across to the Turmish ship, then boarded her. Only the gold-haired priest climbed up to the carrack's deck. The few mottled seabirds that had gathered along the rails scattered into the air when he got close. Squawking and screeching angrily, the birds circled over the two ships. A few of the men attempted to shoot the scavengers out of the sky, but the first mate swiftly ordered the men who'd fired at the birds be put to hard labor for the afternoon. John simply frowned at the waste of good arrows for impromptu target practice.

After a few moments the priest appeared at the *Ouroboros*'s rail and waved to the *Sarnath*. "No one left alive," someone muttered behind John. The fletcher was thinking the very same thing.

The Sembian sailor rowed the small boat back to the *Sarnath* faster than he had rowed away from her. The priest seemed to be bowed in prayer the entire way back.

"Well?" the captain asked when the ship's boat got near. "What did you find?"

The priest tried to stand, but the boat rocked so much that he nearly tumbled into the sea. His companion grabbed him by the hem of his scarlet robe and yanked him back to a sitting position. From their erratic, almost frantic actions, it seemed clear that both men had been frightened by what had been discovered on the abandoned carrack.

"Plague," the priest replied at last. He took his holy symbol—a wooden disk painted a rosy pink—and rubbed it between his hands. "They're all dead."

A rumble of concern and fear ran along the rail, as those who heard the priest's report discussed it with their neighbors. The first mate cursed and spat into the water. "Well, Captain," she said at last, "there's not much doubt about what we should do now."

Again the captain nodded. "Not much doubt at all."

The two men in the boat couldn't hear the discussions held at normal levels onboard the ship, but they must have sensed something was wrong. They both grabbed for the oars and attempted to push the small boat closer to the black-hulled Sembian cog.

The first mate turned to Razor John. "Kill both the sailor and the priest, fletcher."

John gasped. "No!" he said, outrage in his voice.

The first mate raised her callused hand as if she were going to strike the fletcher, then she stopped. "Those men have been exposed to plague," she hissed. "Kill them before they get aboard, or we'll end up just like the *Ouroboros*."

The comment stopped John cold. He stared out at the two men in the small boat, then thought of a plague spreading through the ship, killing everyone on the *Sarnath*. I'll die, too, he realized. And Kiri. That thought, above all, disturbed him terribly.

He met the cold, hard gaze of the first mate. "Why me?"

She smiled a malevolent, evil grin. "Because you're a soldier now, Cormyrian, and I'm an officer. You do what I say. Besides, do you want a ship full of crusaders to die because of two men? You won't beat the Tuigan that way."

Closing his eyes, John came to a decision. He hesitated for only an instant, pulling his black, fingerless gloves tight on his hands, then snatched a blue-fletched arrow from his quiver and nocked it in his bow. The sailor in the small boat looked up just as John let the arrow fly.

The Sembian sank down, an arrow through his heart. The cleric wailed once and got to his knees. "I can cast a spell!" he cried. "I won't spread the plague."

"We just can't take that chance," the captain replied coldly. He turned his gray eyes to John and casually flicked two fingers toward the ship's boat.

The fletcher sighted the cleric's heart and pulled back on the bowstring. The fine cord bit into his fingers, then he let another arrow fly. The Lathanderite futilely tried to get out of the way. Instead of striking him in the heart, the blue-fletched arrow hit his shoulder, knocking him from the boat. He struggled for a moment, then sank. The cleric's wooden holy symbol was left floating on the surface, but soon it, too, dropped beneath the water.

"You eight archers to my right," the first mate yelled, "get some pitch and lob flaming arrows onto the *Ouroboros*. I want her fully engulfed before we leave."

After glancing at the still form in the boat, she turned to John. "You do your job well. Now all you have to do is get used to following orders." When he replied with only a blank look, the first mate added, "This is a war, fletcher, not a contest of skill at the spring festival."

Silently John walked back to the bowsprit. Along the way, a few sailors slapped him on the back and congratulated him on his fine marksmanship.

As he leaned back against the gunwale, the fletcher pondered why no one seemed especially chilled by what had just occurred. After a little while, he decided that the first mate was correct: he'd only done his job. Razor John wasn't proud of the task he'd reluctantly completed, but he went back to working arrows convinced that King Azoun would at least understand he'd killed only to save the ship and further the cause of the crusade.

*   *   *   *   *

The port of Telflamm was crowded with ships of every sort. As King Azoun scanned the harbor from the deck of the *Welleran*, he estimated that about two hundred vessels from the crusaders' fleet lay moored nearby—almost half the total armada. Boats of many sizes shuttled between the docks and the larger ships, carrying soldiers and sailors to shore. The piers were filled to capacity with cogs and carracks, which were being unladen by longshoremen. Crates of food and weapons, horses and livestock, even parts for mobile forges and supply wagons, covered Telflamm's docks.

"We're ready to go, Your Highness."

Azoun nodded. "Then let's be on our way," he said to Farl Bloodaxe. "Will we be to Torg's camp before nightfall?"

The general shrugged. "I don't know these waters very well. I would say more likely before sunrise tomorrow morning." The dark-skinned man shielded his eyes with his hands and looked toward the sun, which was now high in the east over the onion-shaped domes of Telflamm's temples and civic buildings. "Yes, definitely by dawn tomorrow."

"King Torg awaits," Azoun noted cheerfully, motioning for Farl to give the orders to proceed. The *Welleran* was quickly under way north along the coast of the Easting Reach, two other Cormyrian carracks following close behind.

Azoun glanced back at Telflamm once, then began a leisurely stroll around the ship. For the first time since the carrack had left Suzail—a little over a month before—the *Welleran* was quiet. Most of the passengers had been dropped in port so that extra supplies could be loaded aboard the Cormyrian tri-masters. This food and other essentials were destined for King Torg and his dwarven troops, and whatever soldiers Zhentil Keep had seen fit to send. Only a skeleton crew remained aboard the flagship, commanded by Farl Bloodaxe, who had won the men's support during the storm.

With Lord Harcourt and General Elventree secure in Telflamm, keeping the troops in line, Azoun had time to discuss the use of magic in the upcoming conflict with Vangerdahast. The king's trusted advisor was along on the crusade to supervise the use of the War Wizards against the Tuigan. Azoun had no doubts that his old tutor would wreak havoc upon Yamun Khahan's army given the chance.

"From everything I've heard," Vangerdahast had said during one meeting, "the Tuigan don't like magic very much at all. In fact, their permanent capital—if you can call a tent city a capital—is set up in a magic-dead area. Spells won't work there." The mage had stroked his beard then and looked wistfully at the flickering lantern. "A few well-placed lightning bolts ought to shake them up quite a bit."

Azoun leaned on the base of a mast. He laughed to himself, thinking of the gleam that shone in Vangerdahast's eyes whenever he spoke of using spells against the horsewarriors. Azoun was sure that his old friend was getting at least a little caught up in the adventure of the crusade.

In fact, from what the king had seen during the sail from Suzail, the entire army seemed to be growing more excited, more enthusiastic about the campaign. The *Welleran* had come close to many other transport ships during the trip across the Inner Sea. Every time the flagship got near enough that another vessel could see she flew King Azoun's standard, she was welcomed with cheers of greeting.

That joyous sound kept Azoun's spirits buoyed through the quiet trip along the coast that day, and the king's growing confidence in his army began to show in his demeanor. He spent little time during the night worrying about the battles to come. Instead, he thought about his wife and wondered how she was faring back in Suzail. Before he went to sleep, he resolved to have Vangerdahast contact Filfaeril as soon as possible, once the supplies were delivered.

Vangerdahast even noticed that Azoun seemed relaxed and well rested on the morning they reached their rendezvous point on the northern shore of the Easting Reach, just south of the port town of Uthmerg.

"Why so animated this day, Your Highness?" the royal wizard asked as he watched the king briskly pace back and forth at the rail.

"I am happy because our goal is almost in sight," Azoun told the mage. He stopped pacing, then pointed east to the tall-grassed, rolling hills that stretched away from the shore. "And King Torg is sure to be ready to join our army by now."

The wizard squinted toward the shore. The choppy, shallow water prevented the *Welleran* and the two ships accompanying her from getting closer than a few hundred yards from the beach's dark sand. "Then I suggest we get a move on. Do you see any envoys yet?"

Now the king scanned the dark shoreline, too, but saw nothing save a few white birds running in the surf. "No. You contacted them already, didn't you, Vangy?"

"Hours ago," the wizard sighed. He rubbed his chin, then nodded. "If you have no objections, Azoun, I'll have us in the dwarves' camp in a few moments."

With that, the royal magician fell silent and noiselessly mouthed an incantation. His eyes rolled back in his head, revealing milky white orbs. "That will do nicely," Azoun heard the mage mumble. His voice sounded hollow, as if it were coming from a great distance. Before long, Vangerdahast closed his eyes, then shook his head briskly.

"I've located the camp, and I think I've spotted a fine location for us to teleport to. We'd best move right away, however." The wizard grabbed Azoun's wrists. "Don't want some fool dwarf to park a horse or a cart there."

"Farl," the king called. When the general appeared from a hatch nearby, Azoun said, "The escort hasn't shown up, so we're going ahead to the camp. We'll send word as soon as the dwarves are ready to receive their supplies."

The ebony-skinned man nodded, then asked, "Is there anything else I should do while you're gone?"

"Just keep the ship afloat," Vangerdahast said quickly. "Come, Your Highness, we really can't dawdle."

Azoun swallowed and clenched his teeth. "Let's get it over with, Vangy." The king had complete faith in his friend. Still, the gruesome stories he'd heard about mages mistakenly teleporting into stones or trees, or ending up hundreds of yards above the ground after the spell, made Azoun nervous.

Again Vangerdahast fell into a rapid, rumbling chant. A brilliant yellow light flashed into existence around the king and the wizard. Azoun looked down, but before he could note the fact that the deck was suddenly visible through his ghostlike feet, the world disappeared. The only sound of the king's passing was the hollow thud of air rushing to fill the space where he'd stood only a moment before.

White. Blinding, empty white.

That was all Azoun saw for what seemed like minutes. Then the world and all its colors returned. The king rubbed his eyes and looked around. Low, grass-covered hills surrounded him on every side.

"I'm sure if I do that one hundred times, I'll never get used to it," Azoun said softly. He staggered forward a step, then stopped to regain his balance.

Vangerdahast chuckled. "Rather like the way I feel about sea travel, I'd imagine."

Unlike the king, he was not troubled by magical travel. In fact, the royal magician seemed energized by the experience, as if the spell had somehow granted him a little extra strength. "The dwarves' camp is—" The wizard paused, then pointed east. "In that direction, I believe."

Azoun was still staggering slightly when he topped the rise. Though he felt weakened by the teleportation, he still climbed the slope with greater speed than Vangerdahast could manage. Being the first one up the hill, Azoun saw the crossbows before his friend.

"Stand where you are," a red-bearded dwarf growled, leveling his weapon menacingly at the king. He spoke in Common, a universal trade language in Faerun, but his words were tinged with a heavy accent.

"Aye," added his companion, who was shorter than the first and much, much fatter. "You'll not be sneaking around our camp, human." His accent was even more pronounced than the other dwarf's.

"Just a minute," the Cormyrian king said evenly, holding his hands away from his sword. "We're here to see Torg."

Vangerdahast trudged up next to the king. The dwarves shifted their crossbows to target the wizard. "Don't be foolish," the mage snapped, dismissing the guards with a wave of his hand. "This is King Azoun of—"

"Pryderi mac Dylan, you absolute dunderhead, put that thrice-damned crossbow down!"

Both dwarven sentries, Azoun, and Vangerdahast looked up sharply at the loud, bellowing command. A scowling dwarf, waving his hands wildly around his head, stormed up the hill behind the crossbowmen. Neither the Cormyrian king nor his advisor were fluent enough in Dwarvish to understand exactly what was being said, but they got the general idea from the other dwarves' reactions.

The red-bearded dwarf lowered his weapon and dropped to one knee. After he'd pulled his fellow sentry to the ground, he said, "Ironlord, I didn't—"

The scowling dwarf reached the top of the hill. He stood, hands on hips, for a moment, then cuffed the red-haired sentry on the back of the head. "I warned you there'd be royalty about, you oaf," he grumbled in Dwarvish. "Can't you recognize a king when you see one?"

Azoun and Vangerdahast exchanged brief, concerned glances. The dwarf the others called "Ironlord" wore a steel breastplate covered by a black cloth surcoat. A brilliant red phoenix clutching a warhammer spread over the surcoat's front. The dwarf's thick black beard only partially obscured that symbol, for the hair was bound with thin golden chain into two neat forks. The forked beard made the ironlord look a little ominous, and his hard, closely set eyes only heightened the effect.

This was obviously Torg, ironlord of Earthfast.

"Your Lordship," Azoun began in rough, broken Dwarvish. "I am King Azoun of Cormyr, and this is Vangerdahast, royal mage of my court, commander of the army's War Wizards."

The dwarf smiled broadly and studied the king with his dark, steely eyes. "Welcome, Your Highness. You speak passable Dwarvish for a human," Torg said in perfect Common. "My apologies for this . . . scene." He glowered at the kneeling sentries.

Azoun tried to return the ironlord's smile. "It's certainly understandable," he offered, pointing back down the hill. "We appeared out of nowhere. They were only doing their—"

Torg cocked his head to one side. "Appeared, you say? Out of nowhere? What happened to the blasted escort I sent to meet you at the shore?" He raised one hand up to his black beard and pulled a gold chain tight around one fork.

"They didn't show up," Vangerdahast replied. "We waited quite a while, but no one came."

The dwarf's face darkened in anger again. He turned abruptly to the kneeling sentries and snapped, "Gather up a patrol and find the escort I sent out." After a pause, he added, "Bring them to me when you find them." The guards rushed to the task.

Vangerdahast decided then that he was going to have to brush up on the spell that allowed him to comprehend strange languages. Torg's habit of slipping in and out of Dwarvish made the wizard uneasy. Since it was his job to keep Azoun safe while away from the ship, Vangerdahast knew he'd feel more secure if he could understand what everyone said at all times.

Torg exhaled sharply, as if he were expelling his anger. The ironlord then faced his guests. "Please allow me to escort you through the camp personally." He spun on the heels of his thick-soled boots and marched down the hill.

Azoun and Vangerdahast quickly fell into step behind the dwarf. Torg's short legs didn't hinder his speed, the humans soon learned. The dwarven king set a good pace as he stomped toward the camp. Walking behind Torg, Azoun noted that, apart from the gleaming metal of his armor and sword, the dwarf was decked out entirely in red and black. Blood and thunder, he concluded silently.

For his part, Vangerdahast was studying the layout of the dwarven camp. The hill the wizard marched down led to a large, grass-covered plain. Uniform, brown tents spread in straight lines across the open area. The precision of the lines astounded the wizard, who had assumed the camp would be like most human camps: relatively chaotic sprawls held together only by proximity.

Before the two kings and the wizard reached the first tent, they saw the army. Hundreds upon hundreds of short, stocky dwarven soldiers marched in precise ranks. The bright sunlight glinted off their polished armor and the blades of their weapons. Azoun noted with some surprise that the dwarves were carrying polearms.

"You make them drill in full armor?" Azoun asked Torg as they got near a formation. He knew from experience that the hot, early summer sun would be devastating on the armor-clad soldiers.

The ironlord stopped and looked at Azoun, puzzlement showing on his face. "How do you expect them to fight in armor if they don't train in armor?"

"But the sun. The heat will—"

Torg snorted. "It may well be sunny on the day of the first battle. The men will be glad we did this then." The dwarf shaded his eyes and looked up into the sky. "I hate the sun myself. Too damned bright." He turned to Vangerdahast. "Of course, we don't get this much sunlight underground. Another good reason to drill the troops in it."

Surveying the army for a moment, the wizard scratched his head and said, "This is the first dwarven army I've seen with polearms." He motioned to the marching troops. "Why are you training with pikes?"

A wicked gleam flickered in Torg's dark eyes, which neither Azoun nor Vangerdahast missed. "Do you remember the human general I mentioned in my letters?" Without waiting for a reply, Torg said to Azoun, "The human was very familiar with Your Highness's treatise on the use of polearms in warfare. Recommended it so highly, in fact, I read the book myself. Quite enlightening."

Azoun bowed slightly, a little embarrassed by the unexpected praise. "You intend to use the pikes against the Tuigan?"

"Of course."

"But the Tuigan are archers," Vangerdahast exclaimed. "Pikes won't do you any good if they stay two hundred yards away and fire arrows at you." He gestured at the drilling troops. "You'll be slaughtered."

Torg laughed and dismissed the wizard's comments with a wave of his hand. "Yamun Khahan has never faced dwarven troops before, and I'm sure his warriors' arrows haven't been tested against plate armor forged in Earthfast." The ironlord put his short, round fingers to his mouth and whistled. "And we have ranged weapons of our own."

The dwarven captains who were scattered throughout the field signaled to soldiers carrying large drums. The drummers beat a fast, chaotic riff, and the army rushed into a long line, three dwarves deep. As the soldiers in the front rank knelt and planted their pikes in a defensive wall, the back two ranks quickly drew and cocked heavy crossbows. The dwarves made it look easy, but the strength required to ready a crossbow would have made it practically impossible for human armies to accomplish that maneuver in so short a time.

Torg beamed with pride. He raised a hand, signaling the captains again, and a new cadence was sounded. The dwarven troops disarmed their crossbows, slung the heavy weapons on their belts, and regained their pikes. The drumbeat changed yet again, and the troops broke into four large squares, twenty dwarves wide by twenty dwarves deep. The edges of each square bristled with pikes.

Azoun, almost caught up in the display of amazing military training, saw that Torg was looking at him, obviously waiting for a compliment. "Impressive," the Cormyrian king said at last. "Perhaps you can give our troops a few pointers."

The ironlord laughed, a deep bellowing sound that seemed to echo in his chest before breaking into the world. "Indeed," he said, giving Azoun a solid slap on the back. Vangerdahast concluded then and there that he didn't like the ruler of Earthfast very much at all.

Torg ordered the troops to resume the regular drills. With a rumble of drums and the clatter of armor, the squares broke into marching columns. Satisfied with the display, the ironlord led his guests toward a pavilion at the heart of the dwarven camp. As they walked through the tent city, both Azoun and Vangerdahast were amazed at the absolute order of the place. Not only were the tents arrayed in straight lines, but gear was stored in neat piles and even the inevitable garbage dump was kept contained in a tidy, square enclosure.

The dwarven camp was like none Azoun had ever seen or even heard about. He suddenly wished Thom Reaverson had come along. The bard would have found the place fascinating.

"I have yet to hear from the troops your allies in Zhentil Keep are sending," Torg said as he entered the pavilion. The king winced slightly at being called an "ally" of the Keep, but, in this instance the term was accurate.

"They should have been here by now," Vangerdahast noted as he sat at a low, long table. "In fact, they should have reached here more than a day or two ago . . . if Zhentil Keep is honoring the agreement."

Vangerdahast's concern was not lost on Azoun. The king ran a hand through his gray-shot beard and sighed. If Zhentil Keep broke the treaty, it might mean they intended to invade the Dales. In truth, the king realized, they could be attacking even as he sat there, pondering the point. "I should contact the queen," he told the wizard. "She might have heard something recently."

"You'll have time for that in a bit," Torg said, scowling at the reference to the wizard's magic. "I'll send some scouts to the north and west. That'll do for now." He took three brightly polished silver mugs from a metal case and set them on the table. He turned his dark eyes to the pavilion's door and yelled something in Dwarvish.

A smartly liveried squire rushed into the tent, carrying a large wooden keg. The dwarf's beard was short and, unlike Torg, his face was almost free of deep-set wrinkles. Azoun assumed the servant was very young, but he always found it extremely difficult to estimate a dwarf's age.

"Drink," Torg said, opening a silver spout in the keg and

filling the mugs. He handed one to Azoun and the other to Vangerdahast, then hefted the third and raised it in a toast. "To the complete destruction of the Tuigan. May the corpses of the horsewarriors reach to the sky!"

"Indeed," Vangerdahast said weakly, rather appalled at the crass toast. Azoun repeated Torg's toast more enthusiastically. The dwarf's bellicose oath brought back memories of Azoun's time with the King's Men, promising over mugs of ale to vanquish all the evil in Faerun.

The dwarven brew was very bitter. Vangerdahast drank little, but Azoun and Torg shared a few mugs as they discussed the arrangement of troops. Messengers came and went, and scouts were sent to search for the Zhentish force. The afternoon passed, and still there was no sign of the Zhentish troops.

Torg left Azoun and Vangerdahast alone in the pavilion shortly after sunset, promising to return as soon as he'd located the missing patrol. Using a spell, Vangerdahast contacted Filfaeril, but she had heard little from the Zhentish of late.

"The only news is that Lythrana Dargor, that beautiful envoy who visited with us right before you left, might be assigned to Cormyr as a permanent ambassador," said the conjured, misty image of the queen. "She has nothing but praise for you, Your Highness. Don't you think she was quite attractive, Vangy?" she asked, though the question was more of a barb aimed at her husband.

"Ah, you've found me out, my love," sighed Azoun mockingly. "Who could have guessed that I'd throw you over for a Zhentish envoy."

With a slight grunt, Vangerdahast pushed himself to his feet. "This spell takes too much energy from me for you two to be spending it this way," he grumbled. "My apologies, Your Highnesses, but—unless there's some other *matters of state* to discuss—we must end this."

The laughter faded from Filfaeril's ice-blue eyes. "Things here are quiet. Not a grumble from the trappers." After a pause, she added, "Take care, my husband, and do not worry about our kingdom."

"We'll speak again soon," the king replied. The misty image of the queen dissipated, and the pavilion grew quiet.

For more than an hour, the Cormyrian king sat at the long table, toying with an empty mug. Upon closer study, he noticed that the fine silver drinking cups were engraved with grisly scenes of war. Dwarves battled pig-snouted orcs and shorter creatures Azoun recognized as goblins. On another mug, dwarven warriors carried skulls into a vast cavern and stacked them in neat pyramids.

Without looking at his advisor, the king asked, "Is there some way for you to find the Zhentish troops with your magic?"

The wizard sat at the other end of the table, facing the king. His head lolled to one side in a fitful doze. He snorted awake at the king's question. "Eh?" he mumbled. "The troops from the Keep have arrived?"

Azoun smiled and, after a final glance at the strange engravings, set his mug down. "It's getting rather late," he said. "We should either help look for the missing dwarves or try to contact the Zhentish army."

Rubbing his eyes, Vangerdahast said, "You know that dwarves hate magic almost as much as they hate water. Allowing you to contact the queen was risky enough, thank you. Perhaps we should just return to the *Welleran*." The wizard stretched and motioned toward the pavilion's open door. "At least I could get a good night's—"

A strangled gasp escaped Vangerdahast's lips. The three lanterns that hung from the pavilion's supports cast enough light on his face to reveal that it had gone stark white. His mouth hung open a little in obvious astonishment, and his eyes were wide with surprise.

Azoun turned to see what had shocked the royal magician so. His hand slipped automatically to his sword, but when the king saw the armor-clad figure in the doorway, he felt his arm fall limp at his side. Unlike Vangerdahast, Azoun managed to whisper a single name: "Alusair."

A slight, devilish smile crept across the face of the woman in the doorway. She nodded slightly and said, "Hello, Father. It's been quite a long time."

- 8 -

The Mithril Princess

Princess Alusair of House Obarskyr smiled and held out her hands to her father. Still numb from the surprise meeting, King Azoun hurried to his daughter and embraced her tightly. After a moment, he pulled back and studied her face.

In the four years since she'd left Suzail, Alusair had changed quite a bit. Now twenty-five, the princess was possessed of a mature beauty. A few wrinkles gathered at the corners of her oak-brown eyes, and her golden hair haloed her face like morning sunlight. Smiling, the princess stepped back from Azoun and said, "Well, where's the anger I expected?"

The king continued to stare. Somewhere in the back of his mind, he wondered if she was an illusion or if this was merely a dream. "I—I haven't had time to be angry, Allie." He choked back a tear and dropped his eyes. "Your mother and I . . . we hoped you weren't . . ."

"Dead?" The princess laughed and moved to the table. "Hardly. I've been in some tight spots in the last four years, but never that close to the realm of Lord Cyric. The God of Death will have to wait awhile for me."

By now, sufficient time had passed for Vangerdahast to recover from the shock of seeing Alusair, too. "You ungrateful little snipe! I ought to blast you into pieces for the worry you've caused your family!" The wizard curled his hands into tight fists and practically shook with rage.

Alusair moved farther into the tent and sighed. "I've

missed you, too, Vangy." The wizard scowled and looked away. A shadow of anger crossed the princess's features, but she quickly brought up another subject.

"How is Mother? And Tanalasta?" Alusair filled a mug with strong dwarven ale and set it down.

Azoun returned to his place at the long, low table. "Your mother and sister are both fine. Worried about you, of course." He rubbed his eyes and gestured to the camp outside. "What are you doing here?"

With a slight groan, Alusair opened the clasps on her brassards, the armor on her arms. "I've been helping King Torg defend his land against some ambitious orcs and goblins from the north." She slipped the heavy plate off her arms and let it fall to the pavilion's grass floor.

Shaking his head in disbelief, Azoun looked to Vangerdahast for direction. The wizard had turned to face the conversation again, but his features were clouded with anger. "So how did you elude my wizards for all this time?" the king asked at last.

Alusair undid the straps of the cuirass that protected her chest. "It really wasn't that difficult," she said, glancing at Vangerdahast. "No offense to Vangy, but this was all I needed."

The princess dropped the cuirass beside the brassards, then held up her left hand. A bright gold band hugged her ring finger. "I bought it from a mage in Ravens Bluff. A spell on the ring makes it impossible for someone to detect my whereabouts through magical means."

"I knew it had to be something foolish like that," Vangerdahast grumbled.

The king looked closely at Alusair's hands as she adjusted the padded doublet she wore under her armor. They were grimy with sweat and hardened from years of gripping a sword, but that was not what Azoun noticed. "Where is your signet ring?" the king demanded.

Her smile fled completely, and Alusair sat down at the low dwarven table. She moved stiffly, not surprising since she'd not removed the brichette from her hips or the cuisses from her legs. "I threw it away, dropped it into the sea."

"Why?" Azoun snapped as he stood. "That ring could have saved your life. It identified you as a princess of House Obarskyr."

"Which is exactly why I had to get rid of it. I didn't want a bounty hunter to capture me and try to ransom me back to Cormyr." The princess took a long, slow swallow of ale.

"So you tossed your heritage into the sea?" In the quiet minute that followed the rebuke, Azoun slumped into his chair. "Make me understand, Allie. Why?"

"I told you, I didn't want someone to blackmail the family. I don't think you realize how much danger you put me in by offering a reward for my return."

Azoun shook his head and waved his hand angrily. "No, no. Why did you run away in the first place?"

After another sip of the ale, Alusair leaned forward, her head resting on her hand. "The note I left should have explained everything, Father. I just couldn't stand it at court any longer. You and Mother were always tied up with some petty political problem. Tanalasta spent more time worrying about fashion than the state of the country." She took a deep breath and rubbed her eyes with the tips of her fingers. "I don't want to go over all of this again."

"Then why are you here?" Vangerdahast interjected from the other side of the tent. His face was hidden in the shadows, but Alusair could imagine the look of puzzlement it held.

Her eyes still closed, the princess sighed. "I thought it might be time to forget the past." She turned to her father, her mask of cocky self-assurance cracking for the first time. "I thought you would finally accept me for what I am, not what you want me to be."

Vangerdahast walked to Azoun's side. "I'll explore the camp for a while," he said softly in the king's ear.

Once Vangerdahast had gone, Azoun waited for Alusair to say something. After a few moments of continued silence, he gave up. "You threw away your heritage, Allie." The king paused, trying to push the anger from his voice. The more he thought about his daughter, however, the angrier he became. "And for what did you give it up?" the king snapped after a moment. "To become a sell-sword? A freebooter? You could have ruled Cormyr one day!"

' Alusair laughed bitterly. "Tanalasta is older, remember? She'll be queen, alongside whomever you and Mother decide will make a suitable king. Even if I could rule," she added, turning away from the king, "I wouldn't want to."

"You've no respect for responsibility," Azoun replied. "That's your biggest problem. You're a princess. But do you use the gifts with which the Goddess of Luck has blessed you? Of course not." He pointed an accusing finger at Alusair. "You waste your life roaming the countryside."

The princess stood, her back still to Azoun. "This was a mistake," she said, a measure of hardness returning to her voice. "You're just not ready."

Hearing the pain in his child's voice did more to wipe away Azoun's fury than anything he could have done himself. "I can't help but be angry, Allie," he said. "I just don't see why you couldn't live at court. Was life so terrible that you had to run?"

When the princess turned around again, bright tears sparkled in her eyes. The light from the lanterns made each drop look like a diamond as it rolled down Alusair's cheek. "I am not a politician, Father. I don't belong in the court." She wiped her eyes with her doublet's sleeve. "You used to tell me stories about the King's Men, how you used to sneak out and go on adventures. What I did isn't all that different."

"Of course it's different," Azoun said almost automatically. "I was never gone for long, and I always returned."

Alusair started to say something, then paused and shook her head.

"What is it, Allie?" the king asked, holding his hand out to his daughter. "You can be honest."

Looking into her father's eyes, Alusair wondered if she really should speak her mind or let the subject drop. No, she decided, things will never be resolved if I avoid this conflict. "You must regret it," she said softly.

A look of confusion crossed the king's face. "Regret what?"

Alusair swallowed the last of her tears and sat down

across from Azoun. "Coming back. You must regret ever coming back from your adventures with Dimswart and Winefiddle and the others."

"I had responsibilities, Allie. I couldn't—"

"No, Father. Not couldn't, *didn't*." She squeezed the king's hand. "Even when I was a little girl, I heard it in your voice when you told me about the King's Men."

"Perhaps I regret it a little," the king conceded. He gently pulled his hand away from Alusair and steepled his fingers before his face. "But I had a responsibility to Cormyr—as you do—and I fulfilled it. Anyway," he added, smiling a little, "I never could have had a family or done what good I've managed for Cormyr gallivanting around the countryside as Balin the Cavalier."

"And you wouldn't have been forced to do so many petty wrongs either," the princess noted firmly. "You can't worry about each individual in Cormyr, only the state as a whole. So when you tax, you can't consider the minority it really hurts. You take away freedom in deference to law. That's wrong."

Azoun frowned as he considered his daughter's words. "What's the alternative? I do good for the most people by creating and upholding the country's laws."

The princess reached behind her, picked up the cuirass she had dropped onto the ground, and placed it on the table between her and her father. "With a good suit of armor," Alusair began, running her finger along the fantastically carved metal, "and a sharp sword, I can right as many wrongs as I can find between sunup and sundown."

"That's all fine, Allie, but you can't make any significant change as an adventurer. I tried, remember? That's what the King's Men was all about."

Alusair stared at the light reflecting on the armor before her. "I guess I just don't want the responsibility for anyone else. I only kill myself if I try to rescue someone from an ogre or if I decide to take a side in a war." She traced a dent in the armor, recently but not completely mended. "And if I die, I know I fought for a good cause."

Reflexively running a hand through his gray-shot beard,

Azoun stood up and paced around the pavilion. The wind was picking up outside, and occasional strong breezes made the sides of the tent snap and bow. After a few circuits around the long table, the king faced his daughter. "What have you been fighting for, Allie? What have you done with the last four years?"

The princess looked up from her armor. "I've been to Waterdeep, Ravens Bluff, Damara, even the Moonshae Isles. I lived for a while on the money I took with me when I left the castle. After that, I worked as a caravan guard, helped a fishing village make a bargain with a dragon turtle, even hunted for the Ring of Winter for a season or two."

The mention of the Ring of Winter, a powerful artifact that had been missing for many, many years, made Azoun start. Most of the beings who sought it were power-mad and very often evil. "These are jobs any mercenary would take, Allie. How can you say you've been fighting for good causes?"

"I always knew who I was working for, Father. I always knew what their goals were."

Azoun fell silent again and paced for a few more minutes. After that, he asked the princess more questions, but each yielded a short, dry answer. The king learned where his daughter had been, what she had done there, but very little about her life. "And did you always travel alone?" Azoun asked after she told him of the time she'd been captured by a party of drow north of Waterdeep. "I'd heard that you'd run away with a cleric from Tilverton."

The comment had an immediate effect on Alusair. She paled noticeably, even in the shadowy tent, and her voice trembled slightly when she replied. "Yes, Father. I . . . traveled with a cleric from Tilverton, Gharri of Gond. He died as we tried to escape some bounty hunters. They were after the reward you'd put on my return."

Azoun moved to his daughter's side. "I don't know what to say . . . other than I'm sorry for your loss."

"For a long time I blamed his death on you, Father," the princess said, her face betraying the strain the topic was putting on her. "I only recently decided that you couldn't have known what the bounty hunters would do."

The silence that followed the revelation of Gharri's death was longer and more deadening than the last. Alusair sat, her head bowed slightly, remembering her lost love. Azoun stood over his daughter, his hand on her shoulder. The king considered breaking the silence again, but found there was nothing he could say that wouldn't sound maudlin or foolish.

The high, shrill sound of a trumpet crying out over the dwarven camp broke the sad calm in the pavilion. The king heard low, rumbling voices, speaking in Dwarvish. The hushed voices were echoed by faint sounds of metal clanging. With a slight shock, Azoun realized that this was the first noise he'd heard from the dwarven camp all evening. After the drilling had ended at sundown, the camp had become deathly silent, highly unusual for a large gathering of soldiers.

Alusair grabbed her cuirass and stood up. The trumpet called out again, a harsh, trilling note. "Orcs," the princess hissed. "The sentries have spotted orcs."

As Alusair retrieved the brassards that would cover her arms, Azoun moved to the tent's door. Dwarven troops mustered quietly in the darkness outside. The stocky soldiers marched quickly out of their tents, toward the edges of the camp. Their faces were set in grim determination.

"We've got to go, Father," Alusair said. The king turned to see his daughter, her armor slung over her shoulder, waiting to leave. "This isn't a particularly safe spot. I'll escort you across the compound to Torg's tent, then you and Vangy should head back to the ship."

The king frowned. "I'll see Torg, but I'm not all that sure I'm leaving just yet."

With the skittering sound of metal sliding across metal, the princess drew her sword. "You don't have a weapon, do you?"

Smiling, Azoun reached to his high leather boot and withdrew a slender silver dagger. The lanterns cast small glints of light off the stiletto's razor edge. "I've had too many attempts on my life to ever travel unarmed."

The king and the princess crossed the central square of the dwarven camp. Soldiers continued to march through the square, heading toward their assigned mustering stations. The troops were fully armored and carried crossbows and swords. Apart from an occasional trumpet blast or shouted order, the camp remained strangely silent.

"Silence is a virtue for Earthfast's soldiers," Alusair explained as they walked toward Torg's compound. "They're used to fighting underground. Any noise made in the caves and tunnels would echo, and that could hide an enemy's location."

Azoun watched a mail-clad dwarf pull a pointed helmet over his head, then trudge off. "Don't you find it disconcerting?" he asked. "I don't think human troops are ever this quiet."

"I'd know who to place a wager on in a battle, wouldn't you?" Alusair asked in response. She stopped alongside a firepit, its flames low, the fire mostly extinguished. The princess kicked dirt into the stone-encircled pit to douse the feeble blaze. Before her father could ask why, she said, "They're used to fighting in the dark, remember? Any light like this—" She gestured at the smoldering ash with her toe. "It could take away their advantage in a night battle."

The pair soon reached the ironlord's tent, directly across the open square from the pavilion Azoun had occupied. Breathless messengers hurried in and out of the large, black tent. The runners wore leather armor studded with metal. Even with that heavy burden, they dashed as quickly as their short legs could carry them, relaying orders for the dwarven commanders. Two guards holding pikes stood at strict attention in front of the royal tent.

"Tell the ironlord I've brought King Azoun of Cormyr to the safety of his presence," the princess commanded one of the guards in perfect Dwarvish. The sentry nodded his helmeted head once and spun sharply to the door. When he opened the heavy cloth covering the entryway, Azoun heard Torg growling what must have been orders. The ironlord's loud voice contrasted sharply with the quiet of the camp. As soon as the door fell closed again, the voice was muffled to near silence.

"The tent is made of thick felt, laced with metal," Alusair whispered in response to the king's puzzled look. "They designed it especially for Torg to use in this campaign."

The guard exited the tent and held the door open, a sign for the princess and the king to enter. As he went in, Azoun was amazed at the contrast between the dark, silent camp and Torg's bright, noisy headquarters. The dwarven monarch sat on a stone dais across from the door. He already wore much of his armor; a squire was fastening the last straps of the cuisses on the ironlord's legs. To Torg's left, a tall golden birdcage stood. Three small, brilliantly colored birds fluttered about inside the cage, chirping happily.

"We've got trouble, Princess," Torg bellowed in Common as soon as he saw Alusair. "Pryderi mac Dylan found the escort we sent out earlier. Dead, of course." The dwarven king pounded his fist on the edge of his throne. "Orcs, they say. Signs of them all around the camp."

"The Bloody Skull?" the princess asked.

Torg pushed the squire away and finished the straps himself. "No. From what Pryderi found, this is a new band."

Azoun stepped forward. "How many?"

"Hard to tell, Your Highness. Has your daughter told you about our orc problems?"

"Daughter?" the king gasped, looking from Torg to Alusair, then back again. "You know?"

"Who do you think told me about your treatise on polearms?" The dwarven king grinned and turned to the princess. "A happy family again, eh?"

"I told him who I was only a few days past, when it was too late for him to contact you, Father." Frowning slightly, Alusair decided to change the subject right away. "Where's the magician who was with my father when he arrived?"

Turning to the birdcage, Torg leaned forward, placing his face against the bars. The birds danced around the cage, twittering loudly. "Do you keep birds in your palace, Azoun? They are fantastic creatures. Almost the greatest thing the gods set on Toril, don't you think?" He cast a glance at Azoun, then gazed into the cage again. "We use them in the mines. If the air goes bad, the birds die first."

Alusair sighed. "The wizard, Ironlord. Where is he?"

"I caught him wandering about the camp, so I sent him with one of the patrols. Perhaps he can determine how many orcs are lurking out there." The dwarven king threw a cloth cover over the birdcage, then reached for his surcoat. "I didn't want a spellcaster in camp, if I could help it anyway. No insult intended, Azoun, but I just don't trust magic."

Azoun heard a trace of fear in Torg's voice, but he wasn't surprised. Dwarven communities tended to foster natural strength and endurance in their people. Little sorcery was permitted. Dwarves often created weapons and armor that, because of their exquisite making, had magical powers, and dwarven clerics—who called upon their gods for the ability to cast spells—were common, too. However, mages were people to be feared, for their arts were not rooted in the power of the earth, religious beliefs, or simple craftsmanship.

"No insult taken," Azoun said. "Vangerdahast can defend himself if the need arises, and he certainly knew of the dwarven aversion to magic before he came here."

The stoic guard who had announced Azoun's presence earlier entered the tent once again. "Pryderi mac Dylan's patrol has returned," he said in Dwarvish, his helmet muting his voice to a low rumble.

Torg pulled his surcoat on over his armor. After adjusting the black tunic so the blood-red phoenix lay squarely positioned on his chest, he said, "Show Pryderi in." As the guard moved to usher in the new guests, Torg told Azoun and Alusair to take a seat on the stone benches that were on either side of the tent.

The red-bearded dwarf who had threatened Azoun atop the hill strode into the tent. His beard was tangled slightly, and his surcoat was torn and mud-splattered. "Ironlord," he said as he entered, "I have much to report." He dropped stiffly to one knee and bowed his head. "The mage cast a spell and discovered a little about the orcs."

Azoun could understand only fragments of what was being said, but Alusair spoke and understood Dwarvish well.

At the mention of the mage, she said, "Ironlord, Vangerdahast should be allowed into your presence."

"Of course," Torg said casually. "Squire, tell the guards to let him in."

Vangerdahast entered a moment later. The bottom of his long robe was covered with mud, and brambles still clung to his sleeves. Like Pryderi's, the mage's beard was tangled and dirty. He was picking sharp yellow thorns out of his clothes, muttering curses in Common, when he stepped through the door. He bowed perfunctorily to Torg, then joined Azoun and Alusair.

The disheveled Pryderi cleared his throat and continued his report. "The human wizard joined our scouting party after we'd found the escort. We spotted a pair of orcs creeping about—"

Torg held up a hand, and the soldier stopped speaking in mid-sentence. "Can you translate this for your father and the mage, Princess? They should know what's being said, and Pryderi is no master of Common." Alusair nodded and leaned toward Azoun, ready to translate the soldier's report.

"Don't worry about me," Vangerdahast muttered when Azoun asked him to move closer. "I cast a spell a little while back that lets me understand Dwarvish." He removed a large, squirming caterpillar from the hem of his robe and tossed it into the corner.

Pryderi, still resting on one knee before Torg's throne, waited for the ironlord's signal before he continued. "We spotted the orcs creeping about north of the camp. They were obviously spies for a larger group, as they were wearing a uniform of sorts."

Torg leaned forward. "Uniform?"

"Yes, Ironlord," Pryderi said emphatically. "The orcs both wore black leather armor and had armbands that depicted skulls surrounded by a black sun."

"Cyric worshipers," Vangerdahast said to Torg. "That skull symbol belongs to the God of Death."

The dwarven king nodded impatiently. "Yes, mage. I know the symbol well. Many of the orcs in this area worship Lord

Cyric, almost as many as worship the old orc gods."

Folding his arms over his chest, Vangerdahast slumped in his seat. Azoun wondered what had put his advisor in such a foul mood. Obviously, he thought, it's got something to do with the outcome of this patrol.

Pryderi shot an annoyed look at Vangerdahast, then continued. "We had to hide in some thickets near the stream to avoid them." The dwarf motioned to his muddied armor. "It was uncomfortable, but the orcs did not spot us. I was ready to follow them back to their camp when the mage cast a spell that froze the creatures in place."

Torg glanced uncomfortably at the wizard, then motioned for Pryderi to finish.

"We killed one of them right away with a crossbow," the soldier reported proudly. "The other we left to the mage." He made the latter sound far worse than death by a crossbow bolt through the skull.

"Well, mage?" Torg asked in Common, resting his chin on a fist. "What did you learn?"

Vangerdahast stood and took a step toward the dwarven king. "I hypnotized the other orc, Ironlord." Torg responded to this statement by furrowing his thick brows together in confusion. Vangerdahast rubbed his chin. "Ah—subjected his will to my own," the mage finally said. "I made him answer the questions I asked."

Torg and Pryderi exchanged knowing glances. Everything Vangerdahast had done was confirming their mistrust of mages' abilities. "Go on," the ironlord said after a moment. "What did you learn?"

"There are at least one thousand orcs out there," Vangerdahast replied. "Probably more. By the looks of the two scouts, they're very well armed for orcs, too."

Azoun put his hands to his temples to rub away a headache that was welling behind his eyes. "The troops from Zhentil Keep," he sighed. "They must have run into the orcs. That's why no one has heard from them."

Vangerdahast nodded. "That would explain much. When I asked the orcish scout, he said they'd come from the west." The mage pointed at Pryderi. "I might have been able to find out more, but this armored imbecile killed the prisoner."

Torg's face reddened, and he shot to his feet. With a growl, he snapped a question at Pryderi in Dwarvish. The soldier bowed his head and replied softly.

The ironlord planted his hands on his hips. "He said the orc was trying to escape. Is that true, mage?"

Scowling, Vangerdahast said, "A soldier struck the orc when he was slow in answering a question. That broke my spell, and the orcish scout went for his sword." The wizard practically shook with anger when he added, "That buffoon shot the orc before I could do anything."

"Pryderi did the right thing, Ironlord," Alusair said. "The orc might have escaped." Torg nodded and sat down again.

Vangerdahast was struck dumb by the princess's statement. He stood, staring at Alusair. The king quickly turned to his daughter and said, "That's absurd."

The rebuke didn't faze Alusair in the least. "You haven't fought as many orcs as the dwarves have, Father. You can't treat them like humans or dwarves or elves. Even if it would have meant certain death, that scout would have attacked Vangerdahast—just to take someone else with him when he died. The soldiers in Earthfast have been fighting against orcs for hundreds of years. Most of their wives and children have been murdered by the beasts. They know orcish treachery well."

"Besides," Torg noted as he sprawled in his throne, "we have all the information we need right now. If the troops we're expecting from Zhentil Keep ran into the orcs, they've probably been wiped out. And," he concluded, lifting his sword from the ground next to his throne, "they will attack us very soon. All we need to do is wait."

Both Pryderi and Alusair nodded. Vangerdahast returned to his seat next to Azoun. After a short discussion, it was decided that the Cormyrian king and his wizard should stay in camp, at least until the sun rose. Next, the ironlord sent Pryderi to join the army guarding the perimeter and called in his scribe to take down some messages for the home city, Earthfast.

For the rest of the night, a white-bearded scribe sat

hunched over a piece of parchment, making notes in the thick, angular symbols of the dwarven alphabet. Elaborate iron lanterns hung from metal supports throughout the tent, illuminating much of the area, but casting deep shadows into the corners. Vangerdahast slept, stretched out on one of the stone benches, snoring fitfully. Azoun and Alusair sat close together, and the princess told the king about the terrible, bloody battles she'd fought in defense of the dwarven city.

At the end of the last tale, she pointed to the armor she wore. "The dwarves made this for me after that fight with the goblins. It's made of the finest mithril steel." She laughed softly and added, "Torg now calls me the 'Mithril Princess' when I wear it."

Across the tent, the ironlord stretched and yawned. He walked slowly to the door and glanced outside. The first rays of the morning sun were creeping over the hills to the east, filling the dwarven camp with cold, pale light. Torg moved his head sharply to work an ache out of his neck. "I was sure the damnable orcs would have attacked by now," he said morosely. "Perhaps now that it's light they'll find a little courage."

As if in response to the dwarven king's wishes, a messenger burst into the tent. "Ironlord!" he gasped, dropping to one knee. "The orcs have shown themselves. They're on the eastern side of the camp."

Torg reached for his sword. "Ha! Now they'll pay for that escort party they murdered," he cried, startling Vangerdahast awake. The birds at the dwarven king's side were also shocked out of their slumber. They flitted around their cage noisily.

Alusair, already wearing her cuirass, stood and strapped her brassards onto her arms. "Have they attacked yet?" she asked the dwarven messenger.

"Not yet," he replied, wiping the sweat from his brow. "They are arrayed in battle formation in the field to the east."

Azoun turned to Torg. "Ironlord, it might be best for us to avoid this conflict. Perhaps the orcs will listen to reason and march on."

"Reason?" Torg snorted. "Orcs listen to reason, you say? No insult intended, Azoun, but you don't know orcs. They're here to fight."

"What about the crusade?" Vangerdahast asked, his voice still raspy with sleep. "The troops that die in this possibly preventable battle are lost to the Alliance of the West. Besides," the wizard added, appealing to the dwarven king's honor, "you gave your word that *two thousand* dwarves from Earthfast would assist us against the Tuigan."

Torg muttered something vile about wizards into his dark beard, then sighed. "All right. We'll see what your diplomacy can do. It's your funeral, mage. And remember, the first orc to raise a bow or a sword gets a crossbow bolt between its beady little eyes."

Vangerdahast straightened his beard and followed the two kings and the princess from the tent. Torg's entourage was quickly joined by a squadron of elite guards. Like the other dwarven soldiers, the bodyguard said nothing as it marched to the eastern edge of the camp. Vangerdahast kept to himself, too, and reviewed the spells he knew that might be useful in an attack. Azoun spoke softly to Alusair, but that conversation died abruptly when the Cormyrian king saw the line of dwarves standing before him.

The army of Earthfast was arranged in neat, perfectly straight rows at the eastern edge of the camp. For hundreds of yards to either side of Azoun, the battle line stretched, three dwarves deep. Silver armor reflected the growing morning sun, and two thousand mailed hands gripped crossbow stocks or swords. Trumpeters and drummers mixed with the troops, ready to sound the attack. Standards marking clans stood above the helmeted heads. These symbols—stylized hammers, anvils, and various weapons— served as rallying points for the soldiers.

The impressive dwarven line silently faced to the east, where the sun rose slowly over the hills. There, silhouetted in sunlight, stood the orcish army.

The two armies were a study in contrasts. Unlike the mailed dwarves, the orcs generally wore only black leather armor. A few had on chain mail or pieces of plate, but most of the slouching creatures garbed themselves in the uniformly bleak, weatherbeaten skins. The orcs all personalized their clothing with swatches of bright cloth taken from a murdered foe or bits of bone or fur from a vanquished beast. Whereas Torg's troops stood at attention in rigidly organized lines, the orcs huddled in groups or even squatted on the ground, waiting for orders. Some held unpolished, chipped swords, and others carried almost every kind of weapon imaginable—flails, maces, axes, spears, even polearms. Their standards were real skulls or crude pictures of bleeding eyes or broken fingers, held aloft on posts.

Alusair spotted drummers lounging amidst the orcish troops and pointed them out to Torg. The dwarven king nodded and relayed an order to his archers that, if possible, the drummers were to be shot first. They were undoubtedly the means of relaying orders in the orcish ranks.

Torg took his helmet from his squire and cradled it under an arm. He pointed to the center of the enemy's line, where a huge skull, probably belonging to a giant, sat atop a pole. "Their leader, if you can call these savages organized, is probably right there."

At Azoun's signal, Vangerdahast murmured a spell. When the incantation was complete, the mage put his hands to his mouth and said, "Leader of the orcs, we wish to parley." The words, magically boosted in volume by the spell, easily carried over the silent dwarven troops and even the noisy, grumbling orcs. "I hope they understand Common," Vangerdahast said after he'd delivered his message.

There was a commotion around the giant skull standard. Across the fifty or so yards that separated the armies, Azoun could see a few orcish soldiers brandishing swords, gesturing wildly at a particularly large soldier. This orc in turn grabbed another soldier by the throat and pushed him toward the dwarven line.

The abused orc staggered to his feet, shouted a curse or two over his shoulder in Orcish, and took a step toward the dwarves. "No kill," he shouted in broken Common. "Me speaker for Vrakk."

Azoun quietly conferred with Torg and Vangerdahast for a moment. All three men stepped to the fore. The wizard readied a protective spell as Azoun moved past the lines and held out his empty hands. "I am King Azoun of Cormyr," he yelled in Common, enunciating each word slowly for the creatures arrayed before him. "We don't want to fight, but we will if necessary."

Something Azoun said had an electrifying effect on the orcish troops. The soldier that had been pushed forward rushed back to the large orc, presumably Vrakk. The leather-armored troops broke into loud debate. A few waved their weapons menacingly at the king and some continued to sprawl on the ground, but most argued heatedly with their comrades.

Finally the large orc stepped forward, punching a trooper who stood in his way. He took a dozen steps into the space between the armies and slapped his hands to his hips. "You Ak-soon," he growled in horribly belabored Common. After pounding his chest with one long-nailed hand, he added, "I Vrakk from Zhentil Keep. I here to fight horsemen with you."

– 9 –

The Patchwork Army

Dwarves crowded one side of the pavilion; orcs milled together on the other. At the long, low table, King Azoun, Princess Alusair, and Vangerdahast sat together. Torg and Vrakk glared at one another spitefully over mugs of ale. Though there was a murmur of Orcish rumbling through the room, none of the dwarves and no one at the main table spoke.

Vrakk, leader of the orcs, hefted his silver mug and gulped a mouthful of ale. The brown liquid rolled down the side of his gray-green face and dribbled off of his lower canine teeth, which protruded from his large mouth. "We fight for Ak-soon," he said at last. "Masters at Keep no tell us to fight for *dglinkarz*." The orcish leader lifted his piggish snout a bit and sneered at Torg.

The orcs in the tent grunted and snarled their agreement. Many of the sweaty, drooling soldiers repeated the word *dglinkarz* and nodded. The dwarves already had a hand on their sword hilts, so the orcs didn't notice them almost universally tighten their grips.

Azoun looked to Vangerdahast, who shrugged. The wizard had cast spells enabling himself to understand what the dwarves and orcs said, but the term the orcish leader had used seemed untranslatable. "Fight for whom?" Vangerdahast said to Vrakk in Common.

The orc narrowed his beady red eyes. "*Dglinkarz*," he snapped, pointing at the dwarven king. With a sweeping gesture, he indicated all the dwarven troops. "They all *dglinkarz.*" It was obvious from the tone the orc used that it was a venomous insult.

Torg curled his hand into a fist and held it in front of his mouth. "I will not stand for this, Azoun," he growled. "I will not sit idly by while this beast insults me."

The Cormyrian king turned sharply to the orcish leader. "And if I order you to fight alongside the dwarves?"

"If Ak-soon orders," Vrakk said, "we follow." He dropped one elbow to the table, slouched slightly, and scratched the coarse hair on his arm. "That be law from Zhentil Keep."

Azoun leaned forward. "Even if I tell you to fight on the side of—" he paused and glanced at Torg "—*dglinkarz?*"

Scowling so much that his yellowed lower canines almost jutted to his snout, Vrakk nodded. "We follow Ak-soon."

"He may follow you," Torg snapped as he stood. "I will not. All the denizens from the Realm of the Dead could attack Faerun before I'd fight beside this rabble." The ironlord angrily motioned his guards to leave, then stomped from the pavilion himself. The orcs' jeers followed the armored dwarves out of the tent.

Azoun could hear Torg issue a loud string of orders outside. Alusair leaned close to her father and said, "He's commanded the guards to kill any orcs that haven't left the camp in an hour."

"Dwarves not so good warriors, eh, Ak-soon?" the orcish leader bellowed. He slapped the table so hard it rattled, then broke into a loud, snorting fit of laughter. The rest of his party followed suit.

Her hand on the hilt of her sword, Alusair stood. "I'll see if I can talk to the ironlord, Father." She paused, scanned the room of orcish troops, and added coldly, "Unless you want to see a battle start in camp, tell these . . . troops to muster where we met them, in the field to the east. Torg isn't bluffing about killing any orcs found in camp."

Vrakk stopped laughing abruptly. "What you say, girlie? You think *dglinkarz* frighten us?" He smashed his silver mug on the table's edge, denting it. "We no leave until ready."

Alusair drew her sword, an action that was answered in kind by the dozen orcs in the tent. Azoun and Vangerdahast stood up slowly, and the wizard prepared a spell that would extricate the humans from the situation if need be. For a long moment, there was no sound save for the orcs' heavy, grunting breaths.

Surprisingly Vrakk didn't move. He sat at the table, gripping the dented mug, staring at the princess. "You not like Ak-soon, girlie. You like *dglinkarz*, bad soldier."

"Look at that mug you're holding, pig," Alusair hissed. "You see those skulls the dwarves are piling up? Those are orc skulls." She pointed the tip of her sword at Vrakk. "Torg will add your skull to that pile, and I'll be happy to help him."

Azoun slapped the princess's blade down. "Enough!" he shouted. "Get out of here, Allie. I'll see you at Torg's tent in a minute."

"Not until you're safely away from these animals," Alusair replied, still glaring at Vrakk.

"I said *go* Alusair," Azoun repeated sharply. He grabbed his wayward daughter by the shoulders and spun her to face him. "Right now."

The princess knew from the look in the king's eyes that there was no point in arguing further. She assuaged her fear for her father by deciding that Vangerdahast would certainly guarantee Azoun's safety. With only a single, threatening look at Vrakk, she stormed from the tent.

His daughter gone, Azoun noticed that the tension in the pavilion eased noticeably. Vangerdahast was still rigid with concentration, preparing himself to use a spell if necessary, despite the fact that many of the orcs had sheathed their weapons. Vrakk lounged at the table, studying the dwarven mug closely.

"We follow Ak-soon," the orcish commander rumbled, "but we not let Torg take skulls." Vrakk raised his eyes from the dented silver mug and studied Azoun's face. "What you want orc soldiers do?"

The king rubbed a hand across his forehead. "I think it would be best if you gathered your troops in the field to the east, as the dwarves ask."

Without a pause or another word, Vrakk stood and grunted a command in Orcish. The Zhentish soldiers muttered to themselves, but they filed out of the pavilion and headed east. Most of the orcish army was still gathered in the field, but a few had wandered into the dwarven camp. Whenever he saw one of his men, Vrakk would yell out orders. Any orcs slow in responding got a solid blow to the head to remind him of his duty.

As soon as Vrakk and his leather-armored orcs were gone from camp, Azoun and Vangerdahast hurried to Torg's tent. As they crossed the compound, the king and the mage noted that the dwarves were breaking down tents. Like everything else they did, the troops from Earthfast dismantled their bivouac with steadfast deliberation.

"I think I prefer the orcs," Vangerdahast said as he watched a pair of gray-bearded dwarves take down a tent in silence.

Azoun shook his head. "We need Torg and his troops, Vangy. I don't know if we can beat the Tuigan without them."

The guards opened the door to the ironlord's tent as soon as Azoun and Vangerdahast got close. The Cormyrian king noticed that twice as many armed and armored sentries, all wearing the black surcoat of the ironlord's elite guard, stood watch around Torg's tent. The dwarves' spotless armor and perfect military formation as they paced a perimeter around their leader's tent gave Azoun an idea.

Upon entering the dark tent, the king said, "I'm disappointed in you, Ironlord. I'd heard your word was worth more than this." Vangerdahast cast a surprised look at his friend; he hadn't expected Azoun to take the offensive in this matter so quickly.

Torg, who was supervising the packing of his few belongings, frowned. The ironlord's black beard hid the expression, but Azoun and Vangerdahast saw the dwarf's anger in his eyes. "It's no use, Azoun. We're going back to Earthfast. My men won't fight alongside orcs."

The Cormyrian monarch glanced at his daughter. She sat silently at the edge of the tent, her drawn sword resting on her lap. "Your soldiers would fight at my side if you ordered them to, if you allowed them to," the king said harshly, returning his eyes to Torg.

Azoun's tone made the statement sound like an accusation. To Torg, it seemed as if the king was saying that it was only his reluctance—or cowardice—that prevented the dwarves from joining the crusade.

Which was precisely the impression that Azoun wanted to give.

Looking at the sentries outside, the king had realized that there were only two things that seemed important to the dwarves of Earthfast: order and honor. With a little work, he knew that he might be able to show Torg how leaving the crusade was contrary to both of these—despite the troops they had to fight beside.

Bristling at the slightly veiled insult to his bravery, Torg whirled on the king. "We fight only for good causes," the ironlord hissed. "I doubt any cause that draws scum like that to rally to it."

"Indeed," Alusair said from the shadows. "More than that, Father, it makes me wonder what you gave the Keep to secure their cooperation. I hope it was worth it."

"We're not talking about Zhentil Keep or my policies," Azoun snapped. He took a step toward Torg. "I have your word of honor that two thousand dwarves from Earthfast will stand against the Tuigan. Are you going to break that promise?"

The dwarves' actions indicated that they intended to do exactly that, but Torg hedged when confronted with the question. He mumbled something into his beard, then said, "You've broken your part of the bargain, Azoun."

Without hesitation, Vangerdahast pointed a finger at the ironlord. "Far from it," he said coldly. "King Azoun has not broken any such bargain; he offered you nothing in return for your troops but the honor of defending Faerun."

Alusair had moved to Torg's side during the exchange. She sheathed her sword and glared at her father. "This is all political rhetoric. It isn't dishonorable to refuse to fight on the side of . . . of murdering animals."

Clenching his teeth, Azoun forced back the growing rage he felt within him. "By that logic, Allie," he said flatly, "you'd fight for the horsewarriors just because they oppose the orcs. That's foolish."

Alusair put her hands on her hips. "But it isn't—"

"No, Princess," Torg grumbled, putting a hand on Alusair's arm. "Your father is right." The ironlord narrowed his eyes and studied the Cormyrian king for a moment. "I want retribution for the soldiers who were slain."

"That's reasonable," Azoun conceded. He looked at Alusair, but she would not meet his gaze.

"And I will not allow the orcs to travel with my troops," Torg added. "You will take them down the coast in your ships. We will march the rest of the way and meet you in Thesk."

Azoun had known from the start that the troops from Earthfast would not travel by boat. Some clans of dwarves preferred to keep in contact with the earth, the source of their prosperity, the sustainer of their mining cities. The king suddenly realized that Torg's demand that the orcs be taken to Telflamm by ship was, in fact, something the dwarf could tell his generals he received as a concession from the humans. Though he hadn't yet discussed it with the ironlord, Azoun had intended taking the Zhentish troops aboard his ships from the start.

The king nodded. "Your demands are fair, Ironlord. I will transport the orcs."

"This is all rather absurd," Vangerdahast said. "Why is the dwarven army walking all that way when we could easily provide transport for them, too?"

"You may understand magic, wizard," Torg replied, turning his back on Vangerdahast, "but you don't understand dwarves. I gave my word to fight, so I will honor that." He paused and rattled his birdcage. "To ask my troops to travel by sea is to ask them not to be dwarves."

A dwarven officer entered the tent and kneeled. "We'll be ready to leave by highsun," he reported.

Pausing for only an instant, Torg said, "Tell the troops to prepare for the march south."

The officer started to speak, then thought better of it and stood. "By your command, Ironlord," he said and spun sharply on his heels.

When the officer was gone, Torg sighed. "We can set up the logistics of the march later. Now, I want Vrakk to give me the orcs responsible for the deaths of my soldiers."

Within minutes, Azoun, Vangerdahast, Torg, and Alusair found themselves once again in the field to the east of camp. The sun was high over the hills, close to its zenith. A group of five hundred or so dwarves stood at attention in the hot sun, adorned in full armor. The orcs sprawled on the ground, shielding their faces from the bright sunshine with rat-eaten cloaks, packs, or whatever else they could find. At the center of this ragtag group, Vrakk and his lieutenants huddled around the giant's skull standard, arguing noisily. If they noticed Azoun's approach, the orcs didn't show it.

"Commander Vrakk," the king said sharply when he reached the standard, "we must discuss an incident that possibly involved your men."

Alusair and Torg nervously eyed the soldiers, and both of them kept their hands close to their weapons. Vangerdahast stood behind Azoun, a spell ready in his mind. He tapped his foot in irritation, as well. The orcs were not nearly so concerned with their camp as the dwarves were, and even that temporary resting spot was cluttered with garbage and puddles of waste; the smell alone was making the mage queasy.

A short orc with an especially piggish snout started to speak, but Vrakk kicked him in the back. "What problem now, Ak-soon?" the orcish commander asked, a bit of a whine in his voice. "We want to fight, not sit in sun all day."

"There was a dwarven patrol of three murdered yesterday on its way to the shore," Azoun said, the accusation clear in his voice.

Vrakk nodded. "They attack orc scouts," he responded casually. Grabbing a piece of meat from one of the other orcish soldiers, he stuffed the raw flesh into his mouth.

Torg stepped forward. "I want blood-payment," he rumbled. An orcish lieutenant moved between the ironlord and Vrakk, but Alusair drew her sword. Before the orc could respond, the princess's blade rested at his throat. Two dozen other Zhentish soldiers leaped to their feet and drew their weapons. As Vangerdahast prepared to cast his spell, the dwarven troops began a quick march across the field to their ironlord.

Before anyone drew blood, however, Vrakk yelled a single command in Orcish. Thanks to the spell he had cast previously, Vangerdahast could understand what the orcish leader was yelling. Still, he wasn't all that sure the troops would "stand down" as Vrakk demanded.

"Lower your weapon, Allie," Azoun said, taking a slow, careful step toward his daughter. "We're all dead if you don't."

The princess pushed the blade against the orc's throat just hard enough to draw a trickle of blood, then lowered it. The orcs around Azoun's party relaxed slightly. However, they, too, kept their weapons at the ready.

Vrakk pushed the orc on whom Alusair had drawn her sword. Looking down on Torg with dark, beady eyes, he asked, "What about orcs you kill last night?"

"They were spies," Alusair said. "You killed soldiers assigned to escort King Azoun from his ship."

After gnashing his teeth together for a moment, seemingly lost in thought, Vrakk replied, "OK. I give blood-payment. Then Ak-soon take us to fight."

Torg was surprised that the orc agreed so readily. "The blood of one for each dwarf killed." The ironlord held up three stubby fingers.

The dwarven troops had reached the orcish line by now. Torg's soldiers stood silently as the orcs jeered at them. All along both lines, swords stood at the ready.

"Be prepared to grab Alusair's arm and reach for my hand if anything goes wrong," Vangerdahast whispered in Azoun's ear. "This is far too dangerous for us to chance any longer."

Vrakk shouted out three names. A trio of orcish soldiers lazily appeared next to the standard. Waving his arms wide to spread his troops out in a semicircle, Vrakk grunted a command. One of his lieutenants took the three orcs' swords, then shoved the soldiers one by one onto the ground. The prisoners squealed curses, but didn't fight their captors. They knew resistance was futile.

Grandly the orcish commander gestured to Torg, then to the prostrate soldiers. "These three guilty," he said loudly. "I take blood-payment." Without another word, he drew his weapon—a huge, darkly stained bastard sword—and nodded to the lieutenant.

Vrakk's assistant dropped to his knees on one of the murderers' backs. Another orc rushed forward and grabbed the prisoner's left arm at the wrist and pulled it straight. With a shout, Vrakk raised the blade over his head and brought it down, two hands on the hilt. He hit the prisoner's arm between the shoulder and the elbow, right where the red armband with their god's symbol lay.

As one of the lieutenants raised the severed arm up high, another two rushed forward and the punishment was meted out on another murderer. The orcish soldiers cheered and made bets on who would cry out or who might struggle. Azoun stood grimly by, but he noticed that Torg seemed to be pleased by the grisly scene. Alusair and Vangerdahast simply turned away.

The last murderer did try to stand when his turn came, but Vrakk kicked him in the face, knocking him senseless. A few hunks of meat and copper coins changed hands in the orcish crowd, the wagers won and lost by the prisoner's actions. With a third and louder shout, Vrakk raised his sword and finished the task.

With a sharp nod of approval, Torg signaled his troops to return to their camp. He glanced at the sun, then at Azoun and said, "We march in less than one hour. Stop by my tent so we can discuss how best to unload the supplies from your ships." That said, he spun around and marched through the tall grass after his soldiers.

As soon as the ironlord was out of earshot, Vrakk began to growl a series of orders in Orcish. Five Zhentish soldiers, wearing tattered, long robes instead of leather armor, rushed forward. The orcish commander pointed at the three dying murderers and grunted.

As the five robed orcs started to chant and wave small skull-headed wands over the wounded prisoners, Vangerdahast said "Shamans." Alusair wrinkled her nose in disgust as the priests bloodied the skulls on the severed arms.

Vrakk strode proudly to Azoun's side. "They probably live," he noted in broken Common. "Cut arms only way to shut up *dglinkarz*. 'Sides, our god heal so orcs fight and make better deaths."

"But they can't fight after this," Azoun gasped. He motioned to the three severed arms that still littered the ground. "Their wounds—"

Vrakk grunted a laugh. "That why we cut *left* arm. They still fight." He glanced warily at Alusair, then added, "She no tell dwarf. They demand them dead again."

"Don't worry," Alusair said coldly, directing her answer to her father. "If you're going to allow the orcs to break a blood-payment, I won't stand in your way." With that, she stormed off after Torg.

The robed orcs had finished their wild incantation to Lord Cyric. The three wounded soldiers on the ground didn't look much better, but the stumps where their arms had been weren't bleeding as freely. Azoun swallowed hard to push back the disgust he felt. "March your troops to the shore, Vrakk. Find the ships there and wait. You will help us unload some supplies, then board."

The Cormyrian king nodded to Vangerdahast, and the two set out for Torg's tent. The wizard walked with his hands clenched behind his back. Every few steps he glanced at Azoun, who was as silent as the dwarves breaking camp. "I think you did the right thing," Vangerdahast ventured after a while.

Azoun stopped walking. "The right thing?" he exclaimed, shaking his head. "I'm afraid Allie is right. I've offended good allies for the sake of monsters."

"Perhaps," Vangerdahast said sagely. Patting the king on the shoulder, he started toward the tent again. "But you know as well as I that Zhentil Keep will use any slight against these troops as provocation to break the treaty."

Azoun could only agree. The happiness of the dwarves was not worth a war with Zhentil Keep.

Torg was in a fury when the king and the wizard arrived. He shouted at his squire three times as Azoun tried to set up a rendezvous point in Thesk. After one half-hour, however, the spot was decided. The dwarves were to meet the Army of the Alliance between the cities of Telflamm and Tammar, along the trade route known as the Golden Way.

"While you wait, you can drill your troops," Torg told Azoun as the meeting was concluding. "You won't have long. I'll press my men to get them there as quickly as possible."

Torg's mood shifted suddenly, and he smiled for the first time in hours. "Ha!" the ironlord cried and slapped Azoun's arm. "We'll work this out after all!" He stood and gestured broadly. "My troops will be ready for bear when we reach Thesk. Just bring on those horsemen!"

Azoun returned the smile weakly. His hours without sleep were beginning to take their toll. He felt washed out and slightly dizzy. "Come, Vangy," the king said as he stood. "Back to the *Welleran*. You too, Allie."

"No."

The king stared at the princess. "I'm going with the dwarves," she said defiantly. "I won't travel with the orcs."

"Who said anything about you accompanying us to Thesk?" Vangerdahast snapped. "I think you should go straight back to the palace in Suzail." He dug a handful of spell components out of his robe and turned to Azoun. "I can send her right now, Your Highness. Just say the word."

Before Azoun could answer, Torg slapped Vangerdahast's hand with the flat of his sword. "You'll not be casting spells in my tent," he growled. "Besides, Alusair has every right to decide her own fate."

"I've had enough of this," the mage said sharply, rubbing his hand. He looked at the spot where Torg had struck him; a painful red welt had blossomed there. "And you should be ashamed of yourself, Princess, disobeying your father like this."

"I'm her father, not her master," Azoun noted quietly from the doorway of the tent. "She—" He studied Alusair's face for a moment, noting the hard determination that had settled in her eyes. "She can make up her own mind."

Torg shot a spiteful look at Vangerdahast, as if he were saying, "I was right all along and now your king realizes it, too." The wizard ignored the ironlord, concentrating instead on Azoun and his daughter. They stood a few feet apart, but the distance might as well have been miles. Alusair seemed genuinely surprised by her father's words. The king, on the other hand, looked pained, as if it had hurt him physically to admit his child's freedom of choice.

"Come, Vangy," Azoun said after a moment. "We've got troops to get to Telflamm." He stopped and faced Alusair again. "We'll need to communicate with you," he noted, pulling the signet ring from his finger and holding it out to his daughter. "Take it."

The princess stepped forward tentatively. A sly smile suddenly crossed her lips. "The ring has a spell on it, doesn't it?"

"What else would you expect?" the king replied, his daughter's smile lightening his dark mood somewhat. "And like your last ring, burying this one in a few hundred fathoms of water will negate the spell quite effectively—so be careful, won't you?"

Alusair took off the plain gold band that prevented her from being magically tracked and slipped the signet ring on in its place. "I'll see you in Thesk."

For an awkward moment, the two stood face-to-face. Finally Azoun said, "Be careful, Allie," and turned to go.

The princess almost stepped forward then, almost embraced her father as he left Torg's tent. But she didn't. As she made her way to her tent through the silent, orderly dwarven camp, Alusair wondered why she couldn't make that sign of affection.

* * * * *

The dwarves had been on the march for almost eighteen hours when Azoun finally returned to Telflamm's harbor. The sun was coming up over the city, its first rays casting a pale halo around the high, onion-shaped spires that so characterized Telflamm's skyline. The docks were still aglow with torches, and the myriad of vessels crowding the harbor were spotted with faint flickering lights cast by watchmen's lanterns.

The Cormyrian ships were once again empty, having left their cargo of orcish troops to the south of the city. Azoun and Vangerdahast knew that they had no other choice; the Zhentish soldiers were likely to cause more trouble in the city than they had in Torg's camp. Now, all the king had to do was gather his own forces and begin the march to the east.

That proved far more difficult than Azoun had expected.

Telflamm provided too many distractions for the Alliance's soldiers and sailors, most of whom had never traveled more than a few miles from their own homes. Refugees from the onslaught of the Tuigan—now less than five hundred miles to the east—crowded the streets. Along with the refugees came vice and corruption. Thieves flourished, as did a black market in food, clothes, even human life. Brothels sprang up overnight throughout the city, often right next door to makeshift arenas where the foolish and the brave could battle to the death for a handful of gold. The city watch, sorely undermanned for the task of policing a transient army and a horde of refugees, found it easier to take bribes and look the other way.

"I don't care if the local watch isn't any help," Azoun said loudly. He glared at Lord Harcourt, the commander of the Alliance's cavalry. "Why aren't the nobles doing something about this? We should have some type of military watch." He paced nervously around the temporary command center, located in Telflamm's government offices.

The general shrugged. "Well, Your Highness," he began tentatively. "It's, uh, a, uh—"

Brunthar Elventree leaned back in his chair. "What Lord Harcourt is trying to say is that his men are right alongside mine—passed out in an alley somewhere or spending their day in a whorehouse." The red-haired dalesman smiled. "However, I don't see what the problem is," he added snidely. "If you'll let us fight beside orcs, a little debauchery won't—"

"That's enough, General Elventree," Azoun snapped. "One more insubordinate comment like that and you'll be relieved of your command." He stormed across the room and stood in front of the dalesman. "I need your cooperation, now more than ever. I have accepted the orcs to fight the Tuigan. You will enforce that. Do you understand?"

Brunthar slowly sat up straight. The poor lighting in the room cast deep shadows over his face, masking his expression, but making him look demonic. "Yes, Your Highness."

"Then that's settled," Azoun said firmly. "This crusade is floundering. If we are going to be able to face the Tuigan, we need to get the men out of here right away." The king paused for a moment, then turned to the dalesman. "General Elventree, since your men are lying facedown next to Lord Harcourt's, you two will gather the troops together. Any questions?"

The dalesman smiled at the king's slight jab at the nobleman. "No, Your Highness."

Lord Harcourt had been a soldier long enough to realize what Azoun was doing. Even though he disliked the commoners from the Dales, he knew the king had to find some way to draw the army together. "Anything you command, Your Highness," he replied as cheerfully as he could. Straightening his ever present mail shirt, the nobleman stood and bowed.

"Good," the king said. "I'll find Vangerdahast and Farl, and we'll do what we can from here." As the generals prepared to leave, Azoun added, "I want the army on the march by highsun tomorrow at the latest."

Neither Brunthar Elventree nor Lord Harcourt thought that possible, but they didn't say so. Instead they made their way into the streets and started a search for soldiers sober enough to serve as military police. Luckily they were more successful than they'd hoped possible. The city did offer a myriad of distractions, but the mercenary troops hired by the Sembians were generally far too experienced as campaigners to fall prey to the vices of a port of call. Within twenty-four hours, much of the Army of the Alliance had gathered to the south, outside the walls of the city.

Razor John was very pleased to learn of the mustering. Though he, like many of his companions, had never been outside Cormyr before, he rarely drank to excess and never dabbled in other vices, even when he was at home. Why start now? he reasoned. After all, Telflamm offered little that couldn't be purchased in Suzail. The price would be higher in Cormyr, of course, and each particular vice wouldn't be advertised so openly, but that made little difference to the fletcher.

Many of John's compatriots found the invitation to debauchery irresistible. Mal, in particular, had spent his time in Telflamm drinking and fighting. The ham-fisted man had even registered himself for a death duel in an arena. John and Kiri had managed to talk Mal out of fighting, but the temptation was great to let him go through with the duel. The last the fletcher had seen of the soldier, he was holed up in a stinking little waterfront tavern called the Broken Lance.

It was this establishment that John sought as he wound his way through the narrow, dirty alleys of Telflamm's harbor. Homeless refugees and resident beggars lined the streets. Some offered black market goods or services in exchange for money, others merely pleaded for a few copper pieces to get them through the day. The pitiable pleas tugged at the fletcher's heart, but he didn't dip his hand into his purse for the ragged children or diseased old men. John had no money left. He'd given much of his wealth to the poor his first day ashore; the rest had been stolen by cutpurses soon after that.

Razor John thought longingly about the crowded marketplace in Cormyr. How different it was from the squalor in Telflamm. He looked up at the sky, but could see little of it. The dilapidated buildings to either side of the narrow alley leaned together so that they almost blocked out the sunlight completely. It's probably for the best, the fletcher decided bitterly. Too much direct sun and the garbage that filled the side streets would stink worse than it already did.

As quickly as he could, John walked the rest of the way to the Broken Lance. A thief was searching the pockets of an unconscious soldier resting facedown at the front door. As the fletcher got closer, the pickpocket looked up at him and ran off. John was glad the thief had fled, since he wasn't quite sure what he would have done otherwise. After checking to see that the soldier was alive, he entered the bar.

The Broken Lance was a small, dark place. Weak light filtered through sooty windows on one side of the room, and sour-smelling tallow candles burned at some of the tables. A large fire sputtered across from the door, sending oily peat smoke up toward the ceiling, where it swirled around before leaking out through various gaps in the poorly constructed roof. The sound of raucous laughter mixed with bawdy sea chants and bursts of swearing. Rats scurried freely across the floor, ignored by most of the patrons.

Razor John spotted Mal immediately. The big soldier was locked in an arm wrestling contest. A few men stood around Mal's table, cheering and cursing. Most of the inn's patrons sat huddled over their tarnished tankards, swilling watery ale. Mal won the contest just as the fletcher reached his side. The soldier slammed the other man's hand to the table, sloshing wine from the large wineskin that rested there. Coins exchanged hands, and most of the men drifted back to their own tables. Mal rubbed his arm and only nodded to John as a greeting.

"We're supposed to be ready to march by highsun," the fletcher said softly. He took off his black felt hat and held it before him, twisting it nervously.

"Is that what you're here for?" Mal asked incredulously. He leered and added, "Shouldn't you and your lady love be off somewhere? I hear Kiri's—"

"That's enough!" John said forcefully. His feelings for Kiri Trollslayer had grown steadily over the trip to Telflamm, and he wasn't about to let a drunken soldier—especially one who was supposed to be her friend—start ugly rumors about her.

Mal looked in turn at each of the other two men who sat at the table. One of them, a dalesman by the roughspun tan tunic and breeches he wore, grinned broadly. The other was a dark-eyed, well-armed mercenary, with a sizable and rather ugly scar running along his cheek. He simply snorted and took a long draw from the large tankard set before him. It amazed John to see Mal, who claimed to hate Sembians and dalesmen, drinking with these two soldiers. But then, the fletcher knew that Mal would drink with almost anyone.

John frowned. "The king's back from the north with the Zhentish troops. It's time to go."

"Zhentish troops!" The dalesman spat. "I hear they're orcs, the whole bunch of them. Fine lot of good they'll do us in a battle." He swilled some wine into his tankard. "More'n likely they'll slit our throats when we're sleeping."

"Maybe they're here for us to warm up on," Mal suggested darkly. He lifted the wineskin to pour himself another tankardful, then stopped. He swished the wine around in the skin and announced, "Last swallows." Both he and Razor John looked about the room.

The Sembian mercenary watched the two Cormyrians for a moment, then asked, "What do you think you're doing?"

"Looking for someone of the nobility," John offered. "It's a Cormyrian tradition that the nobleman of the greatest lineage or the highest ranking officer in the taproom gets the last drink from a cask or wineskin."

"If there were any officers in this place, you'd not be giving that wine to them," the dalesman snapped, making a feeble grab for the skin. Mal slapped a hand over the man's thin face and pushed him back in his chair.

As Mal was dealing with the dalesman, the mercenary snatched the wineskin from his hand. "The person who bought it gets to decide what to do with the last swallow," he said loudly. A few heads turned toward the table.

Mal swore and stood up. As he leaned forward to grab the skin from the Sembian, the mercenary drew a dagger and held it to Mal's throat.

"No weapons!" the barkeep cried, then ducked into the back room. A few men and women drew their swords. One or two made for the door.

Mal slowly sat back down and slid his hand around his tankard. The Sembian's evil grin only made his scar turn red and, if possible, more ugly. He handed the wineskin to the dalesman. "You bought it, archer. It's yours."

As the dalesman smiled and uncorked the wineskin, Razor John reached for his own dagger. He certainly didn't intend to fight over something as ridiculous as a mouthful of cheap wine, but he wasn't about to let someone attack him either. "Let's go, Mal," he rumbled, taking a step away from the table. "This isn't worth it." When his countryman didn't stand, John looked down in amazement.

Mal sat hunched over his tankard, which he gripped tightly in his left hand. Beneath a tangle of blond curls, his broad, thick-boned face was caught somewhere between an expression of bewilderment and rage. "Damn Sembians," he muttered. "Damned dalesmen. I should've known better than to drink with merchants and farmers."

"At least this wine's going where it belongs," the dalesman said happily. He pulled the cork and upended the wineskin. The last of the red liquid poured onto the dirty floor, startling a few insects. Before the wine had drained through the widely spaced floorboards, the tan-clad soldier repeated a short, ritualistic prayer to the God of Agriculture.

A few people at nearby tables laughed. The Sembian mercenary stood, slack-jawed and staring. Mal, his alcohol-numbed brain only now registering what had happened, cursed again and stood. His dirty, sweat-soaked clothes clung to his muscular form like a second skin.

"No hard feelings," the dalesman said, offering his hand to Mal. "You've got your traditions; we've got ours."

John saw Mal tense his arm, but the realization that he was going to lash out came to the fletcher too late for action. The warrior swung with his left in a vicious backhanded slap. The dalesman, his reflexes dulled by wine, couldn't get out of the way of the tarnished tankard. With a dull clang, the heavy metal mug hit him square in the face, shattering his nose and more than a few of his teeth.

The dalesman hit the floor with a muffled thud, his blood mixing with the dregs of the spilled wine. The skitter of a dozen swords leaving their sheaths underscored the muttered curses and oaths.

Mal, the tankard still dangling in his left hand, stared dumbly at his victim. "Get up," he said roughly, kicking the body with his mud-caked boots.

With a gasp, Razor John dropped to his knees. He put his

ear close to the dalesman's bloody mouth. "He's not breathing." A few tears began to well in the fletcher's eyes. "You idiot!" he screamed. "You killed him over a tankard of wine!"

The Sembian mercenary took a step back and sheathed his dagger. "The generals'll hang you for this. They'll not let murder go unpunished."

The dented, bloodied tankard dropped to the floor with a hollow clang. Mal shook his head, started to speak, then kicked the dalesman again instead. "Get up, you bastard. You're not dead."

Razor John stood and turned toward another commotion that was breaking out near the door. The innkeeper, followed by two soldiers and a member of the city watch, was pushing his way through the crowd. The fletcher recognized one of the soldiers as Farl Bloodaxe, commander of the Alliance's infantry.

"I knew this would happen," the barkeep babbled as he got close. He pointed to Mal. "I could tell he was a bad sort from the moment he walked in here."

"We'll all be glad when your troops leave," the watchman said loudly. Like all of Telflamm's city watch, this man wore a long, bright red overcoat, sashed tight at the waist with shiny black cloth. His high, square black hat was tassled in silver, and a broad, curved sword hung prominently at his side. The guard kicked a chair with the silver toecap of a well-polished boot. "You've been nothing but trouble since you arrived."

"That's enough," Farl said. The ebony-skinned general sighed and looked around. "Any of you care to tell me what happened?"

Over the next fifteen minutes, Razor John, Mal, and a few others told their versions of the incident. Unsurprisingly, Mal claimed the dalesman had drawn a blade. No one corroborated his story, but Mal seemed unaffected by that. When John denied the tale's veracity, the murderer narrowed his eyes and shook his head.

All the time that Farl was conducting his interviews, John felt a growing wave of nausea wash over him. He had never really liked Mal. In fact, the fletcher had agreed to look for the soldier only because he was a fellow Cormyrian and an acquaintance of Kiri's. Still, he had never really disliked him either. Now John saw his countryman for what he really was—a drunken, violent bully.

As quickly as the murder had occurred, Mal's fate was decided. The soldier suddenly became very calm, more quiet, in fact, than John had ever seen him. Irons were placed on his large hands, and Farl ordered the dalesman's body to be taken out and burned. Before the red-coated guardsman could lead Mal to his fate, the doomed Cormyrian soldier leaned close to the fletcher.

"I thought you would have stuck by me," Mal whispered through clenched teeth. "Backed up my story. We're two of a kind, you and me."

"No," Razor John said sharply. "I came to find you because we're both from Cormyr, but—"

"Not that," Mal said. The guard tugged on the irons and pulled the soldier a step away from John. "What you did aboard the *Sarnath* and all." As the watchman pulled Mal another step away, he snapped viciously, "All right. You'll have me hanging soon enough."

Razor John watched in numbed silence as the crowd parted for the watchman and his prisoner. Nausea washed over the fletcher again, and he slumped into a chair. The inn's customers went back to their business, though subdued slightly. John sat for a moment, turning Mal's words over and over in his mind. Then his eyes drifted to the floor, where the dented tankard still lay.

Silently the fletcher picked up the tarnished mug. In his mind, John saw his bow and the arrows he'd used to kill the sailor and the priest who'd visited the plague ship. He'd believed his conscience reconciled with those deeds, but he wondered now how an officer's orders had made his act any different from Mal's.

Tucking the silver tankard under his cloak, John rose swiftly and made his way out of the city to find Kiri and begin the march into Thesk. Thoughts of the incidents at the Broken Lance and aboard the *Sarnath* plagued the fletcher all through the long, hard march away from the coast.

– 10 –

Birds of Prey

Malmondes of Suzail dangled from a rope on a makeshift scaffold south of Telflamm for eight days, a stark example of military justice. In that time, Alusair and the dwarven army made their way south across the green rolling hills of the Great Dale. Now, ten days and almost seventy miles after parting with King Azoun, Torg's soldiers stood on the edge of Lethyr Forest.

As he had each evening of the march, Torg traveled from clan to clan, marked in camp by their different standards. Before the soldiers went about their duties or to sleep, the ironlord gave them a short, direct speech about the crusade. The orcs, he told the army, were an evil they would put up with until the battle was over. Then the Zhentish beasts, or whatever was left of them, would answer to the troops of Earthfast for their insult.

As the soldiers from Earthfast silently set up camp for the night, Princess Alusair studied the dark edge of the forest to the east. The area the dwarves had been crossing was grassland, generally devoid of trees, so the huge expanse of woods presented an imposing front. And though the most direct route to the location where they would join up with the Army of the Alliance was through the forest, Torg refused to consider taking his troops that way.

"Only elves and other such questionable creatures lurk in forests," the ironlord had told Alusair. "I'll not put my soldiers in danger needlessly by taking a shortcut through an obvious haven for traps. We'll go south, then skirt the forest and head east."

Alusair wasn't quite sure who the ironlord thought would set a trap for the dwarves, but she really didn't care. Torg's inflexibility on the matter only fostered a vague but growing dissatisfaction the princess felt with the ironlord's army. Nine months past, in the middle of autumn, Alusair had gone to the Earthfast Mountains in search of a lost artifact. Instead, she found a small but proud group of dwarves defending their decaying underground city against a seemingly endless onslaught of evil orcs and goblins. Always searching for a worthy cause, the princess joined the fight. Her knowledge of military strategy, gained from her father when she was still a child, proved invaluable to the dwarves of Earthfast. The orcs were routed, and the crumbling city was saved.

Most of the time Alusair had spent with the dwarves had been taken up with battles against orcs and goblins. The princess had never felt anything for the soldiers other than respect or the camaraderie one has for an ally in battle. Until now.

Torg cared little for the tremendous confusion Alusair felt. She'd tried to speak to the ironlord about her father on the first day's march, but he had simply dismissed the topic as idle chatter. The princess knew that few of the dwarves had families; the orcs and goblins had slain most of the women and children in Earthfast years ago. Even Torg's queen had been killed in a battle fifteen years past.

That shouldn't make them so cold, Alusair decided as she watched a lone falcon soar up into the twilight. It moved out from the forest's edge and circled idly over the camp. Occasionally, the bird of prey shrieked. The noise echoed mournfully in the warm early summer's night.

The princess sighed and turned toward her tent, wondering over the fact that Torg had sent a letter to Azoun agreeing to supply troops to the crusade at the end of winter, almost four months past. The year was soaring by as quickly as the bird overhead.

The dwarven sentry that Alusair passed on the way to

camp only nodded. Apart from a few softly spoken orders
and the unavoidable noise made setting up tents and building watchfires, the camp was silent. Once, Alusair had
found the peace and quiet relaxing; now it left her too much
time to think. That was the last thing she wanted.

Azoun's actions had puzzled the princess and made her,
perhaps, a bit sad. She'd certainly expected the conflict over
her leaving home. However, Alusair hadn't believed it possible her father would admit she had control of her own life.
She had been ready to take the moral high ground in the dis-
pute, ready to prove to the king how her actions weren't so
very different from his own as a youth. She looked at the
signet ring Azoun had left with her and cursed.

Her father's less dogmatic attitude toward her indepen-
dence might have meant an easy reconciliation a few
months ago, but not after what Alusair had seen in the
dwarves' camp. Her father had openly allied with orcs,
creatures of evil. She saw the alliance as the unpardonable
product of moral backsliding for political ends. Now Alusair
wasn't even sure she wanted to be reconciled with Azoun;
he really didn't seem like the good, noble man she remembered from four years ago.

What should I do? she wondered, reviewing the painful
question in her mind. No easy answer came.

The princess finally reached her darkened tent. For a moment, she considered contacting Vangerdahast and Azoun
using the ring, but decided against it. Instead, she lay on her
blankets and listened to the falcon cry out in the growing
darkness. Alusair concluded from the lessening sound that
the bird was moving back toward the forest. She could still
hear the shrill sounds of its call as she drifted off to sleep.

The rain that fell that night didn't wake Alusair, but she
felt the cold and damp in her joints when she awoke the
next morning. The day dawned gray and cloudy, and a light
drizzle fell over the camp. With as little emotion as they
showed at most other times, the troops from Earthfast
broke camp and moved on. Alusair joined them, sullenly
and silently.

The next three days and nights passed the same way. The

dwarves marched anywhere from ten to fifteen miles a day, quite a feat for a group of two thousand soldiers and a train of supplies. Alusair was certain that Azoun's troops would cover no more than five miles in the same time. The dwarves were much better organized and rarely stopped to rest or to eat. They used fewer wagons than the humans, too, which allowed them greater mobility. The few stout wooden conveyances they did have were pulled by hearty little mountain ponies or mules. Most of the dwarves carried heavy loads in addition to their weapons and armor.

By the second tenday of what she considered a forced march, Alusair started to wonder if she'd be able to keep up. She did, though she paid for the pace every night in sore muscles and blistered feet.

Each night, the princess wearily studied the woods to the east before collapsing into a deep sleep. Falcons seemed to follow the camp, and Alusair found that watching the beautiful birds of prey soar in the sky was quite relaxing. It made her feel free and, more importantly, allowed her to forget her troubles, if only for a little while.

On one particular night, the princess sat in the warm darkness a hundred yards from the edge of camp, closer to the trees. A falcon lofted overhead. She wondered for a moment if the bird was the same one she'd seen on the first night they camped outside the forest. It's possible, Alusair decided after watching the bird turn lazy circles in the sky. The dwarves were scaring up enough field mice and rabbits in their trek across the rolling farmlands to keep a dozen such birds well fed.

Without warning, Alusair's signet ring began to glow brightly. The princess shielded the light with her hand; in the growing darkness, the ring might be an unwanted beacon to creatures prowling around the camp. Every camp attracted scavengers—wolves, jackals, and other, more exotic monsters. Alusair had enough campaign experience to know that it was very unwise to underestimate such creatures.

Allie?

The princess looked at the ring, puzzled. She had heard

her father's voice in her head. Usually Alusair was comfortable with magic, but this was something she had never experienced before.

Princess? Can you hear us? This time the words were Vangerdahast's. An annoying buzzing took hold in Alusair's ears. She dismissed it as a side effect of the spell on the ring.

Holding the gold ring close to her mouth, the princess said, "Yes, I can hear you." She spoke the words softly, so no one or no creature could hear.

What? I can't hear you. Are you all right? Alusair heard her father ask. She didn't like to admit it, but she was happy to hear the concern in his voice.

Vangerdahast sighed in annoyance inside the princess's head. *You are trying to talk into the ring, I'd imagine*, the mage said sharply, his patience fleeing. *Well, that won't work. Just concentrate. I can sense your mind through my scrying spell, but we won't have full contact until you concentrate on us.*

Alusair focused her mind on the sound of the wizard's voice, and the buzz in her ears vanished. *Ah, there you are, Allie*, she heard her father say happily.

She could almost picture Azoun, sitting in his tent with Vangerdahast, hovering over some scrying mirror or crystal ball. Without realizing it, the princess pictured her father five years younger, more as she remembered him from their days in Suzail. His brown beard was less sprinkled with silver, and the deep wrinkles around his eyes were barely noticeable.

We can see you, Princess, but the ring will only allow you to hear us, Vangerdahast explained. *As long as you—*

I'm sure she's figured out how this works by now, Azoun said, abruptly ending the wizard's lecture. There was a brief but pregnant silence, then the king said, *Where are you, Allie? How are Torg's troops holding up?*

Alusair quickly and succinctly reported on the dwarven army's disposition. *At the rate we're moving*, the princess concluded, *we should meet up with you in about twenty-five days.*

That soon? Azoun asked, surprise evident in his voice.

We're about halfway to the meeting spot ourselves, with two more tendays march ahead of us. I was hoping to have some time to drill the troops before we met up.

You'll have about five days, then, Father, the princess thought. A short silence followed, so Alusair assumed there was nothing more to say. With little prelude, she bid her father and Vangerdahast good night and pulled the ring from her finger. The light from the gold ring faded, then winked out.

Studying the expertly engraved dragon on the signet, Alusair rose to her feet. The falcon overhead cried out, and the princess looked up to see it diving toward the trees. The bird shrieked again. This time, however, Alusair thought she heard a shrill whistle from the forest answer the cry.

Now a dark speck against the darker sky, the falcon disappeared into the trees. Alusair paused for a moment and narrowed her eyes in an attempt to see into the murky outline of the woods. After a time, she dismissed the whistle as a product of her imagination or an aftereffect of the spell. With a single glance over her shoulder, she turned from Lethyr Forest and made her way to her bed.

The next day started warm, bright, and sunny—in fact, a rather typical day for the early summer month of Kythorn—but an almost palpable uneasiness hung over the dwarven camp. Alusair learned from Torg that the sentries had reported possible movement by mounted troops at the edge of the wood during the night. The ironlord had passed word through the ranks that every soldier was to be prepared for battle, and the princess assumed correctly that this was the source of the army's restlessness.

Despite Torg's orders, Alusair didn't wear her armor that day, donning instead a clean doublet, rough leather leggings, and high leather boots. She found it far easier to march dressed that way, though perspiration still plastered her short blond hair to her head. The ironlord scowled at Alusair, but made no comment on her dress.

Clouds rolled across the sky far to the south as the dwarves began their march, but the sun still shone cheerily overhead. Torg paid little attention to the fine weather, forcing his soldiers to march through their noon meal. They stopped at dusk, and as soon as the column halted to set up camp, soldiers spotted a horseman leaving Lethyr Forest.

At least he appeared to be a mounted rider from a long way off. As the creature got closer, Torg was surprised to find that a centaur, not a man, raced toward the dwarves at a full gallop. He carried a banner in one hand and seemed to be unarmed.

"Load bows!" Torg growled. A young dwarf at his side dipped the ironlord's standard. The standard-bearers for each clan mirrored the movement, and all along the column, packs were dropped and crossbows cranked to the ready.

Alusair, too, dropped her pack, but she didn't draw a weapon. Centaurs were often very reasonable creatures, dedicated to guarding their forest homes. She doubted that the messenger galloping toward the dwarven king was bringing tidings of war. Even though the princess stood right next to Torg, she didn't bother to tell him this; Alusair knew he wouldn't listen.

The centaur headed straight for Torg's banner. The cloth standard, embroidered with the phoenix and hammer symbol of Earthfast, was the largest banner and flew in the army's front rank. It was reasonable to assume it belonged to the soldiers' commander.

"Hail, dwarves of Earthfast," the centaur called in Common when he got close. Many of Torg's troops shifted uneasily. They had never seen anything like this half-man, half-horse before.

The crossbowmen in Torg's bodyguard aimed their weapons at the herald. "State your business," the ironlord replied crossly.

Alusair and the herald both frowned at the clipped, insulting reply. The centaur stopped abruptly, kicking up clods from the field with his large hooves. He glanced over the column, and a trace of discomfort crossed his tanned, heavily bearded face. "I am the speaker for Tribe Pastilar of the Forest of Lethyr," he said formally, fear edging his voice. "You fly the banner of Earthfast. Are you—"

"Yes, yes," Torg said impatiently. "I am Torg mac Cei, Ironlord of Earthfast. What do you want?"

The centaur herald's massive, muscular chest heaved slightly as he let out a sigh of relief. For a moment, he had thought the scouts had mistakenly identified the dwarves' standard. "You are passing close to our territory," the herald continued, a bit more relaxed, "and we simply wish to know your intentions."

Torg paused and eyed the centaur coolly. Alusair knew that a curt reply here might draw suspicion to the troops, so she stepped forward and spoke up. "We are moving past your forest on the way to Thesk. There we rendezvous with King Azoun of Cormyr to fight a barbarian incursion from the east."

The herald's sunburned face brightened visibly. "We hear much good about Azoun of Cormyr, even in this isolated part of Faerun." He dipped his standard twice in quick succession. It was obviously a signal to centaur troops waiting at the fringes of the forest, and many of the dwarves cast nervous glances at the tree line, waiting for an attack.

Torg, annoyed at Alusair for presuming to speak for him, moved next to the human princess and scowled at the herald. "Now that you know where we're headed, can we be on our way? We stayed out of your woods, so we expect you to leave us alone."

The herald's face betrayed his confusion. "We do not intend to delay your troops, Ironlord. We know how urgently the humans in Thesk need your assistance. But are you not ready to camp for the night?"

"We haven't decided that yet," Torg snapped. He glanced at his standard-bearer and muttered something in Dwarvish. Before the young dwarf could send the signal for the new orders, Torg grabbed the standard's pole and held it straight.

Alusair was stewing quietly about the ironlord's foolish antipathy toward the centaur. She noted that Torg was staring past the herald and turned to see for herself what attracted his attention so fully. There, charging across the field, was a group of four more centaurs.

"Is this some kind of trick?" Torg growled.

The herald swished his tail around his chestnut-brown rump to chase away a horsefly that had settled there. Turning at the waist, he glanced behind him, then looked back at the ironlord. "No. That is our tribal leader. He simply wishes to meet you before you move on."

Torg grumbled a curse in Dwarvish, then let go of the standard. He nodded curtly to the standard-bearer, who signaled the rest of the army to lower their weapons. The army slowly but steadily broke into small groups and started to set up their tents. Alusair and two guards stayed by Torg. The princess thanked whatever god gave Torg enough sense not to openly insult the chieftain of Lethyr's centaurs by meeting him with loaded weapons.

As the four centaurs got closer, Alusair saw that three of them were armed. Whereas the herald carried the tall standard of his tribe, the chieftain's escort hefted long lances. The leader of the centaurs had no weapons himself, but wore a vest of treated animal skins and a broad black belt with a pouch around his waist. A long, thin rod of silver, wrapped with thick twine in the middle, hung from the belt, too.

"Hail, Ironlord of Earthfast," the centaur chieftain said brightly and clattered to a stop. Alusair, who was herself only average height for a human, noted with some amusement that the man-horses from Lethyr were almost twice as tall as Torg and his soldiers. The grass, which came to the dwarves' waists, climbed only a little way up the centaurs' legs.

Torg gave the chieftain a formal, if rather cold, greeting, and the centaur introduced himself as Jad Eyesbright. Before the dwarven lord could say anything in reply, a beautiful falcon dove out of the darkening sky and skimmed the grass a few yards ahead of the ironlord. Alusair held her breath and found her eyes riveted to the beautiful black, gray, and white predator. Torg, too, watched the graceful bird as it gyred back up in the purple evening sky.

The centaur chieftain noted the looks on Torg's and Alusair's faces, then smiled. "You have an appreciation for birds of prey," he noted. "That is good. They are beautiful creatures. That one serves our tribe." He pointed to the falcon as it wheeled above the army.

"It's been following us," Alusair said, her eyes still on the falcon. She let her gaze drift to the centaurs and added, "I noticed it, and another falcon, circling the camp. I thought they followed us for the small birds we frightened into the open."

Jad Eyesbright shook a lock of his long black hair out of his eyes. He thrust his distinctive, almost square chin forward a little as he studied Alusair closely. "Very observant," he said. "How do you know that bird was a falcon? Most humans simply call all raptors 'hawks.' "

"I grew up in a castle that had a very large mew, with hawks, falcons, and owls," the princess said. "I spent a lot of time with the falconers, learning about the birds." A happy memory of helping the hawkmaster train a young black hawk came unbidden to Alusair's mind, and a slight smile crept to her lips.

Torg crossed his arms and tapped his foot on the ground. Had the dwarf been in a close cave of stone, as he often was, his action would have loudly signaled his impatience. In the field, the ironlord's steel-shod boot thudded dully and almost silently against the fertile earth.

Jad Eyesbright had launched into an animated discussion of birds of prey with Princess Alusair, so he missed Torg's none-too-subtle expression of annoyance. The herald, however, did not. The brown-haired centaur cleared his throat noisily, producing a sound much like a whinny.

"The ironlord has been marching all day, Chieftain," the centaur herald said, bowing his head slightly. "Perhaps it would be best—"

"How thoughtless of me!" Jad Eyesbright exclaimed, tossing his hands into the air. He nodded to Torg. "Forgive me, Ironlord. You must want to rest."

Torg stopped tapping his foot. "Indeed," he mumbled. "We have a long march tomorrow, so we'd best get some sleep." He glanced at Alusair, hoping she would agree. The princess, however, was too pleased to be talking to the centaurs to want the meeting to end so quickly. After days of the dwarves' silence, the garrulous centaurs were a most welcome change.

Jad grinned a broad, large-toothed smile. He pawed the ground with his front hooves and bowed slightly. "I'll have some fresh food sent out for your troops. I'm sure you're tired of rations of dried meat." He nodded to one of his escorts, who dashed back toward the forest. "Is there anything else you need?"

Torg, who really hadn't expected the centaur chieftain's generosity, stood fidgeting. "No," he said, a bit nonplussed. After dismissing his guards with a wave of his hand, Torg mumbled, "Come, Alusair. We have battle strategies to go over."

"Alusair?" Jad asked, tilting his head slightly as he looked at the princess. "The daughter of Azoun of Cormyr?"

Frowning slightly, Alusair nodded an affirmation.

"Well," Jad said happily, "we must have a talk. I've heard a great deal about you." The chieftain turned to his guards. "You may go. I'll stay here with Torg and the princess awhile." As the guards braced their lances and cantered about, preparing for the run back to the woods, Jad added, "And make sure that food I asked for gets out here quickly."

Torg sighed, resigning himself to having a guest in camp, at least for a short time. He, however, was going to beg out of entertaining the centaur. "I have things to see to, Chief," the dwarven king began.

Before Torg could add any embellishment to his excuse, Jad nodded and smiled. "Of course, Ironlord. No insult taken." The man-horse twisted at the waist and glanced at Alusair. "I hope, however, that the princess has time to talk."

"Certainly," Alusair said quickly. And a bit too enthusiastically, she noted with a twinge of guilt when she saw Torg furrow his brows. The feeling lasted only a second, as the seemingly endless days of silence with the dwarves pushed back into her consciousness.

Torg shuffled his feet uncomfortably for a moment, then bid Jad and Alusair good night and stalked off to his tent.

"Torg is everything I'd been led to believe," Jad said, his

voice lowered to a conspiratorial whisper. He looked at Alusair, gauging her reaction. His tail twitched nervously behind him.

The princess smothered a short laugh. "And more, I'm sure," she noted, her voice lowered to match the chief's. After pausing for an instant, Alusair tilted her head. "You've 'heard' quite a lot for someone living in a rather isolated part of the world."

For a moment, Jad Eyesbright was silent. He removed a large brown glove that hung at his belt and slid it over his left hand. When the glove was in place, he said, "Information is easy to come by. We stop many travelers in and around the forest, and some of them are friendly enough to tell us the news in Faerun." He motioned toward the ground with his empty right hand.

Alusair understood the gesture and nodded. She took a seat as Jad folded his beautifully muscled black legs under him. The centaur sat with a slight grunt, then squirmed for a moment to get comfortable. "I've heard a great deal about your father from various mercenaries and traders, the same folk who warned me about King Torg's short temper and distrust of anything non-dwarven," the centaur explained casually.

Alusair swatted away a bug. "And me?" she asked.

"Bounty hunters spoke of you most frequently," the chieftain replied. He paused again, then lifted his left hand. Putting his right hand to his mouth, Jad whistled. Alusair started, and two dwarven sentries stationed nearby came running at a trot.

"Oh, dear," Jad said when he noticed them coming toward him. "You'd best tell them there's nothing—"

Before the centaur chieftain could finish his sentence, the falcon arced down from the twilight and swooped onto his gloved, outstretched left hand. Alusair said a few words in Dwarvish. The two sentries silently returned to their posts, pushing through the tall grass.

As Jad grabbed the jesses attached to the bird's legs, the falcon tightened its grip on the glove. The centaur deftly snatched the leather straps with his right hand and slid them into the grip of his left. The bird's sharp talons bit into the leather glove, and it squeaked a short, piercing note. "Yes, yes," Jad said paternally, moving his face close to the falcon's. "You've done your job well." He pulled a small piece of food from his pouch and fed it to the bird.

"He's very beautiful," Alusair said. She studied the falcon's plumage—its darkly hooded head and yellow legs. "A peregrine, if I know my hunting birds."

Jad nodded appreciatively. "Right again, Princess," he chimed.

"And you can communicate with him somehow, if he's been spying for you."

The centaur chieftain held up his right hand. For the first time, Alusair noticed a thin silver bracelet around his wrist. "A present from a mage my tribe once helped. It has a spell on it that lets me talk to, even see through the eyes of, any bird I choose. With the bracelet and the falcons, I've been watching the dwarves for the last few days."

Alusair pulled up a thin stalk of grass and twirled it between her thumb and index finger. She watched the hawk's bright, steady eyes and wondered what it was like to see the world soar underneath as you lofted over trees and lakes and armies. "The freedom must be wonderful," she said after a while.

Jad only nodded. "But what of you, Princess?" he asked. "From the stories I'd heard, I didn't expect to find you going off to fight alongside your father." When Alusair paused and stopped twirling the grass, the centaur offered an apologetic smile. "Forgive me," he said sincerely. "I shouldn't pry."

Alusair smiled weakly, but the direct question had shocked her into uneasiness. "Now I see how you learn so much," she said, a bit sarcastically. "You interrogate anyone who'll talk to you." When she saw the pained expression on the chieftain's face, she added, "I never expected to be fighting beside my father either."

Relief spread over Jad's face. He reached into his bag and pulled out a small leather hood, decorated with tiny gems. The precious stones reflected the last rays of the setting sun as the centaur held it out to the princess. "Could you help me with this?" he asked.

As Alusair carefully hooded the falcon for the night, Jad reached for the long piece of metal. "And this," he said when the hood was secure, "is his perch." The princess took the rod and bent it into a **U**. She stuck the ends into the ground, and Jad coaxed the falcon onto the twined area, where its talons could find a comfortable purchase.

The centaur rubbed his arms. "Much better," he sighed. "Now, where were we? Ah, yes, marching off to war."

Alusair and the chieftain talked casually for over an hour, until even the last, faint traces of the sun had disappeared in the western sky. The moon came out, trailed by the cluster of stars that always hung behind it in the sky. The bright orb of Selune lit up the field, casting a frosty radiance over the lines of tents and the dark outline of the forest. Jad's troops returned with baskets of nuts and berries and even some freshly baked bread. After taking a little for themselves, Jad and Alusair sent the rest of the food to Torg.

As the evening passed, the princess studied the dark-maned centaur chieftain. His friendly, sincere smile and captivatingly dark eyes seemed to reveal him as an honest, kindhearted soul. As they walked slowly around the camp's perimeter, Alusair found herself discussing much about her father and the upcoming battle, though she certainly never intended to do so. Jad, for his part, listened with interest, asking a few questions and relating the little he knew of the Tuigan.

Eventually the strain of the long day's march started to show on Alusair's face. "Perhaps you should get some rest," Jad told her after her third yawn in as many minutes.

The princess could only agree. "We do have a long march ahead of us. The spot on the Golden Way where we're meeting my father is some distance from here."

Jad tossed his head to again remove an unruly lock of hair from his eyes. "I have a wonderful idea," he said brightly. "I can offer Torg a guide, one who could take you through the forest. There are many more direct routes to your meeting place, and that will cut days off your trek."

Shaking her head, Alusair frowned slightly. "I don't think

so." She motioned to the forest. "Torg won't go through there, with or without a guide. I think it's a fine idea, too, but Torg simply won't see past his mistrust of, well, everything."

"We'll see about that," the centaur exclaimed. He trotted off, leaving Alusair to walk briskly in his wake just to catch up. She attempted to stop Jad, but he rushed down the lines of darkened tents toward the open central area. Once there, he easily spotted Torg's tent, larger than the others, with the standard of Earthfast posted at the door.

The guards wouldn't let the centaur enter, but Jad made enough of a racket to draw Torg out. When Alusair finally reached the ironlord's tent, a heated discussion was already underway.

"You're being a fool," the centaur said sharply. Jad pranced back and forth, towering over the dwarven king and his two guards. "I can help you."

Torg pushed the gold-bound black forks of his beard aside and folded his arms across his chest. "I've tried to be polite about this, centaur. Obviously that doesn't work." Spreading his feet apart a little, he said, "Let's try this, then: the dwarves of Earthfast don't need help from creatures like you."

Jad exhaled sharply, making a sound that reminded Alusair of nothing so much as a horse snorting angrily. She was angry herself as she moved to the centaur's side. "Why, Torg?" she asked. "The centaurs can make this journey easier for us, but you—"

"I won't have my troops allying with forest-bound riffraff like him," the ironlord growled, his face growing red beneath his beard.

Jad looked down at Alusair, then at Torg. "Race is no guide to character," he said, trying to subdue his anger. "I've known dwarves who were intelligent and wise. Nothing like you at all." Without another word, he reared on his hind legs and headed away from Torg at a canter.

"Wait!" Alusair called. She glanced over her shoulder at Torg. The ironlord was scowling into his beard, muttering something in Dwarvish. Alusair raced after the centaur

JAMES LOWDER

chieftain.

As she made her way to the edge of the camp, the princess saw the centaur in the bright moonlight. Jad kneeled where he'd set up the falcon's perch. He was struggling with the heavy leather glove when Alusair reached his side.

The centaur turned at her approach. "That—that—" Bowing his head, he breathed deeply. When Jad looked up again, Alusair saw that some calm was reflected in his eyes. "He's made me so angry I can't even talk!"

"I'm sorry," Alusair offered.

"It's not your place to apologize for Torg, Princess." The centaur glanced back toward the camp, then pulled on the leather hawking glove. "To be honest, I don't know why your father called on him for assistance."

"Father has stranger allies than the dwarves of Earthfast," Alusair mumbled, a little bitterness creeping into her voice.

"The orcs you told me about?" Jad asked as he attempted to nudge the drowsy falcon onto his gloved hand. The hawk cried out irritably, and the centaur paused. "Perhaps," he ventured. "Though I'd be willing to guess the King Azoun I've heard so much about had good reason for accepting their aid."

Alusair let the subject drop, more for the feeling of guilt that was beginning to plague her than for any disagreement with Jad's observations. This latest, most puzzling display of Torg's narrow-mindedness was weighing upon her heavily. "I'm just sorry Torg wouldn't allow you to help us," she said after a moment.

Jad snorted. "When I offered the guide to him, the buffoon asked why we weren't coming along to fight. I told him that we're obligated to protect the forest, that we couldn't just leave. Anyway, we'll be here to help if the battle ranges this far west. And I offered supplies, too."

"And he wouldn't hear of it," Alusair concluded.

"Worse still," Jad said, the anger rising in his voice again. "he insulted me, said that I was just laying a trap for them, that I was probably allied with elves or orcs or worse." He clenched his fists and tried to relax.

Alusair rested a hand on the centaur's arm. "I'll tell Azoun of your generosity, Jad," she said. "I'm sure he'll appreciate the offer."

The chieftain looked down at the falcon, which was fidgeting nervously on its perch. "Perhaps there is something I can do to help," he said. He smiled and added, "but I'm sure Torg will think I'm doing it to spy on you."

"You can't give me the hawk." Alusair motioned toward the bird. "You need it to patrol your borders."

"Not really," Jad said, handing the hawking glove to the princess. "We know the woods better than anyone, so it's easy for us to creep close to camps and spy."

When Alusair hesitated, Jad pushed the glove toward her. Eventually he took her hand in his own and placed the leather glove in her fingers. Finally, he unclasped the thin silver bracelet and put it around Alusair's wrist. It was much looser on her arm than it had been on Jad's thick wrist; Alusair held her arm high, and the silver ring slid halfway to her elbow.

Jad briefly explained how the bracelet worked. All Alusair had to do was concentrate on a particular bird, and the bracelet would allow her to see through its eyes for as long as she wanted. The chieftain then added a few cautions about delving too deeply into any bird's mind, and the lesson was over. The princess listened, but her eyes wandered often to the peregrine, now sitting comfortably on the perch, its head tucked down for sleep.

"And I'll expect the bracelet and the falcon returned after you take care of the barbarians," Jad noted, only half in jest. Alusair agreed, and with little further ado, the centaur stood. "My regards to your father," he said as he turned to go. "I hope to meet him someday."

Alusair watched sadly as the centaur chieftain galloped toward the forest. Though the moonlight was bright, she lost sight of Jad Eyesbright in the tall grass long before he reached the tree line. However, even after she could no longer see the centaur, Alusair stood in the field, studying the dark, uneven edge of Lethyr Forest. After a while, she looked around at the silent rows of tents in the dark dwarven camp.

Quickly she coaxed the falcon onto her gloved hand and pulled up his perch. The bird cried noisily, but the unnerving sound was music to Alusair. By the time she headed for her tent, the princess was already anxious for tomorrow to dawn so she could let the falcon soar. The bird shrieked again, and a dwarven sentry frowned at the peregrine as Alusair carried it past. It was clear that the dour soldiers from Earthfast would not appreciate the centaur chieftain's gift.

The princess smiled when she realized they wouldn't.

- 11 -

Speaking in Tongues

The gentle rhythm of the rain on the tent's roof and sides was interrupted by a sharp wind, then the steady, soothing noise continued. Stroking his beard, which he believed was grayer now than when he'd received the letter from Torg four months past, King Azoun sighed. He stared at the jumble of words on the yellowed parchment before him for a moment, then sighed again. When he looked up, the king saw that both Thom Reaverson and Vangerdahast were deeply absorbed in their own work. The wizard was seated in a corner, under the glow of a lantern, while the bard sat directly across the table from Azoun. The lanterns did little to augment the weak daylight bleeding through the tent from the cloudy day outside.

"Are you sure there's no spell you can cast that will allow me to learn to speak Tuigan?" the king asked.

Vangerdahast looked up. "Eh?" he said wearily. A long scroll slid from his hands onto the tent's canvas floor. "No, Azoun, there's not. There's a spell that will allow *me* to speak with them, but that's all I can do. Actually, that should be enough. I can be a capable negotiator if the need arises."

A rather malicious smile crossed Azoun's lips, and he replied, "That's exactly why I'm trying to learn Tuigan—so the need won't arise."

Thom Reaverson stifled a chuckle. He glanced at Azoun, who was smiling, too, then returned his attention to the paper in front of him. Like Azoun, the bard-historian was reviewing a list of common Tuigan phrases, greetings and the like. The foreign words were rendered in Common, spelled phonetically so any westerner could learn them. Both he and Azoun were studying the language in the unlikely event that a diplomatic meeting could be arranged with Yamun Khahan and Vangerdahast's spells didn't work.

Noting the scowl that was slowly spreading over the wizard's wrinkled face, Azoun apologized. "Sorry to interrupt your work, Vangy. I didn't realize you were so wrapped up in those spells lists. I hope you're having more success than I am."

The royal magician rubbed his red eyes. "I should certainly hope so," he mumbled. He pushed the papers spread at his feet into a neat pile, then bent over and reached for the scroll on the floor. The wizard put his hand on his paunch and groaned slightly as he did so.

"This is not easy work," Vangerdahast noted when he'd recovered the scroll. "Each of the spellcasters in the army commands different spells. For the magic units to be of any use, I have to know their potential, know what incantation I can expect from each man and woman." He glanced at Thom, who was still slouched over the Tuigan vocabulary list. "And you, Master Bard. Are you finding the Tuigan tongue easier to glean than your king is?"

Tossing his black braid over his shoulder, the bard met Vangerdahast's gaze. "It's not *that* difficult," he said affably. He looked across the table at Azoun, who was watching him carefully. "Of course, I've had a little exposure to it before."

Azoun motioned to a thin, battered book that lay to his right on the table. "This was Thom's, remember? He'd read it—how many times?"

"Four," the bard answered.

"*Four* times," Azoun noted to Vangerdahast, holding up the appropriate number of fingers. "It's no wonder he's picking this up faster than I am." The king reached for the book and opened it to a random page. "Does Lord Rayburton have much to say about the Tuigan themselves, or did he just take notes on their language?"

Straightening in his seat, Thom said, "His comments on

their dress and the language notes he made are the only things of value. That's why I didn't bring the book to your attention earlier, milord. It's mostly filled with value judgments about the Tuigan's 'barbarism.' "

Azoun raised an eyebrow. "Does Rayburton depict the Tuigan as greater savages than the representative from Rashemen did during the council?"

"Yes, but what makes me doubt his word is the way he describes Shou Lung," the bard replied. "He calls the Shou savages, too, and we know that's not true."

Thom reached for the battered tome and searched for a specific illustration. "Still, Lord Rayburton was an adventurer—one of the first men to cross from the West to Shou Lung without magical aid," he explained as he leafed through the book. He paused and added, "There are some wonderful songs about him. I'll sing you one some time."

"The Tuigan," Vangerdahast prompted.

Thom found the page he was searching for and returned the book to Azoun. "Before Yamun Khahan, the steppe riders were only nomadic clans, far less organized than they are now. Still, from all I've heard, their basic culture has advanced little since Rayburton's time."

The illustration made Azoun gasp. There, in crude line drawings, was a depiction of a horsewarrior flaying a man alive. To the warrior's right, another soldier was slitting his horse's leg and drinking its blood. A line of sticks with heads impaled upon them served as a backdrop for the grisly scene. The king passed the book to the royal wizard, who only shrugged.

"Let's hope, for our emissaries' sake, that Rayburton and Fonjara Galth were exaggerating the Tuigan's cruelty," Vangerdahast noted as he stood and stretched.

The rain continued to beat a lulling rhythm on the canvas, a sound that was punctuated only by strong gusts of wind and the noise from the Alliance's camp. Azoun silently wondered if he had sent the envoys to their deaths. The thought pained him greatly, even though he knew that he and the whole crusading force were in great danger now.

The king and the Army of the Alliance had reached a suitable site for a camp along the Golden Way—as the frequently traveled trade route was called—three days earlier. The men had been exhausted after the slow, grueling march from Telflamm, so Azoun had let them rest for one day before he started drilling them. Trained soldiers and experienced mercenaries made up a portion of the army, so the generals didn't need to teach them how to march or handle a weapon. They did, however, need to break the soldiers into units of manageable size and make them familiar with the signals that would be used during the battle.

Any relief the men might have taken from a break in their march was mitigated by the news from the east. A steady stream of ragged refugees from Thesk had poured past the army all along their trek down the Golden Way. The hungry, exhausted farmers and wareless merchants told wildly varying stories. Some claimed that the Tuigan were bogged down in a battle far to the east, others cast nervous glances over their shoulders and said the horselords were only a day or so behind them. Soldiers from the broken armies of Thesk passed by, too. Some of them joined Azoun's forces. Most fled the plains for the relative safety of walled cities like Telflamm.

By the second day, Azoun had learned the true position of the Tuigan horde. A pair of scouts, Red Plumes from the city of Hillsfar, had dashed into the royal compound at the center of camp and blurted out a report. Tuigan scouts had been spotted to the east, not thirty miles from the Alliance's present position. Azoun had immediately contacted Alusair, but learned the dwarves were still at least two days away. The king then sent a pair of emissaries—a Cormyrian captain to assess the Tuigan's battle strength and a soldier from Thesk who could speak the horsewarriors' hard, guttural language—to meet with the barbarians.

Now, one day later, Azoun awaited word from these messengers and hoped the Tuigan would slow their advance long enough for Torg's troops to join the rest of the army.

A trumpet blast signaling the return of some scouts broke the reverie in the tent. Vangerdahast stuffed his lists of spells into a polished leather pouch and slung it over his shoulder. "It must be getting close to eveningfeast," he said wearily. "I'm going back to my tent to make a few notes before we eat." The wizard nodded at Thom and added, "Keep him at the Tuigan lessons. I know from experience that he's a slacker when it comes to studying."

Thom laughed at the barb, for it was easy to see that the wizard's comment was only a jest. Azoun was renowned as a great scholar, and the bard's own presence at court, along with a number of sculptors, musicians, and other artists, testified to the king's love of the arts.

Squinting against the rain, the wizard ducked out of the Royal Pavilion and made his way across the muddy ground to his own dwelling. Brunthar Elventree, the dalesman who commanded the archers, was hurrying through the compound, too, his head bowed against the rain. "Any problem with the orcs?" the wizard asked loudly.

The rain-soaked dalesman stopped, wiped the wet red hair out of his eyes, then nodded to the royal magician. "Well met, Vangerdahast," he said apologetically. "I didn't—"

The wizard scowled and hugged his pouch tighter to his side. "Forget the greeting," he said coldly. "Just answer my question before I drown." The dalesman had grown a little more respectful of Azoun's position during the march through Thesk, but Vangerdahast still saw him as a brash upstart.

Brunthar shook his head, sending beads of water sailing from his hair. "No. No trouble with the orcs since last night. We've put—"

Nodding and motioning for the man to go on his way, Vangerdahast muttered, "Fine, thank you," and continued toward his tent. He breathed a sigh of relief through his sodden beard, thanking the gods for small favors.

As Azoun and Vangerdahast had expected, the human troops did not accept the Zhentish orcs any more readily than the dwarves had. The Cormyrian soldier who'd been hanged outside of Telflamm for killing a fellow crusader had served as adequate warning against violence for most of the troops. And though insults and cruel, even dangerous practical jokes were often hurled at the orcs, no one had seemed intent on starting a fight with them—until last night.

The fistfight had been only one of a half-dozen in camp that evening. Word of the Tuigan's proximity and the delay of the dwarven troops had put everyone on edge. But while most of the scuffles were easily settled, swords had been drawn at the edge of the orcs' ring of tents, and it took Azoun himself to avert bloodshed.

"We should probably just let them kill each other and go home before the barbarians get here," Vangerdahast muttered to himself as reached his tent. The guard stationed outside, his surcoat soaked onto his armor, gave the wizard a short bow. Vangerdahast returned it perfunctorily and ducked inside.

The tent was dark and musty. Vangerdahast recalled a spell that would kindle a warm light, but quickly dismissed it. The Tuigan might attack at any time, so every spell, no matter how simple, might prove useful. With a string of grumbled expletives, the wizard dumped his pouch onto his cot and fumbled with a tinderbox. After lighting the lantern that hung from the tent's center support, he shucked off his wet robe.

The lantern spread a weak light through the tent, revealing a huge assortment of books, scrolls, and other, more curious items. A live hedgehog lay sleeping in a large glass jar, which itself was bumped up against a box of dragon scales of various colors. Oils and liquids stood in neat rows, their tightly stoppered containers clearly labeled. Mortars and pestals were stored neatly in one corner, next to a large shelf filled with spellbooks. In short, the tent was incredibly organized for the amount of material it held.

But then, that was Vangerdahast's way. He hated clutter and confusion. "An untidy room is the sign of a sloppy mind," he always said. "And people with sloppy minds can't be trusted in a pinch." That saying applied to the fabled mage, Elminster of Shadowdale, too. Vangerdahast had visited the ancient sorcerer's home many times. He was always astounded to find the place in utter disarray—though Elminster claimed to know where every item was.

Vangerdahast doubted that the Sage of Shadowdale even

knew *what* every item in the cluttered tower was, let alone its location.

As he glanced around the tent, the royal mage thought of Elminster, then cursed again. "I wish *ye* were in this gods-forsaken place instead of me," he muttered, using the dialect Elminster favored. Vangerdahast talked to himself quite often when he was alone. It was a habit he'd picked up in his sixty-odd years of magical research, conducted largely in isolation.

That habit did not reflect a deteriorating mind, however. For a man of almost eighty years, Vangerdahast was in good shape, both mentally and physically. An occasional spell had bolstered his health and perhaps added a few years to his life, but all in all the royal wizard was as fit as most men half his age. His weight was a bit of a problem, to be sure, but his paunch had been the result of too little physical activity, not too much wild living.

With a heavy sigh, Vangerdahast folded his robe and placed it neatly on a chair to dry. He then picked up his satchel and removed the lists of spells the army's mages knew. After placing the papers in a small steel box, protected by wards in case a spy should attempt to open it or even move it, the wizard pulled a dry robe from a chest and shrugged it on. For a moment, he considered contacting Fonjara Galth, the representative from Rashemen, but decided against it. Her country was almost three hundred miles to the east, now well behind the Tuigan's front rank. The special powder the witch had left for contacting her would be wasted if used to gather information that might prove inconsequential to the Alliance's current predicament.

"There are other letters to be sent!" Vangerdahast said a little too loudly. His voice filled the tent and surprised him a bit. He smiled sheepishly, straightened his robe, and went to the small table set up next to his bed. After opening a pen case and a jar of ink, the wizard located a piece of fresh parchment and set to work.

To Queen Filfaeril of Cormyr, the note began. *We are now camped in Thesk, part way between the free city of*

Telflamm and the Theskan city of Tammar. We have encountered the enemy through scouts. Emissaries have been dispatched to the Tuigan camp, and we now await their return.

Again a trumpet sounded over the camp, and Vangerdahast looked up reflexively. Just another scout returning, he decided. Frowning, the wizard turned back to the letter.

The army is tense, but in relatively good spirits. The orcs I mentioned in my last missive have caused little trouble with the troops, but they are scarcely welcome. They keep to themselves at the edge of the main encampment, and most of the men have yet to see them but from afar. King Torg still has not arrived with his dwarves.

The wizard paused and considered his next comment carefully. After tapping the pen against his lips, he nodded and added, *The princess was possessed of better spirits when we spoke to her last. I am unsure of the reason, but I think something occurred on the march that has changed her perception of the ironlord. For this, both Azoun and I are glad.*

After rereading what he had written, Vangerdahast gently scattered pinches of fine sand on the paper to dry the ink. After a moment, he composed two more short paragraphs.

Not surprisingly, the king looks forward to the conflict with the khahan. The refugees sadden and anger him, and seeing them drives him on. He has infected some of the men with his cause, too. An army might yet be forged out of these varied mercenaries and farmhands.

Azoun has surprised me more than once on this crusade—as he did the princess in the dwarves' camp, I'm certain. I pray to Tempus, God of War, that he has a few surprises left.

After signing the letter "Your Obedient Servant," the royal wizard again sanded the letter to dry the flowing, ornate script. He deftly rolled the parchment thin and enclosed it in a bone-white metal tube. "Guard!" he called sharply.

There was no answer. No doubt, the wizard concluded with a chuckle, the boy thinks I'm just talking to myself. He had to yell twice more to get the rain-soaked sentry's attention.

"Take this to the king, and ask him if he has any messages going back to Suzail. If not, bring the tube back to me so I can seal it." Vangerdahast handed the sniffling guard the container and dismissed him.

This was the fourth note Vangerdahast had sent to Queen Filfaeril since the army left Telflamm, almost a month past. Like all other "wasteful magic," spells of communication were forbidden unless used in emergencies. Still, the wizard had promised to stay in contact with the queen and keep her updated on the crusade. Vangerdahast abhorred calling them reports, and he used any other word but that to describe them—missives, notes, letters, even dispatches. In fact, the communiques *were* reports, and Azoun kidded his friend about them constantly.

For the king knew that his wife had requested Vangerdahast to send updates to her regularly; Filfaeril herself had told him. It wasn't that she didn't trust Azoun to contact her himself—which he did at least once a tenday—nor did she think he might not tell her everything. Indeed, the queen knew Azoun would never lie to her. It was just that she realized that the king's letters would be far from objective, simply because Azoun himself found it difficult to be objective. Vangerdahast, she knew, would be painfully honest in assessing the crusaders' situation.

The latest dispatch sent, Vangerdahast lay down to relax for a few minutes before the evening meal was announced. His eyes were just fluttering closed when a commotion outside his tent startled him awake.

"Gather the generals!" someone yelled.

"Is the king in his tent?"

The sound of men splashing across the muddy compound was punctuated by other shouts. Vangerdahast had just sat up, his mind still half-clouded with sleep, when Thom Reaverson burst into the tent. The bard's homespun tunic was only spattered with rain, an indication of the speed with which he'd crossed from Azoun's tent to the wizard's.

"One of the emissaries is back," Thom gasped.

"One?" Vangerdahast asked as he stood up, rubbing his eyes. "Where's the other?"

The bard frowned. "Dead. The khahan killed him this morning, right after our men reached the Tuigan camp."

Vangerdahast paused for an instant, then put his hand to his forehead. Waking so suddenly and to such tumult had brought on a throbbing headache. Ignoring the pain as best he could, the wizard followed Thom back to the king's pavilion, where the generals had already gathered to hear the report.

The surviving scout—a Cormyrian captain—sat at the center of the tent, surrounded by Azoun, Farl Bloodaxe, Brunthar Elventree, and Lord Harcourt. A cleric was examining some lacerations on the soldier's forehead, but the captain continued to speak as salves were dabbed into his wounds and bandages wrapped around his head.

"They're monsters, Your Highness," he said just as Thom entered the tent with Vangerdahast. The captain glanced around nervously. "When we met their scouts, Kyrok—that's the Theskan you sent with me—he told them we were delivering a message to their leader. They laughed, but took us into their camp."

The cleric handed the soldier a vial of pale amber liquid to drink, which he did quickly. Without another pause, he continued his report in an excited tone. He told a grim tale of how Yamun Khahan, whom he depicted as little more than a raving madman, treated the emissaries with scorn. And when the Theskan soldier had refused to drink a sour-smelling, milky white liquid, fearing poison, the khahan and his generals had grown furious. The Theskan was beheaded on the spot.

"One of the Red Wizards from Thay was at the meeting. The khahan's historian and his generals, too," the soldier noted hurriedly. "They were all savages." He bowed his head. "I'm sorry to have failed you, Your Highness. I think the only reason they let me live was to deliver that message."

"And their troop strength?" Azoun asked softly.

The soldier shrugged. "At least one hundred thousand. Probably more. Their scouts took us straight to the khahan, and we didn't really see all that much of the camp."

After a brief silence, Azoun dismissed the wounded sol-

dier and the cleric. The generals scattered to various seats
throughout the pavilion, while Thom took up his customary
observer position near the door.

"Sorry I was late, Your Highness. Did the khahan send any
message back with the captain?" Vangerdahast asked after
everyone had settled down.

The wizard noted the frowns that quickly took root on
the faces of the other military leaders. Azoun caught
Vangerdahast's eyes with his own and held the wizard's
gaze for an instant. That was long enough for Vangerdahast
to guess what the khahan wanted—and what the king's reply would be.

"The captain gave me the message before you arrived,
Vangy. Yamun Khahan wants me to come to his camp."
Azoun laced his fingers together before him and paced
around the tent. "He promises my safety and says that the
only way to avoid 'the utter slaughter of my armies and the
destruction of my lands' is to meet with him in person."

Vangerdahast frowned now, too, though his expression
was deeper and more pained than the other generals'. For
an instant, he considered taking back the kind things he'd
said about Azoun in his letter to Filfaeril, then dismissed the
idea as petty. "And you're going."

This last wasn't so much a question as a statement. Everyone in the pavilion had served with King Azoun long enough
to know that he would accept Yamun Khahan's invitation.

* * * * *

The rain stopped some time during the night, and early
the next morning, over the objections of all his advisors,
King Azoun set out for the enemy's camp. He knew he'd be
in danger, but that was of little concern. He'd never have
proposed the crusade if he feared death. No, Azoun realized
that this was the last peaceful alternative to open conflict in
his dealings with the khahan.

The king was realist enough to know that a friendly outcome to the meeting was unlikely. All he really hoped was
that Vangerdahast could keep him safe with magic so he

could stall the Tuigan horde for one more day. With any delay, Torg's dwarves might have a chance to finally join up with the rest of the Alliance. The king realized, in the battle that was almost sure to begin before the tenday was out, he'd need all the support he could muster.

Vangerdahast, Thom Reaverson, and an elite guard of fifty men rode with the king, most on horses borrowed from Lord Harcourt's cavalry. The handpicked soldiers all wore plate armor and silk surcoats bearing the purple dragon. They passed quietly through the jumble of tents, cookfires, and corrals of horses that made up the Alliance's camp. Cormyrian soldiers rushed to see their king, bowing low as he passed. The dalesmen and mercenaries saluted their commander, but thought it silly to bow.

As Azoun reached the outskirts of the main camp, Vrakk rushed in front of the procession. The leader of the orcs was followed by a dozen or so pig-snouted Zhentish troopers. "We go with you, Ak-soon," Vrakk called, pounding a hand on his muscular, black-armored chest.

Vangerdahast opened his mouth to speak, but Azoun cut him off.

"Thank you for your offer, Commander Vrakk," the king said, loud enough for the humans who were gathering nearby to hear. He paused for an uncomfortable instant, looking for a reason to politely reject the orc's offer. "But I need you to stand guard here, in case the horsewarriors plan a sneak attack while I'm away."

Vrakk closed one eye and squinted up at the king. "OK, Ak-soon. We wait here." He stepped aside for the procession, which quickly went on its way. The king nodded to the orcish leader as he passed.

Azoun admired the orcs' bravery, for few men had seemed happy to accompany him on this most dangerous journey. However, the king was adept enough as a statesman to realize the unpolished orcs might open a conflict in the Tuigan camp merely by being there. If Yamun and his men were anything like Torg—or even Azoun's own troops—Vrakk would start a battle simply by being orcish.

Once the procession left the main area of the camp, which

ended with the orcs' circle of tents, they passed into the squalid grounds held by the refugees and lowlifes who had attached themselves to the army. Any large collection of soldiers attracted a certain number of prostitutes, black marketeers, and con men. Armies also drew a small contingent of camp followers—unemployed men looking to earn a few coppers in the service of a knight or young boys hoping to sneak into the ranks and find adventure. While the collection of people swarming around the army contained many of these types, it was largely made up of frightened, displaced farmers and merchants.

The sight of the men, women, and children huddled inside makeshift tents or sprawled in the open, exposed to the elements, brought a pall over Azoun's soul. He had ordered his officers to begin a charity for the poor, homeless wretches, but it was clear from the multitude the procession passed that any meager collection from the soldiers could do little to help. Even the defeat of the Tuigan horde would do nothing to bring back these people's homes and loved ones.

"It's a sad sight," someone said to Azoun.

The king turned sharply and saw Thom Reaverson at his side. The sadness on the bard's face mirrored the sick feeling in Azoun's heart. "I came out here two nights ago to tell the refugees a few stories. Just to take their minds off everything. They are glad you're here, milord. You're a hero to them."

That comment gave the king no comfort. He saw the pain and suffering around him now, and it hurt him to know that he could do little for the refugees. "The war won't help these people," he said softly, glancing from dirty face to dirty face in the crowd.

Thom nodded in agreement. "No, probably not. But if you didn't lead us here, there'd be a lot more like them come fall, after the Tuigan had stormed over the rest of Thesk."

When Azoun didn't answer, Thom reined his horse and let the king pace ahead. It was obvious that he wanted to be alone with his thoughts. Azoun did mull over the sights in the refugee camp, thinking about how little it mattered to him that these people were not his subjects. Then he pictured similar scenes in Cormyr, in Suzail itself, with the last of his army holed up in the castle while the city's inhabitants cowered in the courtyard, begging for protection.

The king's heart flared with anger, and he suddenly wanted nothing more than to be face-to-face, sword-to-sword with the khahan. No, I can't really help the people already victimized by the horsewarriors, Azoun decided. But Thom's right: I can stop the Tuigan from harming anyone else.

That thought fueled the fire in Azoun's heart as he spurred his horse and set a grueling pace for the other riders. The procession was soon beyond the boundaries of even the refugee camp and traveling swiftly down the Golden Way. The trade road over which much of Thesk's wealth moved was a broad path of dirt, worn smooth by frequent use. Though they passed many others on their way to the Tuigan camp, Azoun and his entourage were the only people heading east. Still more refugees trudged down the road or through the huge, rolling fields of recently sown wheat.

From the estimates given him by the emissary who'd survived his trip to the camp, Azoun figured he and his companions would be riding much of the day at a hard pace to reach the Tuigan. However, after only an hour on the road, the king noted that the flood of refugees had thinned to a trickle. By highsun, a party of eleven Tuigan appeared on the road ahead.

Without delay, Vangerdahast, who was saddle-sore and grouchy, cast the spell that would allow him to understand and converse in the Tuigan tongue. Both Thom and Azoun brought the words for a standard Tuigan greeting to mind in case the wizard had trouble. The soldiers all drew their swords.

As he got closer, Azoun saw that the group of horsewarriors blocking the road was made up of ten soldiers, all wearing black quilted armor, muddy boots, and pointed, fur-trimmed caps topped with long, stringy red tassels. They seemed not to notice the hot, Flamerule sun beating down on them through the clouds. The eleventh man was gaunt and bald, with facial features far less severe than the butter-skinned nomads who gathered around him. The bald man smiled amiably and slipped from his saddle when the king got within a dozen yards.

"Greetings, Azoun, king of Cormyr," he said in heavily accented Common. "I am here as the mouth of Yamun Khahan, Illustrious Emperor of All Peoples. Hear my words as his." He then bowed to Azoun, which drew scowls from his companions.

Thanking the gods that he didn't have to test his feeble grasp of Tuigan just yet, the Cormyrian king nodded in reply to the emissary's bow. He glanced at the dark-eyed Tuigan soldiers, feeling the anger that had flared to life in the refugee camp burn within him. "Where is your master?" he asked coldly.

The bald man started back for his horse. "Yamun Khahan waits for us. He invites you to the camp under his protection."

"And my guards?"

"Are welcome, too," the emissary replied, making a broad, sweeping gesture with his hand. "The khahan assumed you would bring an escort. You are, after all, a great leader of soldiers." He wheeled his horse about and pointed to the east. "Our camp is not far away. Please follow me, Your Highness."

Azoun hesitated for an instant, then urged his horse on. Vangerdahast and Thom fell in behind the king, and the Cormyrian guards spread out to encircle all three men. The ten black-garbed Tuigan soldiers split into two groups after the westerners had arrayed themselves. One group of five fell back and followed the entourage, the other rode just ahead of the bald emissary.

After half an hour of riding along the road, which became rutted and hilly as time went on, Azoun began to spot other groups of riders. These bands of men roamed far to the north and south of the road, through the fields and the occasional groups of trees that cut across the land. The king could see only their dark shapes, but he assumed they were Tuigan since the flow of refugees had stopped some time ago.

Azoun glanced back at Vangerdahast to ask the wizard a question. The paunchy old man was lolling slightly in his saddle, his eyelids fluttering. When Thom nudged the wizard, he cast watery, dull eyes on the king. "I'm not feeling very well at the moment," Vangerdahast noted softly. He shook his head as if to clear it, then added, "But I'm sure I'll be fine in a little bit. Just tired, I suppose."

A pall of smoke to the east became visible at about the same time Azoun spotted the other riders. From the blue-gray haze hanging low in the cloudy sky, the king realized that they were getting close to the Tuigan camp. After Azoun and his escort topped two more rises in the road, the huge collection of tents revealed itself to them.

The round, domelike tents lay scattered to either side of the road. Thousands of fires trailed thin wisps of smoke, which then joined together in the blue haze Azoun had spotted earlier. Wicker corrals of horses and sheep dotted the camp, spaced seemingly at random amidst the soldiers' quarters. Men lounged in groups or raced about on horses, the most activity seeming to center around a large white tent in the middle of the camp, right next to the road.

The bald emissary reined in his horse and waited for the king to reach his side before allowing the mount to move. "This is our camp, Azoun of Cormyr. Yamun Khahan waits for us here."

This was the first time the emissary had been close to Azoun, and the king could now see that he was not a Tuigan. Not only were his features less severe, but they seemed to mark the gaunt, bald man as a resident of the oriental lands. "How did you come to be the voice of the khahan?" Azoun asked after a moment. "You are not Tuigan."

"I was once a citizen of Khazari, a land now under the khahan's rule," the man said a little wistfully. "My name is Koja, and I am presently grand historian for Yamun Khahan." He bowed again in greeting. "The khahan sent me to meet you because I have seen you before, at the Council of Semphar. I was still an envoy from Prince Ogandi of Khazari then."

Azoun cast his mind back to the meeting that seemed to

signal the beginning of the problems with the Tuigan. Over a year ago, the countries of Faerun and of Kara-Tur had met in Semphar to discuss the Tuigan and their attacks on trade caravans crossing the steppes between the two great powers. There had been many nations represented at the council, and the eastern land of Khazari had claimed only a small voice in the proceedings.

Koja smiled warmly. "It is not surprising that you cannot remember me, Your Highness. I had very little to add to the discussions." He paused and motioned for the lead riders to move ahead to the camp. They set off at a gallop. "But I remembered you quite well. I even mentioned your speech at the council to the khahan when I first met him."

Azoun looked puzzled. "My speech?"

"Yes," Koja said. "You spoke after Chanar Khan interrupted the meeting. Chanar informed us all that the khahan demanded a tax on all caravans, that he wished to be recognized as sovereign over us all, but you told him—"

"—that Yamun Khahan could expect no gold from Cormyr," the king said, finishing Koja's recollection. "I bade the general inform the khahan that he did not rule the entire world."

"Yamun Khahan has not forgotten that," Koja said, a hint of a warning buried deep in his voice.

Azoun brought his horse to a stop. "Is that why my emissary was slain?" he snapped, his eyes growing hard. "Because of something I said a year past?"

"Of course not," Koja said quickly. He turned from the king and watched a group of forty or so soldiers race from the camp toward them. With a smile, he glanced at Azoun again and concluded, "Your emissary refused to honor our customs and insulted Yamun Khahan in his own tent. He was punished according to Tuigan law."

Vangerdahast, who had been napping in the saddle, snorted awake when the procession stopped. Thom held out a hand to steady the old man. "Vangy," he whispered. "Are you feeling all right?"

The old wizard motioned to the bard as if he were ready to reply. Suddenly his eyes rolled back in his head and he slumped from his horse to the ground, unconscious.

Azoun spun around in his saddle, and the Cormyrian guards all drew their swords. The western soldiers closed a tight circle around the king, but Koja, who had been trapped in the press with Azoun, shouted, "It's no use to fight. Hundreds of soldiers block the way back to your camp."

Thom looked up from the ground, where he cradled the fallen wizard in his arms, assuring the soldiers' horses did not trample the old man. "Vangy's alive," he called.

Azoun drew his own sword and pushed it close to Koja. "If you think this will stop the army, you're a fool."

The emissary reached out with an empty hand. "Please, Your Highness. You have the word of the khahan to insure your safety. Had I known the old one was a wizard, I could have warned you about this place."

The Cormyrian soldiers looked to Azoun, waiting for orders. The five black-garbed Tuigan still guarding the westerners had drawn their weapons, too. They sat atop their prancing horses, wide grins on their scarred faces. "What do you mean, *this place*?" the king asked sharply.

"We chose to camp here because it is like the Tuigan capital in the steppes, Quaraband. This place is magic-dead," Koja replied, gesturing with his empty hands. "The whole camp is located in an area where magic will not work. That is why the wizard is sick."

Glancing at the soldiers racing from the camp, Azoun realized that a fight would be out of the question. With Vangerdahast unable to cast spells of any kind, he and his men would be slaughtered. The king gritted his teeth and ordered his guards to lower their weapons.

Koja breathed an audible sigh of relief, then slid to the ground and helped Thom sling Vangerdahast onto a horse. "You are in no danger, Your Highness," he said, smiling sincerely. "The khahan is, if nothing else, a man of his word."

As they set out again toward the khahan's tent, this time surrounded by fifty guards, Azoun and Thom exchanged concerned glances. And though they couldn't know it, the same thought was running through each of their minds.

Both the bard and the king prayed silently that Lord Rayburton, who'd written that the Tuigan were uncompromising savages, had taken at least some literary license in his depiction of the horsewarriors.

– 12 –

Propaganda

More tea, Your Highness?"

Azoun nodded politely, and Koja refilled the king's cup with warm, salty tea. "I much prefer this brewed in the Shou style," the historian said casually. "They put dollops of butter in their brew."

"Actually," Azoun replied, "this is quite good." He brought the cup to his lips and took a small sip. *Not as appetizing as tea with milk and sugar,* he added silently, *but certainly not bad.*

The king and the Tuigan envoy sat on piles of brightly colored cushions in a large yurt—at least that was what Koja called the round Tuigan huts. Made mostly of felt, the tent was musty after the recent rains. The place was dark, too, as the only illumination came from a single lantern hanging from the center pole. Little decoration lightened the oppressive mood of the yurt, save for a few small felt idols that hung over the door.

"Are you sure Vangerdahast will be all right?" Azoun asked Koja. The king placed his cup on the dirty floor in front of him and leaned forward. It seemed that he was emphasizing his question with body language, but he was actually stretching out his sore back. The king wasn't used to sitting cross-legged on the ground for hours at a time, and his muscles were complaining.

"Yes, Your Highness," Koja replied calmly, though he'd answered this question for the king once before. "The sickness will pass, and when the wizard leaves the area, he'll be able to cast spells again."

Azoun sighed and leaned back with a short, almost silent groan. If Koja had heard him, the Khazari gave no indication of it. And, as it had many times in the last two hours, the yurt fell silent.

However, the king did not relax. The noise from the bustling camp outside the quiet, dark tent kept him on guard. The Tuigan soldiers' shouts and the clanging of weapons being forged and repaired reminded the Cormyrian king that he was still amongst the enemy.

Not that Azoun had been threatened since entering the Tuigan camp. On the contrary, Koja and the various Tuigan khans Azoun had met since arriving had treated him with respect, even deference. And while the king was led to the central yurt to await the khahan, tribal healers who wore masks of birds and beasts had taken Vangerdahast into their care. Because he'd been denied access to the khahan's yurt, Thom had gone with the wizard to keep an eye on things. Still, the king realized that much of the civility he saw from Koja was a show for his sake alone.

The bulk of the Tuigan army had greeted the king's procession with little regard and, in a few cases, open scorn. Most simply went about their business, cleaning weapons and tack, eating, or simply exchanging stories around the many smoky cookfires scattered through the camp. At least on the surface, the Tuigan camp was not all that different from the western one Azoun had recently left, and nothing like the horrifying place Lord Rayburton had described in his journals. Yet, the king was not foolish enough to assume that the many apparent similarities between his camp and the khahan's were anything other than superficial. Hundreds of details set the two camps apart, ranging in significance from the Tuigan's use of dung to stoke their acrid-smelling fires to the violent punishment the khans frequently and openly meted out to their soldiers.

The most important difference Azoun noted between his troops and the Tuigan army was a little harder to define, but it made the two camps seem very different indeed. From Rayburton's book, the king recognized a few of the hundreds of standards dotting the camp, rallying points for the various barbarian clans. Despite this obvious fragmentation, the Tuigan camp seemed unified, whereas the Alliance's camp was home to a loose confederation of troops. In Azoun's army, the orcs were not welcome in many places, the Sembians and mercenaries not welcome in others. Cormyrians fraternized with Cormyrians, dalesmen with dalesmen.

Unity of purpose and casual self-confidence permeated the Tuigan gathering. Why shouldn't it? Azoun mused as he finished his tea. Yamun Khahan has led this army to victory after victory.

The first substantial clouds of doubt rolled over the king's vision of the crusade as he pondered that thought. He was rubbing his chin, buried in contemplation of this, when the yurt's flap flew open, flooding the dim tent with light. Azoun found himself looking up at a broad-shouldered, heavily armored man.

Koja offered a brief greeting in Tuigan to the newcomer, then turned to Azoun. "Your Highness," he said with a slight smile, "this is Yamun Khahan, Illustrious Emperor of All Peoples."

Quickly Azoun got to his feet. The khahan studied the king for a moment, openly sizing up his opponent. He said something to Koja in Tuigan without taking his eyes from the Cormyrian king.

"The khahan wishes you to be seated," Koja said, motioning toward the cushions Azoun had just vacated. "This meeting will not take up much more of your time."

Azoun did as he was asked, but he wondered for a moment why the khahan had kept him waiting for nearly two hours. As the Tuigan leader made his way across the tent to a wooden seat, never taking his eyes off the king, Azoun decided that the wait, like this meeting, was some kind of test. He was certainly annoyed by the delay, but he refused to show the barbarian that he was at all put out.

Yamun silently took his seat. Azoun met the khahan's steady gaze now, and took the opportunity to size up his own opponent.

In the feeble light of the single lantern, Yamun Khahan looked ominous. His prominent, heavy cheekbones and broad, flat nose cast heavy shadows over the rest of his face. Despite these shadows, Azoun saw that a long, ragged scar ran across the bridge of the khahan's nose and over his cheek. Another scar, faded with age, bit into the corner of his mouth, twisting his upper lip into an almost perpetual sneer. The king met the warlord's eyes and found them dark and clear.

Long braids of red-tinted hair framed Yamun's shadowy visage and rested on his flaring silver shoulder guards. The silver ailettes topped a breastplate of gold, sculpted with muscles. At the khahan's waist, a skirt of silver chain mail hung, vaguely reflecting the lantern's glow. In opposition to this finery, the khahan's boots were heavy and worn. Mud clung to them in thick, wet globs, which occasionally slid onto the yurt's dirty, carpeted floor.

The khahan met Azoun's eyes again and smiled, though his twisted lip made the expression more threatening than inviting. He shouted something in Tuigan, and Azoun wished that he'd learned more of the guttural tongue or had his bard at his side.

Two other Tuigan entered the tent and took seats on the floor at either side of the khahan. From their armor and their bearing, Azoun assumed them to be generals. "This is Chanar Ong Kho, illustrious commander of the left flank," Koja announced formally. He gestured with an open hand to the man on Yamun's left.

Chanar Khan scowled at Azoun, then unslung a heavy skin from his shoulder and placed it at the khahan's feet. The king recognized the brash general as the same man who had interrupted the Council of Semphar and presented the khahan's demands to the delegates there. At that time, he had led ten thousand men. Azoun wondered how many more he had under his control now.

Koja motioned to the man on Yamun's right and added, "This is Batu Min Ho, illustrious commander of the right flank." This general immediately bowed to Azoun, dropping his head almost to the floor. When Batu Min Ho raised his face again, the king noticed that the general was, as his name suggested, a Shou. Like a Tuigan's, Batu's dark eyes were set wide over broad cheeks, and his nose was broad and flat. Still, there was a delicacy to his features lacking in both Chanar and Yamun.

"Tell the khahan and his generals that I am honored to meet them," Azoun said, returning Batu Min Ho's bow. "I have heard many great things about their military skill."

Koja repeated the king's words. Coarse, loud laughter burst from Chanar, and Batu simply nodded at the compliment. Yamun remained silent, but leaned forward, resting an elbow on his knee. The straps of his armor creaked with the effort. Slowly he pointed at Azoun and asked something in Tuigan.

The king understood a little of what the khahan said, but waited for Koja to repeat the question before answering. "Why do you think I invited you here?" the bald Khazari asked in Yamun's stead.

"So you could meet your adversary," Azoun replied. "To decide how much of a threat I am."

Yamun nodded when Koja relayed the answer. The warlord regarded the king for a moment, his eyes narrowed. "You know I outnumber you by three-, maybe four-to-one," he said through Koja.

Azoun simply nodded for an answer, and Yamun paused again. "The prisoners I have taken in Thesk warned me of your coming," the khahan growled. "They said you gathered a great army to crush me. What my scouts have seen of your troops makes me think that they are not great enough to even slow me down."

"We shall be able to tell that only if we fight," Azoun said, then turned to Koja. "Emphasize 'if' in that reply."

After taking a sip of his tea, the bald man nodded politely, then relayed the king's message. Chanar laughed again, but Yamun glowered at the khan, which silenced him almost instantly. "Then surrender to me now, Azoun of Cor-meer," Yamun answered, lounging back in his seat and tugging at the end of his stringy mustache. "That is the only thing that will stop me from destroying you in battle."

Koja had just begun to relay the khahan's words when Batu Min Ho leaned forward and spoke. The babble of voices confused Azoun a little. He caught only part of what the bald Khazari was reporting. Still, the king understood the Shou general's question without translation.

Stretching two empty hands before him, Azoun faced Batu Min Ho. "Yes, Batu Khan," he said in rough, halting Tuigan. "I seek peace."

Azoun's reply had a striking and immediate effect on the others in the khahan's yurt. Chanar leaped to his feet, his mouth hanging open in shock. Surprise registered on Batu's face, too, but the emotion did not show as readily on the Shou general. Glancing from the king to Yamun Khahan, then back to Azoun again, the Khazari historian seemed to be waiting for their reactions to determine his own.

For his part, Yamun slouched forward again. A slight smile battled with his scar for control of his lip. "You speak the language of my people," he said slowly.

"I speak only a little Tuigan," Azoun corrected, using the one Tuigan phrase he was certain he knew correctly, then switched back to Common. "Koja, I do need your help. I understand only some of what they're saying."

The Khazari sipped his tea and nodded. "What do you want to tell the khahan?"

"Repeat what I told you, then tell them that I hope we can avoid bloodshed."

As Koja relayed the message, Chanar sat down and said something to the khahan. Yamun's slight smile broadened into a leer as he picked up the leather bag Chanar had placed at his mud-caked feet. Unstoppering the bag, Yamun shouted out a command.

Two servants immediately entered the yurt, bowing to the khahan as they did so. Yamun mumbled another order, and the two young men scurried to the back of the felt tent and clattered through a chest. They returned with a bejeweled, golden goblet and a round ball of red silk.

Koja blanched noticeably, and Chanar pointed at the Khazari and laughed. The khahan handed the goblet to Batu, who upended the golden vessel, emptying some sludgy globs from its bottom. He then wiped it out with a bit of the heavy carpet that lay on the floor. Taking the leather bag from Yamun, a servant filled the goblet with a milky liquid.

The other servant unwrapped the stained silk and held the object the red cloth had covered out to Yamun. It was a human skull, the top of which had been cut away. A silver cup now filled the empty bones. The khahan held the grisly drinking vessel so that its empty eye sockets faced Azoun, and a servant filled it, too, with liquid from the leather bag.

Chanar Khan said something to Koja, and the bald man nodded. "Chanar Ong Kho wishes me to inform Your Highness that the skull once belonged to Abatai, an enemy of the khahan." The Khazari frowned and added, "Do not forget what I told you about your envoy, Your Highness. Failure to drink means certain death."

With mild surprise, the Cormyrian king noticed that Yamun and his generals were watching him closely. They are expecting to frighten me with the skull, Azoun realized, then noted that Koja was obviously unnerved by the grim trophy. Thanking the gods that the area was magic-dead, for it negated the possibility of the skull-cup being ensorceled, the king reached for it.

Before he leaned back and gnawed pensively on his lower lip, Yamun gave the skull-cup to the king. Batu called out a toast in Tuigan, or at least that was what Azoun assumed he cried, then gulped down the thick, sour-tasting drink. A servant refilled the bejeweled goblet Batu held, and it was passed to Chanar Khan. The smiling Tuigan general paused before lifting the golden goblet and motioned for Azoun to drink from the skull.

"'To Yamun Khahan," the king said, "Illustrious Emperor of the Tuigan." Though the milky white liquid in the skull-cup smelled disgustingly like curdled milk, Azoun gagged down two swallows and handed the skull to Koja.

A sour look on his face, the historian leaned close to Azoun. "The drink is called kumiss. It's made from fermented mare's milk." He shuddered and licked his lips. "Some men love it. I have yet to acquire even a tolerance for the nasty stuff."

Only after both Azoun and Koja had drunk did Chanar lift his goblet to salute Yamun. Through all of this, the khahan watched Azoun closely. Finally Yamun himself gulped down what was left of the kumiss in the skull-cup, then returned it to the servant. The two young men put Abatai's skull back in its wrappings of silk, returned it and the golden goblet to the chest, and hurried away.

Yamun asked Koja what the king had used as a toast. When the bald man told him, the khahan frowned. "I am emperor of *all* peoples, Azoun of Cor-meer," he rumbled. "I will prove that to you tomorrow when I empty out your skull and make it like Abatai's."

Hesitantly Koja relayed the statement. Azoun paused for a moment, then stood. "Tell your master that my troops will not surrender. Let your army meet us tomorrow, then. We will be waiting."

"Perhaps I should kill you now," Yamun replied. As Koja voiced the threat, Chanar reached for his curved sword.

Azoun wished in that instant for Vangerdahast to be well and at his side. He had only accepted the khahan's invitation because he believed the royal wizard could extricate him from a situation such as this one. He let that hope pass quickly, however, and steeled himself for his fate. "If you kill me here it is proof that you fear my armies."

Chanar and Batu both stood and drew their swords as soon as the historian had finished the reply. Scuttling backward like a crab, Koja hurried away from the circle of men. Yamun shouted, and ten of his black-armored guards entered the tent. The khahan remained seated; his face did not reveal any anger. He issued another order, and both of his generals spun around to look at him, surprise on their faces.

Immediately Batu Min Ho sheathed his sword and bowed to Yamun. The Shou glanced at Azoun as he made his way from the yurt, but said nothing more. Chanar Khan, however, rattled off a string of questions. The Tuigan general's face was red, and he gestured menacingly with his sword at Azoun.

With a grunt, Yamun finally raised himself from his throne and shouted at Chanar. The general bowed deeply, then backed out of the yurt. His face held an odd mixture of anger and contrition.

Koja stood, walked to the khahan's side, and asked him a question, too softly for Azoun to hear. Yamun leaned close to the Khazari and replied. The historian nodded, then faced Azoun. "The audience is over, Your Highness," he announced formally. "You may gather your men and leave. I will escort you away from our camp."

Azoun bowed stiffly to the khahan. Yamun nodded in reply, then said something to Koja. The bald historian smiled and whispered his answer to the warlord. Azoun waited politely, then followed the Khazari from the yurt. In turn, the king was followed by the ten black-garbed Tuigan soldiers. Within a few minutes, Thom, Vangerdahast, and the Cormyrian guards joined him, and they were quickly on their way out of the Tuigan camp.

The royal wizard was still unconscious, slung unceremoniously over his horse. Thom talked at length about the Tuigan shamans and the unusual rites they'd performed over Vangerdahast.

"The Tuigan stumbled across this magic-dead area a day or two ago," the bard said from horseback. "The wizards from Thay all left as soon as they'd learned the khahan intended to stay here until he met with you."

Koja, who rode on the opposite side of Azoun from Thom, nodded his agreement to the bard's statement, then noted, "Yamun does not trust sorcery, so he wasn't sorry that the Red Wizards went home." When he saw he had both Thom's and Azoun's attention, he added, "Magic has little place in Tuigan culture."

Azoun found it surprising that Koja would reveal that information to him, since he could certainly turn it to his army's advantage. Still, the Tuigan's confidence in the power of mundane swords and arrows was grounded in months of victory. The king knew that his wizards alone couldn't win the war for him.

By the time Azoun and his escort reached the spot where they'd first met Koja, the sun was low in the cloud-filled sky to the west.

"I am happy to have met you, Your Highness," Koja said, bowing in his saddle. "It is sad that we will not meet again in this world."

Azoun heard the sincerity in the Khazari's words and wondered how the obviously peaceful man found life with the Tuigan bearable. A bit sadly, the king returned the compliment, then turned to go. Before he got his horse pointed toward his camp, however, Azoun remembered a question that had been plaguing him since he'd left the khahan's yurt.

Wheeling his horse to face the historian, the king called out, "A moment, Koja. I have one last question for you. What did the khahan tell you after he'd dismissed the generals?"

The bald man maneuvered his horse and trotted it up to the king. "As I warned you, offering any insult to the khahan is death," the historian said simply. "I asked Yamun why he did not kill you for your insult."

"And his answer?"

"The khahan told me that what you said could not be an insult unless it proved to be true," Koja replied. He shrugged. "I don't understand the difference, but tomorrow the khahan intends to show he is no coward, that he does not fear your army."

With Koja's words echoing in his mind, Azoun reined in his horse and faced it back toward the west. Again, the king set a brisk pace along the Golden Way. All the way back to camp he wondered if the patchwork army that awaited his return could ever be a match for the horsewarriors.

* * * * *

Like most of the Army of the Alliance, Razor John waited anxiously for King Azoun to return from the Tuigan camp. With overworked, cramped fingers, he crafted arrows for the upcoming battle. That work couldn't keep his mind occupied, so he listened to the other weaponsmiths exchange rumors about the Tuigan camp.

"Well, I heard they sacrifice someone to their dark god every day at highsun," an arrowsmith said authoritatively. He looked up from the arrowhead he was fashioning and turned to the decrepit bowyer sitting next to him. "I heard that from the mouth of the Cormyrian captain who was in the Tuigan camp."

"Could be why they killed the three other envoys Azoun sent," the bowyer ventured casually without taking his eyes off the yew longbow he was finishing. The craftsman's hands shook, but from what John could see, the bow was expertly fashioned.

"I thought only two envoys went," John corrected. He took a finished arrowhead from a pile to his right and fastened it to a shaft.

The arrowsmith snorted. "Shows how much you know, fletcher. I bet you haven't even heard about the babies the barbarians had spitted on pikes."

Though he thought that particular rumor to be false, since from all reports the Tuigan didn't fight with pikes, Razor John decided to keep silent. He'd learned soon after joining the army that it was practically impossible to argue with a gossipmonger. Fact was something such men falsely cited so often that they couldn't recognize its true form even in the most simplistic of debates.

Shaking his head, the aged bowyer took out a long, heavy string of hemp and fitted it to the nocks at either end of the yew stave. "Them damned horsemen done far worse than killing infants when they overran Tammar." He tested the bow's pull and pretended to sight along an imaginary arrow. "I can't wait to get at those monsters."

The arrowsmith grunted his agreement, then continued to list the atrocities of which he'd heard the Tuigan accused. Many of the various grisly crimes were based upon the reports of "reliable men who'd been there when it happened." The most outrageous claims were mitigated by the fact that they came only second- or third-hand to the arrowsmith.

Tiring of his co-workers babble, John let his mind wander. Unsurprisingly, the first thing that pushed into his thoughts was Kiri. The fletcher had grown increasingly fond of the daughter of Borlander the Trollslayer as the days passed. Had the timing been better, he would even have considered asking her to marry him, but the chances of one of them dying on the crusade were too great to set any such plans before the end of the fighting.

Snatches of other conversations, the ones taking place between the various clutches of workmen preparing for the battle, intruded on John's contemplation of his future with Kiri. Fletchers, bowyers, and arrowsmiths surrounded Razor John almost completely, but the armorers and swordsmiths weren't so far away that he couldn't hear the ring of their hammers or smell the sharp smoke from their fires. He listened to the steady, clanging beat of hammers on hot metal and tried to let the familiar sound drown out all others. It was a warm late afternoon, even for the high summer month of Flamerule, and John was soon nodding off.

A rap on the shoulder brought the fletcher's mind back to his immediate surroundings. The arrowsmith and the bowyer were coughing hoarse, braying laughs, and a few of the other workmen had glanced at John.

"Did I wake you?" someone asked sweetly. John turned to find Kiri Trollslayer standing over him. Her hands planted firmly on her hips, the pretty soldier from Cormyr cocked her head and set her brown eyes on the fletcher's face.

Fumbling with a half-fletched arrow, John got to his feet. "N-No, Kiri. Just daydreaming." He glanced up at the darkening evening sky and amended that. "Well, twilight-dreaming, anyway. Aren't you supposed to be on sentry duty?"

With a laugh, Kiri hooked her arm in John's and took the arrow from his hand. "I have some interesting news," she said as she dropped the unfinished arrow to the ground. "The king is on his way back. He should be in camp by the time the stars are out."

She told John the news in a voice loud enough for the workmen around them to hear, but many had turned to watch Kiri anyway—there simply weren't as many female soldiers in camp as men. The area was soon abuzz with excited chatter.

"He had to fight his way out of the Tuigan camp, too," Kiri concluded, addressing the comment to anyone who was listening. She paused and crossed her arms over her sleeveless tunic, as if daring someone to contradict her.

"Aye?" the aged bowyer said. "Good thing the king has Master Vangerdahast along. The wizard probably cast a few fireballs, or maybe even a lightning bolt or two, to help them along." A chorus of agreement met that comment, and others suggested spells the royal magician had probably thrown during the fight.

"Where did you hear this, Kiri?" John asked sharply, turning her toward him with both hands.

Frowning, she pulled out of the fletcher's grasp. "A rider from the king's escort just returned," she snapped, annoyance clear in her voice. "He told one of the other soldiers on sentry duty."

With a groan, John put a hand to his forehead. "Just like the sentry I talked to after Mal's execution, right?"

Kiri scowled, and a look of genuine hurt filled her eyes. She knew the incident to which John referred quite well. He had talked to her about it a dozen times since it had occurred.

Azoun had ordered the entire army to witness Mal's execution on the day they left Telflamm. As John had stood with his fellow soldiers, watching the murderer dangle from a scaffold, a dalesman assigned to control the crowd had struck up a conversation. The dalesman had then proceeded to tell a wildly exaggerated version of the fight in the Broken Lance. The tale ended with something John still found absolutely astounding.

"And I heard from a friend," the dalesman had concluded, "that the Cormyrian had an accomplice, some cutthroat named Razor John. They say his sword's so sharp—like a razor, you know—that he cuts off heads with a single stroke."

Dumbfounded, the fletcher had simply nodded, then bid the dalesman good-day. On many occasions John had told Kiri the tale and never failed to mention how little he thought of gossips. Those frequent comments all came flooding back to Kiri as she stood before her friend.

"I'm only telling you what I heard," she said, a slight quaver in her voice.

With a frown at his own callousness, John rested his

hands gently on Kiri's shoulders and apologized. The news of Azoun's battle with the Tuigan was spreading like wildfire, from bowyer to armorer, blacksmith to fletcher, but John and Kiri let their conversation drift on to other topics. Still, it wasn't long before a soldier in chain mail, the star and shattered crown insignia of Archendale emblazoned on his white surcoat, dashed into the work area.

"The king is coming!" he shouted. "Down the Golden Way." He turned and dashed off to another section of the camp, sweat beading on his forehead in the warm air.

Workmen dropped their tools and immediately made their way to the broad road that intersected the camp. Thousands of soldiers and refugees already lined the trade road for well over a mile to the east. John and Kiri were content to stay far back from the press, even though they knew they had no chance of spotting the king from where they stood.

As he waited, John caught snatches of stories about the king's escape from the Tuigan camp as they circulated through the crowd. The speculation he'd heard from his co-workers about the spells Vangerdahast had cast in defense of the king was now stated as fact. More than once the fletcher felt tempted to offer a correction to an obvious falsehood, but restrained himself.

Soon cheering was heard from the east, and a new wave of rumors spread through the crowd. Vangerdahast, it seemed, was wounded. Some even claimed he was dead. In any case, the wizard wasn't moving. Enthusiastic plaudits for Azoun's heroic escape from the Tuigan camp were met and redoubled by condemnations of the khahan's savagery. By the time the king's banner reached the spot where John and Kiri stood, the Army of the Alliance was a cheering mob, swearing oaths to Tempus, the God of Battle, and pledging to fight by Azoun's side to the last soldier.

From his horse, the Cormyrian king looked out on the Army of the Alliance in amazement. Troops from Suzail stood side by side with Sembian mercenaries. Dalesmen thrust their swords into the air and swore oaths with Red Plumes from Hillsfar and militia from Ravens Bluff. Azoun even spotted some of Vrakk's orcs scattered in the mob, shouting and cheering along with the humans.

The king's guard spread out as the procession entered the camp, and Azoun made his way through the crowd to the royal compound. Thom followed as close behind as possible, leading Vangerdahast, still unconscious on his horse. The other three generals met them outside Azoun's tent.

Brunthar Elventree of the archers was already smiling when Azoun clapped him on the shoulder. "This is unbelievable," the king exclaimed to the dalesman, then glanced at the cheering crowd. "What forged the group of soldiers I left into an army in only one day?"

The king faced his cavalry commander, Lord Harcourt. Even though it was warm, the old Cormyrian nobleman still wore his heavy chain hauberk. Harcourt simply shrugged as a reply and continued stroking his sizable white mustache.

Carrying Vangerdahast between them, Farl Bloodaxe and Thom Reaverson broke into the scene. The wizard was mumbling in fits, but he was still obviously unconscious. The king's smile fled and was replaced by a concerned grimace. "He's better," Thom offered as they brought Vangerdahast into Azoun's tent, "but we should call for a healer."

After kneeling for a moment at his old friend's side, Azoun turned to Thom. "That's already been done. Will you watch him until the priest arrives?" When the bard nodded, the king motioned for General Bloodaxe to follow him from the tent.

Once outside, Azoun invited his generals to sit around a campfire, then he quickly explained what had transpired in the Tuigan camp. The cheers from the army had died down somewhat, but the men could still be heard alternatively praising Azoun and cursing the horsewarriors. Finally, the king looked to Farl. "Can you tell me what brought the men together like this?"

The ebony-skinned infantry commander drew his mouth into a hard line. "Rumor," he said, plucking nervously at the sleeve of his white shirt. "There are incredible stories circulating through camp, stories of how you were ambushed by the khahan and had to fight your way back."

Clearing his throat noisily, as he often did before speaking, Lord Harcourt added, "They've been telling wild tales about the Tuigan, too, don't you know." He twirled his mustache and frowned. "Some say they sacrifice babies and do horrible things to the women they capture. Nasty business. Even the nobles have been busy with the gossip."

Seeing the concern on Azoun's face, Brunthar Elventree leaned toward the king. "But the source doesn't matter so long as the effect is right," he noted brightly, the heat from the fire turning his face as red as his hair.

"Of course the source matters," Azoun snapped. "It's all a lie! The Tuigan aren't monsters, and I did not have to fight my way back to camp."

A few guards at the compound's edge looked toward the king, and Lord Harcourt cleared his throat again. "Your Highness," he began haltingly. "You may want to lower your voice a bit."

"Why?" both Azoun and Farl asked simultaneously.

Brunthar Elventree poked the fire, sending an angry shower of sparks into the night sky. "Because a word or two like that will shatter whatever spirit this army has mustered," he growled. "You might as well kill the men yourself if you demoralize them now."

Farl fell silent, but Lord Harcourt nodded his agreement. Turning from the fire, Azoun paused a moment to gather his shattered thoughts, then commenced pacing. After a few turns, the king faced the generals again.

"I did not fight a single Tuigan today, so the tales of heroism the troops are telling are lies," he said flatly. "Can you let that be the thing that unites them?" He allowed his gaze to drift slowly from Farl to Lord Harcourt to Brunthar.

It was the dalesman who spoke first. "They'll fight together now, Your Highness," he answered confidently, meeting the king's eyes. "And if they fight as a unified force, perhaps they won't have to die at all."

"Harcourt?" Azoun asked after a moment.

With a nod, the old noble said, "I agree with General Elventree. It's regrettable to let untruths fester like this, but with the Tuigan ready to attack tomorrow, it's for the best. If the men are galvanized by the tales, I say let them believe whatever they want."

Before his king could ask him, Farl Bloodaxe stood and faced away from the fire. "I'll do as Your Highness asks," he said. "We've known each other a long time, so I'll be bold enough to be honest. I believe this is a serious mistake." Turning toward Azoun again, he added, "By not correcting the rumors, we're fostering them."

"If my archers survive the battle," Brunthar interjected, "they won't care what we did to motivate them, so long as we win. If we lose—" he shrugged and poked the fire again "—then no one will be around to argue the point."

Azoun's first impulse was to strike the cocky dalesman, but he knew that the urge was more a reaction to his own indecision than anything General Elventree had said or done. He saw his choice clearly laid before him: either let the rumors circulate freely and unite the army, or tell the troops the truth and possibly demoralize them on the eve of the first battle. And though his heart told him otherwise, the king looked Farl in the eye and said, "Let the men think what they will." After a pause he added, "But I want all three of you to get your troops under control and ready them for the morning."

Lord Harcourt and Brunthar Elventree bowed and left immediately. Only Farl paused before carrying out his liege's commands, and he stood for a moment, studying the king from across the fire.

"You know this is wrong, Azoun," the general said at last. He cast his eyes to the ground and toed a stone.

"There's no other choice, Farl. If you were in my position, you'd see that."

The infantry commander shook his head. "No, Your Highness. Wrong is wrong, and—"

"Go on," the king prompted. "As you said, we've known each other a long time. You *can* be honest with me."

"I'm afraid you'll be made to pay for this somehow, that letting these rumors go unchecked will come back to haunt you."

A weak smile crossed Azoun's lips, and he nodded. "Perhaps," he said wearily. "Perhaps." With a sigh the king sat on a large stone near the fire. "But this is war, and my responsibility is to the troops. I cannot be guided solely by my beliefs."

Farl bowed and turned to go. Before he got more than a few feet away, he stopped. "The soldiers are here because of your beliefs, Your Highness, and the true crusaders will gladly die for the causes you champion . . . but never for a lie."

Then the general was gone, leaving Azoun alone with his thoughts. He stared at the fire for an hour, wondering if this was what Vangerdahast had warned him against in Suzail. If so, the king decided as he rose to check on the royal wizard, then *my old tutor was right. I'm not prepared for war at all.*

– 13 –
Crows' Feast

That night most of the clouds fled the sky, as if they were reluctant to be witness to the upcoming battle. The morning after Azoun's visit to the Tuigan camp began bright but much cooler than the day before. The king, as restless as the clouds, rose early, just as the sky to the east was growing pink. His first office that morning was to offer a short prayer to Lathander, Lord of the Morning, God of Renewal.

"If Lord Tempus does not see fit to strengthen our arm in the battle today," Azoun's prayer concluded, "then let our sacrifice fall to you, Lathander, and lead to the beginning of a united Faerun, one that will rear up to crush the Tuigan."

The prayer done, the king donned the foundations of his armor—a new quilted doublet and hose—and went to check on Vangerdahast. The handful of guards outside the Royal Pavilion snapped to attention as Azoun passed. The guards looked as if they'd stood at attention for hours, but the king didn't miss the empty wineskin or the marks in the ground around the fire where they'd likely passed the night.

"Three more scouts have reported back, Your Highness," one of the guards said, bowing as he addressed the king. "They note that the Tuigan are on the move toward us, but still many miles away."

The king nodded. "As we expected. Send runners to Lord Harcourt, General Elventree, and General Bloodaxe. Have them report to me in a few minutes." He started toward Vangerdahast's tent, then added, "Apprise them of the reports when they arrive."

Without waiting for an acknowledgement, Azoun continued to the tent of his friend and advisor. Cormyrian soldiers bowed to the king as he trod across the royal compound, while others merely saluted. Though his mind was otherwise occupied, Azoun put on a cheerful face and returned the greetings enthusiastically. He knew that now more than ever, he had to present a confident facade.

Even with the frenzied momentum built by the stories surrounding the king's return, fear still hovered over the Alliance's camp. A glazed, faraway look clung in most soldiers' eyes, and the men and women seemed distracted as they hurriedly prepared to meet the enemy. The sounds of their work—wood being chopped for last-minute barricades, swords sliding harshly over sharpening stones, nervous horses crying out as they were armored for the charge— drifted over the camp and heightened the sense of fearful anticipation.

Most soldiers responded to the tension by throwing themselves into their duties. Archers checked and rechecked their bows, counted arrows, and sharpened arrowheads. The nobles under Lord Harcourt's charge polished their armor, as if a good sheen on their plate mail would stop a Tuigan arrow. Other noblemen tended to their horses, securing the mounts' barding or making sure they were fed in accordance with military tradition. Swordsmen readied their weapons and armor, if they had any armor at all. Some men broke down parts of the camp, dousing fires and loading baggage onto carts. No one would admit that the camp was being packed to aid a hasty retreat, but everyone knew why the tents slowly disappeared from the landscape that morning.

Other soldiers spent their hours before the battle talking with friends or drinking around the cookfire. Azoun passed one such group on the way to Vangerdahast's tent. Being Cormyrian soldiers, they moved to stand as the king passed, but he motioned them to stay seated. The soldiers smiled broadly at this, and they cheered when Azoun took a drink from their wineskin before moving on. The king was still in earshot when the soldiers again related descriptions of the wives or lovers they'd left in Cormyr. From what little Azoun heard, he guessed these stories had as much truth in them as the ones about his battle in the Tuigan camp.

Religion weighed heavily on many minds and became important even to those not usually inclined to give the gods their due. Clerics, whose job it would be in the battle to aid the injured and pray for the dead, bustled from tent to tent, campfire to campfire. Many of the priests encouraged the men to turn their thoughts away from the conflict. Others, like the worshipers of Torm, God of Duty, or Tempus, God of Battle, exhorted the troops to fight as their deities demanded. Clerics of Lady Tymora were the most common in the camp, as their goddess was known as the patron of adventurers.

One such cleric of Tymora was leaving Vangerdahast's tent as the king approached it. The dark-haired priest exuded exhaustion as he shuffled, shoulders stooped, away from Azoun.

"Just a minute," the king said, running a few steps to catch the Tymorite. "How is the royal magician?"

The cleric, when he saw Azoun, bowed deeply. He straightened his clean brown robe and turned his blue eyes on the king. "He is no longer delirious, Your Highness, but I fear he will not be ready to fight today."

Something about the cleric tugged at Azoun's memory, but the troubling news about Vangerdahast quickly displaced the thought. The king sighed. "Have you been caring for Vangerdahast since we arrived last night?" he asked, noting the redness rimming the cleric's blue eyes.

"I have had some experience with mages made sick by magic-dead areas," the cleric responded. "As Your Highness certainly knows, Cormyr holds an area or two like the one the Tuigan camped in, caused by the Time of Troubles. That is why I was assigned—"

"Yes, of course," the king said distractedly. "I would like you to come back and see to the royal magician during the battle."

The king left the cleric bowing and entered Vangerdahast's tent. His thoughts lightened a little when he saw how much the orderly tent resembled the wizard's workshop back in Suzail—even to the live hedgehog Vangerdahast kept in a glass. The king had always assumed the bristly little creature was part of a spell, but he wasn't sure. Perhaps it's Vangerdahast's idea of a pet, he mused.

The wizard himself was stretched out on a cot, snoring lightly. A votive candle, rimmed with silver, burned fitfully on a table near the wizard's head. The cleric had no doubt left it there, Azoun decided, for silver was a metal favored by Tymora's priests.

The candle's flickering flame did little to brighten the tent, but it did reveal another man sleeping in the shadows. Thom Reaverson, the king's bard, lay curled on the ground next to one of Vangerdahast's bookshelves. The bard hugged himself tightly and shivered a little in the cool morning air. Smiling, the king lifted a robe from the wizard's trunk and spread it over Thom. Then, as quietly as he could, he left the tent.

Once outside, Azoun ordered a guard to wake Thom in an hour, at which time the bard was to begin packing Vangerdahast's belongings. Since the wizard's tent would be behind the Alliance's lines, the king decided not to have the unconscious royal mage moved. For now, at least.

Actually, what to do with Vangerdahast during the battle was the least of Azoun's problems. A more pressing dilemma was the command of the War Wizards, which would now have to be given to another mage. The king knew the choice would not be difficult to make, for the War Wizards had a strict hierarchy. The next ranking mage would simply take over as commander. However, Azoun had no idea if this other wizard knew of Vangerdahast's plan for the battle.

It was likely that the plans had not been shared. Vangerdahast was secretive, and he tended to reveal only a little about his projects, even to Azoun. That tendency was the source of the king's other big dilemma, as well. With Vangerdahast unable to cast any spells, Azoun had no way to contact Queen Filfaeril or Princess Alusair. The royal mage had made it very clear that only he knew how to home in on the Obarskyr family's signet rings. Vangerdahast always claimed that this insured no one could abuse the tracking devices, but Azoun now cursed himself for not demanding some other way to contact his family quickly.

With these problems weighing heavily on his mind, the king returned to his pavilion and met with the generals. Farl, Brunthar, and Lord Harcourt were sitting around the large table in Azoun's tent, a map of the immediate area spread between them. The king briefly explained that Vangerdahast was still unconscious and outlined the ramifications of that problem.

"The Tuigan should be here in an hour or two," Farl offered, drawing a large red arrow on the map to indicate the enemy's movement. "We've just been discussing alternative troop placements."

Walking to the head of the table, Azoun glanced down at the map and shook his head. "It's far too late to consider changing our plans. Our soldiers will expect us to array as we've practiced." He turned a meaningful eye to the commanders of the archers and cavalry. "As has been proven to my satisfaction, we can't undermine the men's expectations at this late date."

"But Torg isn't here," Brunthar Elventree noted. "Without his infantry support, my archers will be vulnerable."

Farl took a drink from a mug that was holding one corner of the map flat. As the paper curled slightly, he glanced at the dalesman. "The infantry we have now will be enough. Two thousand dwarves wouldn't make that much difference anyway." He smoothed the map and replaced the mug. "I agree with Azoun. We should stay the course we've plotted already."

Clearing his throat, Lord Harcourt added, "The plans we've set are sound. They follow all the dictums and suggestions of the great battles of King Rhigaerd II."

Following his father's rules of war was not what Azoun had had in mind when he suggested an organization for the battle lines. Common sense dictated most of the placement, and the little the generals knew of Tuigan tactics suggested the rest. The king scanned the map and picked up a pen.

"This really isn't a matter for debate. We'll array as we planned," he said, inking the pen. "At least for this engagement . . . though with a bit of luck, we'll hurt the khahan enough that he'll turn now."

The generals all smiled and murmured their approval, but none of them truly believed such an easy victory was possible. Azoun didn't either, but he knew that he had to present his facade of confidence to his commanders as well as his troops. "Of course we can't rely on chance too much," the king added with a sincere smile. "Lady Tymora always favors those who make their own luck."

Azoun bent his attention to the map and sketched out the position he would take in the Alliance's battle lines. After marking a small blue crown, the king handed the pen to Farl, who positioned the infantry.

In a steady, smooth hand, the black general marked two lines to represent the footsoldiers under his command. The first line was centered slightly in front of Azoun's crown and ran wide to either side of the king's mark. "This will be the main body of infantry," he noted with his deep voice, glancing up at the king. "It holds most of our pikemen, spears, and so on."

Farl then added a second, thinner line behind the first. "And this is the second rank, made up of swordsmen rather than men with polearms." As the generals all knew, the second line was not there to stop a Tuigan charge, but to fight at close quarters once the battle got under way. Shorter weapons, like swords and axes, would be of far more use in a press than spears or pikes.

After taking the pen from Farl, Brunthar Elventree inked it again. "The archers go here, here, here, and here." Each location to which the dalesman pointed received a blotchy triangle of ink. When the archers' commander was done, four large groups of bowmen were interspersed along the second line of infantry.

Next, Lord Harcourt took the pen. With sweeping, ornate strokes, he added wings to the lines of infantry. "And the nobles will guard the flanks," he said, then bent down and added a few more marks to the map. "My cavalry will sweep in as soon as the infantry and archers have stopped the barbarians."

The last comment was stated as fact, and Azoun was pleased by the confidence Lord Harcourt seemed to be putting in the less experienced generals. Neither Farl nor Brunthar had been involved in a campaign on this scale before.

Finally the pen passed back to the king. He inked it again and added the remaining details to the Alliance's battle lines. A large **W** denoted the wizards' position, behind the line of mixed infantry and archers. To the mages' rear would lie the camp itself, which Azoun depicted as a number of blocks.

"I want the refugees gathered behind this pavilion," the king noted after he'd finished drawing. "That will put our army and most of the camp between them and the fighting."

The three generals nodded in agreement, and Farl volunteered to see that the king's wishes were fulfilled. That settled, Azoun reviewed the signals the standard-bearers would use to relay his orders, then asked for questions. There were none.

"May the Goddess of Luck and the God of Battle look favorably upon us," the king concluded. As General Elventree and Lord Harcourt turned to go, Azoun clapped them both on the shoulder. "I don't suppose I'll see you before the Tuigan arrive, so fare well. I know you'll both fight bravely."

Lord Harcourt dismissed the parting with a wave. "The barbarians will be routed by sunset," he said firmly as he left.

Brunthar Elventree and Farl Bloodaxe exchanged worried glances. "Let's hope," the dalesman said and followed the cavalry commander to the lines.

"What was that all about?" Azoun asked Farl when the others had gone.

The infantry commander paused, then pursed his lips. "We—Brunthar and I—feel that, well, Lord Harcourt may be underestimating the Tuigan's strength. Given the chance, he'd probably try to rout them with the nobles alone."

Guiding Farl to the exit, Azoun said, "I agree with your assessment, my friend, but Lord Harcourt is a good soldier.

He'll follow my commands when it comes down to a fight, so *his* mistaken disregard for the enemy's strength doesn't matter." When the infantry commander paused at the door, the king added, "Besides, there are plenty of things I'm counting on you for already. Leave the command of the generals to me; it gives me something to occupy my time."

A sly smile on his face, Farl bowed and headed into the heart of the camp to oversee the movement of the refugees. Azoun watched the commander go, then called for a squire to help him don the rest of his armor.

Less than an hour later, after a quick visit to the temporary head of the War Wizards, the king was touring the battle lines. He walked a little stiffly in his full suit of plate mail, but with the practiced gait of one accustomed to the heavy burden of armor. Azoun personally favored training in battle conditions, and he'd often spent an hour or two in the height of summer practicing his swordsmanship dressed in his full armor. Seeing the distress in some of his soldiers' faces as the early morning sun beat down upon their heavy mail made the king thankful it was a habit he had maintained. Even though it was relatively cool for a day in mid-Flamerule, any sun hammering on an armored body could be brutal.

Soldiers scurried along the front, fortifying their positions or simply taking their place in line. As the generals had agreed, the bulk of the army was split into two lines, but the map had not shown that they were spread across the slope of a wide, low hill. This positioning afforded the bowmen in the second rank a good view of the field. Azoun glanced behind him at the four groups of archers and prayed their longbows would prove a match for the short, curved bows the barbarians fired from horseback.

Adjusting his coif of mail, the king wiped the sweat from his forehead. The hill itself will help the archers, too, he concluded silently. The field's long slope will almost certainly slow the Tuigan charge enough for the bowmen to whittle their numbers down a little before the first sally.

"Your Highness!" a messenger shouted and dropped to his knees behind the king.

Azoun spun around to see a dirty, panting youth. "What is it, boy?"

"The barbarians, Your Highness. I seen 'em coming when I was on scout," the youth reported between gasps. "I raced here as fast as my horse'd carry me."

Flipping back a mailed glove, Azoun arched his hand over his eyes and looked to the east. The morning sun was low enough in the sky to be blinding to someone scanning the horizon, and the glare prevented the king from seeing any movement in the distance. Only mile after mile of rolling wild grain, intersected by the dark scar of the trade road, met his anxious eyes. Still, the king didn't doubt the report, and he immediately told the standard-bearer waiting nearby to signal the army to form battle lines.

Azoun patted the scout on the head and sent him to his place at the rear of the army, where he'd be ready as a messenger if the need arose. Trailing the standard-bearer and a few knights behind him, the king walked to the rear of the lines himself. With the help of a wooden ramp, Azoun mounted his fully barded horse. The white destrier pranced nervously, then trotted to the front lines under the king's guidance.

As Azoun watched, a few soldiers scattered caltrops over the field far in front of the Alliance's lines. These spiked metal balls, like the wooden barricades that also littered the field, were meant to slow a cavalry charge. All along the first line, the men tightened the straps on their leather armor or shifted under the weight of their hauberks of chain mail. Spear points and pike blades glinted in the morning sunlight as the weapons sat on the ground near their owners, who also rested in anticipation of the conflict. Wineskins passed surreptitiously from man to man as the waiting began.

The experienced campaigners knew that a period of tense expectation, when the lines were formed but the enemy had yet to charge, would be part of the battle that day. They took the delay in stride. Many listened to the sergeants and captains barking orders or tossing encouragement to the men. Others heard the murmur of hushed, worried conversations, and, closing their eyes, dreamed that they were in a tavern far from this particular battlefield. Whatever they did, the soldiers who had seen a large battle before tried their best not to look for the Tuigan on the horizon.

They knew that the enemy would come soon enough.

In fact, it was only one half-hour after the king had signaled the lines to form that the dust from the Tuigan advance became visible, even against the bright morning sun. The signal to prepare for assault rippled through the standards, and the men got slowly to their feet. Last gulps of wine were swallowed, and prayers were quickly murmured. The more hardened mercenaries placed final bets on the number of men they might kill or how many hours the fight might take. Most of the soldiers simply stood and stared at the dark line growing across the horizon.

"Can you see how they're arrayed?" Azoun asked the armored horseman to his right.

As infantry commander, Farl's position for the start of the battle was near the king, to the rear of the first line. He squinted at the enemy troops rushing toward them and, after a moment, shook his head. "I can't tell from this distance." Farl's horse shifted nervously beneath him, and he steadied it with a pat on the flank. "If there are as many warriors as you said, their front isn't long enough for them to be riding in less than two, perhaps three lines."

Fear knotted Azoun's stomach, and he suddenly knew why the men had been so quiet, so tense in the hours before the battle. The king's work had kept his mind occupied with hundreds of details, and his position had called on him to make a myriad of decisions, all of which drew his attention away from the reality of the conflict. As Azoun sat on his destrier, watching the Tuigan advance, he knew with horrible certainty the battle that might end his life was charging toward him at a fast gallop.

Azoun glanced at the helmet in his hands. The basinet was ovoid, with a high point at the summit that tapered to the ornate gold rim of the Cormyrian war crown. "In a battle against Zhentil Keep this crown might guarantee my safety," he said vaguely as he slid the helmet over his coif of mail.

"But the khahan has expressed a wish to make my skull into a cup, so I suppose this makes me stand out more than a full purse at a thieves' guild meeting."

Having been in many battles before, though none nearly as monumental as the one that faced him now, Farl Bloodaxe recognized the fear in the king's voice. That's good, he thought. Fear keeps men alive in war.

He didn't tell that to Azoun. Instead, the infantry commander leaned close and said, "Thom once told me a story of an ancient Cormyrian king who fought a glorious battle against an enemy who outnumbered him twelve-to-one."

Frowning, Azoun slid his visor closed. "I've heard that story, too, Farl. The king and all his knights but one die in the conflict. Hardly a tale to lighten our moods."

"Our odds are far better, Your Highness," Farl said, closing the visor on his own helmet. "We're only outnumbered three-to-one. At least a dozen of us should make it back to Cormyr." With a flourish he drew his sword and bowed it in salute to the king.

Beneath his helmet, Azoun chuckled. He meant to return a witty retort to his friend's dark humor, but when he glanced at the Tuigan line, it was closer than he had expected. The signal went out again to prepare for first assault. Pikes and spears bristled from the Alliance's first rank, and the tension in the air made the whole army grow as tight as the string on a longbow.

The formation of the Tuigan charge was clear now, but the sun at the enemy's back and the high, waving grain sometimes hid the horsewarriors from Azoun's sight. As Farl had guessed, the khahan had organized his men into three rough lines, each about three men deep. Azoun was amazed that the barbarians managed to maintain a straight, orderly charge as they raced across the plain. If Lord Harcourt can see the precision with which the Tuigan are advancing, the king decided, he's probably modified his opinion of them considerably.

At a few hundred yards, the bulk of the enemy reined in their horses and stopped. A group about half the size of the Army of the Alliance, perhaps fifteen thousand men, raced forward. A steady rumble of drums accompanied the heavy thunder of their horses' hooves pounding the ground.

"They're going to test the line!" Farl shouted, waving his sword in the air. The first line gripped their shields a little tighter and braced their polearms for the impact. In the second rank, captains bellowed orders to the archers, who tested the pull of their bowstrings one last time.

Azoun shifted in the saddle to get a better look at the four groups of archers, then drew his sword. The king could see Brunthar Elventree's standard—the mace, spear, and chain symbol of Battledale in gold upon red cloth—at the rear of the closest formation of bowmen. Like all the groups of archers, the dalesman's was fortified with dozens of long, sharpened stakes. The palisade formed a wall of spikes that tilted down the hill, ready to repulse an enemy charge.

The king gave the signal for the archers to fire when ready, and Brunthar's standard wavered in the light wind crossing the field. Six thousand archers drew their bows as one and leaned back, seemingly to point their arrows at the low-hanging sun.

Just as Azoun turned to the battlefield again, the archers fired. Six thousand arrows sliced through the air, and the thunder of the Tuigan advance was momentarily drowned out by the hollow whistle of the deadly missiles. After arcing up into the sky, the arrows seemed to hang at the zenith of their flight, then, in an instant, they dropped onto the charging barbarians.

The black curtain reached the Tuigan charge about one hundred yards from the Alliance's front rank. Hundreds of horses tumbled into the grass, screaming in pain, tossing their riders under the hooves of other charging steeds. Some arrows struck the riders themselves, often killing their targets instantly. In all, the first volley dropped almost one tenth of the entire charge. This heavy toll might have been a surprise, had not the barbarians' orderly advance made them easy targets for the skilled western longbowmen.

The attack seemed to surprise the charging horsewarriors, for some of them faltered momentarily. The majority of the Tuigan line galloped on, however, leaping their horses over the dead and wounded on the battlefield. And as the charge picked up speed, another sound rang out over the field: a shrill war cry. The Tuigan screeched their rage at the Alliance as they hurtled forward, brandishing their bows over their heads in defiance.

When the horsewarriors were a little more than fifty yards away, Brunthar Elventree signaled the archers to fire again. Another swarm of arrows sliced through the air, the sound of their passing contending with the war cry in the ears of the western troops. At this relatively short range, the longbows did even more damage to the massed Tuigan troops. Thousands of horses and soldiers sprouted brightly fletched arrows. Their shouts of shock and pain wavered under the shrill war cry.

"Ready for assault," Azoun said, and the signal was passed. At the right and left flanks, the armored noblemen who made up the majority of the cavalry readied their weapons and anxiously held their horses in place. In the second rank, Brunthar gave the signal to fire at will, and arrows sailed over Azoun's head in squalls.

The Tuigan reined in their horses and fired their strong short bows. Thousands of arrows bit into the western lines. Azoun reflexively threw his shield up, and he heard two arrows strike it with surprising force. Luckily, the Tuigan seemed to take aim at the front ranks, where many of the men had shields, too. Still, what sounded like a single pained groan went up around Azoun as some of the missiles found their mark.

"Signal the mages!" Farl cried at Azoun's side.

The king lowered his shield and looked to the Tuigan lines. If the infantry commander had been able to see Azoun's face, he would have seen a look of shock; the horsewarriors were wheeling their swift little horses about and fleeing. "We should save the wizards for when we really need them," the king shouted. He pointed at the retreating enemy. "What's going on?" The Tuigan fired over their shoulders occasionally, but it seemed as if they were running away.

Farl flipped back his visor. His face, too, was a mask of surprise. "That had to be a test," he ventured. "Maybe they didn't know the range of our bows or what kind of battle magic we had."

A hearty cry went up from the Army of the Alliance. The king signaled the archers to cease fire and watched as a much-weakened group of riders rejoined the khahan's army. "Losses?" Azoun asked as he lifted his own visor.

After scanning the field for a moment, Farl said, "They lost four, perhaps even five thousand. We wounded more than that." He shook his head. "The khahan must care very little for his men to condone that kind of carnage for a test."

"Or his men think highly enough of him to go to it willingly," Azoun corrected. "Save for an instant when our first volley hit them, they didn't pause. This was a familiar drill for them." He looked across his own first rank. "Have the captains tally our losses. We may just frighten them off."

The dead were counted as they were dragged out of line, and the king was relieved to find that only about three hundred had been killed in the first assault. The thought of any men dying under his command troubled Azoun, but he pushed those guilty thoughts aside.

The wounded were far more numerous, but many of the arrow wounds required only simple dressings or minor healing spells. Most of the wounded bragged about their new badges of honor or invited their neighbors in the ranks to see where the Tuigan arrows had pierced their shields or split their leather jerkins. The sergeants let this nervous bravado continue as the minutes of waiting for a new assault wore into an hour, and the sun rose high over the field.

By midday, crows began to flock to the battlefield. The corpses of the Tuigan horses and soldiers slain in the first assault lay in the field, growing cold in the sunlight. Many of the less-traveled soldiers in the Alliance were shocked to find the birds gathered so quickly. Some even spoke of the dark-winged scavengers as a bad omen or the result of evil sorcery. The experienced mercenaries knew the crows were neither of these things. The large black birds, so common in fields throughout Faerun, were like any other animal; food attracted them, and a battle always proved to be a seemingly endless source of carrion for their greedy beaks.

Still, the crows' steady cawing unnerved some of the troops. Brunthar had to discipline a few archers for wasting arrows by shooting at the birds, and Farl found himself yelling at a member of the king's guard for betting on which Tuigan body the birds would land on next.

At last someone shouted, "Here they come again!" A murmur of odd relief ran through the western lines.

"By Torm's mailed fist," Farl said, "they're scouting us again!" He slammed his visor down and raised his shield on his arm.

The crows quickly leaped in to the air, out of the path of the galloping horses. Azoun attempted to ignore the coarse squawking as he gazed out upon the advancing Tuigan line. There were perhaps twice as many riders charging toward the Alliance as last time. The odds were now even.

As before, the longbows rained arrows on the Tuigan charge twice before the horsewarriors stopped. Azoun then ordered Brunthar to have the archers attack in unison again as the barbarians turned to fire. This third sheet of arrows, launched just as the khahan's men were readying to fire themselves, had a terrible impact. Not only did the attack take a toll in Tuigan lives, it spoiled many of the mounted archers' shots. But this wasn't the only surprise the king had prepared for the second Tuigan charge.

As the horsewarriors reined in their mounts fifty yards from the Alliance's front rank and the longbowmen launched their own counterattack, the wizards entered the war.

With a crackling hiss, over two hundred flaring balls of fire leaped from the rear of the western army's ranks and struck the Tuigan charge. Like liquid, the fireballs splashed against the horsewarriors, killing hundreds and horribly burning many more. Had the field not been dampened by recent rains, a massive wildfire would have spread from the attack. As it was, blazes broke out all around the barbarians' line, sending thick black smoke coiling across the field.

Unaccustomed to such an awesome use of magic, many of the Tuigan faltered. Panicked horsemen wheeled their steeds about for a retreat or tried to fire their bows as ordered. The Alliance's archers loosed another volley, and a few of the wizards behind them completed a more complicated incantation begun a few moments earlier.

In twenty-eight spots along the Tuigan charge, the ground burst up, showering the horsewarriors with earth and uprooted grass. In each of those ravaged places, a massive creature of stone climbed out of the ground, swinging huge fists of rock and dirt. The stone creatures had cold, expressionless faces and eyes made of sparkling gems that reflected the fires still growing around the enemy.

Azoun sat motionless as the earth elementals lumbered into the Tuigan line, scattering horses and soldiers. From ten to fifteen feet tall, the creatures found it easy to dash the troops from their path, and the Tuigan arrows had little effect on their hard, rocky bodies.

Rays of glittering golden dust and swarms of glowing blue darts accompanied the arrows that rained down on the retreating enemy. The Army of the Alliance shouted out their victory as the Tuigan wheeled in the burning field and tried to escape the shambling monsters and shower of magic that drove them from their horses and crushed them into the earth.

"They didn't even have a chance to fire a second time," the king said to Farl. He raised his sword high into the air and added his voice to the army's triumphant cry.

The infantry commander shouted something the king could not hear. After an instant, Farl flipped up his visor and slapped Azoun on the shoulder. "Your Highness, look!"

Following the general's outstretched arm, the king saw what so upset Farl. Far to the right, the Alliance's cavalry was breaking from the flank, sweeping in on the retreating Tuigan line. "By the gods," the king whispered, the color draining from his face. Lord Harcourt's banner charged through the ranks of cavalry as they raced toward the fleeing enemy.

After an instant of hesitation, the king grabbed his own standard and shouted, "Call them back!" to the young knight carrying it. The king's banner, emblazoned with the purple dragon of Cormyr, ordered a retreat. The signal was to no avail; the nobles continued their charge.

"What does Harcourt think he's doing?" Azoun cried bitterly to no one in particular. "Has he gone mad?"

The cavalry meant to guard the left flank saw its counterpart's charge and followed suit. In helpless anguish, the king watched the silver dots he knew to be armored knights race across the field and cut off the Tuigan retreat. Some of the fighting was obscured by smoke, but it was clear that the better armored western nobles were having an easy time wiping out what little remained of the broken Tuigan charge.

A messenger, sweaty from an obviously furious dash through the lines, made his way to the king's side. "Words from Lord Harcourt," he said, neither bowing to nor saluting the monarch.

Azoun shook a mailed fist at the boy. "What's going on?" he snapped. "Why did he charge?"

"Th-the nobles, sire. They, uh—"

Seeing the fear in the messenger's eyes made Azoun realize what he was doing, and he tried to calm himself. His face still red with anger, the king said, "The message, boy. Don't be afraid."

"Lord Harcourt sends his apologies, Your Highness." The boy swallowed nervously and glanced around. "The nobles disobeyed his orders and charged."

"By the gods, why?"

The boy wiped a gummy hand across his forehead. "Lord Darstan and some others said they could easily chase down the horsewarriors when you, one wizard, and a few knights escaped from the Tuigan camp on your own. I heard 'em say it, Your Highness."

The shock from that statement had little time to settle on Azoun. A deep, rolling rumble crossed the field, and for an instant, the king thought the wizards had cast another powerful spell. A single look at the battlefield revealed how wrong that guess was. Through the patches of smoke and fire, Azoun could clearly see the entirety of the khahan's army advancing at a gallop across the body-strewn field.

The black line on the horizon spread as it moved closer, and the king realized why Yamun Khahan had waited until now to attack in force.

"They're going to surround us," he said, turning to Farl. "The khahan was hoping to bait the cavalry forward so he could surround us easily."

The infantry commander scowled. "Without cavalry on the wings, the Tuigan will outflank us without trying." He spurred his horse and charged away from the king, shouting orders.

By now the rest of the Alliance had realized what was happening, too. The wizards, unprotected by any kind of armor, pushed from the rear of the formation to the short space between the first line of infantry and the mixed line of swordsmen and archers. Shoving their way to protection, the mages threw the second rank into turmoil. In a few places scuffles broke out, though the captains saw to these with harsh efficiency.

Assessing the situation as quickly as possible, Azoun decided to force both lines up the hill farther. In a normal assault, the archers' palisades would be used only if the frontal assault drove the first rank into retreat. Then, the wooden spikes would hamper a full-scale charge. However, if the Tuigan got to the rear of the Alliance and forced the second rank downhill, the palisades would be useless.

"Front rank retreat to the second rank's position!" the king cried, waving his sword to motion the retrenchment. The standard-bearer echoed the order, and sergeants and captains barked out the command all down both lines.

For a well-trained army, this maneuver would have proved little problem, but the Army of the Alliance had had only a limited amount of time to drill. As a result, the retrenchment took far too long. By the time the ranks were in place, the Tuigan had outflanked the army and were closing in on three sides.

Azoun didn't see Lord Harcourt's standard waver, then fall, as the bulk of the khahan's troops rolled over the Alliance's cavalry. The nobles had wiped out the last of the retreating Tuigan line, but at the cost of their lives to a man.

The fires and the earth elementals slowed the charge a little, too, but not enough. Eighty thousand barbarians, crying out for vengeance, screaming for western blood, emerged from the smoke, brandishing their bows.

Without warning, a Tuigan arrow bit into Azoun's leg. Fired at a distance of only thirty yards, the black shaft pierced the king's cuisse and pinned his leg to his horse. The destrier reared as Azoun threw back his head and screamed in agony. The sky he saw through tears of pain was black.

Above the Army of the Alliance, the crows swarmed. Their numbers seemed to blot out the sun, and their cries drowned out Azoun's scream. Almost hidden in the sea of black feathers, a lighter-colored falcon circled the battle, watching the Tuigan surround the crusaders.

- 14 -

Duty

Black wings fluttered in front of her eyes, obscuring the battle on the ground below. She swooped lower, closer to the conflict. The carrion birds bumped and battered her, making her view jump, but soon the Army of the Alliance came clearly into sight again.

Tuigan troops completely ringed the western army.

Alusair cursed bitterly, and her black-and-white view of the battle wavered. After she forced herself to concentrate on the magical link with the falcon, the vision cleared again. For being so high above the lines—higher even than Suzail's tallest tower—Alusair was amazed at the detail she could discern. Through the bird's eyes, the princess saw the plights of individual soldiers, even the flights of single arrows.

For all her searching, she couldn't find her father. She'd spotted the royal standard, which was being buffeted about in the press, but the king wasn't near it. That was a very bad sign. As Alusair knew, Azoun needed to be in contact with the purple dragon standard to issue commands; without him, the army was fighting on instinct alone.

Refusing to believe her father dead, Alusair decided that he must have been pushed away from the standard-bearer. The mental effort it took to draw that conclusion weakened the link to the falcon, and for an instant, the battle disappeared completely from her mind.

"Damned magical—" Alusair stopped, kept her eyes

tightly closed, and took a deep breath. When she opened her eyes, she saw Torg standing over her, his hands balled into fists and resting on his armored hips.

"Well?" he asked impatiently.

"Only a few more miles and we'll see the Alliance," the princess said sullenly. "The Tuigan have them surrounded, so we'd better hurry."

Not waiting for more of an explanation, Torg barked a string of orders to his captains. The dwarven army heaved itself wearily to its feet and prepared for the march. Before the army proceeded across the low, rolling hills, however, they dropped their packs and tethered the mules that towed their wagons.

"We won't be needing tents to fight the barbarians," was all Torg would tell Alusair by way of a reply.

Her heart heavy with concern for her father, the princess contacted the falcon, once again using the bracelet the centaur had given her, and told it to circle the battle for a while, then return to her. Next she, too, stripped her pack and put on her full armor. Sweat trickled over much of her body almost immediately after she donned the heavy plate. The princess's thoughts were on other things, though, so she hardly noticed it.

Setting a quick pace, Torg set off for the battle. The dwarves had yet to see a Tuigan patrol, and Alusair hoped their appearance would be a surprise. For his part, the ironlord didn't care much about the tactics of the fight to come, only that it come quickly. If the army gained a few skulls for the caves of Earthfast, so much the better. The number of dwarves who might die to take them didn't matter, either, just as long as they perished in a righteous fight.

Smoke rose on the horizon. From what she'd seen through the falcon's eyes, Alusair knew it was from the fire the wizards had started with their spells early in the battle. The dark clouds rolled into the sky and seemed to transmute into thousands of individual black birds. This grim sight set the dwarven troops on edge long before they heard the first faint echoes of the battle drift over the hills toward them.

"Damn all humans!" Torg shouted suddenly. He slapped his mailed hand noisily against his leg and pointed to the left. A few hundred yards away, three Tuigan scouts were rising from the tall grass. The barbarians dashed away before the ironlord even considered sending soldiers after them.

"It can't be helped," Alusair offered. Bracing her helmet under her arm, she wiped the perspiration from her brow. "We should be able to see the battle once we top that next hill."

The princess was correct. When the dwarves reached the spot she'd indicated, they saw the two armies thrown together in bloody, chaotic combat before them. Far to their right, the Alliance's camp was spread in the bright sun. Without warning, a falcon swooped low over the fields, then caught an updraft and sailed high over Torg's troops. For a moment, Alusair considered using the bracelet again to get a better vantage on the battle. She quickly dismissed that notion when she saw a line of horsewarriors break from the conflict.

"Array for combat!" Torg shouted. He swatted the standard-bearer when the boy didn't move fast enough for his liking. Alusair frowned at the cruelty.

The dwarves scattered and formed a triple line across the hill. The first two ranks placed their pikes at their feet and drew their crossbows, while the third rank braced their polearms as a protective palisade. As five thousand Tuigan horsemen rumbled up the incline, away from Azoun's left flank, Torg's troops swiftly cranked their heavy bows. They loaded the powerful weapons, then waited with their characteristic silence to meet the charge.

"They'll ride close once, then turn and fire," Alusair reminded Torg. "Just as they did with the Army of the Alliance. They'll try to draw you out."

The ironlord raised the visor on his helmet. "I'm not fooled so easily, Princess." He smiled and straightened his beard, bound in heavy chains of gleaming gold for the battle. "And the Tuigan have never faced a dwarven army in battle before."

Slamming his visor back into place, Torg ordered the standard-bearer to relay a command to the troops. As the horsewarriors galloped closer, the dwarves' front rank raised their bows and sighted on the enemy. When the Tuigan reached seventy-five yards, the dwarves fired.

A loud, reverberating retort followed the firing of the bows. Heavy crossbow bolts sped toward the Tuigan and tore fearfully into their ranks. Horses tumbled and soldiers screamed, but the mass of the enemy line rushed toward the dwarves, unaffected by the death and pain around them. At fifty yards, the barbarians reined in their horses and returned fire.

Alusair flinched as the shower of powerfully launched Tuigan arrows arced into the sky and struck the dwarven line. The princess knew what to expect from the attack, so she wasn't really afraid. Like the rest of Torg's troops, Alusair wore plate armor wrought in Earthfast, legendary for its strength. That day's battle added to the stories about the mountain kingdom's craftsmen.

A thunderous clatter echoed in Alusair's ears as arrow after arrow struck armor and bounced off. In only a few instances did the missiles penetrate the dwarves' plate mail, and then only because of a carelessly exposed joint or slightly open visor. As the rain of arrows lessened, the ironlord ordered his troops to fire again. The second line loosed their crossbows, and more bolts ripped into the retreating Tuigan line.

"They won't try that again," Torg said loudly. He looked down the intact dwarven line, then out at the hundreds of wounded barbarians in the field. "Not even orcs are stupid enough to use an unsuccessful attack twice in a day."

With a twinge of guilt, Alusair found herself admiring Torg again. The ironlord was thoughtless and perhaps even cruel, but he knew the battlefield well. "May Clanggedin and all the other dwarven gods prove the rest of your plan as successful, Your Highness," the princess said. She glanced at the horsewarriors and added, "For we will test it very soon."

With a loud and trilling war cry, the Tuigan charged again.

As the double line of riders drew nearer, Alusair could see that they wielded lances and silver curved swords instead of bows. It was clear that they were going to push for hand-to-hand combat.

Showing little anxiety, even though the barbarians were barreling down on his troops, Torg bade the standard-bearer signal again. Deftly the soldiers hung their cross-bows from hooks on their brichettes and picked up their pikes. The Tuigan were less than forty yards away when the dwarven lines broke. Their bows clanging softly against their armored hips and legs, Torg's troops formed their battle squares.

It was obvious that the Tuigan had never encountered this tactic before. Their commander, riding next to his standard, halted his charge and attempted to slow his men, but the barbarians rushed to engulf the four squares of dwarves. Capturing so compact and easily surrounded an enemy looked simple at first. The horsewarriors soon discovered otherwise.

"To the right! Crush them between the squares!" Torg bellowed and waved his sword from the center of one group. The dwarves pushed to the right as commanded, driving the horses and riders into the pikes bristling from the next square.

Alusair, in the center of a different square, watched as the Tuigan tried to press the attack. The horsemen found themselves spitted on pikes or knocked from their mounts. The latter often provided worse then a quick death by blade, as the rest of the barbarian attack crushed the hapless victims under horses' hooves. And as more riders rushed to the battle, those caught in front against the immovable wall of well-armored, well-armed dwarves were slain with greater ease.

The bodies of the Tuigan dead were piled high around the squares. Wounded horses thrashed at the dwarves' feet and became a fleshy wall bracing Torg's troops from close assault, but not really hindering the reach of their long-handled pikes. The carrion crows had begun to circle around this bloody battlefield, too, though Alusair found the birds' noisy, insistent cawing less disturbing than the dwarves' disciplined silence. Even when faced with the Tuigan charge, the soldiers from Earthfast leaned silently into their grisly work, occasionally grunting as a pike struck home.

Finally, over the screams of the wounded humans and the clash of metal upon metal, the princess heard the steady beating of drums. Slowly at first, the Tuigan broke off. The dwarves took the enemy's retreat as ample opportunity to slay some of the humans from behind. As Torg could have predicted, not a single dwarf broke rank.

The ironlord bellowed his laughter over the humans' screams and the birds' cries. He raised his beautifully crafted, blood-soaked sword high over his head and shouted his triumph. Without pause, the rest of the army from Earthfast joined in. The dwarves' victory shout was very different from the Tuigan's shrill, trilling war cry. It sounded like it came from deep within the earth itself, rolling and rumbling from the dwarves as if they echoed the noise of stone grating against stone deep within the mines they dug.

The cry chilled Alusair, but she'd heard it before. Perhaps it was the moans and screams the princess noticed behind the victory shout that made her shudder, or the blood she saw splattered across the pikes as the soldiers thrust them into the air. Perhaps it was the knowledge that a long afternoon of fighting lay ahead before her father would be safe. Whatever the cause of her discomfort, Alusair realized that now was not the time for celebrations.

"Ironlord," she cried as she pushed through her square. "We must move quickly if we are to help the Alliance."

Their shout ended, the dwarven soldiers eyed the princess warily as she shoved through the ranks. She had left her post without permission, an offense none of them would ever consider committing, and they silently showed their scorn for the action. Alusair ignored the glares she got and muscled past the few dwarves who purposefully stood in her way.

"I know the tactics we should follow, Princess," Torg sighed as Alusair finally got near. "We will move as soon as we've collected trophies for the caves of Earthfast." He wiped a fleck of blood from his gauntlet and ordered the men to reform into two lines to advance.

"Collect your severed heads *after* we've saved the rest of the Alliance," Alusair snapped. She pointed toward the battle still raging a few hundred yards away. The Tuigan who had survived the assault on the dwarves, about half of the number that had charged, were now forming a flank to face the ironlord's troops.

Torg frowned. "You're right," he grumbled. "We'd best get this over with."

The dwarves advanced swiftly, but didn't get too close to the Tuigan lines. They fired volley after volley of crossbow bolts into the enemy ranks, wreaking havoc. More than anything, the dwarven army proved a seemingly incurable distraction to the Tuigan's right flank. The horsewarriors' arrows had little effect on the heavy dwarven plate mail, and whenever a direct assault seemed imminent, Torg would order his men to form squares.

Whoever was directing the Alliance's troops at that end of the line took full advantage of this distraction. The western infantry rallied and pressed hard against the Tuigan right, driving them closer to the dwarves' crossbow barrage. Given little choice, the commander of the Tuigan in that part of the battle ordered a desperate assault on the troops from Earthfast.

Torg's squares proved as effective in this combat as they had in the first encounter with the Tuigan. The ironlord slowly but surely moved the groups of pikemen down the hill, forcing the barbarians back to the western lines. With amazing speed, the dwarves and the western infantry destroyed the Tuigan flank, capturing its standard and the general who commanded it.

The rest of the battle dragged on through the afternoon, until the sun began to dip in the west. Smoke still billowed darkly across the field from the various brush fires that chewed away at the tall grass. Few arrows were launched now, but the air was still full of impatient dark shapes. Many of the crows had landed and fed, but more arrived all the time, drawn by the coppery smell of blood and the cries of their kin.

It wasn't until the bright orb of the sun had sunk half below the horizon that the sound of drums echoed over the battlefield. In as orderly a fashion as possible, the Tuigan pulled back from the western line. Unsurprisingly, especially after the disastrous cavalry charge earlier in the day, no one moved to follow the enemy. A few longbows were hefted and arrows shot halfheartedly at the retreating horde, but the majority of Azoun's troops stood in dazed silence. More than anything, they were surprised to be alive.

"Princess!" someone called in a deep, loud voice.

Alusair scanned the mass of western soldiers for the speaker. Men and women lay everywhere, wounded or dead. In a few places, soldiers cried softly for their fallen comrades, and prayers were muttered in musical, lilting voices all through the western lines. In the midst of all this, someone pressed toward the dwarven army, his hand held high.

"Your Highness! Over here!" the armored man shouted, waving his gauntlet in the air.

The press of soldiers parted for an instant, and Alusair saw that Farl Bloodaxe, his helmet tucked under his arm, was the one calling to her. The Cormyrian general smiled when the princess met his eyes, but that couldn't hide the exhaustion on his face nor mask the beads of grimy sweat that rolled down his dark skin.

As the general came close, Alusair said, "Well met!" and shook his hand. "I'm not surprised to find you were in command of this end of the line. You rallied well and took advantage of our press."

Farl gestured to the soldiers all around him. "The troops are responsible for that. Not me." A worried look crossed his face, and he leaned close to the princess. "Have you seen your father?" he asked quietly.

Blanching slightly, Alusair shook her head. "I was hoping to do that right now."

Without much comment, Farl and Alusair made their way through the western lines. The general briefly explained how he'd not seen the king since early in the battle. He was concerned for the monarch, because the fighting had been especially fierce at the center of the front rank. Alusair listened in grave silence, and she noted that more and more corpses lay in the ranks as she made her way to the king's standard.

The crowd of gaping onlookers made it easy for Farl and Alusair to find Azoun. The general called for captains to break up the crowd and reform the men into companies, while the princess shoved the soldiers out of her way and rushed forward. She choked back a gasp when she saw the king, surrounded by clerics and sprawled unconscious on the ground.

"The king will be fine, Madam Knight," a fat, red-faced priest of Lathander said. He placed a restraining hand on Alusair's shoulder and attempted to turn her away. "The clerics do need room to work, however, so—"

"That's my father," Alusair snapped, and the priest's pudgy red cheeks flushed a deeper crimson.

He stammered an apology, but Alusair wasn't listening. Without a glance at the clerics who had turned to look at her, she went to her father's side and knelt.

They'd removed the king's helmet and chain mail coif, even loosened the straps holding his cuirass tight around his chest. Azoun looked pale, and sweat plastered his hair and beard to his face. Though he was unconscious, his breathing seemed labored and his mouth was twisted into a grimace of pain. The reason for the expression was obvious. A broken arrow jutted from the king's left thigh. The missile had penetrated the heavy silver cuisse, and now blood stained the bright armor.

"He'll be all right," a cleric murmured soothingly. Alusair saw the man's deep blue eyes and noticed the shining silver disk—the symbol of Tymora, Goddess of Luck and Patron of Adventurers—hanging around his neck. "But we should move His Majesty from here to a place where we can work our healing."

The princess started. It was clear from the cleric's tone that he was actually asking her for permission to move the

JAMES LOWDER

king. Alusair hadn't expected to fall into a leadership role
with the Army of the Alliance, and she was certain that she
didn't want the responsibility.

"Perhaps Vangerdahast or General Bloodaxe should give
you your orders," Alusair began. "I don't—"

The infantry commander's deep voice whispered in the
princess's ear. "With all respect, Your Highness, you'd best
show the troops that someone they respect is in command
here. Vangerdahast is quite ill and confined to his tent."

Farl's sudden comment startled Alusair, who was already
on edge. She glanced at the crowd, grown larger now because of her presence. Even the general's orders could not
disperse the Cormyrians who'd come to see the elusive princess, the daughter of Azoun who had helped to save them
from the Tuigan. Memories of regal processions through
the streets of Suzail flooded Alusair's mind. She could not
help but notice that the hope and awe on the soldiers' faces
was very similar to the emotions shown by the poor who
had once watched her in Cormyr. Their need was obvious
and overwhelming.

"Your orders, Your Highness?" Farl asked, loudly enough
for the crowd to hear.

Alusair winced. She had already decided that she would
have to put on a show of authority for the Alliance, but she
hated being forced into anything. And it was clear Farl was
doing just that. With a flash of anger in her eyes, the princess stood and glanced at the infantry commander.

"Regroup the soldiers into companies, General," she replied. She looked to the crowd and added, "The Tuigan
could very well come back tonight. My father will expect us
to be prepared when the healers are done with him."

"Will the king live?" someone called from the crowd. The
anxiety in the hidden soldier's voice was clear.

Forcing a smile onto her dirty face, Alusair paused. After
waiting a moment for effect, she put her hands to her
mouth and shouted, "King Azoun lives, and he will be at the
head of this army by sunrise. Until then, my words are his."
She faced Farl again. "Break up this crowd, General," she
said softly. "I'll meet with you and the other commanders as

soon as my father has been moved."

After bowing deeply, Farl Bloodaxe went to work on the milling throng. Alusair helped the clerics lift her father onto a litter, then refocused her attention on reorganizing the Army of the Alliance. Her first task, she decided as she made her way through camp, would be to talk with the Tuigan general the dwarves had captured in the battle. How the remaining troops should be arrayed depended largely on what they could expect from the khahan, and the general might give her some indication of the barbarians' disposition to night fighting.

The princess found the commander of the Tuigan right flank sitting sullenly amidst a mass of silent dwarves. The khan's standard lay shredded on the ground at his feet, and four armed guards stood watch over him. No one had dressed the bloody head wound the general had sustained in the fighting, so Alusair ordered a dwarven healer to bind the man's cuts while she waited for a translator to arrive from the War Wizards.

The sun had almost set completely when the wizard finally arrived. His long gray robe was tattered and greasy; multicolored smudges from spell components clung to his fingers. Despite his obvious exhaustion, the mage efficiently translated Alusair's opening flurry of questions. The answers the Tuigan commander gave were brief and not very informative.

The princess sighed and studied the khan for a moment. Batu Min Ho, for that was the name he had given the translator, looked to be of Shou descent. His broad features were tempered slightly; his nose was not as flat nor his cheekbones as pronounced as other Tuigan's. Still, he was dressed in the armor favored by some of the barbarian elite: a heavy breastplate over a chain mail hauberk, rough boots, partial cuisses of studded leather on his legs, and thick leather gauntlets dotted with steel on his hands. The disturbing thing about the general was his calm, even though he surely must have known his life was in grave danger.

"Will the khahan offer ransom for you, General?" Alusair asked at last. After hearing the question translated, Batu

- 253 -

merely shook his head.

Frowning, the princess leaned forward and looked into Batu's eyes. "Will the khahan attack tonight?"

At first there came no reply. Batu stared at his interrogator for a moment, then at the translator.

"He wants to know if you are the daughter of King Azoun, the man he met in the Tuigan camp," the wizard reported. "He assumes your position in the army indicates a relation to the king, but also notes that you resemble Azoun in many ways."

The princess was surprised to learn that her father had visited the enemy camp, but she let that shock pass and concentrated on questioning the general. "I am Princess Alusair of Cormyr, daughter of King Azoun," she replied. After a pause, she added, "My father sends his regards."

After bowing to Alusair from his seat, Batu met her gaze again. "Then the king has survived the battle?" he asked through the translator. He raised an eyebrow in surprise, an act that shifted the bandage wrapped around his head. "Yamun Khahan offered a great reward for your father's head. I was certain someone would collect that reward."

A shudder wracked Alusair, but she tried not to show it. She took a sip from a waterskin that lay at her feet and offered it to the general, who stoically refused. "Will the khahan come tonight?" she asked again.

The wizard translated the question, and Batu paused for quite a while before answering. From the expression on his blood-smeared face, Alusair guessed that the general was formulating a safe answer. Finally Batu said, "I cannot guess the thoughts of the khahan, Princess, nor would I reveal them to you if I could. I will tell you this much, however. Your armies have presented the greatest challenge the Tuigan have faced in many months. Your troops fight most valiantly."

It was Alusair's turn to pause, for she wondered where she should lead the questioning. Two of the dwarven guards started to build a fire to chase off the growing twilight, distracting the princess for a moment. When she turned back to Batu, she found him studying her.

"Would the honorable princess be so kind as to answer one question for me?" he asked through the mage. The princess nodded, and the general bowed slightly. When he looked up at Alusair, his eyes were dark and his expression grim. "What do you plan to do with me?"

"We are civilized, Batu Khan," Alusair replied without pause. "You will be our prisoner until the end of the war. You will be taken from the fighting and kept from harm."

That answer seemed to displease Batu Min Ho. The general sank into contemplation for a moment, then said something so softly that the wizard wasn't sure he heard it correctly. The comment wasn't meant for anyone else, but the general had noted, "Then there will be no more illustrious battles for me." He bowed stiffly to the princess and asked to be allowed to rest.

The discussion obviously over, Alusair ordered the four dwarven guards to escort Batu to the Alliance's camp at the rear of the battle lines. The khan and the dwarves had not gone more than a dozen steps from the princess when a scuffle broke out.

"Look out, Lugh!" a guard shouted in Dwarvish.

The clash of steel on steel rang out as Alusair rushed toward the fight. Batu Min Ho, a short dwarven blade in his hand, stood over a fallen guard. The three other dwarves circled him warily, their swords held out in front of them. Drawing her own blade, the princess stepped toward the Tuigan commander.

Batu met Alusair's gaze, and a curious smile worked across his lips. After a feint to drive the dwarves back, the general held the sword's point to his stomach. He softly repeated three names—Wu, Yo, and Ji—and fell forward. Batu didn't even cry out as the bright steel pierced through his armor and impaled him.

Other dwarves, hefting their silver-bladed pikes, were now charging toward the disturbance. The khan's original guards, still holding their swords, examined the general's body to see if he were truly dead. Satisfied that the suicide had been successful, they left the body where it lay and turned their attention to their fallen comrade.

The ever-efficient dwarves swiftly carried the dead guard away to be interred in the communal cairn they were building, and Alusair looked up from Batu Min Ho's corpse. The khan's strange, final words ran through her mind over and over again, and she wondered who or what he had called for in his final moment. In fact, the death took such command of her thoughts that the princess didn't realize she had walked far into the Alliance's lines until she was hundreds of yards from the flank.

She found Farl talking quietly to a dark-haired man clad in a muddied sky-blue tunic and hose. Where the color stood out on this man's clothes, it presented a stark contrast to the other soldiers' dark tunics or their leather or steel armor. Both men bowed formally when Alusair came near. "Any word of my father?" she asked.

The blue-clad man bowed again, an act that tossed his ponytail over his shoulder. "Your Highness, I am Thom Reaverson, the king's bard and royal historian. I just came from His Highness. The clerics have healed the arrow wound, but he is still unconscious."

"That's not what I hoped to hear," the princess replied, "but it's certainly not the worst news I've had today." The bard smiled warmly at her, and Alusair found herself returning the gesture. "Could you go back to my father's side and keep me apprised?" she asked after a moment.

"Of course," Thom said. "I'll look for you near the Cormyrian standard, Your Highness." He hurried off at a jog toward the Alliance's camp.

Alusair didn't watch him go, however. As soon as the bard had been assigned his task, the princess moved on to other matters. "What's the army's status, Farl?"

After leading the way to a pair of rickety canvas-and-wood camp chairs set up around a nearby fire, the infantry commander gave his report. The Tuigan attack had cut the Alliance's number by half. With only a handful of exceptions, the cavalry had been wiped out, and a third of the wizards had been killed or wounded in the fighting. "I've got the men gathering the dead," Farl reported, "but I'm afraid it's a monumental task."

A quick scan of the battlefield revealed hundreds of torches flickering in the darkness outside the Alliance's lines. These torches illuminated the field for the details sent to retrieve western corpses and search for the wounded. So far, no body found outside the lines proved to be alive; the Tuigan had trampled most of the corpses in their retreat. A low moan continually hovered over the western camp as the injured and the grieving vented their sorrow together.

A sick feeling settled in the princess's stomach as she considered the situation. She rested her elbows on her knees and bowed her head in thought. "Pull three-quarters of the troops off corpse detail," she ordered at last. "I want them breaking down what remains of the Alliance's camp. We should be ready to move if the need arises."

Farl frowned. "But the corpses of our soldiers—"

"—will be of no use to us now," the princess sighed. She noted the shocked look on the general's face and added, "The gods will certainly understand if the heroes who died fighting here are not given the proper burial rites."

"Yes, Your Highness."

"When that's done, organize the remainder of the troops into three shifts. I want the men rested up in case the Tuigan come back," Alusair ordered calmly. "One shift of the three should remain alert, waiting for the horsewarriors, while the others sleep."

Nodding, Farl looked around at the Alliance's lines. "I've already started on that, Your Highness. If the men weren't so frightened, they might be easier to command." He paused and looked into the fire. "I-I share their concern, Princess. I don't think we have the strength to make another stand here."

A pressure had begun to weigh upon Alusair the moment she'd discovered her father was injured, the moment she'd been forced to take command of the army. The princess felt that pressure increase now. Her shoulders tight and her stomach in knots, she placed her hand on the general's arm.

"Then we'd best be ready to move by midnight," she said softly. "Perhaps we can find a more defensible place to the west."

Farl didn't reply at first. Eventually he stood and bowed. "I'll see that your orders are carried out." He paused, then added, "I'm glad you're here, Princess. I don't know how the men would have reacted to your father's injury if you hadn't taken command."

Alusair appreciated Farl's compliment, but the notion that she was one of the only things holding the Alliance together frightened her. She realized then that it was this responsibility that weighed so heavily upon her. Running a hand through her knotted blond hair, Alusair wondered if this pressure was what her father felt every day.

To take her mind off that and other thoughts, she established a makeshift command headquarters in the midst of the western lines. Despite this effort, the princess found that, once she'd set the army to its various tasks, there was little for her to do but wait and think and watch the bright bonfires that had sprung up around the battlefield. Those fires, which might have been the center for a rustic celebration in Cormyr, were the resting place for the western dead. One by one, corpses were hefted onto the blazing pyres, their souls sent to the afterlife unceremoniously on clouds of foul-smelling smoke.

The funeral pyres brought more unwelcome contemplation, and she was attempting to force her mind away from various morbid topics when she heard a spent arrow snap beneath someone's foot. Glancing behind her, the princess saw Thom Reaverson, a smile on his young face. At the bard's side was another man, dressed in a heavy black robe, its hood concealing his face.

"Hello, Allie," the hooded man said.

Alusair sprang to her feet and threw her arms around her father. When the king groaned, the princess backed up a step. From where she stood, Alusair could see Azoun's pale face and haggard expression. She also noted for the first time that he leaned heavily to his left upon a walking stick.

Before his daughter could say a word, the king held up his right hand. "Thom told me you were here, so I came to see you." He shifted his weight on his leg, trying to get comfortable. "I just wanted to tell you I'm all right, and I wanted to see how you fared in the battle. I was . . . worried."

The king didn't need to explain the disguise. After seeing how ill her father looked, Alusair could guess the reason for it. "You don't want the men to see you when you're so weak," she said quietly.

Azoun nodded. "In the morning, after I've rested, I'll return from the dead, their triumphant hero." Alusair could not miss the note of self-scorn in those words. She wanted to comfort her father, but he'd already placed his hand on Thom's shoulder and turned to go.

"Wait!" the princess gasped, running a few steps to get beside Azoun. "What are we supposed to do until morning?"

The king cocked his head, and Alusair thought she saw a little color flush back into his face. "Thom told me that you've taken command until I get better," he said, pride bolstering his weak voice. "And from what I hear you're doing everything I would." He hobbled a step, then stopped and added, "I'd move the troops tonight, though. We'll have a better chance of putting some distance between us and the Tuigan under cover of darkness." Thom cast a sympathetic glance at the princess, then the king and the bard moved on.

For a moment Alusair considered telling her father she didn't want the responsibility for the army, that he or anyone else should take it. But as her father limped back toward the western camp, his face hidden in the hood, the princess realized that he already knew that. Alusair realized, too, that she would take command of the Army of the Alliance, not because she had some vague duty to honor or pride, but because Azoun needed her help.

The weight she felt upon her shoulders that night wasn't lessened by her acceptance. In fact, she felt the responsibility all the more because she knew what it was and knew that the burden could not be lightened. But Alusair was reconciled with that, and she went about organizing the retreat of the army, knowing that her father depended upon her. She was certain she would not fail him.

– 15 –

Heart's Counsel

I left Cormyr, left a soft job guarding caravans, for this," the mercenary cursed. He wiped the sweat from his brow with one blistered hand and held the small ax in the other. When no one responded, he swore under his breath and went back to work.

With a grunt, the tired, hungry man resumed chopping a point onto the end of a long wooden pole. Hundreds of other soldiers crowded around him, sharpening other poles to be used in the defensive palisades. Exhaustion showed plainly on all their faces, and few men spoke. The occasional conversations that sputtered to life in the ranks died quickly, as if fatigue had swallowed the soldiers' words as well as their strength.

Like the blistered mercenary and the others in the work detail, Razor John had slept little in the last day and a half. He, along with what remained of the Army of the Alliance, had left the site of the last battle shortly after midnight. They'd struggled west down the Golden Way all night, stopping only briefly for morningfeast. A constant fear that the Tuigan would suddenly sweep down on the retreating army from the east had hung over the troops all night and all day. Now, an hour or two before sunset, the western soldiers still wondered where Yamun Khahan and his army of barbarians were.

"They're just toying with us now," the mercenary muttered.

CRUSADE

"Perhaps they'll stay away for a while. Perhaps we hurt the Tuigan worse then we think, Yugar," Razor John offered hopefully. He paused to take off his shapeless black felt hat and scratch his sweaty scalp. The fletcher's sandy hair, once almost long enough to cover his ears, was now cropped short for easy care. This, coupled with the bags beneath John's eyes and the tired stoop in his gait, made him seem haggard and more than a little mournful.

The mercenary snorted a laugh. "They grow 'em stupid in your family, don't they, fletcher? We're outnumbered six- or seven-to-one. The damned barbarians are probably sitting a few miles east of here, laughing at us."

Turning his red-rimmed eyes on the mercenary, Razor John bit back a retort. He'd made the comment about the Tuigan more as a way to lighten the youth's foul mood; he was certainly wise enough to know that their situation was indeed desperate. But Yugar, a young, inexperienced Cormyrian mercenary, seemed intent on finding fault with everything.

With an exaggerated swing of his lanky arm, Yugar tossed down his ax. "And I was fooled into thinking there was money in this idiotic crusade." He slapped his forehead with a grimy palm. "Worse, I believed Azoun's babble about our responsibility to the rest of Faerun."

There had been times in the last two days when Razor John had questioned his own wisdom for venturing so far from home to fight an unknown enemy. And nothing had challenged his resolve more than the death of some of his friends in the first battle. He could still see their mangled corpses staring up at him as if shocked by their own deaths. Luckily, Kiri Trollslayer had escaped harm, but several soldiers John had befriended had perished the day before. But even those deaths had not convinced him that Azoun's crusade had been foolish.

"Why don't you just slink away?" the fletcher hissed as he slammed his ax into the wooden pole. "The army will be better off without you, coward."

Yugar laughed again, this time loud enough to turn a few heads. The Cormyrian mercenary ignored the blank stares

- 261 -

of his comrades and picked up the claymore at his feet. "They call me Yugar the Brave back in the Stonelands," the boy boasted. He spun his sword a little awkwardly and lowered the point at Razor John. "And you'd best apologize or you won't live to see the Tuigan again."

Something inside the fletcher snapped. Without thinking, John slapped the mercenary's blade away and landed a fist against the boy's jaw. Yugar tumbled backward over the pole he'd been working on. As the mercenary's claymore spun through the air, the fletcher rushed forward and planted a heavy-booted foot on his thin chest.

"Braggarts like you make a mockery of everything we've given up—no, everything *I've* given up for this crusade," John said, pressing his steel-shod boot down over Yugar's heart.

"Let me up!" the mercenary bellowed in impotent rage. He cursed and clumsily swung his arms, trying to get a grip on John's leg.

With lightning quickness, the fletcher pulled the dagger from his belt and brandished it over the prone soldier. "I'm here because I believe in Azoun's cause, sell-sword, not for the silver I'll earn for killing Tuigan." He lowered the blade menacingly. "Don't mock the crusade or the king again. I won't stand for it."

As soon as the fletcher raised his foot, Yugar rolled toward his sword. He glanced back at Razor John, then slowly stood and picked up his weapon. For an instant, the fletcher wondered if the boy was going to attack. An angry shout settled the question.

"I'll have you both standing unarmed and naked before the next Tuigan charge if you don't get back to work!" Brunthar Elventree shouted.

Razor John sheathed his dagger and pulled his ax from the pole. The fiery dalesman who commanded the Alliance's archers moved to the fletcher's side.

"Is there a problem here, soldier?" Brunthar growled, gesturing at Yugar. "Have you mistaken him for a barbarian?"

Razor John looked up at the general. A broad, bloodstained bandage covered much of the dalesman's bright red hair, and a large lump of cotton wadding lay over his right ear. John knew that General Elventree had lost part of that ear to a Tuigan sword in the first battle. "No, sir," the fletcher replied.

Narrowing his eyes, Brunthar studied John for a moment, just long enough to make the fletcher uncomfortable. "I won't have any more fights between you, then," he said at last. He flicked his eyes to Yugar, and when he saw the mercenary was still scowling, Brunthar pointed to another cluster of workmen. "Get moving. I want you preparing spikes with those men."

Yugar muttered a curse, but turned away quickly and headed toward the other workmen. Brunthar had heard the remark, though. He was considering how to make the young mercenary regret the stupid comment when a commotion broke out behind him. When he spun around, he expected to see another brawl; the presence of both King Azoun and his daughter certainly surprised the commander of the Alliance's archers.

The king was dressed in a tunic of royal purple, with hose to match. He limped heavily upon his wounded left leg and used a walking stick of plain, dark wood for support. Except for the walking stick—and the Cormyrian battle crown that rested upon his wrinkled brow—Azoun looked like many of the soldiers who prepared for the battle. In her chain mail hauberk and silken surcoat of purple, Alusair was clothed the same as any member of the king's guard.

"Your Highness," Brunthar said, bowing formally. "I hope you are feeling well this afternoon."

Azoun nodded and lifted his walking stick in a casual salute. The dalesman's formal greeting was a great sign of deference, the king realized, so he did not let the opportunity to return the favor pass. "Our healers seem to be able to call upon their gods for miracles," he replied. After a cursory glance at the fortifications the archers were preparing under Brunthar's guidance, the king added, "Very impressive work, General Elventree."

"Thank you, Your Highness," the dalesman replied. "Everything is as you and the princess requested."

"But better than we had hoped to build in so short a time," Alusair offered, following her father's lead. "Let's hope the rest of the Alliance will be as prepared for the battle as your men."

After bowing again, Brunthar looked toward the sun. "The meeting is at sunset?" he asked.

"Indeed." The king motioned with his walking stick toward the stretch of the Golden Way that snaked out from the western lines. "Out in front of the first rank. We'll see you there."

Azoun and Alusair set off on their tour of the lines again, leaving Brunthar and the archers to their work. For the last hour, the king had been walking through the camp, his daughter at his side. The review was mostly for show, to let the troops know that he was healthy and in command of the Alliance again. It was a painful exercise in rumor-quashing, however, and the king often found his leg wound throbbing angrily at the exertion.

"General Elventree has certainly changed in the last month," Azoun noted. He grimaced slightly as he made his way over a small ditch. "When he first took command of the archers he had no regard for my position at all."

"Is that why you were so careful to compliment him?" the princess asked.

Azoun nodded, then gave a short bow in response to the greetings of a group of archers. "Partially. Brunthar has proven himself a good commander. The dalelords were correct in sending him." He paused and marveled at how much he had opposed the idea of a dalesmen commanding the archers.

"What are the other reasons?"

"Just a moment, Allie," the king said when he spotted a messenger running toward them. After receiving word about the most recent scouting forays, Azoun said, "If we seem to be calm, seem to handle the preparations for battle with some confidence, the troops will take strength from our example. If I praise Brunthar, his men will know they are doing what we expect—"

"So they'll hope they are prepared for the next assault,"

the princess concluded. She frowned slightly and swatted a mosquito. "I thought so. I mean, that's why I said what I did to General Elventree."

Noting the look of concern on his daughter's face, the king asked, "Does that bother you?"

Alusair considered how to form her concern, how to put it into words. Finally, she adopted the most direct approach; though rather blunt, it seemed the most accurate. "It seems like we're lying."

The reply didn't surprise Azoun. In fact, ever since he had allowed the rumors about the Tuigan and his "escape" from their camp to circulate, he'd been troubled by that same thought. After all, those rumors had been partly to blame for the disastrous cavalry charge in the last Tuigan encounter. Azoun had come to no conclusions, however, so he simply didn't know how to respond to Alusair's comment.

Father and daughter remained silent for a time. Alusair knew the king well enough to realize that he was wrestling with the problem, not ignoring it. They'd spent many hours in Azoun's study in Cormyr embroiled in similar debates, and the pattern was always the same: in the course of a discussion, Alusair would pose a particularly challenging question. Rather than toss off a quick reply or dismiss the problem, the king would consider the issue, pacing back and forth, occasionally glancing at a book or two.

The scenery around Alusair and Azoun now had little in common with that study. As they walked, they passed the groups of archers preparing palisades. Many of the soldiers were finished chopping points onto the poles, and some were even setting the eight- to ten-foot-long spikes into the ground. Alusair had never been in a cavalry charge that had been forced to face that kind of defense, but she was certain that it must be terrifying to break against a line, only to find huge sharpened stakes braced in the ground, leveled at you or your mount. She shivered and dismissed the grisly thought.

After a time, in which Azoun distractedly returned the bows and greetings of his troops, the king and his daughter looked away from the line of palisades and moved back to-

ward the Golden Way. The sun was beginning to sink in the
west, and a few of the Alliance's commanders had already
gathered in the road for their meeting.

"I don't lie when I encourage the troops, for I believe that
they—that *we* can actually win," the king replied at last. He
stopped and looked back at the soldiers toiling away, some
setting spikes, others placing small barricades before the
first rank. "I have my doubts, but it isn't my place to share
those with the soldiers. They need a leader, not a doom-
sayer."

Alusair paused for a moment. "Farl told me about Lord
Harcourt," she began. The pain that registered on the king's
face at the mention of the cavalry charge made the princess
regret bringing up the subject. "This isn't the time—" she
added quickly.

"If not now, when?" the king replied, a bit too sharply. He
spun around as swiftly as his wounded leg would allow and
headed toward the meeting. "I don't know what to say
about Harcourt and the nobles," he admitted as he trudged
along.

"Perhaps you shouldn't have let the rumors about the
Tuigan circulate," Alusair offered bluntly.

Alusair wasn't saying anything that Azoun's conscience
hadn't suggested to him over and over already. When he
told his daughter this, she nodded. Then it was her turn to
be silent. For a moment, it seemed that the conversation
would end there.

When he stepped onto the road, however, Azoun put his
hand on his daughter's arm. "When you were in command
of the army last night, how did you make your decisions?"
he asked.

"I did what I thought was right."

Azoun nodded. The reply was exactly what he'd expected. "That was how I decided to let the rumors about my
deeds in the Tuigan camp circulate. From the counsel I received, I concluded that the army would be far better off if I
didn't dash their enthusiasm."

"Then you didn't take the most important counselor into
consideration," the princess said. She pointed at the king's

chest. "You didn't listen to your heart. You didn't do what your conscience told you was the right thing to do."

Azoun could feel the tension growing between him and Alusair. He took a deep breath and tried to respond as calmly as possible. "There are thousands of lives depending upon my decisions, Allie. You can't know—"

"Oh, but I can," she replied. "Before I knew you were well enough to take command again, I believed I would have to lead the army in the next battle. I felt the pressure."

Farl Bloodaxe bowed as he came close. Unlike many of the soldiers, the ebony-skinned commander had taken off his armor. He again wore the dark breeches and billowing white shirt that made him look more like a pirate than a general. "Excuse me, Your Highness, Princess, but the others have gathered as you requested. We await only your presence."

Azoun was almost relieved at the interruption. He and Alusair had closed the gap that had separated them for so long, but it was clear that many things still held them apart. "Thank you, Farl," the king said. "We'll be along in a moment."

As the general turned to go, the king remembered Farl's words the night before the first battle: *The soldiers are here because of your beliefs, and the true crusaders will gladly die for the causes you champion . . . but never for a lie.* Turning to his daughter, Azoun took her hand in his own. "Perhaps you're right, Allie," he sighed, squeezing her hand. "At the very least, you've given me something to think about."

They embraced briefly, which assured both of them that their argument had done little to set back their reconciliation, and went together to the meeting.

Azoun and Alusair found the three surviving generals— Farl, Brunthar, and, much to their surprise, Vangerdahast— as well as Torg and Vrakk, in animated discussion. The commanders sat on camp stools around a low-burning fire. Azoun greeted the royal wizard warmly, and more than anything, seeing his old friend again lightened his mood.

But Azoun quickly found that Vangerdahast had not fully recovered from the sickness that struck him down in the magic-dead area. The firelight revealed the mage's features, pushing away the shadows of the growing twilight, and the king saw that Vangerdahast was quite pale. A palsy shook the mage's left hand, too, but he tried to keep the quivering limb hidden in the sleeve of his long brown robe. When he noticed the king's concerned stare, Vangerdahast frowned.

"I was just telling the other generals," the wizard said crankily, "the magic-dead area seems to have erased the effects of the spells and potions I'd experimented with, the ones that kept me healthier than my eighty-odd years." His frown deepened into a scowl, and he pointed at the king with an age-spotted hand. "But that doesn't mean I'm unable to command the War Wizards."

"You're absolutely correct, Vangy," Azoun replied with as much enthusiasm as he could muster. While he didn't doubt that the royal wizard could easily keep the Alliance's mages in line, the revelation of Vangerdahast's present malady shocked him.

"We're wasting time, Your Highness," Torg grumbled. The dwarf looked as petulant as ever. Azoun guessed correctly that the mere presence of the orcs' commander was enough to upset the ironlord. The dwarf's position in the circle, on the opposite side of the fire from Vrakk, certainly reinforced that guess.

Torg's bigotry is the least of our worries now, the king concluded. Still, he smiled and nodded. "You are correct, Ironlord. The Tuigan won't dally so we can swap stories of the wounds we've gained in the fight so far."

Without ceremony, the king took a seat between Vangerdahast and the spot reserved for Alusair. Turning to Farl, he asked, "Have your scouts spotted any movement in the khahan's ranks yet?"

With a shrug, the infantry commander said, "No, Your Highness. They're still camped close to where the last battle took place, about twelve miles east of here."

"Nor have I spotted anything with the falcon," the princess added. "They seem to be waiting for us to commit to another battle."

"I don't understand it," Brunthar Elventree said. "Why

didn't they run us down after the battle? They let us escape!"

Azoun drummed his fingers on his right leg. "Perhaps we surprised them," he offered. "The general we captured told Alusair that we'd given Yamun Khahan the strongest resistance of anyone in the west."

"But you lost almost half your troops," Torg reminded the king. He picked up a wineskin that lay at his feet and took a swig.

Vrakk growled deep in his throat and leaned forward. The firelight revealed the true ugliness of his face—the short snout, beady black eyes, and bristling, course hair. His black leather armor, now slashed open in three places, did much to heighten that sinister appearance. "We send many Tuigan to Lord Cyric," the orcish commander rumbled, invoking the name of the Lord of the Dead.

"Vrakk's right," Alusair noted, a slight hint of scorn for the orc hidden in her voice. "By Farl's count we killed thirty thousand barbarians. That's three for every man we lost."

"Leaving Yamun Khahan with seventy thousand horsemen to our army of fifteen thousand," Azoun concluded. He rubbed his wounded leg reflexively and paused. "We cannot survive another battle like that."

"And the khahan won't be foolish enough to go around us and avoid a fight. That would leave an army to his rear," Farl added.

Vangerdahast, who had been watching the fire, mulling over some point, finally looked up. "Yamun Khahan will certainly attack us tomorrow," he said without preamble. "Perhaps we surprised him, perhaps not. In the end, it really doesn't matter why he's let us live this long. He'll make sure we have no way to retreat back to Cormyr."

After a moment Azoun concluded, "Then we can assume the Tuigan will come soon. Perhaps even tomorrow. That means this night holds the only hours we have left to prepare."

A little stiffly, the king stood and pointed to the western lines. "I want each of you to tell me what you'd do if you were Yamun Khahan, approaching our position."

JAMES LOWDER

All eyes were turned to the Alliance's lines. Though the sun was almost set behind the western army, the generals all knew the position by heart. They had stumbled upon the spot in their retreat up the Golden Way. Tall, sturdy trees spread in a long line from either side of the road. Without fast cavalry to cover the army's flanks, the trees insured that the Tuigan could not surround the western troops as they had in the last battle. Better still, the timber would force the Tuigan to attack across a narrow front, limiting the usefulness of their vastly superior numbers.

Torg only regarded the scene for an instant before he spoke. "They'll charge," he said, as if the matter required no more thought. "They have us outnumbered, so why waste time?"

Brunthar shook his bandaged head. "What about their archers?" he asked. "In all the other engagements, they've tried to break the lines using bowmen."

"True," Alusair said, "but in the last battle, General Elventree, your men proved that our longbows have better range than their shorter bows."

Clearing his throat, Vangerdahast added, "And the mages showed how useful a few fireballs could be in dealing with barbarians." He waved his hand to dismiss the notion. "I agree with Torg. They'll simply charge us and get it over with."

Azoun nodded. "Farl?"

"Yes. They'll charge," the infantry commander said. The wind tugged fitfully at Farl's white shirt as he paused. "They've no magic to rout us from the trees, and it'll take them forever to ride around the woods and attack us from behind."

"Vrakk?"

"Don't know," the orc grumbled. "Generals missing something. Ak-soon missing something . . . but Vrakk not know what."

Torg looked away, disgusted, a gesture that drew angry glares from Farl and Azoun. The orc rubbed his green-gray snout for a moment, then finally shrugged and said, "They charge."

"Fine," Azoun concluded. "Yamun Khahan will come here, perhaps tomorrow, and toss seventy thousand barbarians at us." He glanced back at the western lines. "How do we stop him?"

Again the generals fell silent. The crackle of the fire and the cawing of the seemingly ever-present carrion crows did only a little to mask the sounds of the palisades being erected. The sharp reverberations of hundreds of axes hitting wood, of mallets pounding the spikes into the ground, sounded through the woods and across the field.

"Before the cavalry broke rank, the combination of long-bow fire and magic seemed to slow the Tuigan down quite a bit," Alusair said at last. "But that was when they were stopping to lob arrows."

Azoun nodded enthusiastically. "Both those things will be important in the battle," he said. "Arrows and spells can whittle down the number of Tuigan lances and Tuigan swords the infantry will have to turn aside."

"But not stop seventy thousand of them," Brunthar said gloomily. "What about building more blockades to slow the charge down? We won't have the advantage of the hill here. The Tuigan can race pretty much unimpeded to our front rank."

"Good," Azoun said. He motioned to the left and right. "Perhaps we should concentrate on barricades at the edges of the field. That'll narrow down their attack even further."

Vrakk, who had not missed any of the dwarven king's angry looks in his direction, chimed in with a half-sarcastic remark. "Why don't Torg and his *dglinkarz* dig big hole for Tuigan to fall in?"

The ironlord immediately dropped his hand to his sword. Farl and Brunthar stepped between the dwarf and the orc, and looked to Azoun for guidance. The king was grinning broadly. "That's it!" he said, though only softly at first. "Of course!"

The leaders of the Alliance stopped, and even Torg wondered what the king had stumbled upon. Azoun pounded his fist into his other hand and looked around at the dark field. "But not one big hole, Vrakk. Thousands of little ones."

The orcish leader grinned evilly. "Ah! Is good idea!"

Azoun noted the confused look on the faces of his other generals. With the broad smile still on his face, he said, "The arrows and spells were most effective when the Tuigan stopped to fire at us, right?" Without waiting for an answer, he continued. "So we'll make them stop—or at least slow them down enough to be good targets for the archers and mages."

"Holes," Alusair repeated, comprehension slowly dawning upon her. "We won't put up barricades, we'll dig holes across the field."

The other generals had caught the gist of the plan by now, and they enthusiastically embraced it. By digging a wide band of holes at a distance of fifty yards from the Alliance's lines, the generals could be sure that many of the horses in the Tuigan front ranks would stumble, tossing their riders and slowing down the rest of the charge. In the midst of the animated discussion, Farl slowly shook his head.

"My troops and the dwarves could easily dig the traps overnight," the general said loudly. Everyone stopped and faced the infantry commander. "But what makes you think the Tuigan are foolish enough to charge such an obvious trap?"

The king turned to the royal wizard. "Well, Vangy?"

For the first time that evening, a smile crept onto the wizard's age-withered face. He patted his beard, now more white than gray, and said, "Even Elminster could disguise a field full of holes. It'll be easy—though the casting will take some of our wizards away from the battle."

"That's no problem," Azoun concluded, clapping his hands together. "The illusion need only be maintained long enough for the first wave of riders to hit it."

The matter settled, the king and his advisors talked long into the evening, reviewing troop strengths and establishing battle plans to cover every contingency they could dream up. The moon, partly covered by clouds, was shining as brightly as it could when the meeting finally ended.

Farl went off to double the watch on the perimeter, so that Tuigan spies would not see the dwarves hard at work in the field. Despite his annoyance at the orc for suggesting a plan that utilized his troops, Torg was enthusiastic about the task that lay ahead. He knew his troops would perform exactly as required. The other generals said good evening, too. Azoun and Alusair knew that Vrakk, Brunthar, and Vangerdahast would sleep little that night, but bade them good night in return.

The king and his daughter talked for a short time on various minor topics, then the princess went off in search of Thom Reaverson. She had promised the bard earlier in the day to relate some of her adventures. Azoun in turn walked back to camp, favoring his leg slightly. The damp night air seemed to make the pain worse, and the king wondered if he was going to put up with the discomfort for the rest of his life. The clerics had done the best they could, so it seemed likely.

It will hurt at least until tomorrow, he concluded grimly.

The dwarves had already begun their long, grueling task by the time Azoun reached the Alliance's front line. And though he couldn't see the troops from Earthfast, the king could hear their tools biting into the road and the field. The sounds weren't all that different from the hammering and digging going on around him, as Farl's troops completed their barricades and the archers finished the palisades. Hopefully the Tuigan wouldn't be able to uncover the trap through the sound alone.

For a moment, the king wondered what he should do. The pain from his leg was getting more intense, though not unbearable, and he was very tired. Sleep certainly seemed in order. However, another trip through the ranks might provide a little comfort for the troops, provide a bit more reassurance that their leader was working late into the night, too. Perhaps, then, sleep might come more easily to the soldiers.

Remembering his daughter's advice, Azoun sighed. His heart was very clear on how the night should be spent. Limping slightly, the king set off for the nearest campfire and the group of weary soldiers clustered around it.

– 16 –

Gamesmanship

The Golden Way stretched east before the Army of the Alliance, weaving a broad path through the fields of swaying grass. Clouds filled the sky, and the dawn sun, just rising in the east, shed only a pale light over the battlefield. It was a relief to Azoun's generals that the Tuigan wouldn't be able to use a bright sun at their backs to blind the Alliance's archers.

A quiet tension reigned over the western camp. Actually, no one would call the collection of scattered fires surrounded by bedrolls a formal camp. The soldiers had done little more than set up their defensive lines, with the wagons of supplies behind them. Most now were sprawled in an exhausted sleep near where they would fight later in the day. If the gods were kind and the Alliance won—and many believed that it would take the gods' power to equalize the odds in the battle—they might set up a real camp. If they lost, it wouldn't matter.

Not that the western troops had given up hope. Azoun had discovered, much to his surprise, that there were few soldiers in the ranks sodden with despair. The king's trek around the camp the previous night had revealed that most of the army still believed in the crusade, that they weren't afraid to die as long as the cause was good. The soldiers felt, as Azoun still did, that they were all that stood between their homes and the Tuigan horde.

At first he had thought the men were only telling him what they believed he wanted to hear. After all, few of the soldiers had spoken to a king before, and most of the Cormyrians spent their time bowing instead of discussing their plight with Azoun. To test this, the monarch had passed the word through Farl that anyone wishing to leave camp could do so before dawn without fear of recrimination. It was a risky ploy, and one opposed by all the Alliance's generals; Azoun had hoped it would reveal the army's true disposition and forge a sense of unity in the troops that remained.

It worked far better than he had imagined.

"You must have counted wrong," Vangerdahast gasped, shaking his head. "I don't believe it."

Alusair smiled and handed the parchment to her father. "Farl said that, too, Vangy. We had the captains count *twice*."

Relief showing clearly on his weary face, Azoun threw his head back and sighed. "Only one hundred gone," he murmured. "One hundred out of over fifteen thousand."

"And most of those were mercenaries," Alusair reminded the king. She took the parchment from his hands and reviewed the figures noted there. "I don't think we lost a single Cormyrian regular, dwarf, orc, or even a dalesman. Only hired swords."

Still numb from the surprise, Azoun looked out over the lines. Some of the men were sleeping, their heads covered to block out the weak sunlight. Morningfeast occupied most of the troops, but a few nervous men and women checked and rechecked the palisades and ditches. "They're all good soldiers," he said.

"Idiots, you mean," Vangerdahast corrected sharply. He looked away, still shaking his head. "I'm going to review the War Wizards."

Alusair looked up from the parchment. "None of the wizards left either," she reminded the mage. "Does that make them idiots, too?"

Vangerdahast stopped short and wheeled around. "Having your father needle me is enough," he snapped. He shook a finger at the princess, then his features softened. "Gods, your whole family exists only to shorten my life. Anyway, I never even bothered to count the War Wizards," he noted as he turned away again.

"Wait, Vangy," Azoun said, taking a few steps forward. "Why not?"

Without turning around again, Vangy held up his palsied left hand. "They know that I'd come back from the grave to haunt them all if they left me here to fight the Tuigan alone." He shuffled past the barricades and disappeared into the western army.

"I believe he might," Alusair said to herself. She rolled the parchment up and stuffed it into her belt. "I'll give the numbers to Thom for the chronicles, Father."

The king was still looking in the direction where Vangerdahast had disappeared. "I couldn't make him stay in Cormyr, you know," he said absently.

"Who?" Alusair asked, moving to her father's side. "Vangy?"

Azoun nodded. "I wanted him to stay in Suzail in case there was trouble. Someone else could have commanded the War Wizards." The king shook his head as he remembered the mage's vehement defense of his position as general. "Sometimes I don't understand why."

"Because he's your friend," Alusair offered.

"He's been like a father to me, too," noted Azoun. He looked out across the Golden Way. "Gods, how he didn't want me to lead this crusade. He was so unreasonable."

Alusair laughed. "Fathers are like that," she said and headed off to find Thom Reaverson.

The king, who was already wearing the padded doublet and chain mail coif that went under his plate armor, decided it was time to fully arm himself. As he donned the rest of his shining silver armor, Azoun took reports from returning scouts. At first they had little to tell, but soon it became clear that the Tuigan were on the move again.

"Send for Vrakk and Torg," Azoun told one messenger. He slipped his surcoat over his breastplate so that the purple dragon reared squarely on his chest. Finally, he looked to the standard-bearer. "Signal the troops into position."

The king's standard rose high into the air. The effect the purple dragon symbol had on the army was astonishing. A murmur ran over the mass of troops, and those still sleeping were quickly roused. Armor was donned and weapons gathered. Archers planted their bunches of arrows point first in the ground at their feet, making them easy to pick up in battle. Wizards reviewed spells in their minds, and soldiers softly recited prayers to their gods. The men who hadn't eaten morningfeast grabbed their meals of hard biscuits and dried meat and rushed to their place in line. Captains and sergeants began to prowl the ranks, shouting orders and arranging the troops in the strongest formations possible.

The dwarven king appeared at Azoun's side. Like Azoun, Torg was dressed in his full plate armor. Whereas the Cormyrian monarch's short beard was tucked into the chin of his mail coif, the ironlord's hung down across his chest, bound as always in gold chain. The finely polished metal of the dwarf's armor and the gold entwined in his beard gave off a dull reflection of the morning sunlight.

"By your request, Azoun," Torg rumbled happily. "I'm ready for battle." As if to prove it, the ironlord drew his beautifully crafted sword and waved it in front of him. "Let the Tuigan come."

A few moments later, Vrakk, commander of the Zhentish orcs, arrived. "Good-morning, Ak-soon," he said sleepily in his usual belabored Common. "My soldiers protecting archers, like you say." He unslung his black leather armor from his shoulder and dropped it onto the ground. In a rather haphazard manner, the orc fitted himself for battle.

Regret instantly colored Azoun's thoughts. The night before, Vrakk had requested that he leave command of his army to another so he could serve in the king's guard. The orc had been an able soldier and had kept his troops in line, so Azoun was happy to agree. How Torg had heard of the matter so quickly the king couldn't guess, but within an hour, the ironlord had demanded similar honors. Wanting to avoid an incident so close to the time of battle, Azoun had also appointed Torg to serve in his bodyguard.

Now the tension between the two commanders only added to the anticipation of conflict.

Alusair and Vangerdahast had also joined the king at his

standard by the time the scouts reported the Tuigan to be less than three miles away. A cloud of dust hovering on the eastern horizon told the king that the seventy thousand enemy riders were fast approaching.

While Vangerdahast still wore a brown robe, much like the ones he wore every day at the castle in Suzail, the princess was girded in her ornately engraved plate mail. The bright metal was dented in a few more places than when Azoun had first seen it, but it looked as if it had passed through the first battle without much damage. Silently, Alusair's father hoped the dwarven plate would protect his daughter as well in the battle to come.

"Cast the illusion whenever you're ready, Vangy," the king said as a squire rechecked the last straps on his armor. Azoun flexed his left leg and grimaced slightly. The left cuisse had been repaired since the first battle, the arrow hole filled and hammered smooth, so that wasn't the problem. From the pain he felt, the king knew that his wound was going to trouble him, despite the attentions it had received from the clerics earlier in the day.

As the king considered this, Vangerdahast had the standard-bearer signal the War Wizards. Then the royal mage faced the battlefield and started a low, musical chant. He swayed slightly and moved his hands in a complicated arcane pattern. Trembling, Vangerdahast cast the components of the spell—a stone, a twig, and a bit of grass from the battlefield—into the air.

No one saw the spell components disappear, for all eyes had turned to the field itself. There, the handiwork of the dwarves lay exposed in the weak sunlight. Thousands of holes littered the field, stretching in a semicircle from the woods on the army's flanks. But as Vangerdahast and the wizards he had signaled completed their incantations, the holes disappeared. More precisely, the illusion of a rolling, grass-covered field split by a trade road hid the ravaged ground.

"Excellent," Azoun said and clapped his friend and tutor on the shoulder.

Vangerdahast wobbled slightly. The spell weakened him

far more than it would have before the magic-dead area sapped his strength. Still, the wizard puffed out his chest a bit. "Precise down to the type of grass," he said proudly. "The Tuigan will never know what they hit."

Turning to Alusair, the king said, "Your turn."

Beneath the dwarven plate armor, the princess still wore the bracelet the centaur chieftain had given her. She used the magical device now and summoned the hawk from the trees nearby. The bird quickly took flight and soared out over the western lines. Concentrating, Alusair could see the Tuigan horde through the falcon's eyes, spread out in a wide line, closing in on the Alliance. The bird swooped nearer, and the princess caught sight of the object of her search. There, in the center of the massive Tuigan army, was a yak-tail banner, the war standard of Yamun Khahan.

The falcon caught an updraft and soared higher, out of the range of the Tuigan bows. Circling behind the enemy line, the bird followed it for another mile or so. After Alusair was sure that the khahan's banner wasn't going to shift places in line, she pulled her mind back from the falcon.

"The banner you described is in the center of the Tuigan line, Father." Alusair shook her head to clear it. Using the centaur's magical bracelet always left her feeling a little drained.

Torg and Vrakk both looked at Azoun, an unspoken question evident on their faces. "I saw the khahan's banner when I was in their camp," the king said. "He had it planted outside his tent."

Grinning, the ironlord grabbed his helmet and dropped it into place. He lifted the visor and said, "Now we know who to aim for."

The dust cloud grew larger and larger, until it seemed to cover the entire horizon. Azoun signaled the army to ready its weapons, and the anxiety that gripped the troops pulled their muscles a little tighter, forced their hearts to beat a little quicker. In the center of the first rank, the king and his guard put on their helmets and drew their weapons. Unlike the last battle, the entire army was going to fight on foot this time. If the Tuigan were routed again, Azoun didn't want anyone pursuing them the way the cavalry had. Knowing that no soldier was foolish enough to chase fleeing cavalry on foot, Azoun had ordered that no one, from himself to the lowest paid mercenary, be given a horse.

The Tuigan appeared on the horizon, at first only a black line against the dust cloud they were churning up. The thunder of their horses' hooves drowned out the murmured prayers and muttered curses in the western lines, and the hundreds upon hundreds of carrion crows that had roosted in the nearby trees took to the air again. In only a few moments, the horsewarriors rode far enough that Azoun could discern a few individual riders. Over the sound of the hooves and the crows, the Tuigan war cry rose.

"Ready the archers and mages!" the king yelled to the standard-bearer. After closing his visor, Azoun said a brief prayer to Tymora, the patron of adventurers, and lifted his shield.

* * * * *

Razor John was afraid.

From where he stood, at the center of the army's second rank, he couldn't see the field very clearly. The section of road the king had chosen to defend was level. Trees protected their flanks, but the troops to the rear of the array found their vision hampered by the geography. Still, the fletcher could make out the massive dust cloud rolling toward him from the east. It was clear that the barbarians were going to attack, and a horrible, numb feeling had taken hold of John's heart. He was certain he would not live to see the sunset.

Even though he feared for his own life, the fletcher was more concerned about Kiri Trollslayer. She was stationed with the infantry in the army's first rank. Perhaps, John concluded darkly, we'll both be killed. At least we'll go to the Realm of the Dead together.

The king's standard, rising up above the crowded first line of infantry, waved a command. John didn't know what the signal meant, but the commander of the archers,

Brunthar Elventree, soon made the order clear.

"Ready to fire!" Brunthar shouted from nearby.

John watched as the dalesman lowered a helmet gingerly over his bandaged head. Brunthar hadn't worn any armor in the first battle, an act that was partly to blame for his wounded ear, but now he wore a visorless steel helmet and heavy chain hauberk.

As he gripped his bow, Razor John wished that he had armor, too. Like most of the archers, he dressed in the rough-spun tunic and trousers he wore on any normal day. The reasons for this were simple: plate or chain armor would hamper his ability to move and fire quickly, and leather armor provided little protection against arrows. And since the archers were all in the army's second rank, arrows would be all they had to face from the Tuigan.

"You!" Brunthar bellowed, cuffing John hard on the ear. "Stop daydreaming and prepare to fire!" The general stood a foot from the fletcher, scowling and staring with hard, anger-filled eyes.

"Yes, sir," John murmured and quickly pulled an arrow from the ground.

The fletcher sighed as Brunthar moved off, barking orders and pulling other soldiers to attention. When the general was a few yards away, John bent over and picked up his battered black felt hat, which the dalesman's blow had knocked off his head.

"If he not hit you, I would," someone grunted to John's right. The fletcher turned to the speaker, an orcish soldier with one broken tooth jutting up from his yellow-green lips. "Sleep here and you not wake up, arrow-man." The orcish infantryman leaned against the wooden spike planted in the ground next to him and casually poked the earth with his sword.

Before John could reply, Brunthar's voice called out another command. "Nock arrows!" After walking past John, repeating the command, the general stopped and stood on a wooden block, which would afford him a better view of the battlefield.

Like the king and his other advisors, Brunthar Elventree

was certain that Yamun Khahan would not waste time trying to draw the Alliance out of its secure position between the trees. He expected the barbarians to charge with their full army without prelude. But when he stood upon that wooden block and looked out over the field, he was surprised to see a group of only one thousand riders racing ahead of the Tuigan horde, brandishing their bows.

"Gods," Brunthar cried. "They're fools!"

Stunned, the commander of the archers watched the charging riders. When the Tuigan were within seventy-five yards, the king's standard waved the command to fire, which Brunthar relayed immediately.

"Fire," he cried. "Range for seventy-five yards!"

The order was carried down the line, as sergeants called out the range. The archers leaned back slightly and, despite the fact they were unable to see their targets clearly, fired. The swarm of arrows that arced out onto the field was amazingly accurate. The shafts cut down quite a few Tuigan, but the surviving riders raced on toward the western lines.

For an instant, Brunthar thought the riders were going to charge into the illusion that hid the holes the dwarves had dug the night before. Luckily, as the Tuigan got fifty yards from the Alliance's front rank, only forty feet from the nearest hole, they reined in their horses. With a swift, fluid movement, each barbarian drew a single arrow and dipped its tip into a small leather bag dangling at his side. The arrowheads smoldered, then burst into flame.

Again the signal for the western archers to fire was sent, but it was too late. The Tuigan line sent the burning arrows into the sky. They trailed streams of flame as they passed over the western troops, then disappeared into the trees to either side of the road. The western archers cut down most of the remaining horsewarriors, but that was little consolation. Thin trails of smoke were already working their way out of the forest.

The orc standing next to Razor John struck himself on the forehead with the palm of his hand. "That old trick," he growled. "Orcs use fire to drive elves from trees in plenty battles."

The fletcher barely heard a word the Zhentish soldier said. His mind was occupied with the growing coils of smoke that were wafting over the western armies. For an instant John imagined himself driven from the security of the western position by the fire, at the mercy of the Tuigan. As in the nightmares the fletcher had suffered for the past few nights, the barbarians appeared in his mind's eye as grotesque ogres, drooling blood and wearing little other than uncured animal hides and human bones.

Panicked murmuring broke out in the western ranks as the fire spread. To quell the growing fear, Brunthar jumped down from the wooden box and paced before the line. "Stay in formation!" he shouted. "The king will take care of us. You know that."

Silently the dalesman hoped Azoun would think of something fast.

Brunthar didn't have to wait long to find out if the problem was under control. The thick clouds overhead grew dark, and soon they were roiling angrily in the sky. The rumble of thunder echoed over the plain, and a few large drops of rain splattered on the dalesman's armor. He looked up at the clouds just as the downpour started.

Standing next to Razor John, the orc snorted as the pelting rain fell. "Wizards make storm," he muttered. "Now armor wet and stinky."

A cheer went up in the Alliance's lines as they realized the War Wizards had foiled the barbarians' plan. A low, insistent rumble answered the cry, but some of the men dismissed it as a peal of thunder. Anyone who could see the Tuigan line knew otherwise.

The khahan had ordered his entire army forward. The terrible rumble crossing the field was the sound of their horses pounding the sodden ground.

* * * * *

"Here they come!" Azoun shouted, and the signal went up to prepare for an assault. The king glanced at Vangerdahast.

"Are you ready?"

The wizard smiled wickedly, but Azoun could see a quiver shake his cheek. The strain of casting the spell to make it rain had obviously worn down the aged Vangerdahast. "Ready as I'll ever be," he said.

All eyes turned to the Tuigan charge. The rain was slowing their mounts somewhat, especially those racing through the fields rather than up the Golden Way itself. The downpour had already loosened the topsoil enough that the horses kicked up clods of muddy earth with each step.

At fifty yards, Azoun spotted the khahan's banner. The nine yak-tails that hung from the pole were dripping with water, and the mud churned up by the charge had hidden their color. It was clear nevertheless that Yamun Khahan rode near the standard; it was the tallest and most prominent in the Tuigan line. As ordered, the western archers began to rain arrows down upon the Tuigan. On the right flank, the dwarves let fly a thousand crossbow bolts and quickly reloaded. Sheet after sheet of deadly missiles dropped upon the seventy thousand barbarians as they rushed forward. "Now, Vangy," Azoun said and pointed to the center of the enemy line.

Without hesitation, the wizard drew a pinch of diamond dust from a pouch at his belt. Spreading it in an arc over the ground, Vangerdahast uttered a brief incantation. "There," he said weakly. "The khahan is all yours." He staggered a few steps and added, "I'd best get back with the other War Wizards. I can do no more here."

Azoun couldn't take his eyes off the center of the Tuigan line. The horselords raised their curved swords high and shrieked a frightening war cry. Even though he knew that at least some of the barbarians would be stopped by the holes dug across the battlefield, the king felt a shiver run up his spine. If the Tuigan got through, it was clear they intended to take no prisoners.

The war cry trilled over the battlefield for a few seconds more, until with startling suddenness, the Tuigan line hit the traps. At first only a few horses stumbled, but that was all it took to cause havoc in many parts of the charge. Because of the small front the western army presented, the horsewarriors were forced to ride much closer together than they normally did. Now, when one rider fell or one horse staggered, others quickly followed.

As the full bulk of the Tuigan charge hit the semicircle of holes, it became clear how effective the trap was going to be. Rider after rider urged his mount into the illusory terrain, only to have it drop one leg into a deep hole. The sickening sound of bones breaking filled the air before the horses started to shriek in pain and confusion. Soldiers tumbled out of saddles. A few were lucky enough to be tossed clear of the press, but most were not. The former were quickly cut down by the western archers, the latter crushed by falling horses or the troops charging behind them.

To Azoun, it looked as if an invisible wall had been thrown up to stop the enemy charge—a wall with one noticeable gap.

The riders at the center of the Tuigan line, those closest to Yamun Khahan and his standard, found the path to the western army strangely free of barricades. Their horses pounded over the muddy ground while others on either side of them were stopped by unseen forces. The khahan could not know it, but he and his bodyguard had crossed over a plane of force, a magical bridge called into existence by Vangerdahast for the sole purpose of trapping the Tuigan leader. As soon as the yak-tail banner and the fifty or so men around it crossed that magical bridge, the royal magician let it disappear. When the plane of force was gone, the holes beneath it gaped hungrily for Tuigan horseflesh.

As the riders behind Yamun Khahan fell victim to the dwarves' trap, King Azoun looked to his right. His daughter stood, fully armored, waiting for the command to attack. The king had been wounded and unconscious when Alusair had joined the first battle. When he'd awoke, Azoun had learned she was safe before he'd found out she'd ever been in danger. Now he realized that his order might send Alusair to her death, that Filfaeril might not get to see her daughter alive again.

For an instant, he considered ordering her to the rear, out of danger. Azoun quickly shook aside that thought. The princess belonged on the battlefield as much as he did. That realization did not erase the fear the king felt for his daughter's life, but it allowed him to raise his own sword and give the signal he'd been waiting all day to give. "At them!" King Azoun cried and raced forward.

The two hundred soldiers who charged with the king had been handpicked. Along with Torg, Vrakk, and Alusair, there were dalesmen and Sembians, Red Plumes from Hillsfar and Purple Dragons from Cormyr, all the best soldiers in the Alliance. The two hundred shouted angry defiance at the khahan and braced themselves for the fight. "Now," the king whispered into his closed visor. "Do it now, Vangy."

As if in response to the king's plea, fifty lightning bolts joined the rain and the longbow arrows in the sky. They shrieked over the western lines and tore into the helpless, tangled Tuigan. The bolts momentarily blinded those who had looked upon them, and deafened the soldiers to the cries of the barbarians who were scattered by the lightning like sparks from an exploding firecracker. For the first time in many months, a Tuigan charge wavered, then failed.

Inside the semicircle marked by the wall of crippled horses and crushed bodies, King Azoun was ordering his two hundred to encircle the khahan's bodyguard. The trapped Tuigan were obviously looking for a way to escape, but the king was certain he would provide them none.

Azoun tapped his sword upon his shield twice, and the standard-bearer dipped the purple dragon to the ground. The archers, who had until now been aiming at the mass of Tuigan held up by their fallen comrades, pointed their missiles at the group of riders huddled around the khahan. Longbow arrows whistled over the king's head, and half the khahan's bodyguard dropped from their saddles. The surviving Tuigan caught inside the king's trap scattered, and the handpicked western force rushed to dispatch them.

Gripped with foreboding, Azoun watched Alusair rush from his side toward a barbarian rider. The princess, not carrying a shield, gripped her longsword with both hands and slashed at the Tuigan as he rode past. The blow connected, dropping the warrior to the muddy ground.

As the king took a step toward his daughter, the unhorsed Tuigan stood up. A large, hulking man, the barbarian wore a suit of typical Tuigan armor: large metal plates sewn onto leather. His conical, pointed helmet had fallen off when he'd hit the ground, so his braided, mud-spattered hair was all that protected his head. The princess took immediate advantage of that fact. Before her father could take two steps, Alusair feinted a blow to the barbarian's midsection. When the hulking man moved to block it with his curved sword, she struck at her real target. Her blade hit the Tuigan's unprotected head and split his skull.

With a glance back at her father, Alusair moved into the press of warriors in front of the king.

From the edge of the main battle, Azoun saw a Tuigan whirl his horse around, as if he were ready to charge the western lines alone. Unlike the warrior Alusair had faced, this barbarian wore a breastplate of gold, sculpted with muscles. A skirt of chain girded his waist, and from the top of his conical, fur-trimmed helmet, a horsetail dangled. The sky lit up again as another group of lightning bolts passed overhead. For an instant, Azoun thought that the Tuigan's dark eyes reflected the light with malevolent intensity.

"Yamun Khahan," Azoun said to himself. He took a step forward and tightened his grip on his shield and his sword.

The khahan must have seen Azoun, too, for he kicked his black charger into motion. As his mount bounded over the muddy ground, the ruler of the Tuigan shouted something in his own guttural language. The Cormyrian king didn't know that the khahan was shouting an oath, calling upon his legendary status as the chosen of the Tuigan sky god, but that didn't matter. All Azoun saw was the well-muscled horse with its angry, cursing rider heading toward him. He lifted his shield and bent his knees slightly, preparing to dodge the khahan's attack.

A short soldier in beautifully crafted armor stepped in front of Azoun, holding his sword before him like a lance. The king tried to push past the stocky dwarf, but the ironlord would not be moved. Torg mac Cei wanted the honor of slaying the khahan: the Tuigan leader's skull would be a fine addition to the mounds in Earthfast. Stepping back, Azoun attempted to lure the khahan away from the dwarf. The ironlord had little chance of striking a blow against the mounted barbarian, and it was only his colossal pride that made him try.

As Azoun expected, Torg's stand was indeed futile.

Yamun Khahan raced forward, pointing his horse directly at the ironlord. When the armored dwarf moved out of the way, Yamun sliced down with his curved sword. Torg's armor was perhaps the finest ever crafted in the halls of Earthfast, but it could not protect him from Yamun's powerful blow. With a screeching sound, the Tuigan blade struck the armor on the ironlord's neck and bit far into his back. Torg was dead before he hit the ground.

"Azoun of Cor-meer!" the khahan shouted as he wheeled his horse around to face the king. The Tuigan jammed his heels into the mount's side and drove it forward.

Azoun had not missed the trick Yamun Khahan had used on Torg, and he assumed the barbarian would use his horse to force him into a poor defensive position, too. The king moved long before the khahan's mount reached him, feinting first to the right, then dodging left. The ploy almost didn't work, and the khahan's sword scraped Azoun's helmet and knocked his shield away. Gritting his teeth against the pain from his wounded leg, the king decided that he'd best not try to feint again.

Yamun Khahan threw his head back and laughed as his horse drove Torg's corpse deeper into the mud. For an instant, time seemed to slow down for Azoun, and he saw the myriad of individual battles going on around him as if they were occurring in slow motion. A few yards away, Vrakk and Farl were fighting desperately against Tuigan soldiers they had knocked from their horses. Arrows were streaming overhead, interspersed with occasional flashes of fire and beams of magical energy. Alusair, he realized with a sudden start, was nowhere in sight.

The king's heart caught in his throat, and he wanted to

cry out. In that same instant, however, the khahan's black mount leaped forward, kicking up a shower of muddy water. In four paces it was bearing down on Azoun.

Sidestepping only slightly, the king slapped the horse's front legs with the flat of his blade. The beast skidded to a stop, then lost its footing in the mud and toppled. As the horse fell, Yamun rolled from the saddle. The khahan wanted to stay clear of his mount, the only thing that would give him a chance to fight on. As he soon learned, the battleground was fast becoming a mire; with a curse, the self-styled Illustrious Emperor of All Peoples slid onto his back in the mud.

Azoun stepped forward and brought his sword up to attack. It seemed for an instant that the khahan was helpless. Weighted down by his heavy breastplate, he writhed in the mud like a turtle flipped onto its back. But when Azoun got close enough to strike, Yamun lashed out with his steel-shod boots and kicked the king in the knee.

Normally the blow would have had little effect. Azoun's armor protected him from any obvious damage from the attack, and the khahan had even struck against the king's uninjured right leg. The mud beneath Azoun's feet was just a slick as that beneath the khahan, though, and once his balance was upset, Azoun found his wounded leg of little use in keeping him on his feet. The Cormyrian king toppled into the mire at the khahan's side.

With a monstrous cry, the Tuigan leader grabbed his enemy's arm and brought a mailed fist down on his helmet. The blow knocked the visor from the king's basinet. Now, with the sight limitations brought by his visor gone, Azoun looked upon the khahan. His vision was slightly blurred from the blow, but the king saw that the barbarian crouched next to him, his lips curled into a savage snarl, his wet, red-tinged braids dangled wildly from under his pointed golden helm. Yamun was reaching for his curved sword, which lay in the mud a few feet away.

Azoun called upon all his years of training, all his years of adventuring, as he tried to heave his armored form out of the mud. The best he could do was roll onto his side, but that was enough. As the khahan retrieved his sword and turned, Azoun grabbed his own blade and struck. The blow severed the hand in which the barbarian held his curved weapon. With a howl of pain, the Tuigan emperor toppled forward.

Most of what followed was a blur to the king. In the days that followed, he would only vaguely remember struggling to his feet and raising his sword high over the injured Tuigan. The one clear memory that clung to Azoun for the rest of his life was of Yamun Khahan meeting his gaze just before the blade struck. The barbarian showed no fear as the steel drove deep into his chest, cleaving his heart in two.

The rest of Yamun's bodyguards were dispatched quickly, and to the westerners' astonishment, some of the Tuigan caught in the trap surrendered when they saw that their khahan was dead. Alusair returned to the king's side, the enemy's standard in her hand. A mixture of relief and immense pride gripped Azoun as he watched his daughter break the standard over her knee, then toss the shattered staff and the sodden yak tails onto Yamun's corpse.

By the time the rain stopped, a little less than two hours after it had begun, the barbarians of the Tuigan horde had either retreated or surrendered.

– 17 –
Pages in History

In the tense hours that followed the battle, scouts chased after the retreating Tuigan horde and watched for signs that they were regrouping for another attack. For Azoun, the waiting that afternoon was more terrible than the short lull before the two previous battles, when the enemy had been sighted but had yet to reach the western lines. However, as the day wore on, it became clear that the surviving fifty thousand Tuigan were not going to make another charge.

The Army of the Alliance, now only ten thousand strong, had won the day.

"I've got the latest reports," Alusair announced as she entered the makeshift command center to the rear of the fortified western lines. The princess, who had removed most of her armor, wore a sweat-soaked, padded doublet and grimy hose. Her short blond hair was plastered to her forehead, and her shoulders were slumped with exhaustion.

To King Azoun his daughter looked lovely. Though his left leg was still sore—the battle with the khahan had reopened the arrow wound, and the clerics had only recently stanched the bleeding—the king stood when Alusair entered the ring of camp chairs. These were the main component of the command post. The other, a sturdy wooden table covered with maps, was currently surrounded by the surviving western leaders: Farl Bloodaxe, Brunthar Elventree, Vangerdahast, and Vrakk.

"Where do we stand?" Azoun asked as he hobbled to

Alusair's side.

"The scouts report that the Tuigan are scattering," she said. By now, the generals had turned their attention to the princess. She nodded a greeting. "I used the magical bracelet and the falcon to track the main force of barbarians myself. They're miles from here, heading east."

The king sighed with relief. "Is the horde still breaking up?"

"It seems so," Alusair replied. "Small groups of barbarians sheer off from the main group every so often. A few of these groups are probably scouting parties, but not all of them. Sometimes these small bands are chased off by force."

Vangerdahast shuffled to the king's side. "Inter-clan warfare is starting already." He nodded sagely. "Without the khahan to hold them together, the various factions are preying upon each other, vying for control of the army."

"You've become quite an expert on the Tuigan," Farl Bloodaxe noted.

"I've been talking to Thom," the wizard replied. "He's done a bit of research on the Tuigan. In fact, he's down with the prisoners now, gathering notes for his history of the crusade."

The mentioned of the prisoners visibly darkened the mood of the gathered generals. Brunthar and Vrakk glanced behind the command center, to the area where the seven hundred Tuigan prisoners were being kept. Dwarven troops ringed the area, and clerics moved in and out frequently, tending to the wounded barbarians. The troops from Earthfast had been assigned to guard duty after they'd built a cairn for their fallen leader, partly because the king trusted them to follow his orders and partly because there was some disagreement among the human troops about what should be done with the Tuigan who had surrendered.

"You are going to have to decide what to do with the prisoners soon, Your Highness," Farl said. "It looks as if the barbarians won't attack, at least not in the next few days. Still. . . ."

The black general let his words trail off, but Brunthar Elventree picked up on the thought immediately. "What if the Tuigan *do* attack again? What if they're only biding their time?"

Frowning deeply, Alusair shook her head. "That's not the question, General Elventree. It seems clear that we've broken the barbarian army." She looked out over the collection of prisoners. "But we still need to decide their fate."

Farl sighed. "Many of the Tuigan caught in the trap gave up, but they weren't seriously wounded. They know the khahan is dead, so they have no reason to fight."

"Kill them," Vrakk growled, drawing his sword. "No prisoners."

Without pause, Brunthar added his support to that idea. The dalesman leaned toward the king. "I'll take a group of archers out to dispatch the scum," he murmured. "They're just using up our supplies now."

Azoun hobbled to his chair and sank into it. He steepled his fingers and bowed his head in thought. "What do the rest of you think?" he asked after a moment.

"We cannot kill prisoners who ask for mercy," Farl replied. "We would hope the Tuigan might offer the same mercy to any westerners they captured."

"They attacked us," Brunthar interrupted, as if his point were relevant. "Besides, we are talking about barbarians, not westerners. These are the people who killed an envoy because he wouldn't drink sour milk. These are the warriors we came to Thesk to stop."

After shuffling a few paces in the mud and stroking his beard, Vangerdahast turned to the king. "If we keep these men as prisoners, we'll have to set up a camp for them behind our lines." The wizard paused and looked at the western fortifications. "Do you think our troops will want to share their supplies with men who, only this morning, were intent on killing us all?"

Azoun looked up sharply. "What about you, Allie? What do you think?"

The princess wanted to give her opinion, but she realized that her father probably already knew what she would say. Instead, she held her gauntleted hands before her and shook her head. "No, Father. My counsel, the opinions of your generals, they don't matter now. This is a decision for you alone to make."

The king stifled a bitter laugh, for he recognized how much Alusair wished to make this a test. Once, Azoun would not have even hesitated in his judgment. In the days when he'd ridden with the King's Men, he had meted out justice according to the sentence of his own pure heart. His position as monarch had changed that, and both the king and the princess recognized that fact. The concessions given to Zhentil Keep so that they would join the crusade were only the latest in a long string of petty wrongs done for "reasons of state."

"I know that look, Azoun," Vangerdahast said, shaking a finger at the king. "If you let these barbarians live, they'll only burden the army. And if the Tuigan do attack again, the prisoners might break free, might cost the lives of your own countrymen . . . or your daughter's life, perhaps."

Of course, Vangy is right, Azoun decided. He always is, in matters of logic and in all things political.

But never in matters of the heart.

The king stood. "Allie, tell the clerics to continue to care for the prisoners and give shelter to them." Vrakk growled, and both Vangerdahast and Brunthar gaped in surprise.

"This is madness," Brunthar shouted. "In the Dales we'd never even consider letting our enemies—"

Vrakk thrust a meaty, gray-haired hand over the general's mouth. "Beware, dale-man." He released the startled human, then pounded his leather-armored chest. "In Dales we might be enemy. Zhentish kill for less insult than you ready to say."

The orcish commander narrowed his eyes and studied the king. "I follow, Ak-soon," he said, showing his yellowed teeth, "'cause you may send more men to Lord Cyric this way. He no care if they be Tuigan or not." That said, he stomped off, presumably to rejoin his countrymen.

The outburst had silenced Brunthar, but not Vangerdahast. The old wizard moved close to the king and pushed his face forward until it rested only inches from Azoun's. "This is war. You've no time to play paladin now." When the king didn't respond, the mage looked away. "I knew it would come to this. Don't even try to make me understand."

"I won't," the king said softly. He shrugged in response to the astonished look that comment drew from his old teacher. "I really don't think you'd understand the reasons, Vangy. It has to do with the things the good man must uphold, not logic, not political necessity."

Alusair walked to her father's side. "Shall I help gather supplies for the prisoners?"

"Please. And take General Bloodaxe with you," the king replied. He faced the infantry commander. "I'm sure you'll be able to gather the items needed to care for the prisoners, Farl. Your men should be glad to donate much. After all, they came to fight for a good cause, didn't they?"

The infantry commander gave the king a wry smile. "I've heard that," the general said. With a brief bow, both Farl and Alusair made their way into the ranks.

"I want the men to know that the Tuigan prisoners are being protected by my orders," Azoun said to Brunthar. "I think it would be wise if you told your men that." He paused, then added, "Unless the barbarians pick up weapons or attempt to harm someone, they are safe. Do you understand?"

Without a word or a bow, Brunthar spun on his heels and stomped off.

"This may cost you everything," Vangerdahast hissed after a moment. "The men won't like this one bit. They might even revolt."

"No, Vangy, they won't," Azoun said evenly. "Most of the soldiers are here to protect Faerun, to fight for the cause I put before them four months ago in the Royal Gardens." He gestured at the western troops, still arrayed in battle formation. "They trust me to lead them in a good cause. They may not see the reasons why I tell them to let the prisoners live, but they trust me. They'll follow my orders."

Azoun stood and placed a hand on his old friend's shoulder. "I've paid a great deal for this crusade. If I would have stopped those rumors about my 'glorious escape from the Tuigan,' the nobles wouldn't have charged in the first battle. I'll always have Harcourt's death on my conscience because

of that, and the gods only know what Zhentil Keep will do
with the time I've granted them for free reign in Darkhold."
He swept his hand through the air, as if dismissing the guilt
that plagued him. "Until now, I've committed sins only by allowing evil to occur. I will not kill the prisoners, though not
because all the codes of war say it's wrong. No, because my
heart says it's wrong, and my heart holds the most important code of all."

Vangerdahast studied the king's face for an instant. The
monarch the wizard saw standing defiantly before him
looked the same as the one who had started the crusade.
And though the gray-shot brown beard and wrinkled brow
were familiar, a long-absent spark shone in Azoun's dark
eyes. With a start, Vangerdahast realized that he hadn't
seen that fire in many years, not since the king was a young,
idealistic cavalier.

* * * * *

Sunlight slanted in through the single window of the ruined farmhouse and poured through the gaping holes in its
thatched roof. The light revealed the dust and ash that
danced about the room, but Thom Reaverson didn't notice
it. The bard sat bathed in sunlight, bent over a makeshift
desk. He squinted at the parchment and continued to write.

*Some of the troops were unhappy with the king's deci-
sion to let the prisoners live, but apart from grumbling
around the campfires, there was little negative reaction. A
majority of the army simply took Azoun's word that keeping the defeated Tuigan alive was the course for good men.
Luckily the prisoners themselves proved to be no trouble,
and Azoun freed most of them in the first tenday after the
battle.*

Tapping the end of his pen lightly on his chin, the bard
considered what else he should record. After a moment,
Thom inked his stylus and set to work again.

*The dwarves of Earthfast buried Torg, ironlord of their
people, in a cairn of stone on the day of the Second Battle of
the Golden Way. The dwarven lord's resting place stands*

only a few yards from the trees that served the Alliance so well. The pyres where the clerics burned the corpses from the battle will likely leave no permanent mark on the countryside, but they, too, were built near the site of the conflict.

The dwarves left a day later. Princess Alusair attempted to convince them to stay, at least until the king was certain the Tuigan were not going to mass another attack. "The battle is over," they told her. "There is nothing else for us to do here." Many in the Alliance were not sorry to see the dwarves go. Throughout the campaign, they remained aloof and isolated.

"I don't see how the princess fought beside those cold little men for the three months before the crusade," Thom added to himself. From everything Alusair had revealed, the bard saw Earthfast as a lonely, embattled place, devoid of hope. It was hard to believe that Azoun's daughter, who seemed full of life, had stayed there.

That was before I met her, Thom decided. That was before she and the king were reconciled.

He shook his head and tried to dismiss the idle thoughts that dragged him away from the chronicles. Today was the first time in the month since the Second Battle of the Golden Way, as the conflict was now known, that the bard had stolen a chance to write. And since he wanted to have the notes on the crusade finished before the army returned to Cormyr, Thom had to get back to work.

Stretching once to get comfortable, the bard started to write once more.

It was clear on the day following the battle that the Tuigan were actually retreating. Scouts returned to report that the barbarians were covering an astonishing distance each day—a figure I would relate here but for fear of being called a liar. The death of Yamun Khahan at the hands of King Azoun, the illustrious hero of the crusade—

"Getting a bit carried away there," Thom said softly. Azoun had given the bard strict instructions after the battle that he was not to be valorized over the common troopers in the chronicles. "You'll surely ask me to strike this out,"

Thom noted, "so I'll do it now and save you the trouble."

After marking through the last phrase with heavy, dark lines, the bard repeated the last fragment he'd penned. " 'The death of Yamun Khahan at the hands of King Azoun—' "

—broke the spirit of the barbarian invaders. The prisoners made it clear, with some help from the mages, that without the khahan to lead them, their horsewarrior brethren would surely scatter to the four winds. Experience has taught the Alliance that this was the case.

As the crusading army has moved east, following the retreating horde, it has met with little resistance. Pockets of Tuigan warriors, broken from the main column, have made valiant stands against our forces. Yet flight seems the more common strategy for the tiny bands of Tuigan. As soon as they spot the Alliance, they hurriedly break camp and ride away, pushing their swift ponies to the limits of endurance.

Of great relief to Azoun's generals, too, is the civil war that is obviously tearing at what remains of the Tuigan army. Princess Alusair, with the aid of the falcon and magical bracelet given her by the centaur chieftain, has been able to keep careful track of the barbarians. The sons of the khahan seem to be locked in bitter contention with one of the horde's generals, Chanar Ong Kho. More small bands of warriors break off every day and disappear into the open plains of Thesk.

A few of the barbarians captured in the Second Battle of the Golden Way are released each day to join these groups of fleeing comrades. "The Tuigan are prisoners from a war that's over," Azoun told his generals. "There is no reason for us to prevent them from going home, as we all will soon do."

Thom paused to study the page he'd just completed. Apart from the single blotch where he'd marked over his comment about the king, the sheet was neatly crammed with tight, controlled handwriting. He laid the paper flat to dry, then started a new page.

Even without fighting, traveling through Thesk has not been easy for the Army of the Alliance, and the going promises to be harder still the farther east we go. Few of the fields have been cultivated in the wake of the invasion, and

*the retreating barbarians have been killing much of the
game. Food, while not terribly scarce, is still a concern,
since the army's supply lines grow longer each day and
more vulnerable to attack from other dark forces in the
area.*

*The villages along the Golden Way are deserted, and most
have been pillaged by the Tuigan. Where the peasants simply abandoned their homes, some of the structures remain
intact. In towns and villages where the people made a
stand—*

Sadly Thom looked around at the interior of the shattered
farmhouse. The cottage was one of the only buildings left
on the outskirts of the town of Tammar. The thatch that normally covered its roof had been pulled down in many
places, perhaps as food for hungry Tuigan horses. The fur-
niture was little more than splintered fragments, and even
the hut's wooden door had been smashed in. If any other
possessions once lined the walls of the cottage they were
gone now, but whether the peasants or the barbarians had
taken them Thom would never know.

The bard closed his eyes for a moment, then glanced at
the parchment. The carnage left in the horde's wake would
have to be noted, but not today. Such dark topics were best
left for other times, days when the sun wasn't shining so
brightly and the late summer air wasn't so warm and relaxing. Thom blew the partially finished page dry, gathered the
other sheets he'd finished that morning, and tucked them
under his arm.

I think it's time for a walk, he decided as he collected his
pens and the rest of his writing tools. Then I'll head back to
town and get something to eat.

With full intention of carrying out that simple plan, the
bard stepped over the broken doorjamb. Being free of the
crooked, shadow-heavy cottage made him feel better than
he'd expected, so he whistled a bright tune and set off in no
particular direction.

"Well met, Master Bard," called a voice from behind.

Without turning around, the bard knew that it was King
Azoun who had hailed him. When he did look, Thom wasn't

surprised to see that Vangerdahast accompanied the king. The presence of a third person—a little, bald Khazari priest who'd been captured in the Second Battle of the Golden Way—did make him pause for an instant.

Koja, as the bard had come to know the Tuigan historian and former advisor to Yamun Khahan himself, strode beside King Azoun. Though he had been captured in the last battle, he wasn't really a prisoner, for the king had offered the man his freedom long ago. Koja had asked to stay with the Alliance, claiming that there were many Tuigan who would gladly see him dead now that the khahan was no more. His sincerity in this had been obvious, so Azoun let him stay.

"Interesting news, Thom," the king said happily. From the expression on Azoun's face, the bard could tell that it was at least partially good news, too.

Vangerdahast, still aged from the affects of the magic-dead area, tottered along beside Azoun. The wizard, once rather hale and hearty for a man in his eighties, now looked tired and haggard. His face was a nest of wrinkles, and his hands quivered slightly. The wizard clutched a staff, and his weight drove its tip into the ground with each plodding step.

"We're finally going home," Vangerdahast said before Azoun could elaborate on his comment.

For a moment the fact didn't register in Thom's mind. He stood, slack-jawed and staring, as Azoun nodded to confirm the wizard's claim. "B-but, the Tuigan," he stammered.

Vangerdahast smiled, an act which made his eyes disappear into the mass of wrinkles around them. That pleasant expression almost astonished Thom as much as the news, for Vangerdahast had been in an understandably sour mood ever since his longevity spells had been nullified. "I've just received word from Fonjara Galth—you remember her, eh, Thom? The witch from Rashemen?" Thom nodded and the wizard continued. "Her cronies finally closed the route between the Horse Plains and the West, the one through the Lake of Tears."

"And the Red Wizards who had attacked Rashemen after the Tuigan had stormed through that land have now retreated south, back to their own borders," Azoun added. "Thesk, Rashemen, and the other local armies can put their full attention into routing the remaining barbarians."

The Khazari priest had been standing silently to the side during the conversation. Now, however, he bowed to Azoun and said, "I do not wish to contradict you, Your Highness, but I will repeat what I told you earlier: I do not believe the Tuigan will be dealt with that easily. It is far more likely that the majority of the army will scatter throughout Thesk rather than return to the Horse Plains. They will be as difficult to catch as the wind itself."

"But their families?" Azoun said. "Their homes—"

"They're nomads, Your Highness," Thom noted, a look of concern on his face. "Families and homes mean little to them."

Koja rubbed his bald scalp in slight agitation. "Before Yamun Khahan gathered the various tribes together, they lived by raiding and pillaging each other's camps and the trade caravans that passed through the Horse Plains." He looked around at the open grasslands that surrounded the Theskan town of Tammar. "This is good grazing land, and it is populated so sparsely that they will be able to elude the armies that hunt them."

Vangerdahast's smile vanished. "That's not our problem," he grumbled.

After a short silence, Azoun agreed. With Thay abandoning its plans of conquest and the Tuigan on the run, the Army of the Alliance could return to the Heartlands. "Our responsibility is fulfilled," the king noted, and the four men set off for the center of Tammar, where the majority of the army was billeted.

"Your Highness," Koja said as they walked, "what was your impression of the khahan?"

The question took the king by surprise, and after recalling their brief meeting, Azoun shrugged. "He seemed to be quite intelligent. No," he corrected quickly, "not that. Wise, perhaps. And very driven. Why do you ask?"

"When I was first sent to the Tuigan capital of Quaraband, I was to report back to my prince, tell him what the khahan was like," the priest replied. "I burned those notes long ago, but I think I might try to put something about Yamun Khahan on paper." After a pause, Koja added, "Master Reaverson tells me you are interested in history. Perhaps you will read these notes if I write them?"

"Of course," Azoun said, turning to face the priest. Koja was looking at the shattered road, however, and a wistful smile clung to his lips. "You will miss the khahan, won't you?"

"I was his *anda*," Koja said wistfully, then scowled. "I don't know if I can translate *anda* into your tongue—friend, perhaps, is closest." He cast his gaze to the clear blue sky. "Yamun chose the perilous path on his own, however. He chose to be a great man."

Sentries greeted Azoun as he and the others passed into the fringes of the western camp. Tents and campfires covered the broken streets of Tammar, scattered amidst the ruins of the buildings. Soldiers relaxed. A few loud groups sang bawdy songs, while others played at dice. Discipline was lax, perhaps too much so, but the men had fought and marched hard since arriving in Thesk, and Azoun knew that they deserved a rest.

"Is that the philosophy of your land?" the king asked as he passed a group of archers testing their skill against a blackened post. "That a man *chooses* to be great?"

The priest answered without hesitation, and Azoun noted the pedantic tone Koja's voice took on as he spoke. It was a tone Vangerdahast often adopted when discussing politics. "In the *Yanitsava*, the book of the Enlightened One's teachings, it is written that, 'Some men take the thread of their life and weave their own destiny.' The priests of the Red Mountain believe that these men are evil, that they do not accept the will of the Enlightened One, that they force their own will over the pattern of the world."

"And you, Koja," Azoun said. "Do you believe that?"

The priest laughed. "I was once a lama of the Red Mountain, but I am now as much that as I am an envoy of the Khazari. My time with the Tuigan taught me that I am a far better historian than philosopher."

Koja then turned to Azoun. "Still, I know this much about men like Yamun Khahan: the world cannot bear their presence for too long. Yamun tried to make the world over in his image, to weave a picture that would encompass the entire globe." He gestured with an open hand at the army spread around the two of them. "But the world always has other great men to oppose such plans."

"Your Highness," Farl Bloodaxe interrupted. The general, dressed casually in the tunic and breeches of a Cormyrian soldier, bowed formally. "I've just passed the word on to the infantry captains, and Brunthar has done the same with the archers. The army should be ready to move tomorrow morning."

"Good," Azoun replied, placing his hand on Farl's shoulder. "See that the men draw fresh water from the wells tonight and double the foraging parties. I'm sure the troops will want to get back to the coast as quickly as possible, so the fewer times we need to slow to hunt for food the better."

Thom and Vangerdahast caught up to Azoun, and Koja bowed and went off with them. When the others had gone, Farl stepped close to the king. "There seems to be a problem with the orcs, Your Highness. When I told Vrakk the news, he informed me that the Zhentish troops weren't leaving."

After giving Farl a few more suggestions about stocking the supply wagons, Azoun went directly to the orcs' camp. The men had grown used to the Zhentish soldiers, but Vrakk and his troops still maintained their own compound, away from the humans. They had proven their worth in battle, and the other soldiers would have likely let the orcs integrate their tents with the rest of the Alliance. For some mysterious reason, Vrakk always refused.

As the king entered the Zhentish camp, he decided that that was probably a good thing. The orcs had chosen the most run-down section of Tammar for their home. Their torn and dirty tents were pitched only a few yards from where the town's garbage had been dumped and the funeral pyres had been built for the townsfolk. The place smelled rancid, but the orcs didn't seem to notice. They lounged in their tents, hidden from the bright sunlight.

Only a few Zhentish troopers seemed to be awake, and most of these were sprawled around smoking campfires, swilling wine and eating their midday meal.

Vrakk was seated near one such collection of orcs. He still wore his black leather armor, and Azoun noticed for the first time that, while the orcs' surroundings were like a sty, their piecemeal armor and scavenged weapons were relatively clean.

"General Bloodaxe tells me you are reluctant to leave," Azoun said casually. He held his hand up when another orc offered him a wineskin. "Thank you, but, no."

Vrakk snarled at the orc with the wineskin, and the smaller, brown-furred trooper slouched down and concentrated on the hunk of meat he had burning in the fire. "Orcs not go home," Vrakk replied. "That our orders."

"Orders?" Azoun asked. "From whom?"

"Zhentil Keep," the orc replied. Vrakk's tone revealed that he was surprised at Azoun's ignorance. "We new outpost. They order us stay in Thesk."

A frown crept across Azoun's face as he regarded the orcish commander. "And you've had these orders from the time you left the Keep, haven't you?"

Vrakk smiled, or what passed for that expression with the orc. His large teeth showed yellow and filmy in the sunshine. "Keep say we stay with Alliance till Tuigan gone. They say orcs trust Ak-soon to let leave in Thesk."

I gave my word to those villains, the king concluded silently, and they've used me to place a damned Zhentish outpost of almost nine hundred orcs in the middle of an ally's territory. Azoun sighed. "I don't suppose you'll be setting up your camp here in Tammar, so take your share of the supplies and leave right after sunset. I know your troops can travel by night, so that shouldn't be a problem."

The Zhentish commander found this agreeable, and wasn't offended at all when the king refused his invitation to share the noon meal with him. Though Vrakk appeared rather ignorant, he knew exactly why Azoun was distressed by the revelation of their plans.

"I will tell the Theskan authorities that your troops stayed in their territory," Azoun warned solemnly as he prepared to leave. "They'll consider you trespassers, Vrakk."

The orc's toothy grin widened. "We good soldiers, Aksoon, but we better raiders, better thieves. Thesk big place with plenty spots to hide." He grabbed the wineskin from his brown-haired comrade and took a long swallow. " 'Sides, we learn plenty about war from you. We be safe."

That thought didn't comfort Azoun at all. As he walked back to the royal compound, the king wondered if Koja was right. For all the good that he had intended to do on the crusade, Azoun now saw very little evidence that he'd succeeded. The town of Tammar, like so many other villages and hamlets in Thesk, Ashanath, and Rashemen, lay in ruins, the buildings toppled and the fields uncultivated. The Tuigan army was broken, but not gone from the West. The small groups of bandits that remained would likely plague traders and farmers for years to come. And now the orcs. The Theskan government would not be happy to learn that a band of professional Zhentish soldiers was loose in their land.

I've freed Thesk from Yamun Khahan and made it safe for bandits and spies, Azoun concluded darkly.

The king scowled at himself for being so morose. "I've won far more than that," he said as he looked around at the Army of the Alliance.

The troopers were celebrating the news that the war was officially over. Men went happily about the task of breaking down the camp, and the soldiers Azoun passed greeted him loudly. Some even cheered him. However, it was more than the mood of the camp that made the king realize that he'd won more than was lost. As he looked out on the faces of the archers and infantrymen, he no longer saw the motley collection of dalesmen and Sembians, Cormyrians and mercenaries, that had left Suzail those many months ago. Azoun saw a unified force, a group of men and women brought together to fight for Faerun.

And if these disparate soldiers could be forged together for such a cause, why not their countries?

With that ambitious thought in mind, the king crossed

royal compound. His pavilion still stood, its brightly colored sides flapping gaily in the light breeze. For a moment, he considered giving the order to have it dismantled; the rest of the army would likely sleep on the ground tonight so that they would not be delayed with packing their tents come morning. Perhaps when I'm done talking to Alusair, he decided, and turned toward her tent.

Azoun found the princess stuffing her few belongings into a rough canvas sack. The falcon that Jad Eyesbright had loaned to her sat on a makeshift perch, its head covered with a leather hood, next to Alusair's armor. Whenever the princess would bump into the dwarven plate mail, the bird would give a little screech in complaint of the disturbing noise.

"Hello, Father," she said as the king entered. Alusair tied the canvas sack and tossed it near the door. "I've heard the news. You're leaving tomorrow morning?"

"What do you mean, '*you're* leaving?' " Azoun asked. He sat down on the tent's sole cot and shook his head in disbelief. "Aren't you coming home?"

Alusair sat down next to Azoun. "Yes," she said. "But not just yet."

The king choked on his words, then sputtered, "Not now? When, Allie? Your mother and sister expect you—"

"Please," the princess broke in. She bowed her head. "I don't want to argue. Not now."

Gripping Alusair's hands tightly, the king fought back the confusion that was growing inside of him. In the course of the crusade, his relationship with his daughter had grown beyond the conflict that had stood between them. Azoun was proud of Alusair, and he thought she realized that. "It's all right, Allie. Just tell me why."

"I have things I have to do before I can come home. I've made some promises over the last few years, and I have some debts to settle." She laughed. "I have responsibilities to fulfill."

The king didn't miss the irony in his daughter's words. "When will you come home, then?"

Alusair sighed, a bit raggedly. "I think I'll be home in a few months. Probably before winter sets in." After a short pause, she added, "Thank you for understanding, Father. This is just something I have to do."

"My reaction shouldn't be a surprise, Allie. You have your own life. I just want you to make your family part of that life again." The king glanced at the canvas sack beside the door. "You're leaving this afternoon, aren't you?"

With a nod, the princess stood. She gathered up the pieces of her armor and started to bundle it for travel. "I want to get to the Forest of Lethyr as soon as possible," she said as she spread the armor out. "The centaur chieftain asked me to return the falcon and the bracelet when the fighting was over."

"A falcon's quite a burden on campaign," Azoun noted idly, trying to appear at ease. "They take a lot of care and attention. You don't give it to them, they go wild again. Not much good for hunting or scouting after that."

The princess made a few comments about the falcon and how wonderful it was seeing through the bird's eyes. Then, as she was stacking the cuisses and brassards of her armor in the breastplate, the king reached over and rearranged them.

"If you stack the armor this way," Azoun said as he cupped the pieces together, "it'll make a tighter bundle." He smiled at his daughter. "I have had some experience with this sort of thing . . . though that was a long time ago."

"Not so long that you've forgotten it," Alusair replied. After an awkward pause, she leaned close to her father and embraced him.

For an hour or so, the king and his daughter talked. Azoun told her about his times with the King's Men, and the princess responded with fragments about her adventures. They laughed, and for a short time it seemed as if they were back in Suzail, before the war, before the princess had run away. Too soon, it was time for Alusair to go.

They said good-bye without tears, and Alusair promised to keep the king's signet ring so the family could find her if the need arose. It was almost a happy parting, for both Azoun and Alusair knew that when next they met, they would be father and daughter again, and more. They would also be friends.

As he watched his daughter ride away on one of the few horses the army could spare, Azoun decided that his greatest victories of the crusade would never be recorded in Thom's chronicles. His ancestors might know that Azoun IV once brought peace to Thesk with his victory over the Tuigan, but they would probably never realize he also made peace with his daughter and with himself. After all, such sentimental matters were not the stuff of histories.

Long after Alusair disappeared into the tall grass of the plain, the king could see the falcon spiraling in the sky as it followed her. The bird, which in time appeared as no more than a dark speck, held Azoun's attention until it, too, faded into the horizon. With a contented sigh, the king returned to camp, where the Army of the Alliance awaited his command.

Epilogue

"Sure flights! Razor points!"

John the Fletcher paused and wiped the sweat from his forehead. Though autumn was swiftly fading into winter, pushing a heavy cart along the Promenade was hot and tiring work. Not as bad as fighting Tuigan, he decided with a smile. He hefted his cart and called out his wares again.

"Sure flights! Razor points! Buy your arrows from John the Fletcher! Only the best from Razor John!"

Like most of the Army of the Alliance, Razor John had returned to Suzail a few months ago. He had been a bit surprised to find his business doing well, but his apprentice had taken readily to the heavy workload. More importantly, new customers were frequenting the shop. Razor John was, after all, a war hero.

Not that he had done anything superlative during the crusade. None of his customers ever actually asked John about the battles themselves, and they really didn't care to hear the truth. John was a war hero because the people of Suzail, in fact the citizens of most of the crusading countries, had decided that Azoun's venture against the barbarians had resulted in a heroic conflict. Bards readily took up their lutes and wove stories about the crusaders, always vastly outnumbered and fighting for their lives. John, like the rest of the Alliance, was part of a popular legend—based partially in truth, of course, but growing more fantastic every day.

A horse-drawn wagon forced its way up the Promenade,

and John heaved his cart to the side of the road. "Damned teamsters think they can drive their rigs anywhere," he grumbled as the wagon passed. He shoved his cart forward again, right into a woman carrying a basket of apples.

The elderly lady, a heavy shawl pulled over her stooped shoulders, turned, ready to scold the owner of the cart. She stopped short when she saw the medal Razor John wore over his heart. "Pardon me," she murmured and went on her way.

John shook his head and looked down at the silver disk. The medal had a longbow engraved in it, with the words "Order of the Golden Way" etched around the image. It had been given to each of the archers who'd fought on the crusade, and ones like it—engraved with either pikes or horses—had been cast for each infantryman or cavalryman. The latter was a posthumous honor.

The medals garnered the wearer a great many courtesies in the city. The deference shown John by the elderly woman was only a small sample. The fletcher had found that the silver disk increased his business on the street, got him better service in taverns, even attracted the attention of single ladies. Not that John was all that concerned with such matters; Kiri had survived the crusade, too, and they were planning a wedding for the spring.

Razor John wore the medal because he was proud of the service he'd done Faerun. He'd gone on the crusade believing in Azoun's cause, and the attention the expedition now received only made John feel that much more pride in the Alliance and all it stood for. There was even talk in the inns that King Azoun wanted the bonds between Cormyr, Sembia, and the Dales to become more permanent. Such a union would make any invasion of the Heartlands almost impossible.

John looked to his right. The sprawl of government buildings known as "the Royal Court" lined the Promenade for a long way. Tax collectors and other city officials scurried about in the court's twisted hallways, and the policies enacted there had a great effect on John's life. However, those structures seemed insignificant when compared to the impressive castle that rose behind them. The fletcher stared up at the palace and wondered if the king would be able to unite Faerun.

At that moment, Azoun himself was wondering the same thing. He paced back in forth in the castle's highest tower, his hands clenched behind his back. Every few steps his left leg twinged slightly, but that wasn't a surprise. The arrow wound tended to give him trouble right before it rained.

Moving to the chessboard that lay on a table at the side of the room, the king shifted a knight, then resumed his pacing. His chess game had improved since his return from Thesk, much to Queen Filfaeril's dismay. She now beat the king only three games out of four.

"I hope you're done reading Thom's text, Your Highness," a voice called from the stairs. "The clerics are here to pick up the last pages."

Azoun turned to see Vangerdahast emerge from the open trapdoor. The wizard looked much more healthy these days; he'd spent most of the last two months in his laboratory, restoring the vitality the magic-dead area had stolen from him. His face was still wrinkled and his gait a little slower than in years past, but the wizard was once again the "Vangy" that Azoun knew and loved.

"Of course I'm finished," the king said. He reached down and handed a sheaf of parchment to his friend. "If you see Thom before I do, you can tell him the chronicles are just fine."

Without comment, the wizard took the pages and placed them neatly in his leather satchel. From there they would be delivered to the priests who awaited them in the palace's main hall. The clerics, worshipers of Denier, the God of Art, had been commissioned to copy Thom Reaverson's history of the crusade. The chronicles were then to be bound with Koja's notes on the Tuigan and his life of Yamun Khahan. Demand for the resulting book, which was to be stunningly illuminated by the priests, was already high, and the growing interest in the crusade promised to make the work even more sought after in the months to come.

"Yes, our bard does need encouragement these days," Vangerdahast noted sarcastically. "I understand that he's been offered quite a lot of money by one of our nobles to write a family history."

The wizard's comment brought no response from Azoun. He was confident that the bard would stay at the palace, at least for a little while. After all, when Alusair returned home in a few days, Thom was planning to finish his notes on her adventures. Those stories could then be added to the history of House Obarskyr.

Azoun had resumed his pacing, and Vangerdahast started for the trapdoor. The wizard was reaching to close the door behind him when the king suddenly looked in his direction.

"Thank you, Vangy," Azoun said sincerely. "By the way, have you heard anything from Lord Mourngrym or the other dalelords?"

"They'll come, Azoun. The crusade has earned you enough influence that they'll have no choice," the wizard said—a bit sourly, the king noted. "To be honest, I don't know why you're wasting your time. They'll never agree to unification with Cormyr. Neither will Sembia." When he noted the determined look crossing the king's face, he added. "Of course, that's just my opinion."

The wizard knew better than to argue certain matters of state—like the unification of the Heartlands—with Azoun since the crusade. The success of the foray against the Tuigan had bolstered the king's opinion that the tenets of Law and Good could be used to govern. In the wizard's opinion, that made Azoun rather intractable. Still, the old mage found that he respected the king more these days, even if he did believe his plans to be unrealistic. Like most people, Vangerdahast found it hard not to respect someone so dedicated to the welfare of others.

With a short bow, the wizard disappeared into the stairwell and closed the trapdoor behind him. The heavy wooden door forced a breeze into the small tower room, making the tapestries wave on the walls. The echo of the iron ring clanking against the wood had barely died before the king was pacing again.

In his mind the arguments for uniting Cormyr, Sembia, and the Dales turned over and over, arranging themselves into the best logical order. Azoun occasionally dismissed a reason for the extension of the union, and every few steps a new argument for or against the plan would present itself to him. At the heart of the king's thinking lay one thing: The crusade had proven, on a very limited scale, that such an alliance was beneficial.

No one could deny that. Relations between the three countries and the independent city-states that had offered troops for the crusade had never been better. With the exception of Zhentil Keep, of course. The increased activities of the raiding parties out of Darkhold troubled everyone, and the Keep now found itself politically isolated more often than not.

Most importantly, the crusade had shown Azoun that he could change the world. After all, the Alliance had been founded upon his ideals, his dreams. Certainly he had faltered once or twice, falling prey to the easy solutions of political necessity. Even now, the dalesmen pointed the finger of blame at Azoun for the problems with Darkhold. After explaining the treaty he'd signed with the Keep, the king had offered no excuse for his actions. The guilt was his, and he accepted it.

That was what his conscience advised him to do, and more and more these days Azoun followed that guide. It also told him to forge a new country from the Heartlands, a new empire dedicated to Law and Good. If possible, he was going to do that, too.

The king stopped pacing for a moment and opened the window. Suzail spread before him in the late autumn sunshine, still peaceful, still prosperous. The whole of Faerun could be like this, he thought.

Koja's comment about the world and great men came unbidden to the king's mind. His humility rebelled at naming himself great, but Azoun realized that the priest had been talking about him as much as Yamun Khahan. He pondered that thought as he watched the gulls wheel over the docks, the tradesmen and peasants hustle down the Promenade.

Closing the window, the king shut the chill breeze out of the room. If Koja is correct, Azoun decided as he began to pace again, then I must achieve what I can in what little time I have.

FORGOTTEN REALMS
FANTASY ADVENTURE

THE MAZTICA TRILOGY

Douglas Niles

IRONHELM

A slave girl learns of a great destiny laid upon her by the gods themselves. And across the sea, a legion of skilled mercenaries sails west to discover a land of primitive savagery mixed with high culture. Under the banner of its vigilant god the legion claims these lands for itself. And only as Erix sees her land invaded is her destiny revealed.

VIPERHAND

The God of War feasts upon chaos while the desperate lovers, Erix and Halloran, strive to escape the waves of catastrophe sweeping Maztica. Each is forced into a choice of historical proportion and deeply personal emotion. The destruction of the fabulously wealthy continent of Maztica looms on the horizon.

FEATHERED DRAGON

Forces of terror rack Maztica, destroying cities and forcing whole populations to flee for their lives. The one hope for survival is the promised return of Qotal, the Feathered Dragon. Erixitl of Palul holds the key to that return, but only if she succeeds in her final and most difficult quest. Available April 1991.